If You Walked in My Shoes

Gwynne Forster

If You Walked in My Shoes

KENSINGTON PUBLISHING CORP.

DAFINA BOOKS are published by

Kensington Publishing Corp.
850 Third Avenue
New York, NY 10022

ISBN 0-7394-4886-2

Printed in the United States of America

ACKNOWLEDGMENTS

My sincere thanks to my editor, Karen Thomas, whose support enabled me to stretch myself in writing this book.

My thanks to my husband, my stepson and my daughter-in-law for their strength and support through family illnesses, including my own. And I am also grateful to my stepson for his generosity and unselfishness in enabling me to travel wherever my work takes me.

Above all, I thank God for the talent he has given me and for opportunities to use this precious gift of creativity through the written word.

If You Walked
in My Shoes

Prologue

A loud shriek erupted from her throat but that didn't deter him. She clawed and kicked, but Leon Farrell would not release her.

"Don't. Please don't," she begged, changing tactics when she realized she was losing the fight. "Stop. Leon, please stop. Oh God," she screamed as he ripped into her. Seconds later, he threw his head back, shuddering, and she raked his face with the long talons at the end of her fingers, drawing his blood. But drowning in the abyss of his orgasm, he felt no pain. He didn't look at her, just pulled himself out of her and ran. Ran like a coward, leaving her to deal with the aftermath of his monstrous act.

What was she going to do? Her papa would kill her, for he had forbade her to go anywhere with boys. But for weeks, Leon had begged her to let him walk part of the way home with her after school. She had finally agreed, but they hadn't even held hands as they walked along the narrow dirt road, past widely separated, unpainted houses, fields of dried corn stalks, pine tree stumps and nearly dilapidated barns that marked the little hamlet on the outskirts of Charlotte, North Carolina. He was the boy the teachers called a gentleman, and look what he'd done to her. Shoving her against a tree beside Moody's old barn and violating her. As she trudged on home, tears blurring her vision, Coreen Holmes knew she couldn't tell anyone, for the ugly, unsympathetic gossip would only victimize her further. So she vowed to blot the experience from her mind. Little did she know, however, that for the next thirty years, that act and its consequences would dog her thoughts, her conscience, and her steps, setting her on a life of deceit and pretense.

Thirteen years later, Frieda Davis heard her bedroom door creak open, sat up in bed, and turned the switch of the lamp that sat on her night table. Her bottom lip sagged, and her eyes stretched beyond their normal size.

"Papa!" she called to her adoptive father, who ambled toward her wearing only his underwear. "Papa, what are you . . . ?"

His thick, calloused hands clamped over her mouth, and she felt the weight of his two hundred and fifty pounds upon her small, immature frame. She closed her eyes, unmindful of the tears as pain such as she had never known assailed her.

"If you know what's good for you," he said, after emptying himself into her, "you'll keep your mouth shut about this."

"Papa. Papa," she cried. "How could you? You . . . you hurt me."

"Next time, you'll like it."

As if he had done nothing more than tuck his child in bed for the night, he strolled out and closed the door. One month after her twelfth birthday. Two days after she had her first period and wore her first bra, he took her virginity. She got up, crept into the bathroom, and washed herself, fighting tears and hating him. Little did she know that for the next seventeen years she would be a slave to the memory of that act, that her only and consuming passion would become a lust for revenge.

Chapter One

There wasn't a single thing that Coreen Holmes Treadwell could do but wait. Wait for the courage to face millions of people or, God forbid, wait for the strength to decline the greatest boost her career had ever had or was likely to get again. Or she could wait until the Senate Congressional Investigating Committee forced her hand. Not that Coreen was a coward; far from it. But what if, by gaining all that she longed for, had dreamed of and worked for, she then lost everything dear to her?

She lay on her side breathing as quietly as possible, nearly petrified, her body rigid. During the eighteen years of her marriage to Bates Treadwell, they had developed the habit of awakening early, often before dawn, and talking. Just talking. Sometimes he'd hold her hand, or she would hold his, and they would talk about all kinds of things. Funny things. Things that mattered, and some that didn't and never would. Naughty things. Sometimes cruel things. But they talked.

On that morning in early December when the eerie sound of the whistling wind would ordinarily have sent her into his arms, she kept herself apart, pretending to sleep. With the weight on her mind, she couldn't hold a conversation, not even about the simplest thing, and she didn't feel like explaining why. Coreen Treadwell was scared. For twenty-nine years, she had lived with the guilt of giving up her child for adoption and with the fear that it would be her ruin.

In all those years, she had not shared with anyone the remorse that was her constant companion, not with her husband or even her mother. What was worse, in the early years following that birth, she looked for the result of her mishap in the face of every strange little girl or boy of appropriate age that she encountered, for she hadn't allowed her aunt to tell her the child's gender. In that state of denial, she hadn't wanted to know anything about the baby. More than once, a mother or father had stared at her in perturbation as if she were a potential kidnapper. In recent years, her tragedy flowered in the face of every woman and every man around thirty years of age into whose countenance she looked. Always wondering. Always guessing. Yes, and always relieved that she saw no resemblance to herself or to Leon Farrell, who she hoped would rot in hell.

"I know you're not sleeping, Coreen. So what's the matter? Don't you feel good?"

No point in pretending longer. Bates was always on the alert for evidence that he wasn't getting his share of something, or worse, that he was being slighted. "You were so quiet over there," she said. "I thought you were asleep."

He pulled her closer. "Well, I'm not asleep. I've been thinking we haven't had a vacation since we got married. The boys are grown now, on their own, and you've been a wonderful stepmother. We ought to do something for ourselves."

"I know." He was right, but she couldn't think of that right now. She had worked herself half to death to get where she was in her profession, and one wrong move could sink her. Like a balloon. You used all your breath filling it up, getting it big and pretty, and the prick of one little pin would flatten it like a pancake, make you look foolish. She couldn't afford a mistake. If only . . .

"What did you say, hon?" she asked him, trying her best to focus on whatever it was that seemed so important to him.

"Where's your head this morning? You haven't heard a word I said."

"I'm sorry. Let's talk later. I have to write this brief, and I can't get it out of my mind."

"Well, why didn't you say so?"

She gave silent thanks as he rolled out of the bed, grabbed his robe, and headed for the bathroom without pressing his point. She hated lying to her husband, but over the years she had learned that Bates—like so many of the people she met in the course of her work—couldn't always handle the truth, though he swore he wanted to hear it no matter how much it hurt.

By the time she made it to the kitchen, Bates had breakfast on the table and he and her younger stepson, Glen, who was visiting them that weekend, sat at the table in the dining alcove at one end of the kitchen, waiting for her. It was her least favorite room in the house; to her, it signified the servitude to which she had once been consigned. Not even the yellow and blue decor and modern chrome fixtures and appliances were attractive to her. She tightened her robe around her and sat down in the ladder-back chair, the one thing in the kitchen that she loved. Then she smiled at Glen and patted his hand.

Coreen considered it her good fortune that the man she decided to marry had two boys who needed a mother, their own having died at Glen's birth. After her ordeal with childbearing, she'd sworn not to repeat the experience.

She loved Glen as much as if she had given birth to him. When she married Bates, the little boy needed her, had literally sought refuge in her. During his widowhood, Bates worked all hours, leaving the boys to themselves, and Glen was starved for nurturing. Although he loved her, Glen wasn't above taking advantage of her weakness for him. Coreen knew she had contributed to Glen's failings as a man who was spoiled, self-centered, and a womanizer, while Eric, his older brother, had the attributes of an admirable human being.

"You're looking washed out this morning, Mom," Glen said after kissing her cheek. "Don't work so hard."

She patted his shoulder. "I'm up for president of my national association," she told him, more to make conversation than to bring up a subject that induced in her as much fear as pride.

"Yeah. Daddy told me. You'll make it, and the next step will be head of the international. Right?"

"I guess." Shivers ran through her as she said it. She had to get past the coming week, and God alone knew what would come next.

"I'd better be going," Bates said. "You know Saturday is usually my best day. Business hasn't been so great lately. The travel business never is heavy around Christmastime. People too busy buying Christmas presents, and things haven't picked up since New Year's. But folks ought to be heading for the Caribbean and Central America now to get away from this cold weather we're having."

She lifted her face for her husband's kiss. "See you this evening," he said, and remembering that Glen would leave in the afternoon, embraced his son before leaving home.

Coreen put sausage, biscuits, and a slice of chocolate cake, Glen's favorite, in a bag, and walked with him to the door. "Come back soon," she said. He hugged her, promised he would, and she was alone to deal with her demons.

She tidied the kitchen and made the beds. Why did men expect women to do that dirty work even when they also had a job outside the home—a well-paying job, at that—while the men came home and behaved as if they were royalty? She stopped her foot just before, in her furor, she slammed it into the base of the toilet. If she ever became wealthy, she was going to replace her weekly cleaning woman with a full-time housekeeper. Barely contrite, she straightened the bathroom and finished the cleaning, chores she hated, but at least they took her mind from what she dreaded thinking about. She could throw away the opportunity of a lifetime, or she could accept it, risk ruining her career and maybe her marriage.

The phone rang and she let it ring until the caller's patience spent itself. She couldn't count the times she'd sat on the side of that bed wiping tears and wishing she'd been somewhere else or with somebody else. She had been seventeen with her stars blazing and success all but guaranteed. Her teachers said she was talented, bright, and she knew she was: valedictorian of her high school class and able to choose among three colleges that offered her a full scholarship. In those days, she spent hours dreaming and planning. Mama was so proud of her, and her papa even treated her with a new kind of respect.

"This is my daughter, Coreen," he would say to people they met, though everyone in that small place of two thousand, five hundred people knew who his daughter was. Coreen wondered if his pride in her was the reason why he stopped his loud, brutish behavior, especially his yelling at her mama. He didn't strike her or her mama, at least not that she knew of, but she was a little afraid of him.

Suddenly, the deacons at church were asking her to speak at the Baptist Training Union and to teach Sunday school classes to children under age six. And one day her English teacher told her confidentially that she would have the lead in the end-of-year school play. She'd never been so happy. The next afternoon, her mama—wearing a dark and worried expression—took her to a doctor forty miles away in Raleigh where they learned Coreen was four months pregnant.

She'd been suspicious, losing her breakfast every morning and gorging herself on her mama's canned pickles. And oh, how she hated Leon Farrell for pushing himself into her while she fought, screamed in pain, and begged him not to do it. She didn't even like him that much, and she had hated him every day for the last thirty years. Pregnant! But she hadn't wanted to believe the Lord would be so cruel to her when she hadn't done anything to deserve it. She hadn't told her parents, because she wasn't allowed to go anywhere with boys. Her papa would have gone into a rage if he'd known she let Leon walk part of the way home with her. Sometimes she hated Leon Farrell so much that her head seemed on the verge of splitting with her anger.

Coreen dragged herself up from the bed and out of the past, wiped her tear-stained face with the hem of her skirt, walked out on her back porch, and breathed in the crisp morning air. She didn't see her evergreen pine tree bent nearly double in the wind nor the brown leaves that had piled themselves up in a corner of Bates's nice clean garden. She saw herself mortified. Humiliated. Well, what was done was done, and she had to live with it. She waved at Cee Cee, her next-door neighbor, and went back inside. She wasn't sure her mama ever forgave her for being pregnant, and she didn't know whether her father learned that she'd had a child; she hoped not, because her mama would have felt his wrath. Shaking her head, she wondered how birth parents really felt about their children. She didn't remember either of her parents coddling her and telling her they loved her. Many times, she had felt her mama's caring, but she never heard those words of love from her mama's lips. She lifted her shoulders in a slight shrug. One shouldn't speak or think unkindly of the dead, and both of her parents were gone.

The following Monday morning, Coreen walked into her office past the sign that read "Director, Women's Social and Welfare Agency" and prepared for her first appointment. The young girl she expected always arrived late in what Coreen understood was aimed to show disrespect. The girl needed help and knew it, but she despised those who tried to assist her. Coreen's staff found it impossible to give the girl useful guidance or assistance, so Coreen took on the job herself.

On that morning, twenty-five minutes after the appointed time, the girl arrived with a young man. Coreen walked into her conference room and stopped, feeling as if she'd just taken the blade of a swinging hatchet. Seconds later, her breathing restored and her composure nearly in place, she managed to take her seat. The boy looked enough like Leon to be his son. It had taken those few seconds for her to realize that, even if he were Leon's son, he was far too young to be hers. Not for the first time, she wished she had at least asked her aunt whether she'd given birth to a boy or a girl. In her misery, distress and, yes, anger and resentment, she hadn't cared.

"Who's your friend?" Coreen asked Becky, an overweight but attractive young girl of sixteen.

"Rudolph," she said, barely audibly, with her gaze locked on her shoes.

"Are you the father of Becky's baby, Rudolph?"

He slouched down in the chair, and she wanted to grab the bill of his baseball cap and jerk it around to the front of his little head, a head too small for anyone his size.

"Are you?"

"That's what she says."

Coreen watched, doing all she could to hide her disgust, as Becky squirmed in discomfort. "That isn't the answer to my question, Rudolph."

"It's all the answer you're getting." He slouched farther down in the chair, the crotch of his sloppy jeans almost even with his knees. She knew that if she continued that line of questioning she would only earn his deepening hostility, but some information was indispensable.

"Are you going to help Becky through this pregnancy and with the support of this child?"

He leaned forward, and a glare approximating a threat leaped from his narrowed eyes. "I'm here, ain't I? Back off, lady. Nobody's gonna force me to do nothing I don't *want* to do." He emphasized the word *want*. "If she hadn't been tailing behind me all the time, begging me to notice her with her tight skirts up to her ass and her boobs falling out of her T-shirt, it wouldn't a happened. She offered, and I took."

Coreen worked hard at controlling her bottom lip, for she felt it trembling the way it did all those years ago when her papa would get mad with her mama and storm around the house swearing at the top of his voice. Maybe Leon had thought she chased him, but she hadn't. She had just let him know she thought him a nice boy, a few cuts above the rest. *Nice?* So much for her schoolgirl judgment! A nice boy wouldn't have raped her.

"Next time, don't yield to the temptation," she snapped, coming back to the present and reminding herself of who and where she was. "And you won't have to pay, which is what you'll be doing for the next nineteen years." His lips parted in a snarl as if to reply, but she cut him off. "And when you're in this office, watch your mouth."

He stood, and she poised her right foot above the bell in the floor beneath her desk that would bring a guard within seconds if she touched it. Whatever he had intended dissipated like smoke in a gale of wind when Becky pulled his hand and reminded him, "You better be careful, Rudolph. You got seven more months on probation."

He sat down, and she managed to complete the interview, but she held out little hope that Becky and her child would escape a distressful life. For the remainder of the day, she tried without success to blot out of her mind's eye the picture of Rudolph looking so much like Leon, the Leon who hadn't cared whether he ruined a girl's life. The Leon who had been smiling and charming one day and a frightening brute the next.

Periodically, Coreen reminded herself that she ought to call that woman in Washington, and she had better write her speech in case she decided to use it. She didn't do either. Her stomach cramped when she thought of it, and she wanted to pull off her turtleneck sweater as perspiration dampened her clothing. Immobilized by her fear and unable to work, she closed her desk, got her briefcase, and left the building.

What she needed was a good session of her sister-in-law's foolishness. She used her cellular phone to call Lizette Treadwell. "Hi, sis. I thought I'd stop by for a few minutes. You busy?"

"I was, but you picked a good time. I just finished my last customer. I had two cancellations today. People don't like coming out in the cold. Besides, it's damp and cloudy, and you know the sistahs and their hair. Porgy's gone to rehearsal, so my time is my own. Come on by."

Coreen liked her sister-in-law, but Bates criticized her constantly, so they were not as close as they might have been or as Coreen wanted them to be. Lizette's earthy ways irked Bates, for she reveled in who she was—a down-to-earth woman who called it as she saw it, didn't care for superficial people, and flaunted her sexuality and her right to enjoy it. Bates claimed their parents would be ashamed of Lizette, but Coreen found it difficult to believe that parents would be regretful about a daughter who had succeeded in her own business and who was admired in the town where she lived.

Lizette settled them in the little sitting room in the back of her beauty shop. Her pride in the matching velveteen sofa and two chairs, the olive green broadloom carpet, Drexel tables, and Sony television—her private world away from the hustle of the shop—was obvious. She turned on the television and poured them each a glass of ginger ale.

"I'd take a beer," Lizette said, "but Porgy hates beer and can't stand the idea of me drinking it, especially when he's not with me."

"Controlling, huh? Bates is like that about some things, but all in all, he's a good man. I know how lucky I am."

Lizette pulled air through her front teeth and looked toward the ceiling. "Depends on who you're comparing him to. He's got the only travel agency in town, and it's been floundering for years. Oh, he's great provided you do things his way. If a woman wants to take her vacation in Jamaica in August, does he have to tell her it's a stupid idea? He should sell the tickets and let her see how hot it is when she gets there. He's not the weatherman, for Pete's sake. Annie Jordan will never forgive him for talking her out of traveling to the one place she'd dreamed of going for years."

"I know. He can't resist saying what he thinks."

"A little self-control would be good for his bank account."

Coreen knew the truth of Lizette's words, a truth that bothered her about Bates. Always had. He couldn't resist letting you know how smart he was, and if he was pushed, he didn't hesitate to expose another person's shortcomings. His lack of sympathetic understanding for people he could look down on was the main reason she hadn't been able to share with him the problems that troubled her and the decision she must make that had her so frightened.

"He's gentle, and he loves his family," Coreen said, feeling as if she had to apologize and hating it.

"Gentle is good," Lizette said, "if that's what tunes your strings. Me, I like it a little rough sometimes."

Coreen rested her glass on the doily atop the walnut table beside her and stared at Lizette. "What do you mean, rough?"

Lizette leaned back, covered her large brown eyes with her thick black lashes and let a smile drift over her brown face, wrinkle-free in spite of her fifty years. "Girl, don't get me started."

Reluctant to probe since she knew Lizette's penchant for candor, Coreen cleared her throat and after a few seconds let herself speak. "Are you telling me Porgy is rough with you? I never would have imagined that."

Lizette crossed and uncrossed her long legs. She reveled in her five-feet-seven-inch height and rarely went anywhere without wearing her three-inch heels. She showed her teeth in a broad grin.

"Coreen, honey, Porgy is perfect."

"Then why don't you marry him? You've been together for—"

"For sixteen years and us living together for twelve of them. Porgy knocks himself out keeping me satisfied in bed and out of it, 'cause he's not sure I won't leave him. If I marry that man, he'll take me for granted, and I ain't giving up all this good loving just to get a band to go with this diamond." She looked at the jewel on her third finger, left hand, grinned, and buffed it on the side of her skirt.

Of all the convoluted thinking! "Did he ever ask you to marry him?"

Lizette moved her head and shoulders slightly from left to right and raised both eyebrows, obviously impatient with the question. "Every time we make love, he asks me. Every single solitary time."

Coreen couldn't help thinking maybe she should have strung Bates along, made him wait longer than the eight months they knew each other. She hadn't even wanted to make love with him before they married. For all she knew, he thought she was a virgin. She hadn't let a man touch her in the eleven years since she gave birth, and it sometimes surprised her that, after her experience with Leon, she had permitted Bates to make love to her. Their first time wasn't easy. She didn't know what Bates thought about it and hadn't broached the subject.

Lizette leaned back in her chair and clasped her hands behind her head. "Coreen, you need to jerk that supercilious brother of mine out of the clouds. Y'all need to get down. I bet if I sneaked into your bedroom I wouldn't hear a thing but polite conversation. Girl, every woman deserves some good old mind-blowing sex, and Bates is the type who doesn't know a thing but the flat-of-your-back missionary position."

Coreen considered sex the least of her worries right then. "What's wrong with that?" she asked, making conversation.

Lizette rolled her eyes. "Boring."

She had wanted to spend time with Lizette because she needed diversion, respite from the problem that plagued her. She hadn't wanted the added burden of thinking she was missing something vital. But she had never lost herself in anything or anybody as Lizette obviously had, and now she had that to nag her. She left her sister-in-law feeling less of a woman than Lizette, yet she didn't want to be like her.

Walking the block and a half up Poplar Neck Road to her car, Coreen had to brace herself as the wind that drove in from the Atlantic Ocean across the Albemarle Sound slammed mercilessly into her back, almost forcing her to run. From spring through autumn, she loved Bakerville, a quiet town on the east coast of North Carolina just south of Elizabeth City, but not during winters when the winds whipped and swirled in freezing torrents from the Atlantic. She drove home, taking the straight route across Courthouse Square to 38 Queen Street North, a brown stucco Tudor house whose appearance said that its occupants lived well.

Once there, she busied herself stringing beans for supper. As she perched on the high stool beside the kitchen counter, preparing the vegetable, the half pound of beans increased in volume until they seemed to surround her. And she was pitched back into her seventeenth year, the most painful time of her life. In the nearly five months while she waited out her pregnancy in Pick-Up, North Carolina, secluded in the home of her maternal aunt, she must have strung two or three dozen bushels of beans, snapped, washed, and prepared them for canning—beans that would be sold for her aunt's income during that winter.

Her maiden aunt had no mercy on her young niece, who she regarded as a disgrace to the family. Forced to pick lettuce on her knees with her impregnated belly almost dragging the earth as she crawled, Coreen had shed tears until her eyes would no longer cry. She ironed, cleaned, cooked, and thought she would die of the pain in her back. She didn't know whether it was the thin mattress on which she slept or the back-breaking work her aunt imposed on her that caused the unremitting agony.

She hated herself and the way she looked, padding around in that red clay yard with swollen feet and legs, ugly, old-looking, and unkempt, her hard belly sticking way out in front of her. She hated herself and her aunt, too, but most of all, she hated Leon Farrell.

"Where are you, hon?"

At the shock of Bates's voice, she jumped from the stool, almost knocking it over, and quickly focused on the present.

"I'm in the kitchen." She hurried to the foyer where she knew she would find Bates hanging up his coat.

"How was business today?" The banal question was guaranteed to get the same answer he always gave, which was, "So-so, hon. So-so."

He handed her a bag, leaned forward, and brushed her lips with his, and to her astonishment he said, "Pretty good. Matter of fact, I did four tours today. One of them included South Africa, and a trip that far spells money. Not bad at all." He allowed himself a satisfied smile when she glanced into the bag and saw the little packages of "Body Smarts," the chewy raspberry candies that she loved.

"Uh . . . by the way, Jessie Holcomb dropped by. He said his boss told him you were going to testify before the Senate Hearing Committee. You know, the one on child welfare that we've been seeing on TV." Cold tremors shot through her as he continued, staring into her eyes, reading her while he spoke. He made a show of smiling, but the chill his eyes projected added to her discomfort. "Jessie's boss is head of the Democratic Club, so I guess he knows what he's talking about." He shrugged. "Anything to it?"

"I . . . uh . . . I haven't decided what I'm going to do about it, I mean . . . whether I'm going. I have an awful lot on me at the office right now, and I'm way behind. I've had to—"

"What are you talking about?" His frown, everything about his demeanor, told her that he didn't believe her and wouldn't listen to any explanation she gave. "Coreen, you're the most ambitious person in Bakerville, and if you tell me you won't jump at the chance to show off and get national recognition, I'll tell you you're lying. You're not in hiding, are you? I mean, you don't have a criminal record, do you? And another thing, how could you get an opportunity like this one and not even mention it to your husband?"

It came up so fast, so unexpectedly. She had no words for him, could only shake her head. "Then what the hell are you talking about?" he asked her. "You're always running to every two-bit convention and conference, speaking wherever anybody asks you to go and paying your own expenses, blowing money we could be putting in the bank. 'Getting my name out there,' you always say. Now you get an opportunity for some bona fide acclaim, a chance to get your name before the entire country, and you're talking about not going because you're so busy *here*. Nobody who knows you would believe that lie."

She dropped the bag of candy in the chair and whirled around, her fear eclipsed by the fire of anger. "What do you mean by calling me a liar? All you have is the word of a political party gofer, a man who survives by toting tales, circulating rumors, and taking payoffs."

Bates didn't back down as she had known he wouldn't. "You and everybody else in Bakerville know that Jessie Holcomb never spreads lies. If you hadn't promised—"

"I didn't promise."

"Why not? Didn't you admit to Glen that you were hoping to be elected president of your national professional organization? Sure you did. Appearing before that committee would cinch your election. If you don't take this opportunity, you'll have some explaining to do." He walked off, and the next thing she heard was the basement door slam. That meant he was mad and that he'd stay down there, simmering, until he got over it. She went back to the kitchen to finish stringing beans.

If she could only talk to someone. But who? She didn't take people into her confidence, because her papa had crammed into her head what he called a fact—that nobody kept another person's secret, that if you had one, better keep it to yourself. Who could she tell about the awful feeling that she was being gutted, that she was sick with fear that she would have to pay for Leon's crime yet another time? Now that Bates knew of her invitation to testify before the Senate committee, she was damned if she did and damned if she didn't.

I won't let this get me down. I've groped my way through worse mine fields and potential hazards. She gasped for breath as her heart thumped wildly in her chest. *Here I am head of an agency for disadvantaged girls, and I don't even know what kind of life my own child has. Sometimes I think providence is playing jokes on me.*

She pounded the counter with both fists. *It wasn't my doing, and I refuse to give my blood for it.* Refueled, as it were, with the reminder of her innocence in the matter, she rinsed her face with cold water, blotted it with a paper towel, and finished stringing the beans. She had planned to roast a chicken, but didn't feel like the extra work it entailed, so she defrosted hamburger meat, scrubbed some potatoes, and made a salad.

"I'm doing just what my mama did," she said aloud, stomping her foot as similar domestic scenes floated through her memory. "Work all day and then come home, cook and keep house for a man who sits down on his behind and lets me do it. Maybe I'm not so damned lucky." She was about to turn out the light and leave the kitchen when the phone rang.

"Good evening. Coreen Treadwell speaking."

"Ms. Treadwell, this is Judith Cavanaugh. I'm sure you remember me. I'm assisting the Senate Committee on Welfare. Sorry to call you at home, but you had left your office when I tried to reach you there. May we expect you Friday morning?"

She groped for the counter and leaned against it. "I . . . uh . . . I haven't yet decided to appear."

"Ms. Treadwell, our Friday morning session depends on your appearance. If you can't give me your word, we can issue a subpoena, but that won't make you look good. Which will it be?"

She could feel her shoulders sag. "All right. What time and where?"

"You'll get it all by messenger tomorrow morning, including your travel papers and hotel accommodations. Thanks so much for your cooperation."

Coreen dragged herself into the living room and sat there in the dark, her mind a blank. She couldn't even feel her fingers. She merely sat there.

Bates walked back and forth in the basement recreation room, furious with Coreen for holding out on him and mad at himself for not telling her exactly what he thought. If she had a reason for not telling him she'd been asked to testify in Washington, he needed to know what it was. As much as they talked every morning, she could have found an opportunity to tell him just about anything. He had suffered ten years of polite silence and misunderstanding with his first wife, Rose, God rest her beautiful soul, and he wasn't going to live like that anymore. Wasn't that his reason for insisting they talk every morning when they were fresh, didn't feel any bitterness, and weren't tired?

It occurred to him that lately she hadn't been too communicative. Tight-lipped as a chicken. She never had been open; if she didn't want to tell something, she didn't tell it. For eighteen years, he had felt excluded from what really mattered to Coreen. And if she had a close personal woman friend, he hadn't heard of her. All of her mail, personal and professional, went to her office. He didn't think that implied she had secrets, but that it was her way of keeping order in her life.

Coreen hadn't wanted to live in the house he shared with his first wife, but it was one of the finest in their upscale neighborhood, so they kept it, and she settled for refurnishing it. She did that to suit herself without regard to any preferences he might have had. When he objected, she was contrite, explaining that her father took no interest in the home and didn't care how it looked. She didn't want him to use her Teflon pots and pans for fear he might ruin them. And since he was too stupid to lower the flame under a pot or to clean one without using steel wool, he let her do the cooking. And he let her make the beds because he couldn't make them to suit her.

After stumbling over a bicycle, he looked around at the seldom used pool table, dartboard, ping pong table, swimming and fishing gear that cluttered up the place. Coreen had insisted that his sons have everything that every other child had. He hadn't much liked spoiling them that way, but she molded them into a family, which he and his sons hadn't been in the five years of his widowhood.

The pressure of the wooden boards against his buttocks when he sat down reminded him that he should either have the chair reupholstered or throw it out. Cupping his chin with both hands, he thought of his marriage, of his wife's obvious unhappiness. He loved Coreen and hated seeing her tired and washed out just because she had to have things a particular way. Her way. He propped his elbows on his thighs and supported his head with his hands, wondering what he could do to show Coreen that life happened every day and not sometime in the distant future. His wife had been a wonderful mother to his sons and he wanted them to have a good life together, but to his mind Coreen didn't seem to recognize happiness. She didn't even appear to have it as a priority.

His annoyance abated. Only a woman who had known suffering could have Coreen's outlook. If only she wasn't so secretive. He trudged back up the stairs where he found her sitting in the darkened room.

"What's the matter, Coreen? Something's eating you."

"I'm . . . I'm tired."

He sat down and rested his left hand on her thigh. "You want me to cook? What are we having besides beans?" He knew he stunned her, but if a good shock would get her to open up, he wasn't averse to using that means.

She stared at him as if he were an occult phenomenon. "You? Cook supper?"

"Yeah. Provided you don't tell me how to do it and you're willing to trust me with your pots and pans."

She took his hand and walked with him to the kitchen. "All right. While you're cooking, I'll start on my statement for the Senate committee."

He stopped walking and looked down at her. "You don't have to do it. If it bothers you so much, tell 'em no."

She looked past him, not at him, unlike her usual in-your-face response, and he didn't like that. "Like you said, it's good for . . . for me and . . . and for us, too, so I'm going."

He'd give anything to know why the prospect of appearing before that committee made her teeth chatter. He put the ground beef away, defrosted and baked some pork chops, steamed the beans, made corn bread, and called Coreen to supper.

"I didn't realize you could cook like this," she told him, savoring her third piece of corn bread. "I thought your culinary talents didn't extend beyond breakfast. This is good."

"After Rose died, I did all of our cooking. I'd cook supper sometimes now if you weren't so particular. When are you supposed to be in Washington?"

"Friday. So I guess I'll leave here sometime Thursday. I don't have the travel orders yet."

He stopped eating. "I'm getting the impression that you only decided within the last hour. Since I got home."

"Well, like you said, after that exposure everybody will consider me an expert. So I figured it's maybe just what I need. Everybody will know who I am."

"I can't believe you didn't think of that before." He took the dishes to the kitchen, looked in the freezer for ice cream, and thought better of it. He wasn't in the mood for desert. He had always known Coreen to be truthful, but she was in there spinning tales, and if he confronted her they might discover how solid—or fragile—their marriage really was.

Chapter Two

Tears glistened in Frieda Davis's eyes as she watched two men drop the last shovel of dirt on the coffin in which Beatrice Davis, her adoptive mother, reposed. A person who had worked as hard and endured as much pain and harassment as her mother ought at least to have been buried on a day bright with sunshine and in a season of sweet-smelling flowers. The cold and bleakness of this Saturday morning seemed to Frieda the final mockery of an unhappy life. The woman had given her as much love and caring as her husband, Frieda's adoptive father, would allow. She had done her best to behave as a good daughter to her adoptive mother, but Claude Davis hadn't made that easy either.

Beatrice Davis had no control over her husband. Frieda would always remember him as a contemptible, selfish man who took what he wanted from whomever he chose to get it. When he died, she hadn't cared, didn't miss him and never would. At last, the workers smoothed the sod on her mother's grave, patting it firmly, and with the blustering January wind in her face, tears finally trickled down Frieda's cheeks, stinging like icicles. Tears for her adoptive mother and for herself. During Beatrice's long illness, Frieda had not been able to help her mother as much as she would have, because she dared not risk an encounter with her adoptive father.

After adopting her, Claude and Beatrice had two daughters

of their own. Beatrice didn't make a difference between them, but Frieda hoped Claude had. The fingers of Julie, the older of her adoptive sisters, curled through hers as the choir and mourners sang "Nearer My God To Thee," that standby Baptist funeral hymn, and the undertaker covered the grave with flowers. Then she walked with her two sisters back to the car for the drive to the house she hadn't entered since she ran away the day after finishing high school at age seventeen.

When she saw the house, Frieda hesitated and nearly stumbled. But she forced herself to walk into that purgatory on earth, the place that gave birth to her ugly, painful memories. When she stopped at the doorway and leaned against the doorjamb, both Julie and Portia, her younger sister, turned to look at her, although their facial expressions didn't suggest that her behavior was abnormal.

"You can have your old room," Julie said. "It's been so long, so many years since you were here with us. We want to catch up, to find out everything that's happened over the years."

Over the last twelve years, what hadn't she done? Everything a person could do to make a decent, honest living. "I can't stay, Julie. I could barely make myself walk in here. And if I didn't know how you and Portia feel with Mama gone, I'd be at the station waiting for the bus to Baltimore. But Mama was good to me, and I had to come to pay my respects to her."

"You didn't come when Papa died, and I wondered why you didn't send flowers or a card," Portia said when Julie went in the kitchen to make coffee. "I can't believe he passed only three weeks ago, and Mama was still walking around then, though she could hardly put one foot in front of the other one. She said she had a pain in her chest, and the next minute she was gone. But Papa was sick a long time, Frieda."

Frieda had hoped they wouldn't want to plow through the past. She had never told anyone why she left home, but the pleading in her mama's letters for her to forgive her father was proof her mother knew. She despised Claude Davis and had no intention of whitewashing him to his biological daughters.

She rubbed her right hand across her forehead. "I left here because of him, and if I had come back for his funeral, I would have been as big a hypocrite as he was. Flowers? I wouldn't have sent *weeds* to his funeral."

"What are you talking about?" Julie stood in the door between the dining and living rooms holding a tray of coffee and cake. "What do you mean, Frieda?"

"You don't want to know. I can't bear to think of it, much less discuss it."

Julie rested the tray on the heavy oak coffee table, almost sitting on the floor. "You can't let it drop there, Frieda. What happened?"

Frieda sat forward, aware that her face was a liar's mask, and assumed a nonchalant air. "Look, the two of you mourned him; I didn't. So I don't want to unearth all that old stuff and destroy his memory for you. Let's drop it."

"We're not going to drop this," Portia said in an agitated voice. "I had problems with him, and they started as soon as you left here."

Frieda's gaze traveled to Julie, and chills streaked through her when she observed the look of recognition on her sister's face. "Me, too," Julie said in a barely audible voice. "It was awful. And all this time, I thought it was only me."

And all the time she thought he did that to her because she wasn't his own child. If only she had known, she could have protected her sisters.

"He abused me from the time I was twelve until a week before I left here." Frieda told them. "He threatened to kill me if I breathed it. I can't tell you how many times I tried to sneak up behind him and plunge a kitchen knife into him. But I couldn't get the courage to go through with it."

"I finally told him that if he ever touched me again, I'd tell Mama, even if he killed me," Julie said. "At first I was confused. He'd do those things to me, and then he would cry and try to hug me and tell me he loved me. Oh, you don't know how I hated him."

"I told him I was going to kill *him*," Portia said. "After that he shrank away every time I got near him. I went to his funeral for Mama's sake. I didn't care how much dirt they threw in his face."

"I think we ought to sell the house, split the money among the three of us, and get on with our lives," Julie said. Frieda was glad that Portia agreed, because she certainly did. She never wanted to see the place again.

"At least I won't ever have to go back inside that torture chamber," Frieda said to herself that evening as she kissed her sisters good-bye at the station and boarded the bus to Baltimore.

She had no stomach for the supper Julie and Portia packed for her. As the bus thundered through the darkness, she was once more in Bixby, North Carolina, a tiny, lower middle-class village on the outskirts of Charlotte, terrified as Claude Davis opened her bedroom door and swaggered to her bed. After the first time, she cringed whenever she had to be alone with him, whether it was in the kitchen, the garage, or outside in the open air. For five long years, she suffered his brutality. Then one night while watching television, a week before she finished high school, she saw a movie, *Caroline's Secret*, that chronicled a situation similar to the one in which she found herself. When he came to her later that night, she told him that if he touched her, she would go to the police. He didn't believe her, and when he attempted to crawl into her bed, she broke the light on her night table over his head. "Pig," she'd sneered. The last word she ever said to him. Eight nights later, the day after her graduation from high school, she ran away.

That little victory—stunning him with a blow to his head—did not satisfy her. Every day from that night onward, she plotted ways to get even with him, but in the end his death robbed her of that pleasure. She leaned back in the seat, closed her eyes, and while visions of the past mocked her and rended her, tears soaked her clothing. Someone would pay. And who remained as the proper recipient of her revenge but her birth mother?

If it's the last thing I do, I'm going to find my birth mother and tell her what she did to me. I don't want to know why she gave me up; I don't care about that. I need to tell her to her face what she consigned me to.

Around noon that same Saturday, Coreen walked up the ramp at Northeastern Regional Airport, looked over her shoulder at the commuter plane that brought her back home to Bakerville, and waved at it. *Thank God for the planes and the pilots that took me safely to Washington and back home to Bakerville,* words such as she whispered after every safe flight. She dreaded plane rides almost as much as she had feared testifying before that committee, and she breathed deeply in relief that both were behind her.

She hadn't been confronted with embarrassing or hostile questions. The senators had actually wanted her views on the plight of disadvantaged girls, the root of their problems and how they might be remedied. They treated her as an expert. Her, Coreen Holmes, whose first seventeen years were spent in a working-class neighborhood, one hundred and fifty feet from the railroad tracks and closer still to the local jail, jumping puddles in the unpaved road where she lived—modest circumstances by any estimation. Coreen Holmes, who turned her life around after getting one of the hardest blows a young girl could weather. Her steps quickened as she thrust her shoulders back and headed for the rental car. If luck was with her, all of Bakerville and especially her staff saw her performance, one that could guarantee her rise to the top of her profession.

Feeling better than she had in days, Coreen took Route 32 at a faster clip than she usually drove and was soon in Bakerville, where she decided to surprise Bates at his travel agency. Not many people would argue a customer out of a deal guaranteed to net them several hundred dollars, but she stepped in the door just in time to prevent Bates from doing that.

Lydia Felton rushed to her. "Coreen, I'm so glad to see you. I can't get Bates to set up my tour the way I want it. He keeps telling me I'll have to double back to Florence if I go there before I go to Pisa and Sienna, and I don't care. I want to go to Florence first. I'm paying, and that's the way I want it."

Coreen greeted Bates with a kiss on the cheek. "Well, you know how he is, Lydia, always careful not to cheat or mislead anyone." She turned to her husband. "Honey, as soon as you finish that, can we leave? I have a lot to tell you."

She ignored his glare, and he wrote the tickets, put them in an envelope, and handed them to the woman. "That cost you three hundred dollars you didn't have to spend."

Lydia left, her face wreathed in smiles as she tucked the tickets into her handbag.

"You can't know how relieved I—"

"I don't interfere with your business, and I'll thank you not to meddle in mine. That woman will be back here tomorrow or the next day asking me to change her itinerary, because somebody told her she was throwing away money. Let that be the last time you do something like that."

"Look, I'm sorry. Please let's not allow that to start a riff between us. I'm in such a good mood, and I've got so much to tell you. Let's eat dinner out."

Bates leaned back in his desk chair and looked at her in a way that she wouldn't say was unfriendly, but warmth wouldn't describe it either.

"Maybe not this evening. Eric called and said he'll be in tonight, and he's bringing a friend."

"But I hadn't planned anything special, so—"

He interrupted her. "It's only one-fifteen, and he won't be here until around seven. We have plenty of time."

So he wasn't anxious to hear about her experience before the committee, or maybe he had watched it. Well, he wouldn't catch her standing on her hind legs with her tongue hanging out and her paws bent in front of her, a little puppy begging for recognition.

"In that case, I'd better drop off the rental car and catch you at home."

She strode out before he could react, but however her exit appeared to him, crestfallen was the way she felt. They encouraged their sons to come home whenever they chose, but she wished Eric had picked a better time to come and bring a guest. For some reason, Bates was displeased with her, and not because she interfered with his sale. It didn't bode well for an evening in the presence of others; Bates wouldn't bite his tongue if there was something he wanted to say.

At the first peal of the bell, Bates rushed to open the door, anxious as he always was to greet his elder son. He reached out to envelop him in his arms and stopped as his gaze landed on the woman behind him. From her olive complexion, long black hair that might or might not have been permed, and chiseled features, he couldn't figure out her ethnic origin. But she sure didn't look very black to him.

"Dad, this is Bright Star." And as if reading his father's mind, he added, "Star's Chickasaw Native American. Star, this is my father."

"Glad to meet you, sir."

He didn't know what his next move should be. Never having met a Native American woman or man, he wasn't sure how to greet her, so he extended his hand and hoped she'd shake.

"We're happy to have you, Star. Come on in, son. Coreen's back there in the kitchen."

Eric must have known that he knocked him for a loop—bringing that good-looking woman home with him without warning his parents—for he winked and exposed his teeth in a satisfied grin before clasping his father in his arms.

"You two get acquainted while I check out Mom."

"Uh . . . have a seat, Star. You don't mind if I call you Star, do you?"

"No, sir. That's what I expected you'd call me."

He'd never been tongue-tied, but what did you say to. . . ? "How'd you get to be an In—a Native American? I mean . . . oh, for goodness sake, what I mean is—"

The twinkling of her eyes put him off. Then she laughed, and he could see why Eric brought her home with him. "Mr. Treadwell, I'm sorry for laughing, but that was funny. Anyway, I think you know the answer."

He liked her, and he sure hoped she wasn't all facade and no substance. A woman ought to have something going for her other than looks. "What do you do, Star?"

"I design computer software. That's how I met Eric. He needed a program that would simulate new corn varieties with specific cross fertilizations and I got the job."

Bates leaned forward. "Did you manage to do it?"

She settled herself in the chair, comfortable and self-assured. "If I hadn't, I wouldn't be sitting here. When it comes to his work, Eric doesn't fool around."

"I can believe that. He was hardly five and already demand-ing that everything and everybody be straight. Wouldn't take no tea for the fever. Never lie to him."

"And I like that about him."

He'd better find out all he could about her before Eric came back. "I don't know much about the Chickasaw. What part of the country do your folks live in?"

"You'll find the Chickasaw throughout Mississippi, Louisiana, and especially Oklahoma, but I didn't grow up with them. My parents died in a flood, and an Oklahoma Choctaw family found me and raised me. They adopted me, but they gave me as much of my Chickasaw heritage as they could. Fortunately, the lan-guages are similar, and I can speak with the Chickasaw."

"How're you two getting along in here? Mom, this is Bright Star. Star this is my mom, my stepmother."

Coreen stepped toward Star, who rose and went to meet her. *Well, I'll be danged,* Bates thought. *They hug just like everybody else.*

"I'm so happy to meet you, Star. Welcome. Eric surprised us with this visit, and I didn't have time to make you a really nice dinner, but next time I'll show off." She laughed, intentionally downplaying the impact of her words. He liked the way Coreen had of making people feel comfortable while saving the light for herself.

"Honey, Star's a real Native American. She told me she's a Chickasaw, but that a Choctaw family adopted her and raised her. Her folks are from out there in Oklahoma."

Coreen's smile faded, and he watched as this woman who had the self-possession and aplomb of an undefiled saint seemed to shrink before his eyes and to fidget like a restless child. He was about to ask her what was wrong, when she announced that she had better check the dinner and left the room. He had hoped that with the Senate hearing behind her, Coreen would return to her normal self—strong, resolute, and purposeful, but gentle and soft-spoken. He closed his eyes. She could be so sweet and caring, the way she was with his boys when they were growing up, and the way she was with him when he needed that femi-nine person who lounged at the edge of her public persona.

His breath shortened when it occurred to him that Coreen might not be well and hadn't told him. He shook his head. No, it wasn't that because she slept like a log. It was something else, and it wasn't trivial. He didn't like it.

Coreen leaned against the refrigerator door, sweat dripping from every pore of her body, and wiped her face and neck with a handful of paper towels. "Lord, please don't let any of them come in here before I get myself together," she whispered. Of all the women in the world, why did Eric have to find one who was adopted? She didn't want to know about the woman's life, her problems growing up, or anything else about her. Every day of her own life, guilt plagued her about the child she gave up, the child she hadn't let herself look at or know anything about. She pounded her fist on the nearby stove. She'd been only seventeen with a woman's burden, but she never heard one sympathetic word from her aunt. Overworked. Lacking any prenatal care or preparation for that awful twenty-four hours of pain during which she wanted to die.

Coreen straightened up and forced herself to deal with the dinner. "I don't deserve this torture," she said, "and I refuse to let this thing whip me."

She froze a smile on her face and made herself personable and outgoing while they ate dinner, although she could barely wait for an opportunity to be alone.

"Do you know how to prepare any Native American dishes," she asked Star, making talk.

And Star's reply suggested she knew that. "Why, yes, ma'am. After all, I lived with my adoptive parents until I went away to college. We didn't live on a reservation, but in Tulsa where my adoptive father works for the IRS, so I had all kinds of friends and ate all kinds of food. I cook all kinds, too."

Adoptive! Adoptive! If she heard that word one more time, she would scream. As she stopped herself from placing her hands over her ears, her gaze fell on Bates and the quizzical expression on his face.

"You all eat all of this food," she said, "while I get the dessert together." With that, she made it to the kitchen where she snatched a deep breath. If she could just make it through the dessert, she could plead a headache and go to bed. Later, Eric said, "Star and I will clean the kitchen, Mom," and she wondered if her anxiety had been so obvious.

"Is there any way you can get a few days off from work and . . . well, just rest?" Bates asked her later that night as he walked into their bedroom still damp from his shower. "You've been under a lot of stress, and neither the job nor anything else is worth your sanity."

She let her negligee fall from her shoulders, threw it across a chair, and prepared to crawl into bed, grateful for his misunderstanding of what had nearly petrified her. Just when she had a moment of peace, just when she basked in her triumph before the Senate committee and had avoided national humiliation, she received in the person of Bright Star a gut-wrenching reminder, one that could be with her for the remainder of her life. She suspected that Eric cared for Star, and she didn't wish her son ill, but . . .

"What did you think of Star?"

"Uh . . . too soon to tell," she hedged, and she knew he didn't like that.

"I didn't ask you for a character analysis, Coreen. I want to know what your gut instinct is about our son's girl."

"You think she's his girl?"

He let the towel fall away from his hips and strode over to her. "What do you think? He's twenty-seven years old, and she's the first female he's ever brought home with him. Surely you don't think she's his fencing buddy. Didn't you look at her? She's the type of woman a man marries, provided he gets the chance."

"At least she not a bimbo."

"*What?* What made you say that? You'd never catch Eric with a bimbo. He demands substance, and you know it. Now, Glen. That's another matter."

"I don't want to talk about them," she said, covering her faux pas. "Besides, they're both wonderful sons to me, and I'm grate-ful."

He slid into bed, propped himself on his left elbow, and looked down at her. "What else did you have in mind?"

She'd faked all night, so she might as well fake this, too, because sex was as far from her mind as north was from south.

He fooled her, whispering softly of his concern for her, reminding her of their younger days.

"When I looked past Eric's shoulder and saw that lovely young woman standing behind him, I thought about you and how I felt when I brought you home that first time to introduce you to my boys. I was so nervous and so scared you wouldn't like them." As he spoke, softly and rhythmically, hypnotically, he stroked her face and let his hands move gently up and down her arms.

"I loved you so much, but I knew we would have to end it if things didn't go well with you and my children. You were so beautiful, so loving, and so feminine. I prayed harder that night than I'd ever prayed."

His lips trailed over her face, barely skimming her eyelids, ears, nose, and cheeks, moving to her neck, adoring it as one savored a gourmet meal. Restless and agitated as her libido stirred, she lit up when he bent to her breast, knowing as she did that he needed no other accomplice to attain his goal. He worked at her until she became first pliant—when his game escalated to a torture of her senses—and then the aggressor, taking him into her and writhing helplessly in ecstasy until he spent himself and rocked her to sleep.

She awoke the next morning to the aroma of coffee. "How you feeling this morning?" he asked her. "I got us some coffee. I don't expect Eric and Star will get up anytime soon."

She sat up and rubbed her eyes. "I put her in the guest room. You're not telling me they slept together."

He nearly spilled the coffee on her. "I'm not telling you *where* they slept, because I don't know and I don't care. How many times did we sleep together before we got married? Huh? The first time we did it was a little less than two months after we met. So don't hand me any moral outrage. I hope she's as good to him as you were to me last night."

She shifted her gaze, reminding him that she didn't like to remember how wild she could be in their lovemaking. "You sneaked up on me."

"I know. If I hadn't, I'd have gone to sleep rock hard. Something cut the wind out of your sails last night and right before my eyes, too. Want to tell me about it?"

She had known he would bring that up, for very little escaped him, and he rarely considered it prudent to keep quiet about a thing if it perplexed him. She hated lies and liars, but how could she tell him why knowing Star was an adopted child shook her to the pit of her being? How could she tell him it seemed like God was tracking her, forever holding her deed in front of her, waving it like a skull and bones flag billowing from a mast on a pirate's ship? Whenever she got over one obstacle, another hurdle confronted her.

"You can't know what these past couple of days did to me. Washed me out. You know how I like to manage things. Being at the mercy of such powerful people was a frightening experience."

With his back to her, he finished that cup of coffee, picked the carafe up from the floor, poured himself another cup, and drank that. Then he turned and hooked his gaze into her, all but daring her not to look at him. "How'd it happen that you were practically dancing the boogaloo at the agency yesterday afternoon. You were a bird out of a cage, free of your worries and fears, practically bursting out of yourself. You were even feeling successful, certain that your performance at the hearing guaranteed you another rung up the ladder. So what happened since then? Somebody else call you to testify somewhere?" He stood and looked down at her. "Coreen, do I look crazy to you?"

He deserved better and she knew it, but she couldn't risk his judging her and refusing to absolve her the way he did everybody else. She reached for his hand. "Bates, please don't create a problem where none exists. I'm straight. I try to be a good woman, a good wife and mother, and good at my job. Please don't erect a barrier between us. I couldn't bear it. I'm not here because I can't go anywhere else; I'm here because I need you."

He continued to look at her until at last, shaking his head as if mystified, he said, "None of this is reasonable, Coreen; things are suppose to add up. Nothing you've said explains how you could . . . Look, I want you to see a doctor. We've got to rule out manic-depressive psychosis. I can't think of anything else that would make sense."

She knew she didn't have a mental illness, especially manic-depression, which was a serious and rarely alleviated condition. Not wanting to mire herself into a deeper pit, she squeezed his fingers, urging him to sit on the side of the bed where he'd been before getting vexed with her. "I'm not ill, and I don't have any psychological problems. You know a letdown always follows the euphoria I was feeling. I'd been so anxious that getting that hearing behind me was almost more joy than I could bear. Do you believe me?"

"I want to, Coreen. I have to. But, baby, try to keep it between the lines. I'm getting too old for this roller-coaster, zigzagging stuff."

She let the tips of her fingers skim the side of his face. "Since when was fifty-two old? Besides, old men don't carry on the way you did with me last night."

When he grinned and said, "You're just saying that because it's true," her relief was palpable.

"I don't know how Star's adoptive parents raised her, but I was thinking how nice it would be if we all four went to church this morning."

There it was again. She battled her will and smiled. "I expect she pays homage to the Great Spirit."

"Well, that's the same as the Lord, isn't it?"

"I don't know and I don't think we should ask her. Speak to Eric about it." She allowed herself a long, lazy, catlike stretch and got up. "I don't think I'll go to church, but if you're going, I'd better get breakfast."

"Of course I'm going."

His frown alerted her to her errors. He went to Mt. Airy

Baptist Church every Sunday morning, and she didn't cook breakfast on Sundays; he did. Unless he was sick, he had cooked every Sunday morning since Glen went away to college. But in her relief that she had escaped the ferocious inquisition of which she knew him capable, she made a blunder that he wouldn't forget. He might not say anything about it then or for days, but she knew she would face it eventually.

Eric and Star left for the University of Maryland in College Park around eleven that morning, and she got busy straightening the house. "Acting like my mother again," she grumbled, though admitting to herself that she enjoyed the fruits of her labors, that she relished their elegant home when it was in a state fit for a queen. She finished the chores as quickly as she could, dressed warmly, and drove out Route 32 to Stanley's Meat and Fowl market where she bought two dressed ducks, country sausage, and smoked spareribs. With her purchases in a cool box, she drove back to Bakerville and parked behind the library, which opened from one to three-thirty on Sundays.

"No. No. I'd better not do this," she told herself. "Some of these gossips working here will want to know why I'm searching the catalogue for information on adoption." Maybe she would do that the next time she was in Elizabeth City where not many people knew her. She had hardly started the motor for the drive home when she nearly slammed her foot on the brakes. Elizabeth City wasn't safe, either. The whole country had stared at her likeness for three hours the previous Friday. She walked into her house feeling whipped, hardly aware of how she got there. Maybe she should tell Bates everything. But she didn't think she could bear his disapproval and certainly not his scorn. He didn't like knowing that her status in the community, and now nationally, exceeded his, and she didn't believe he would hesitate to knock her down a few pegs if he thought she deserved it.

That didn't mean he didn't love her; he did, and she knew it. But he needed a confidence builder, and as with a lot of men in his position, he didn't hesitate to use her for that.

* * *

Coreen walked into the building at 122 Poplar Neck Road and strode to the elevator, hardly having given a thought to what she could expect from her staff. With some surprise, she welcomed their warm greetings.

"You sure looked good on TV," a messenger said while waiting with her for the elevator.

" 'Morning, Ms. Treadwell," a secretary said, beaming, as Coreen got off the elevator. "You sure told it to 'em just like it was. I was glued to that set downstairs."

"She sure did," another staff member who had joined them said. "Bet they weren't expecting anybody like you. I tell you I couldn't get over how you answered those questions. Not a bit nervous."

"What's Hillary Clinton like?" one of them asked.

"I didn't see her. She's not on that committee."

"We sure are proud of you," another said.

Coreen thanked them, and after a short walk from the elevator to her office, found her office key and inserted it into the lock. After turning the key a few more times than was ordinarily necessary, the door opened and she walked in. *What on earth?* Her desk drawers stood open, their contents spilled over the floor, and the doors of her closet and bathroom were ajar. The desk chair lay on its side in front of the desk.

Her heart pulsed like a runaway train. She sat on the edge of the desk and looked around, assessing the damage and trying to calm herself. Suddenly, she dashed across the room, removed the huge reproduction of a landscape, and breathed in relief. The reproduction covered a safe in which she kept files of sensitive cases, papers that she hadn't had time to microfilm and store in the confidential files. She walked around the desk and pressed the button that summoned the guard.

The tall man of stately manners and appearance walked into her office, looked around, rubbed his chin, and asked her, "You wanted to see me, ma'am?"

She had, on occasion, wondered about Oscar's mental capacity, but this time she had no doubt. She made herself smile. "Do you think someone left the front door unlocked at any time this past weekend?"

"I wouldn't think so, ma'am. I found it locked each morning when I came to work."

A former heavyweight boxer turned deacon of Bates's church, it didn't pay to question Oscar's logic. "Have any other staff reported a problem to you this morning?"

He shook his head. "Nobody, ma'am."

"I see. Perhaps we had better get my secretary in here and see whether she can tell us anything."

"She's gone to her sister's wedding this week, remember?"

"Yes. I'll have to call the police. This is . . . Oscar this is enough to make me ill."

"Yes, ma'am. I never saw anything like it. We don't let any of the clients on the elevators 'less they have an appointment with somebody." He scratched his head as if in search of an explanation. "Anybody hate you?"

She flinched at the suggestion. "I don't know. I wouldn't have thought so." She excused him, telephoned the police department, and sat on the edge of her desk waiting for the officers to arrive. Days, maybe years, of work lay cluttered around her feet in disarray. Very shortly, the officers arrived, dusted the office for fingerprints, photographed the chaos, and left. She called her deputy and two of the caseworkers to help her put her office in order.

"This is the work of one of these girls," Maddie Franks, her deputy, said.

"Well, if any of them has a police record, the police will have them in no time," one woman said as she crawled around the office raking in handfuls of papers.

Coreen was quiet. It seemed as if she took one step forward only to be jerked a couple of steps backward. Why had the person chosen her office, and how did he or she get past the guard? She didn't remember denying assistance to any of the girls they served, and while an employee might get angry with her, each one cared too much about the service her organization provided to scatter records in that way.

"You all had better stop and eat," she told them around one-thirty in the afternoon. She had no appetite for food. She felt personally violated, almost as if Leon Farrell had done his deed a second time. The women left for lunch, and Coreen sat in the middle of her ruined office, her eyes dry although tears poured down her insides.

She reached beneath the desk for her phone and answered it. "Oh, Bates. You wouldn't believe what I found when I walked into my office this morning."

"A bunch of red roses?"

"*Roses?*" She described the scene around her and waited for his words of solace.

Instead she heard, "What time did you get to work this morning?" She told him, and his lengthy silence wasn't the response she expected. He said, "You found this out five hours ago and hadn't called to tell me about it? Why are you telling me now?"

"Look, I was so shocked that I—"

"You didn't think your husband could help. Right? Well, I can imagine it's upset you, but I don't like the fact that you didn't think enough of me to tell me. You don't need me, Coreen. You can tell me you do till you're green in the face, but it won't be true."

"Honey, I . . . What is it, Oscar?"

"You talk to Oscar, that fountain of knowledge. I'll see you at home." He hung up.

She'd deal with that later. "Yes, Oscar."

"I've been intending to ask you about this, ma'am. My niece, my sister's daughter, wants to put her baby up for adoption, and she doesn't know where to go. She's seventeen, and we told her she had to be eighteen to do that. Isn't that right?"

She stared at him. *Lord, please don't let me get paranoid.* "I'm too busy to deal with that, Oscar. Speak with Ms. Franks when she comes back from lunch." *And for heaven's sake leave me out of it.*

Oscar left her office, and she remained as she had been before he walked in, seated on the floor staring at the shambles of her office, shaken as the significance of what she saw dawned on her. Someone wanted to hurt her, if not physically, then professionally.

She laughed, balled up a sheet of paper, and threw it across the room. Then she laughed harder. And harder. Until the laughter dissolved into tears that racked her body. She wrapped her arms around her middle and let them flow. After an hour, when she had herself once more firmly in control, she went into her bathroom, washed her face, combed her hair, and got back to work. It would take more than that to break her. Much more.

Chapter Three

A week after finding her office, her private sanctuary, ransacked, Coreen sat in her desk chair, the place now neat and orderly except for the files, and opened the brown wrapper that lay among her morning mail. She knew she would find there several issues of the *Sentinel*, Pick-Up, North Carolina's biweekly paper to which she had subscribed for the twenty-four years since she graduated from college. Not that she had an interest in or an affection for Pick-Up; very much to the contrary. She wanted to know if any news had leaked out about her five-month stay there, her pregnancy, and of her having borne a child. With no other living relative, she had in recent years also scanned the paper for news of her aunt, although not out of concern for Agatha Monroe's well being. Curiosity better described her motive.

Scanning the front page of the first issue she picked up, a notice in the lower righthand corner brought a gasp from her. Her aunt had died several weeks earlier without leaving any known relatives. When she turned to page three, she read a description of her aunt as a God-fearing woman who lived a righteous life. It stated further that Agatha's church and her insurance policy with the Daughters of Zion Tents buried her in style.

What a charlatan, she thought. No God-fearing person would have treated another as her aunt had treated her. *Well, she's gone, and that's that. I wish I could be sorry, but all I feel is relief that there's nobody now living who knows I ever had a baby. My real name wasn't even given to the birth registration office.*

Realization dawned on her, and she flung her arms wide, scattering the pages of the *Sentinel* and then slapping her palms on the desk. Her secret died with her aunt. Humming Springsteen's "Glory Days," she skipped and danced around the office as she put her files in order.

"My goodness," she said to herself. "I can start my campaign now. Nothing stands in the way of my election as president of my national association."

In her elation, she didn't remember that Bates was still vexed with her for failing to tell him about the condition in which she found her office the previous week, that since then, he hadn't said any more to her than was necessary. Indeed, she wondered how he was handling his libido, as it tended to roar out of control every third night and sometimes more often than that.

She telephoned him. "Hi, honey," she began, after he answered. "Why don't we go to Sparky's Lobster Pot for dinner tonight? I've got a taste for some of those crab cakes."

He skipped preliminaries. "What's going on with you? Don't you think you owe me the courtesy of an apology for cutting me off in order to say something to Oscar, of all people? I doubt he remembered a word you said to him five minutes after he left you."

"But, Bates, surely you're not still angry about that."

"What if I am? I do not want to go with you to Sparky's so you can be Miss Importance and have everybody genuflecting and grinning at you like a bunch of hyenas. I'm eating at home."

She could almost feel her chest sinking into a concave mass, hollowed out like a dog's dish. "Well, if that's what you want."

He deserved better than she had given him recently. She hadn't been forthcoming about the committee, and then there was the matter of forgetting to tell him about her office. She didn't blame him for being vexed at her, but he regarded himself as a devout Christian and in her book that meant he should be more forgiving. The more she accomplished, the more difficult and exacting he became. *Or maybe the less considerate you are,* her conscience nagged.

How long before they had a crisis? Bates didn't think in terms of heading off trouble; he preferred to confront it head-on and usually worsened the problem. Maybe she'd better focus a little more on home and keeping her marriage together. If Bates made up his mind to do something drastic, he didn't let reason interfere with his plans.

Bates knew he was looking for a fight. He was Coreen's husband and he meant to remind her of the meaning of the word "wife." Shortly before five-thirty, closing time, his friend Jessie Holcomb walked into the store, as Bates called his travel agency.

"Man, it looks like snow. I mean, you can practically taste it. I'm going by Tim's and get a few bags of salt. I ain't up to shoveling no snow."

"Yeah. You'd rather make that white guy rich than shovel a little snow. If I put a hundred bags in here and charged half of what Tim charges, I bet I wouldn't sell six bags, but Tim wouldn't have a bag left."

Jessie gave Bates a good look at his flawless white teeth. When he stopped chuckling, he said, "That oughtn't to bother you none. Then old Tim would have to buy yours. You'd still sell 'em."

Bates glared at Jessie. "Man, you don't want to get me cranked up on the subject of black folk not patronizing black folk. Anyhow, I hope to hell you're joking."

"What's eating you, man?" Jessie asked him, scrutinizing Bates as if he preferred to figure it out for himself. "It ain't like you to be so cross."

"Humph."

"How's Coreen, anyhow? She's a real celebrity. Did you see those senators nodding their heads while she was speaking and asking her questions like she was the encyclopedia? Everybody's talking about it. Imagine sitting up there in the Senate and telling those white folk how to run the country. Man, she's something *else!*"

"You can say *that* again."

Jessie cleared his throat. "Things ain't going well with you and Coreen? I never woulda thought that. You better get it straightened out before it gets twice as big as it is now."

Jessie loved to give advice, and it was said around Bakerville that he cherished his wisdom more than anyone else did. He patted the inside pocket of his jacket, saw the big "No Smoking" sign, and slumped into a chair. "Lorna's over at her mother's place in Caution Point. How about I pick up the salt and we check out Lou's Watering Hole for a few minutes after you close up?"

Bates directed his gaze past Jessie at the huge travel picture of sunny Monaco, looked toward the door and the gray January weather beyond it, and raised his left shoulder in a shrug.

"Don't mind if I do." It wouldn't hurt Coreen one bit to have to worry about when he was coming home.

Three hours later, just before nine in the evening, he stood at the door of the Watering Hole ready to go home, and gazed at the four inches of snow on the sidewalk and the mass of grainy white particles falling so thickly that he could barely see across the street. Nervous and repentant about his misdeed—allowing his wife to guess as to his whereabouts and safety for the first time since he married her—Bates hurried to find Lou, the owner.

"Mind if I use your phone? I gotta call home."

Lou heaved his nearly three hundred pounds from the stool on which he sat. "Go ahead and try," he said nodding toward the phone behind the counter. "None of the other guys were able to get a signal. Maybe you can."

Bates grabbed the big man's shoulder. "You telling me the phone's down?"

"Yeah," he said, as if it didn't matter, "and no point in going around there to the pay phone. It's been out of order for months." He took a slug of draft beer. "Get off your high horse and have a few beers like everybody else. You been dawdling here for three hours over one cup of cold coffee. Two or three beers won't drag you down here with the rest of us."

Bates looked steadily at the man to indicate his displeasure, but he wasn't about to take on a former boxer nearly twice his size. Besides, he doubted anything he did would pull him down to Lou Hinkins's level.

"Still think this was a good idea?" he asked Jessie, who seemed imperturbable about their being stranded in a lower-class bar for as long as the storm lasted.

Jessie took another swig of his beer. "I don't remember putting no gun in your back. You walked in here a free man."

"What about Coreen? Suppose the electricity goes out or something like that? Your wife's out of town; mine's home by herself worried to death."

"Oh, come on, Bates. Coreen's been by herself all evening, and it didn't worry you one bit till you saw the snow. Just make up your mind you ain't gonna get none tonight, and think of all the energy you'll save."

"You like the sound of your voice better than I do right now." He looked at Jessie, relaxed and at home in the company of Bakerville's hardest beer drinkers. "What the hell was I doing here in the first place?" he asked himself, and took his seat across from Jessie at a table in the corner. He didn't hang out with the boys as Jessie did. It didn't appeal to him. And in the eighteen years of his marriage to Coreen, he couldn't remember not going directly home from work. He was mad at her, but that didn't mean he had to behave as a teenager, getting even. He leaned back in the chair and sighed, remorseful for his impulsive act. It would be a long night, and nothing he could say to Coreen would make amends. Nobody could beat his wife at suffering if she put her mind to it.

Bates worried without cause. Annoyed at his refusal to go with her to Sparky's for seafood, Coreen cooked a supper of beef stew, rice, string beans, and baked corn bread, ate her meal, and went to bed a little after seven-thirty. She left his food on the stove.

When she awakened the next morning to find that she'd slept alone, her anger dissolved into anxiety, and she wrestled with the fear that Bates could be dipping into some other pot of honey.

Then furor rolled through her as she imagined her husband wallowing in another woman's cocoon. Not that he had ever before behaved in a way that suggested he might be philandering; he hadn't. But when a man got to be fifty and started worrying about his sexual prowess, his wife had better be on the lookout. She put on a robe, and went downstairs to make coffee. One glance at the kitchen window clarified the situation.

Coreen tested the phone line. How many times had she asked Bates to buy a cellular phone? If he had one, they would never be out of touch. But he scoffed at the idea: nobody was going to catch Bates Treadwell walking down the street talking on a cell phone. She pulled air through her front teeth. As if that was the only use to which a cellular phone could be put.

She poured a cup of coffee, got her cell phone, and dialed Lizette, her sister-in-law. Then she flipped on the little television that rested atop the refrigerator. Bakerville appeared as dead as a burnt-out log, as motionless as an ancient cemetery. Nothing moved before the television camera. She had never witnessed such stillness. Gray, cold, and bleak. Even the usually blustering January wind had been stilled.

"Hey, girl," Lizette said when she detected Coreen's voice. "Thank God for cell phones. That is some snow out there. Heaviest I've seen since the winter of '89. I'm going to get my cooking done in case the electricity goes off, and then Porgy and I are going to spend the rest of the day doing what comes naturally. You and Bates ought to try it, and while you're at it, add a little spice. 'Course, if I know you, you brought work home."

She had brought work home, and she also wondered how Lizette found it so easy to talk about something so personal that wasn't her own business. "The spice will have to wait," she said, suddenly embarrassed that Lizette always seemed to have a better, more interesting sex life than she had. "Bates didn't get home last night. He worked late," she hastened to add, "and got snowed in. He'll be here as soon as it slacks up."

They talked for a while, but Coreen soon tired of small talk. Her mind was on Bates and where he was. A call from Glen to her cellular phone raised her spirits.

"I forgot to tell you that I taped your appearance on the committee," he said, the pride in his voice unmistakable. "You handled it like a pro, Mom."

"Thanks. I sure was glad when it was over, though."

"I had some folks over for drinks the other night, and I ran the tape for them, showing off my mom."

She heard little else of the conversation. How many other people had taped that session, and how long would it be before somebody, maybe someone she'd never met, recognized her? She told him good-bye but was barely aware when he clicked off. Whatever made her think that because no member of the Senate committee challenged her or because her aunt could no longer speak of her that her secret was secure? Suppose somewhere an adopted boy or girl looked exactly like her and saw her on television? Why hadn't she thought to wear glasses?

Maybe I'm worrying for nothing. I sure hope so. A scandal would ruin me professionally and wreck my relationship with my family. Using all the will she could muster, she forced herself to focus on something else.

With the phone line down, she couldn't do the research she'd planned with the use of her desktop computer, so she rummaged through her briefcase for something to do and found some notes on Becky Smith, four months pregnant by a boy who didn't respect her and who was on probation for interfering with a picket line.

Becky isn't hopeless; you can help her if you put your mind to it, her conscience nagged.

She didn't want to risk involvement with Rudolph, the girl's boyfriend and father of her child, but she saw herself in that girl. A girl who had a promising future until she got involved with the wrong boy and who could now look forward to a wretched life. She decided to look for a halfway house for Becky. The chances of getting counseling for Rudolph didn't seem good, but she would check with his probation officer and see what, if anything, could be done for him. She made relevant notes and put the material back into her briefcase.

Why didn't Bates come home? Walking from room to room and wringing her hands wouldn't help, but she did it anyway. Finally, late in the afternoon, from the dining room window she saw a few people struggling against the wind and the slight snow that swirled in its clutches. If he didn't come home now, she didn't know what she would do. Surely, he wasn't still mad because she hadn't told him about her office. She tried to think of any other grievance he could have, but nothing came to mind. She threw out the previous night's dinner and cooked as if she expected Bates at five-thirty, the time he usually got home.

When a key turned in the front door lock at about a quarter past seven, she was about to run to the door, but restrained herself. After all, if he had left work at five as he usually did, he would have been home before the snow fell. She took her time getting to the foyer.

The cold air chilled her as she walked into the hallway, and when she reached the foyer, her heartbeat accelerated at the sight of him standing there alive, even if seemingly almost frozen. She opened her arms and took him, chill, dampness, and all, to the warmth of her body.

"I'm so glad you finally made it home," she said, as if she'd never doubted his whereabouts.

"You're not half as glad as I am. I couldn't even call."

No point in reminding him of the advantages of having a cell phone. "I know, and I was shocked speechless when I woke up in the bed by myself. Come on in and get warm."

He pulled off his coat and jacket. "I hope you got something to eat. I'm practically starved."

She didn't ask where he was and didn't plan to. He would tell her the truth, and if he hadn't spent the night at the store, she didn't want to know it. Besides, if a black, married man in this community went to the home of a woman other than his wife, most African Americans in Bakerville would know it within twenty-four hours.

While he took a warm shower, she heated the food and set the table. Bates was a good man, and if a lot of people watched or taped her Senate appearance, she might one day need his indulgence and forgiveness. Besides, wasn't she the cause of most of their misunderstandings?

Bates usually said the grace, but that night she bowed her head, took her husband's hand, and said, "Lord, we thank you for this food and, most of all, for giving us the love of each other. Amen."

Why did he look at her that way, as if examining her, and then shaking his head as though not comprehending her mood or motive. "And thank you, Lord, for the privilege of being here in my own home," he added, picked up a fried drumstick, and began to eat.

She pushed back the talons of fear that began to spread like wild vines throughout her system. Bates hadn't explained, and he needn't expect her to ask. "Glen called this morning," she said, "but I haven't heard from Eric. I hope he's not snowed in."

He chewed his food in a manner that seemed to her contemplative. Something was on his mind, and she knew he wouldn't keep it to himself very long.

"How come you haven't asked me where I was last night?" He pointed his fork at her. "Didn't you care?"

"Why haven't you told me?" she shot back, ready to stand up for herself. "When a man doesn't come home straight from work, he's supposed to say why. You leave work at five-thirty; the snow didn't start for another two hours."

"When I looked out the door, the snow was already banked around four or five feet high, and I couldn't see across the street. That satisfy you?"

"Is it supposed to?" She wanted to ask him which door and what street, but she had to chose her battles and this one wasn't worth the scuffle. "I made you a peach cobbler," she said, moving toward the kitchen. "I figure a day like this calls for hearty food. Want some vanilla ice cream on it?"

She heard the reflection of his grin in his voice when he said, "Nobody's going to tell me I'm not clever. I got me a woman who knows what to do in the kitchen and lets it all hang out in bed. Baby, I was hard all night. Best time to get it on is when it's cold and dreary outside and nice and warm in the house. Did you make any coffee to go with dessert?"

She brought him the dessert and coffee and sat down to enjoy her own. "I hope it's good."

He smacked his lips. "Sure is. Say, did you know Bessie Jane's Muriel is pregnant? She can't be more than fifteen or six-

teen, hasn't even finished high school, and I heard she either
won't or can't tell Bessie who the father is. Believe me, the apple
doesn't fall far from the tree," he said, referring to the girl's own
birth to an unwed mother. He rattled on, but she didn't hear another word. At work, at home. One omen after another. She had
an eerie feeling that something or someone was about to unlock
the book that contained her past, and that she probably wouldn't
have her husband's sympathy and compassion.

Frieda Davis stepped out of her small apartment that Sunday
morning, prim and neat in her white uniform, white stockings,
white shoes, and gray tweed coat, and hurried along Franklin
Street, past the white marble and limestone steps for which
Baltimore was famous, on her way to Mt. Zion AME Church.
Frieda took seriously her duties as secretary to the Ladies Aid
Society and member of the usher board. She wore the uniform
and white gloves whenever she served as usher, and it pleased
her that she enjoyed special recognition as the small congrega-
tion's nurse.

Except for an occasional movie with her girlfriends, the
church was Frieda's social life. On that morning, however, she
listened to the minister's sermon with a feeling of hostility, because he seemed to speak directly to her.

"Judge not that ye be not judged," he said over and over,
pointing his finger, lowering and raising his voice for effect. He
sang a short hymn, and she relaxed in her seat at the back of the
church near the entrance. But her respite was short, for he took a
few sips of water and began another theme: "Vengeance is mine,
saith the Lord."

Frieda's bottom lip worked furiously, and her eyes blinked
rapidly. *Then I'll just sin,* she swore silently. *I'll just have to get forgiveness,* she said to herself, *because I'm going to have my revenge.
After what I went through, I'm not going to let anybody or anything
stop me. Five years of torture from the man who was supposed to be a
father to me. Ramming himself into me, hurting me and using me like
I wasn't even human, like I was no more than a spittoon. How could
she give me to somebody like that? I don't care what it takes; she'll pay.*

She left as soon as the minister said the last amen, failing for the first time in her memory to take her Sunday lunch with her fellow parishioners. Larry, a hopeful suitor, caught her as she reached the apartment building at 2911 Franklin Street where she lived.

"Where you going in such a hurry, Frieda?" he asked her. "I thought we'd have lunch at church like we usually do, maybe take in a movie or something. What's the matter? You sick?"

She whirled around, ready to take her hatred for her adoptive father, Claude Davis, out on Larry or any other man who ventured near her. "So when did I go to any movie with you on Sunday afternoon? Eating over at church is one thing; all the folks do it. I know you been sniffing around me for months, 'cause I been watching you. But let me tell you right now, buddy. You gets nothing here, so go look somewhere else for a waste bucket. And close your mouth. This ain't the first time you been knocked down a couple of pegs."

She stepped inside the building, locked the door, and trudged up the stairs to her fourth-floor apartment. Once inside what she regarded as her refuge, her own haven—poor though it was—she lit the gas stove in her tiny kitchen and stood in front of it to get warm. The man had the nerve to look as if she'd hurt his feelings. Too bad. She was not in the mood to tolerate the stuff men handed out. If the Lord had put any good men on earth, he sure had scattered them thinly.

After consuming two peanut butter and jelly sandwiches and several cups of coffee, her mood lightened, and she welcomed the telephone call from one of her girlfriends.

"Girl, what happened to you this morning? You got out of there like lightning. Anybody woulda thought you saw a ghost." Frieda held the phone away from her ear while her friend Thelma allowed herself a hearty laugh. "I got pig feet, potato salad, and smothered collards for supper. I just have to make some buttermilk biscuits. Lacy's bringing that old Roundtree movie, *Shaft*. Come on over at about five."

A smile roamed over Frieda's face, finally dissolving into a grin. She loved the old Roundtree movie, and she certainly wouldn't pass up a good meal with her two girlfriends.

"You know I won't miss that. But you shouldn't encourage Lacy to eat pig feet and potato salad with all that weight she's carrying. I keep telling her Mack left her 'cause she got so fat."

"Pshaw," Thelma said. "She didn't have nothing when she had Mack. Otherwise, she wouldn't a spent all her time eating. She weighed about a hundred twenty when she got married. Look at her three years later; two hundred fifty if she weighs an ounce."

Frieda pulled air through her front teeth. "You'd let yourself go, too, if you had to wake up every morning and look at something like Mack. Girl, don't get me started on that excuse for a man."

"Aw, come on, Frieda. He wasn't all that bad; he worked hard and took good care of Lacy," Thelma said, retracting words she uttered less than a minute earlier. "You gotta stop putting down every man on the planet. Some of the brothers are pretty nice to hang out with."

"Yeah. Right. Show me one. I just sent Larry packing. That man gets on my nerves."

She imagined Thelma settling down in the rocker beside her bed, rocking and getting ready to preach. Thelma did not disappoint her. "Larry's a nice fellow, but the way you treat him, I'm surprised he even speaks to you. You'da been better off with Larry than with that bus driver you took up with. He wasn't worth two cents."

That was one man Frieda tried to keep out of her mind. She drew a long breath. "Neither in bed nor out. Everybody's entitled to be foolish once in a while. I'm sick of men. Period. Now get off my case, will you?"

Thelma exploded with one of her raucous laughs. "You go 'way from here, girl. I gotta make the biscuits, otherwise I'd be reminding you of Reverend Hall's sermon last week. You got to love your fellow man, or else—"

"Spare me, Thelma. I know that biblical text, and it doesn't say a thing about how close you have to get to 'em to love 'em. From now on, I plan to do the loving from a good distance."

Frieda did not accept that she was unduly hard on men; to her way of thinking, she had never received anything uplifting from a man. As she saw it, they didn't give her anything but pain, annoyance, and grief.

"When you get to be perfect, Thelma," she said, tempering her voice so as not to sound angry, "then you can ride herd on me. If you knew where I've come from and what I've climbed over, you'd have a different opinion of me. If I'm bitter, I've got good cause."

Thelma's silence was proof that she'd heard more than she was prepared to listen to. Speaking, whether from knowledge or ignorance, was something in which Thelma did not ordinarily hesitate to indulge.

After a considerable time, Thelma said, "I never heard you talk like that, Frieda. We all think you got it made, you being a nurse and all. Still, when the right man comes along, you gon' shift your gears. I just know it."

Frieda rolled her eyes toward the ceiling. "I sure hope you get your mind on something else before I get over there. Let me get a little rest. See you later."

She took her journal from the drawer of her night table, crawled into bed, and wrote a few lines. Then, as she usually did, she flipped back some pages to entries made when she was in her early teens and allowed herself to relive some of the harshest moments of her life.

"I'll never forget it," she swore as she pounded her fist on the table beside her bed. "One day, I will even the score."

As Frieda and Lacy headed home from Thelma's apartment that night, Lacy said, seemingly to herself, "Ever since Mack left me, I can't seem to get on with my life."

To show her disapproval of Lacy's sentiments, Frieda walked faster, although she knew her friend would be hard pressed to keep up with her. "If I hear another woman say something like that, I'm going to scream," Frieda said.

Frieda's agitation evidently did not impress Lacy, who calmly replied, "If you'd fix yourself up, you wouldn't have to make do. I wish I was slim and good-looking as you. You wear those dreary colors, and you don't do a thing to your hair. Well, I guess you don't care." Her steps slowed, and Frieda had no choice but to slacken her pace. "Trouble is, I *do* care," Lacy went on, "but I can't lose weight, no matter what I do, and I'm never going to be good-looking, probably not even in my next life."

Frieda sucked her teeth, stopped walking, and glared at her friend. Women like Lacy made life difficult for other females. She knotted her fists and planted them on her hips.

"Lacy, you got a fixation on your mouth and your vagina. You always filling both of 'em up with something that's got no business there. Leave 'em empty sometime, and you'll be a lot better off."

"That may be easy for you to say," Lacy grumbled, "but if you enjoyed filling both of 'em up as much as I do, you wouldn't be so glib with your advice."

Loneliness overcame Frieda when Lacy's barb found its target with the precision of an arrow shot from a master archer's bow. That was the problem, Frieda thought. *I'd like to know what's so great about it. Maybe it's because of the way it started out for me, pinned down beneath a two-hundred-fifty-pound child molester I was supposed to call Father. Much as I've tried to get interested in sex and enjoy it, even when I liked the guy a lot, I've wanted it to be over as fast as possible. Nothing. Absolutely nothing.*

Lacy grasped her left arm, and Frieda snapped out of her musings. "Have it your way," she said to Lacy, hoping to shift the conversation to another subject.

But as they walked on, Frieda's own thoughts remained on Lacy's comment. One more gaping hole in her life. Another natural right of which she had been deprived. Her chest expanded as she breathed deeper, settling the question that always loomed at the edge of her thoughts, mentally bracing herself for a day of reckoning.

"See you Sunday," she said to Lacy as they separated at the next block. "Don't forget you promised to alter a couple of dresses for me."

"I won't."

Frieda walked into her apartment, went to her clothes closet, opened her little safe, and took out her birth certificate. "I might as well start working on it," she said to herself, "and I'm going to do that tomorrow. Lord, you forgive me, please, but she's got it coming."

In the meantime, Coreen greeted the news of her election to the office of president of the American Society of Social and Welfare Agencies with mixed feelings. An ambitious woman by any measure, on the one hand this evidence of recognition by her peers elated her, but on the other hand she feared that the additional exposure would draw too much attention to her. Never far from her thoughts was the possibility that somewhere a child could be looking for her or, if not, one who resembled her might make the right connection. For years, she had buried that possibility in the archives of her mind, but now, thanks to her growing national prominence, she could think of little else.

With the knowledge of her new status fresh in her thoughts, she left her office at five o'clock that Monday afternoon, as January gasped its last wintry breath, and hurried along Poplar Neck Road. She took that route to Lizette's beauty shop— known to the women of Bakerville as Lizette's House of Style— in order to avoid the arctic-like blast from the Albermarle Sound. But as she reached the corner, she had to brace her slim figure against the gust that met her face-on, slowing her steps and stinging her eyes. Water rolled down her cheeks as if she cried, and she sniffed repeatedly to contain the moisture from her nostrils.

She never had been able to figure out why Lizette put her shop practically at the edge of the town's center, where few African Americans had cause to venture. But it flourished there, and Coreen was glad that it was only three blocks from the agency at which she worked.

At last, winded and feeling as if she'd been wrapped in an icicle, she stepped into the beauty parlor. Not even the odor of hot curling irons taming human hair, the irritating smell of perfumed hair spray, and the cloying fragrances worn by the more than half a dozen women there—none of it lessened Coreen's delight in the warmth that replaced the frigid air outside. As she walked in, Lizette's customers stood and applauded her entrance. Stunned by the reception, she broke her stride, ready to run back out into the biting air.

"Girl, you were all over the local news this morning," Lizette told her as she washed Coreen's thick hair. "I told every woman that came in here today about my high-powered sister-in-law."

"Thanks. I hadn't thought people here would be interested in it."

Lizette removed her long fingernails from Coreen's scalp. "You kidding? Girl, you're a national celebrity. How does this set with my brother? He's not above being jealous, you know."

Coreen bolted upright. She hadn't spoken with Bates since hearing the news of her election that morning, one more reason he would have to think he wasn't important to her.

"I called him twice, but his line was busy and I forgot to try again. Excuse me a minute, Lizette." She took her cell phone from her pocketbook and dialed Bates's number at the travel agency.

"Hi. I'm at Lizette's," she said after greeting him. "I tried calling you a couple of times this morning, but your line was busy. Then two crises landed on my desk, and you may imagine the rest. I suppose you know by now that I won the election. You're talking to the president of ASSWA."

"What time are you leaving Lizette's?" he asked as if she hadn't mentioned her success.

She slapped her hand over the cell phone and looked at Lizette. "I think he's furious." To Bates, she said, "Soon as Lizette finishes with me, but I don't know how long that will be. The shop's full, and she has only one helper today."

"See you when you get home." He hung up.

She put the cell phone back in her purse, "Lizette, there are times when I wish I had the guts to show him that he's not the only man in this world. I'm forty-six, but I still look great."

Lizette's fingers pressed their grape and orange talons into Coreen's scalp with greater force and vigor. "That kind of thinking isn't healthy, Coreen. I don't doubt that Bates can be a pain in the ass, but a fifty-two-year-old man with most of his hair and who doesn't look like a seven months pregnant woman won't go begging if you start acting out."

"Oh, I'm not serious. Desperate is more like it. If Bates got a big order or a corporate contract, he'd have something to crow about, but he lingers in that cubicle of an agency surrounded by out-of-date travel books, twenty-year-old travel photos, and stale air making half a dozen sales a week, often less. And I'm flying. I haven't told him I got a raise, because I'm already making more money than he does."

"Honey, you just gave a soliloquy on the black man's blues. Men his age didn't have the opportunities we women had. But these young black fellows . . . they're going to Yale, Harvard, Stanford, Howard, MIT, and places like that. Ain't no flies on them."

If you only knew where I came from and how I got here! "We've survived many a crisis, and I suspect we'll get over this hurdle, too. Hurry up, Lizette, please. I don't want him to think I'm sulking. I know I should have kept trying till I reached him. Bates is difficult when he thinks he's right, but when he *knows* it, impossible hardly describes him."

Lizette got the blow dryer and began drying and curling Coreen's hair. "Just don't get so remorseful that you let him walk over you. Men can love the hell out of you and still do that."

"I know. How's Porgy?"

Lizette stopped twirling the curling irons, and her face bloomed like a flower opening to the sun. "Honey, Porgy's fine. Lord, what that man did to me last night! I tell you, he had me begging for mercy. Don't get me going. I start to think about that trash Porgy puts down, and he's nowhere near me, and, girl, I start to feel downright unnecessary. Porgy is *some* man."

"And you still don't want to marry him. I don't get it."

Lizette combed out the front curls and handed Coreen the mirror. "You think I want some man pulling rank on me the way Bates does you? Long as Porgy's not sure of me, he—"

"I know. You said that before. Hope you know what you're doing." She swung around in the chair, raised the mirror and checked the back of her hair. "Looks great, sis. See you in two weeks." She paid the cashier on her way out, but by mutual agreement, she didn't tip her sister-in-law.

"Miss Treadwell," a woman unknown to Coreen shouted as

Coreen left the beauty parlor and started up Rust Street. She stopped, fearing the worst, that someone she didn't want to meet had found her. "I saw you on local TV today when I was feeding the baby. I never dreamed I'd actually meet you in the street. How you doing? My name is Sandra. Would you please shake my hand so I can tell everybody you did?"

At first, Coreen had to force the smile, and then it bloomed naturally as she imagined what her late aunt would think of her new celebrity. Same girl who crawled along the lettuce and strawberry rows with her distended belly dragging the ground had grown into a national figure.

"Hello, Sandra. I'm no better a person than the bag lady who sits near the courthouse every day; the difference is our circumstances." She shook the woman's hand. "Stay warm. 'Bye."

Happy to have the wind at her back, Coreen trudged back to the agency at which she worked, got in her car, and began the drive home. She didn't hurry, taking Route 32 and the underpass beneath Courthouse Square to reach her home at 38 Queen Street North on the other side of town. She parked in the garage, but walked around to the front door, aware that she prolonged the time until she would have to face Bates.

He opened the door before she could insert her key in the lock, and she had never seen his facial expression more harsh or his demeanor more rigid.

"All I have to say, Coreen, is that you're heading for a fall, and one of these days you'll want me to catch you to keep you from breaking your neck. How you acted today is definitely not going to guarantee that I will."

"I'm sor—"

He raised his hands, palms out. "That's it. Whatever you intended, you didn't do right. I don't want to hear any more, and I'm not saying any more. What are we having for dinner?"

Annoyed at his superior attitude and unwillingness to allow her to explain, she walked past him into the house. If that was his revenge, she'd let him have it, but one day they'd have it out. *And what of you and your secrets? Isn't that what's behind all this?* She didn't try to do battle with her conscience.

"Some of your pork chops would be perfect," she called to him over her shoulder.

"I expect they would be, but I'm not cooking tonight."

She changed her clothing and headed back downstairs to cook supper. "Set the table," she threw over her shoulder. "It'll be ready in twenty minutes." If the tone of her voice implied that he could take it or leave it, she didn't care. He hadn't walked in her shoes.

Chapter Four

Two days later, a wintry Sunday, Frieda wrapped the navy blue woolen cape around her body and braced herself against the grainy snow that pelted her face like tiny icicles as she trudged through Baltimore's worst blizzard in a dozen years. With the streets impassable for motor vehicles, she had no choice but to walk the fourteen long blocks from Maryland General Hospital, where she worked, to her apartment. Picking her feet up and putting them back down as she plowed through the thick snow took most of the strength left to her after eight hours of lifting and bathing patients, making beds, and listening to patients's worries, complaints, and problems. She didn't mind passing out medicine and taking temperatures, because the shortage of LPNs meant that nurse's aides did some of the nurses' work, but she had too many patients.

At least I've got a job, and I can save me a little money every month to buy me a house. Then, won't nobody be able to tell me nothing. And soon as I can, I'm going to study for my LPN, and those nurses can stop looking down their noses at me. She tightened the cape to her body, bent her head, and struggled the last few blocks to the apartment building in which she lived.

After a warm shower, she made a pot of chamomile tea and put on the woolen robe that she took from her adoptive mother's closet thirteen years earlier, when she decided to run away from home, couldn't find her coat, and didn't have time to look for it.

Whenever Frieda sat in the wing chair beside the sofa, old and worn from use by she didn't know how many previous owners, she automatically propped her feet on the coffee table, picked up the remote control, and turned on the television set, the only item in the living room that she'd purchased brand-new.

Half listening and half dozing, she heard the words, "I thought I was born in Wilmington, North Carolina, until I wrote for a copy of my birth certificate. Would you believe I was thirty-five years old and had never seen my birth certificate." Frieda jerked forward, spilling the warm tea on her lap.

"That's strange," one of four women sitting around a table said. "How'd you get through school?"

"One of my adoptive parents usually registered me, and I didn't go to college, so I haven't needed it."

Frieda ran to the telephone and called the cable television station. When she left home, a figure of stealth in the night, she hadn't looked for her birth certificate. "Would you please ask that lady wearing the orange sweater in the program you're showing right now who she wrote for her birth certificate?"

"Will do," the voice replied. "She'll tell you after the next commercial."

Upon learning that she could get the certificate from the state registrar, Frieda shoved aside feelings of weariness, ignored her hunger pangs, and wrote the state registrar. "I know you can't tell me who my birth parents are, but would you please send me a birth certificate and tell me where I was born."

The next day after leaving work, she hobbled through the snow to the library, looked up the state registrar, and mailed her request. She knew she wasn't born in Rocky Mount and guessed her birth had taken place in a North Carolina town not too far from there, so she sent the letter to the state registrar in Raleigh, the capital.

If the snow-clogged streets had permitted, she would have danced all the way home, so excited was she to have begun her plan for revenge. Her voice sang as if with glee when she answered the phone.

"Helllooo."

"Either you sick or you need to borrow some money," Larry said to her. "I never got a hello like that one from you before."

"Shows what you know," she replied. "I don't borrow and I don't lend, and I never felt better in my entire life."

"Must be some reason why you being so friendly. 'Course, I'm not one to question my good fortune."

Larry couldn't talk to her for two minutes without putting his foot in it. "What good fortune?" she asked him. "Did you hit the numbers or the lottery?"

"Now, Frieda, you know I don't gamble," he said in his awnow, whipped-puppy tone that she detested.

She allowed herself a good laugh. "You don't say! Honey, you risk a lot every time you tail behind me, because you're getting nothing here. You only got one life, and you're betting the wrong part of it on me."

His voice deepened, and she supposed he meant to sound seductive. "A man's got a right to go after what he wants. That's the American way."

"Humph," she snorted. "It's also the American way for a man to work and make something of himself. It's one thing to be poor struggling along by myself, but danged if I'm gonna be poor with a man. I know you can make a good living painting signs, provided anybody needs 'em. When did you last get an order?"

"Now, Frieda, give me a chance."

"You ever heard of chemistry, Larry?"

"What you take me to be? I used those bottles and wicks and things in science class. Course I know about chemistry."

Frieda closed her eyes and moved her head from side to side as if she couldn't fathom the man. She hadn't wanted to paint him as ignorant, but he exposed his mental shortcomings without any help from her. "I wasn't talking about science, Larry. I'm talking about the electricity that sets off sparks between a man and a woman. You know what I'm saying?"

"Sure I do. It's what keeps me hoping you'll come around."

"No, and that's the problem. We don't have any chemistry at all, you and me. Now, take Rose, you know, the stout soprano who sings in the gospel choir at church. She can't sleep nights for thinking about you."

After a long silence, he said, "No kidding. You sure of that?"

She stifled the laugh that threatened to kill her chance to be rid of Larry for all time. "I wouldn't mislead a man about such a thing."

"Well. Thank you, sister Frieda. See you in church Sunday. God bless you."

It didn't surprise her that Larry would be satisfied with any woman able to tolerate him. He hung up, and she treated herself to a sigh of relief. Poor Larry. Rose's reputation as a man-eater was not without merit. Frieda found a calendar and a writing tablet and began working on her plan for revenge. Excitement coursed through her as she imagined getting even with her birth mother.

Coreen loved her husband and their two sons, and although she made their interests her priority, she couldn't forget where she came from and her struggle to overcome the odds she'd been dealt. Her heart went out to every girl and woman who came to her for help, and catering to their needs consumed more and more of her time. She would plan to be home early, take a bubble bath, oil and perfume her body, plan a candlelight dinner with her husband, and enjoy a romantic night with him. Then she would remember a pregnant girl who needed a place to stay, another one who needed health care, a mother without food for her children, and find herself still in her office at eight o'clock in the evening.

Already the days grew longer, and dusk had not settled when Coreen drove into her garage that early March evening at around seven o'clock. She had spent the last three hours of her working day trying to find a place for Becky Smith to sleep that night. Rudolph had kept his word to support Becky's child, and he paid for Becky's prenatal care, but refused to pay the girl's living expenses.

Bates wouldn't understand any of that, she knew, and braced herself for either an onslaught of recrimination or a silence aimed to punish her.

He met her at the door and knocked her off balance with a smile that she couldn't decipher. "Hi," he said. "I stopped by the market and got some catfish. Fishermen were bringing it in as I bought it. You're just in time. I'm ready to drop 'em in the deep fryer."

She reached up and kissed him with more fervor than she ordinarily would have standing at the door with her briefcase in one hand and their dry cleaning in the other one.

"You sure picked a good day to give me this treat. I'll set the table."

He took the dry cleaning from her. "I already did that. Go change. We can eat in about fifteen minutes."

She dashed up the stairs, reached the landing, and stopped. Bates wasn't a man to smile and act nice when he had occasion to grumble and complain. If she were half an hour late, no matter the circumstances, he'd have something negative to say about it.

Lord, I hope he's not getting ready to throw me a curve. I'm too tired to deal with attitude tonight. After washing up, she changed from her business suit to a red jump suit, combed her hair down, refreshed her make-up, and went down to the kitchen.

"I'm going to have some chardonnay. You want some?" he asked her.

She didn't want any wine with catfish, but she didn't tell him that. "Why not?" To her mind, the two didn't go together, and she wondered—not for the first time—if Bates's background was as lofty as he made it appear.

"So how'd it go today?" he asked her and handed her the white wine.

Here it comes, she thought. "One challenge after another. How so many people get themselves in a mess every day is beyond me. Eighty percent of the problems I face every day could have been avoided if the clients had used simple common sense. It's enough to make you cry."

Her eyes widened as he set the food on the table: leek soup, stewed turnip greens, jalapeño corn bread, pickled beets, and a heaping platter of crisply fried catfish. He sat down, bowed his head, and said grace.

"Beats me how you can empathize with those people. If they make their bed hard, why shouldn't they lie in it? Nobody did anything for me when I was trying to make my way." He shook his head as if even the concept was incomprehensible. "I guess it's something you learned in school."

She didn't dare tell him she learned empathy and compassion in the hard-knock school of life. "This food is wonderful, Bates. And this catfish tastes as if you just pulled it out of the water."

"Yeah. It is good. Eric called just before you got home. Bright Star's grandmother died, and he's taking her to Oklahoma tonight. Didn't say how long he'd be there, but if we need to reach him, we can call his cell phone number."

She stopped eating. "Are they so close that he has to *take* her home?"

He ignored her question. "Seems Bright Star doesn't know much about her own family; she'd adopted, you know. She found this grandmother a few years ago and developed an affection for her. Anyhow, Eric's doing what he should do, if the woman means anything to him."

At the mention of the word adoption, her nerves seemed to snake-dance all down her back. "But does he know that much about her? I mean if he goes with her to a . . . a burial or whatever it is they have, won't her folks think they're closer than they are?"

Staring at her over the rim of his wine glass, he said, "That's not your business, Coreen. Eric is a man well able to take care of himself. I don't want him subjected to Mama's whims. If there's anything I can't stand, it's a man who allows his mother to emasculate him. Leave it alone."

Coreen stopped eating and looked at her husband. Annoyance suffused her, and as she seethed, she didn't see the man she married eighteen years earlier. Before her sat a middle-aged tyrant whose receding hairline had begun to elongate his face and whose thickening middle made her think not of sex but of treadmills. She gritted her teeth as she acknowledged that the measure of his conceit was the only thing about him that hadn't become impaired over the years.

Her common sense told her not to say anything she'd regret. He'd forgotten whatever he'd planned for the evening and had succumbed to whatever made him so combative. Still, she had never let him bully her, and she wouldn't then. "It *is* my business, she said. "I have as much of myself invested in Eric and Glen as you have."

"I don't say you haven't," he said, speared a piece of catfish and put it on her plate, "but I do insist that you can love your son without trying to orchestrate his life. You want him to stay single forever? Huh?" He waved the fork the way a teacher waved a ruler at a recalcitrant pupil. "Well, I want some grandchildren, and Glen is such a womanizer that I can't expect them from him."

He stopping eating long enough to release a heavy sigh. "My only problem with Bright Star is her ancestry. Her grandmother may have filled her in on some important facts about her people, but does she know the health histories of her parents, emotional instability . . . you know what I mean. She's adopted, so who knows what kind of tendencies she has."

Adopted! Adopted! She resisted covering her ears with her fingers, because he would have sworn that she wanted to shut out his voice, but the word made her uneasy. She changed the subject. "I'm surprised Glen didn't call."

"I'm not," Bates said. "Glen wouldn't call; he'd figure that if you needed him, you'd call him." Bates stood and began collecting the dishes. "I'll straighten the kitchen. You just unwind."

"Thanks," she said. "I feel as if I've just run the twenty-six-mile New York Marathon. Honey, I am pooped. If you will excuse me, I'm going to bed." She refused to plead a headache; that was too corny.

His head snapped around, and his gaze belched annoyance. "Rather early for that, wouldn't you say?"

Her shoulders sagged, then she stood more erect and told him, "It is, but my body says I've been worked over by a wrecking ball. Thanks for dinner. I'll see you in the morning."

Coreen pulled herself up the stairs by her willpower. Maybe men didn't understand that where lovemaking was concerned, a woman needed consistency. If she told Bates that his snapping at her killed her budding desire with the precision of an expert dart thrower, he wouldn't believe it.

She undressed, found a full-length nightgown, extinguished the lavender-scented candle on the dresser, and crawled into bed. If she lived to be one hundred years old, she doubted she'd understand why the odor of lavender geared Bates up for sex. Put lavender somewhere near his nostrils and he'd be ready to go in a minute. She closed her eyes, and she was back in Pick-Up, North Carolina, harvesting her aunt's lettuce. Back twenty-nine years, crawling along the endless rows of lettuce with a butcher knife in her hand and her distended belly dragging the ground.

As if her knees remembered the torture, pain scored them as when they bled from the scraping that crawling on the rocky soil of Pick-Up inflicted upon them. She gripped her pillow tighter, but even as a tear dampened the corner of her eye, she didn't whimper. If only she could unload the burden she'd shouldered alone for twenty-nine years, perhaps she could have some peace. Maybe when she went to Brussels in her new role as head of her national professional society, she'd talk with a preacher or a psychiatrist, someone who would listen and not think badly of her. No one knew her in Europe, and she wouldn't risk exposure. Footsteps thumped up the stairs, and she squeezed her eyes shut and prayed for sleep.

Bates finished cleaning the kitchen, turned out the lights, and started up the stairs. A puff of smoke in a windstorm was as close as he could get to describing the speed with which Coreen could switch gears. And after all the trouble he'd gone to in order to ensure himself a good night of loving. He hadn't done anything to turn her off, at least not that he knew of. Something was wrong if, after eighteen years of marriage, a man still didn't understand what made his wife tick.

He stripped, took a cold shower, although he hated them, and crawled into bed. Maybe she was asleep and maybe she wasn't. In either case, it wouldn't do him a damned bit of good to check. He said his prayers and went to sleep.

He rolled out of bed at five o'clock the next morning, looked down at Coreen, and decided he'd better get out of there. He wasn't in the habit of forcing himself on his wife, and considering the ache in his loins, anywhere was safer than standing there looking at her all balled up like a kitten, soft and sexy. He let out an expletive that he didn't consider fit for anybody's ears, including his own.

"It won't kill me," he said with a shrug that belied his feeling. Then he dressed, turned on Coreen's computer, and began his daily search of the Internet for new ideas about tours. For years he'd thought himself a happy man. Now, he wasn't so sure.

Several weeks later, Frieda Davis pulled off her shoes, put her feet on the coffee table in her living room, and began separating her mail from the catalogues, political advertisements, and community notices that cluttered her mailbox. One second she idly perused the junk mail and the next her gaze landed on an envelope with the return address of the North Carolina State Registrar, bringing her up from her chair as she knocked over the green plastic bowl of parched peanuts and the brown and gold imitation Greek urn of paper lilies.

My Lord, I can't believe it. She sat down again, slowly, as if uncertain of the chair's location. When her fingers wouldn't do the job, she rushed to the kitchen, got a knife, and slit the envelope.

She hadn't expected to see on her birth certificate the names of her birth parents, and their absence failed to trigger an emotion. But before her eyes were the words, Pick-Up, North Carolina. The place of her birth. She twirled around, laughing aloud. Laughing until she slid down to the floor, on the verge of hysteria.

Eventually regaining composure, she got her calendar and

made notes. Late April or early May would be a good time to go there. She reasoned that it wouldn't be too hot, and people would be outside working around their houses or in the fields, if it was as rural an area as she suspected. After setting the dates for her annual two-week vacation, she lifted her voice high and loud in "Amazing Grace," went into her kitchen, and prepared her dinner.

I'm not even going to breathe this in my prayers, she told herself. Nobody kept another person's secrets, and for what she had in mind, surprise was the key to success.

Coreen's new status as president of American Society of Social and Welfare Agencies (ASSWA) did little to soothe her that late April morning as she sat in her office listening to the police detective as he informed her that whoever trashed her office worked in the building.

"But couldn't the person have hidden here somewhere?" She waved her hand around to suggest the chaotic state in which she'd found her office that January morning. "Couldn't he have wrecked the office that night and walked out past the doorman the next morning without having been challenged? Isn't that more likely?"

The officer shook his head. "Maybe, but not probably. Several of your employees left money in their desk drawers, and Lila Henry left her mink coat in her office, which is just across the hall from yours. None of it was missing, so the motive was not theft, Ms. Treadwell. That person was after vengeance. We'd like to interview every individual who works in this building."

"Go ahead, Officer. I hope you're wrong."

"Starting right now?" he asked.

"Whenever it's convenient for you, but bear in mind that I hold staff meetings on Monday mornings from nine to eleven."

"Thanks, ma'am. I'll work around that."

She didn't try to figure who among her staff would do such a thing; she didn't want to know. The door closed behind him, and she started on her mail; answering it represented her least attractive task, but as head of the agency, she had to maintain good community relations.

"Ms. Treadwell," her secretary called over the intercom. "Becky Smith is here to see you, but she doesn't have an appointment. She says it's urgent."

Coreen remembered her promise to herself that she would do all she could to prevent Becky's slide through the cracks. "Send her in."

"What's the problem?" she asked the girl, who looked as if she might deliver the child at any time.

"I just don't know what I'm going to do with this baby, Ms. Treadwell. I don't have any money, I've never had a job, I can't go home to my folks, and Rudolph disappeared. Not that I blame him. He was going to school daytime and working nights in order to send me money for the doctor."

She sat forward. Somewhere in that statement lay a clue that she needed. Her eyebrows shot up. "Wait a minute. Why don't you blame Rudolph for leaving you with this burden?"

Becky's shoes absorbed her interest, or was it the parquet floor?

Coreen got up from her desk, walked over to Becky, and placed an arm around the girl's shoulder. "Becky," she said in as soft and gentle a voice as she could manage, "is Rudolph the father of your child?"

The girl's face twisted into a mass of misery, and tears cascaded down her face as she shook, sobbing. "I shouldn't a done that to him, but I didn't have nobody else to help me. Rudolph is mean when he gets mad, but other times he's so nice."

"Did you tell him he isn't the child's father?"

She shook her head. "I wish I had told him. When he found out about Ernest, it was too late for me to tell him the truth. He wouldn't listen."

Coreen sat on the corner of her desk facing the girl. "What is the truth, Becky?"

Taking a deep breath, the girl focused on the floor again. "Well . . . uh . . . we all used to hang around the soda bar over near the railroad station."

"And . . . ?"

"Well, I was over there with everybody one night and—"

"Don't feed me a line, Becky. Who is 'everybody'?"

"The fellows. I was the only girl there. One of the boys put some speed in a bottle of Coke and passed it around. I didn't know he'd done it, Ms. Treadwell. Cross my heart. I swear."

"Then what happened?"

"Well, Ernest—he was the oldest—bet the fellows that he'd screw me right there."

"And you let him?" she asked, not bothering to hide her disgust.

"I didn't *let* him, Miss Treadwell. They held me down, and he did all those things to me, all kind of things right in front of those boys. He's a lot older than the rest of us."

"How much older?"

"Maybe four or five years."

"I see. Didn't you scream?"

"I couldn't. One of the boys put his scarf in my mouth. When I got home, I went to the bathroom to take a bath. Ms. Treadwell, I was so scared. I wanted to die. I couldn't even bathe because my papa was in there being sick and Mama was on a rampage. I hid my underwear, but she found it and knocked me around with her fists. When she discovered I was pregnant, she put me out of the house. Rudolph helped me, and I begged at the bus station and in front of some restaurants so I could pay for my room, such as it was."

Coreen closed her eyes and exhaled a long breath. "How many times have you been here? Four? Five? And this is the one time you told me the truth."

Becky nodded but didn't look at her.

"All right. I'm going to send you to a halfway house over in Edenton. It isn't far, right on the Albermarle, and it's very attractive. They'll take care of your confinement, and you'll stay there until the baby is two months old." Becky fiddled with her fingers and shifted in her chair.

"Don't you like that arrangement? I'd have thought it perfect."

An expression of desperation settled on the girl's face. "It's not that. It's . . . it's I don't want to keep this baby. I hate Ernest, and I don't want anything that reminds me of him."

An audible gasp slipped from Coreen's mouth, and she supposed her face bore the look of one who had just been stabbed. "You don't want to . . . to . . ."

Becky stuck out her chin. "I'm not going to keep it, Ms. Treadwell. So wherever you send me, please tell them I want the baby put up for adoption."

She stared at Becky, looking at herself thirty years earlier, and knowing that counseling wouldn't change the girl's mind. Furthermore, she empathized with her. "Living with that won't be easy. You may never forgive yourself for giving your child away."

"I didn't ask for it; getting it was forced on me. Anyway, would you like to spend the rest of your life being reminded of a gruesome rape? Would you? I have to give birth to it, but I sure don't have to keep it, and I am not going to."

Coreen walked back around her desk and sat down. "All right, but you'll have to sign these papers." She took some forms from the shelf behind her chair and handed them to Becky.

"Thanks, Ms. Treadwell. When can I go to that place? I'm getting so uncomfortable, and I don't have the energy to look for food and some place to stay."

"Be here at two this afternoon." She shook hands with the girl. "I wish you luck, Becky."

At the door, Becky turned and said, "I know you wish me the best. If I'da had a mother like you, I wouldn't be in this mess."

The blood drained from Coreen's face, and she slumped into her chair, shaken. Before she could dial the Weeks Halfway House, her phone rang. "Miss Treadwell on line two," her secretary called through the intercom.

Thank goodness it wasn't a business associate. She didn't have to be in top form with Lizette. "Hi, Lizette. What's up?" She did her best to sound lively and upbeat.

"I'm having some girlfriends over for bridge tomorrow night. Porgy thinks I ought to be more sociable. Like I don't socialize in this shop ten hours a day, Tuesday through Saturday. Want to come?"

"I doubt any of your friends would play a second game with me. I'm a lousy bridge player."

"All right, but you can come and talk, can't you? You're a celebrity, and I want the gals to know we're on good terms."

"Stop flattering me. If I'm out with the girls on a Saturday night, my husband will have a fit."

"Yeah, I guess he would. It's been so long since I lived in the house with Bates that I forget sometimes what an ass he can be."

She wanted to end the conversation and with it the feeling that Lizette had a freer, more interesting life than she had. "I'll let you know," she said. "Bates might have something planned."

"Like freaking out in front of the television? My brother is such a bag of laughs. Okay. Come if you can. Love ya."

Coreen stared at the phone receiver long after Lizette hung up. She didn't want to conclude that freedom and personal independence counted for more than commitment, but she didn't know what to think. Porgy allowed Lizette the freedom to do as she pleased, but even though she had all the social and legal rights and privileges of marriage, Bates expected her to account for every minute of the time she spent away from him. *Where you going? How long ago did you leave work? Why don't you do this? Why didn't you do that?* Maybe it wasn't bondage, but she could hardly distinguish that from her husband's possessiveness.

Oh, hell, when did I start twisting things up? Lizette is the one in left field, not me.

In her frame of mind, she didn't care to eat lunch with her colleagues, so she got a turkey sandwich and a bottle of cranberry juice at the delicatessen a few doors from the agency, crossed the parking lot, and walked down Popular Neck Road to the beach. Strolling along slowly, she leaned into the wind that whipped in from the ocean, bringing with it the smell of fresh, salty air and the slight chill common in late April.

She took the sandwich from her hobo bag and munched as she strolled along the beach, eying her shadow in the sand. When she reached the point at which Queen Street emptied itself into the beach, a mile from Poplar Neck Road, she stopped and looked out at the water sloshing, roaring, proclaiming its authority and invincibility. Water for as far as she could see; water to the end of the horizon. The mighty Atlantic Ocean that could rise up and swallow her in a second. Observing the ocean's power and majesty was usually a healing force for her, even as it sloshed, swirled, and roared, but on this occasion, she could think of nothing but the tide of events—unknown but certain— that seemed destined to sweep her away from all that she held dear.

Oh, she could quit her job, give up the office in her professional society that she had worked so hard to attain, and recede into the confines of her home. But she and her work were one, and giving it up would be one more undeserved, disagreeable experience in her life. She couldn't do it.

"Every time I move up a step, somebody or something reminds me that as long as I live, I'll be Coreen Holmes, not one bit different from Becky Smith." She turned and headed back towards the agency. "Maybe just a little luckier." The wind at her back quickened her steps, and she hurried to her office. As she walked, she asked herself, not for the first time, why she chose social work for a profession knowing that her duties would mirror her life.

"Guilty conscience, I guess," she said, and straightened her shoulders, forced a smile to her face, and opened the door.

"Wonderful outside, Oscar," she said, her tone airy. "It's a lovely afternoon."

In her office, she recalled her words to Oscar. "Am I getting to be shallow? Lord forbid."

At five minutes before five o'clock, she made notes as to what she had to do the next morning, cleaned off her desk, got her briefcase, and headed home. She was going to turn over a new leaf. If Bates wanted to be cantankerous, he'd have to look for a target other than her.

"What happened to you?" he asked her when she walked into the house. "You mean to tell me you actually left your beloved office before seven o'clock?"

She was damned if she did and damned if she didn't. "Hi, honey," she said. "Who's cooking? You or me?" It took a lot of skill to argue by yourself, and if he needed a fight, she hoped he got one, because she had no intention of accommodating him.

"Uh . . . uh, I hadn't thought about that," he said. "You want to go to Sparky's?"

Score one for her. "Love it. Let's have a glass of wine. How'd it go at the store today?"

After uncorking a bottle in the kitchen, he brought that and two glasses to the living room where she waited for him. "It wasn't too bad. Sold two tours and several airline tickets. Could have been worse," he said. "You know, one of these days, I want us to have a full-time cook and housekeeper. I've never gotten used to doing housework, grocery shopping, and cooking—not even when I was taking care of the boys after their mother died—and as soon as I get on my feet, we're going to get some household help."

She smiled in agreement and wondered how much of what he said was true. He always gave the impression that his background was one of wealth, if not privilege. Lizette possessed none of Bates's highfalutin' ways, but she knew siblings often differed.

"I know you want the best for us, Bates, and I want you to know I'm satisfied."

He patted her hand. "I know. A man couldn't have a better wife. Let's have another one. Wine costs money; no point in letting it turn to vinegar."

Of course not, she thought, reflecting upon his compliment. *As long as I agree with him, he thinks I'm perfect, but if I say one word in disagreement, he gets out of joint.*

During dinner at Sparky's, she drank three glasses of wine, more than she could recall drinking on any occasion. And why not? Bates looked younger, more virile, and more handsome with the passing minutes, and for reasons she didn't question, everyone and everything in the restaurant amused her. "What do you say we invite the boys and their SOs for dinner next weekend?"he asked her.

"Uh, sure. Why not? We haven't all been together since Christmas. Call them when we get home."

When they got home, she started up the stairs—wondering when the number of steps had increased—turned, and looked back at Bates. "You coming up?"

"I thought I'd . . ." He looked up at her. "Is that an invitation?"

She continued her ascent. "If that's what you'd like," she flung over her shoulder. She hadn't meant to suggest they make love as he'd interpreted the remark, but what the heck, she hadn't been too giving lately.

He bounded up the stairs with such speed that if she hadn't known better, she'd have thought someone sprayed lavender around him. "You bet your tight little tush, I'd like it."

Minutes later he had her in bed, and all she could think of was the difference between man and woman. With effort, she slowed him down.

"Baby, you do dish out some fine dessert," he told her later.

"I had the right ingredients."

She wished she had paid more attention to the amount of wine she drank. Release hadn't come easily; it would have been a lot more fun if her head hadn't grown to the size of a melon. She leaned over, kissed him on the cheek, closed her eyes, and submitted to the pain in her head.

Refreshed after more sleep than she usually got, she arrived at work the next morning, eager to begin planning her first trip to Belgium as head American delegate to the annual conference of her international professional society, the ISSWA.

" 'Morning, ma'am," Oscar said. "I been waiting for you to get in. My niece didn't get nowhere with Miss Franks. Can she talk with you?"

She stopped and swung around very slowly. "Talk with me about what, Oscar? I told you she would be assigned to Miss Franks."

He scratched his baldish head. "I know, ma'am, but they didn't get along too hot."

She didn't want to deal with another girl who had an unwanted pregnancy and sought adoption as the solution. "I'll speak with Miss Franks."

"Please, ma'am. Miss Franks don't understand. You got two boys. She ain't never had no kids, and she don't know what it takes to raise 'em."

"All right. I'll see her this afternoon at four o'clock." *Why am*

I doing this to myself? Guilt, her conscience whispered. By the time she reached her office, her steps quickened in anticipation of a good set-to with her deputy.

She phoned Maddie Franks. "May I see you, please?"

"What's the problem with Oscar's niece?" she asked her assistant.

Maddie rolled her eyes toward the ceiling. "You mean Lorraine? She's impossible. One day she wants to give the baby up for adoption, and the next time she comes here, she tells me she isn't going to have it. I'd be happy never to see her again."

Coreen squeezed the rubber bunny that she kept on her desk for such moments of exasperation. "I told Oscar I'd see her at four today. I'm going to talk with her about responsibility for five minutes, after which I'm going to bring her to your office. Tell her that's her final appointment with you."

"I sure will. Thanks."

After Maddie left her office, Corren remained as she was, staring at her silver-tipped fingernails. *What I ought to do is find myself another job, but I can't. I'm too old to start fresh. Besides, I'm good at this; I know my job like the back of my hand. If only these damning reminders of adoption weren't always staring me in the face. I can handle most anything but that.*

She took a deep breath, let her hands hang at her side, then shook her shoulders, arms, and upper torso until the tension left her feeling relaxed and energetic. Uplifted, she opened the window and sniffed the salty air, fresh like the wind that brought it.

"Life isn't so bad, maybe," she said aloud. "I'll deal with whatever it hands me. Nothing's worse than what I've already weathered."

"I'm indisposed for the remainder of the morning," she told her secretary. "I have to work on my statement for the conference."

While Coreen planned her first trip outside of the United States, Frieda charted her first visit to the place of her birth. She didn't share her goal with anyone and therefore couldn't ask anyone for help. Except for Pick-Up's location, she couldn't find any information about it that would help her carry out her plan. After an evening at the library, she spent hours on the Internet trying to glean something about the character of the place, but without success. Discouraged, she began to wonder whether the place was more than a truck stop.

Finally, on the morning of the last Saturday in April, deciding that she had lost too much of her vacation time, Frieda stashed her suitcase in the trunk of a rented Chevrolet, put her road maps in the glove compartment, and headed for North Carolina. After registering in a motel twenty miles from Pick-Up, she began her trip into the unknown. She didn't know how much of the truth she should tell people, but finally decided that she'd get the most sympathy if she said she was looking for her mother. If the people weren't forthcoming, she'd say her health and maybe her life depended upon finding her birth mother, but she would stay as close to the truth as possible. As it was, she already had enough to pray about.

"I don't know a soul down in Pick-Up," the cleaning woman at the motel told her. When asked about the Chamber of Commerce, the woman replied, "Lady, they ain't got no commerce, no chamber either. Everybody there is trying to get out. Jobs scarce as hens' teeth. What you want to go *there* for? It's just a general store that's got a post office with a first aid station right in it and a filling station out front. 'Course it's got two churches, one Baptist and one Methodist, 'cause them two is always arguing 'bout who's going to hell."

She made the general store her first stop. No one spoke to her as she wandered around the shop, seeming to investigate the merchandise but, in fact, gathering her courage to ask questions. She'd never seen anything like the place, for its goods ran the gamut from crocheted baby booties to kerosene, from butter to handguns. After a time, she ventured toward the cash register and stopped when she realized that she was the only African American in the store. If this was the only place of business, where would she get information?

If only she had one name! "Y'all find anything you want?" an old man asked her.

"Not yet," she said. "Sir, would you know where the black

people live around here?" She figured that he wouldn't understand "African American."

He looked off in the distance and put his thumbs in the pock-
ets of his overall bib. "I always thought they lived all over the
place. Drive down Route 91 till you see a white wooden church
with a little school right beside it. Turn in that road, and you
ought to meet some colored folks in that area."

She thanked him. "Any place around here to get a bite to
eat?"

He wiped his nose with the back of his hand. "If you can wait
half an hour, my daughter will be here, and she can fix you a
sandwich or she may have some fried chicken back in the back.
Have a seat over there at that little table by the stove."

The daughter returned shortly thereafter, and while Frieda
waited for the fried chicken and biscuits, the woman gave her
her first clue.

"Who you looking for back there in Prayer Town?" Frieda
supposed her face mirrored her surprise at that name, for the
woman added, "We call it that 'cause you never heard of such
praying and singing. Real gospel, going-to-heaven stuff."

"I was born here," Frieda said, "and I'm trying to find out
something about my birth mother."

"Adopted, huh?" Frieda nodded. "Well, if I was you, I'd go
to Rev Harper's church service. I bet he can help you."

"I didn't want to wait till Sunday but—"

"Sunday's tomorrow. Everybody around here goes to church."

Frieda thanked the woman, finished her lunch, which she
considered tasty by any standards, and drove down Route 91
until she saw the church and the school beside it. She turned off
the highway, drove past a woman who carried a tin tub of
clothes on her head, backed up, and stopped.

"How you doing, miss," she said, and immediately regretted
the casual greeting, for the woman's face suggested great age.

The woman set the tub on the ground. "You're not from
around here." It wasn't phrased as a question.

"No, ma'am, I'm not. I'm looking for Reverend Harper."

"He's down the road about a mile. I'm going right past there."

Frieda made certain the tub didn't contain water and then offered the woman a ride. "I'm twenty-nine years old," she said after introducing herself, "and I'm trying to find the woman who gave birth to me. I don't know her. I know I was born here in Pick-Up."

"Hmmm. Thirty years ago. I don't remember seeing a girl pregnant who wasn't married. That would be rare for these parts; the people here are very religious. I'll ask around, and if I find out anything, I'll tell Rev Harper. Thanks for the ride, and the Lord be with you."

Minutes later, Frieda knocked on Edwin Harper's door, the entrance to the only home she had seen in Pick-Up that had ever been painted. She rang the bell and set in motion the wheels of her future.

Chapter Five

Frieda stared down at the short, stocky woman who opened the door. Whatever she had expected, it was not the Native American whose long braids reached her belly and who smiled at her as if she were an old friend.

"Howdy. Kinda warm out today," the woman said. "Rev's not home, but I can give you some lemonade, if you'd like. Come on in."

Conditioned by big-city suspiciousness and fears, Frieda thought first that she might be faced with a dangerous trap and couldn't decide whether to accept the invitation.

"We can sit out here and drink it, if you want," the woman said, "but it's cooler inside."

"Thanks. I'll go in and cool off if you don't mind, ma'am."

Frieda followed the woman into the big airy living room and looked around at the plastic-covered chairs and sofa, artificial flowers, family photos hanging on the walls, and crisp white curtains billowing at the windows. The scent of roses and magnolia teased her nostrils, and her gaze followed the direction from which the odor—soft and feminine like the mistress of the house—seemed to flow. She walked over to the open window to see a profusion of flowers and nearby, a thriving vegetable garden, the lot of it as neatly manicured as the living room was tidy and homey.

"I brought you a slice of lemon cake, miss."

Frieda thanked her. "My name is Frieda Davis, and I wanted to see your husband about my birth mother. I need to find her, and I don't even know who she is."

"Not sure I can help you with that. Rev just married me and brought me here a few months ago, and you must be somewhere near thirty. I expect he can tell you something, though. Everybody calls him Rev. I heard it so much that I started doing it. He won't be home till suppertime, but you can come back then and break bread with us if you like."

She ate the cake and finished the lemonade. "This was wonderful, Mrs. Harper. If I don't see you around six this evening, I'll be at the church tomorrow morning. I appreciate your hospitality." From what she had sampled, the woman was probably a good cook, but her mind didn't tell her to drive back there for dinner; she didn't need a reverend's posture and demeanor to remind her that she was sinning.

"Call me Etta. You're welcome. Drive on down the road, and maybe you'll see some of the older folk. Most will be working in the fields, though. After supper, when they're sitting out on the porch smoking out the mosquitoes, is the best time to catch them."

"I'm trying to find my birth mother," she told each person she met. "I'm twenty-nine, and I was born here in Pick-Up. I guess my mother was young and not married. I need to find her; she'd my only hope."

Frieda didn't hesitate to embellish the truth; she had decided to find her mother, and she couldn't consider the consequences for the woman who gave birth to her. At the end of the day, around six o'clock, her search had not yielded one clue. Exhausted, she drove back to the motor lodge, pulled off her shoes, and sat on the side of the bathtub to soak her feet. Experiences that day did not discourage her, but fueled her determination.

Sunday morning found Frieda in the little white church on Creek Road. It took more patience than she normally applied in any situation to sit through the two-and-a-half-hour service. She couldn't focus on the proceedings because her thoughts rested on her search for her mother. And her anxiety as to whether the minister could give her a valuable lead made her increasingly agitated. The long sermon, gospel singing—some of it exquisite—and the choir of little children were what she would have expected in a small country church, but forty minutes of announcements—one given by each of the thirty-three adult parishioners present—seemed too much.

At the end of the service, she went to the minister and introduced herself.

"Oh yes, sister. My wife told me you would be here this morning. I'll speak with you in my office."

She waited until he spoke with each adult and child present and then followed him to his office, a room to the left of the pulpit.

"So you're trying to find your birth mother? Sister, you know the state seals these records for a reason. Some birth parents don't want to be found, and some adopted children want to make their birth parents miserable. Have you petitioned to have your case opened?"

Her heart seemed to tumble out of her chest. "Sir, that would take years, and I don't have that much time."

"Why not? How old are you?"

"I'm twenty-nine, Reverend, and I want to live to see thirty."

"I see. So you have a health problem. Well, I don't know if I can help you. Can you give me any information?"

She shook her head. "I only know I was born here. I got that much from the state registrar. I'm adopted."

"I don't promise anything, but I'll go through my records and see what I can find. Tracking somebody I don't know back thirty years won't be easy, but I'll do my best. Let's say a word of prayer. Lord, grant it that in this and in all that we do, we inflict no injury upon any person. Amen."

Frieda flinched at the words of his prayer and hoped he didn't notice. "Thank you, Reverend. I'll be at your house tomorrow at six, but I won't stay for dinner." She didn't think she could pass his scrutiny if he decided to judge her truthfulness.

She rang the minister's doorbell promptly at six the next evening. "Come on in," Etta said. "Rev just got here, but he'll be with you in a minute. Sure you won't stay for supper? There's plenty."

"Thanks, but I'm hoping he has the information I need, and I can head back home tonight."

"Well, sister," the minister said in his booming voice, "I may have something for you. A member of my flock, Agatha Monroe, passed on a couple of months ago, but a few minutes before she died, she confessed to some un-Christlike behavior. Her niece didn't want anyone to know she was pregnant and came to live with her while waiting for her baby's birth. According to Agatha, she arranged for the baby's adoption. She said she treated the girl very badly, mainly because she was jealous that she didn't have any children. Agatha never married and turned into an angry, self-pitying woman."

He closed his eyes and appeared to decide whether to continue. "Well, she wanted me to write the girl and ask her forgiveness, but she never got the name out before she went on to meet her maker."

Frieda grabbed her chest and leaned forward, her heart pounding as if it were rioting in her chest. "That's all. Nothing else?"

The reverend locked his hands behind his head, leaned back, and looked above her image toward the ceiling. "I'd think that's a lot of information, if you're that baby. You have your great aunt's name, and I can get you a copy of her death certificate from the undertaker. I believe it has her Social Security number, and I know it has her date of birth. If you send that information to the Bureau of the Census, you can get the names of everybody who lived in the house with your aunt beginning with the first census taken after she was born. Go see every one of them that's still living. I've gotten that information for several of my older parishioners who didn't have birth certificates and needed them."

"I don't know what to say, Reverend, except thanks. I . . . I'm stunned."

"Well, if you're sick and need your mother's help, you'd better get busy. Write your name and address here." He handed her a pad and pencil. "I'll send you the death certificate tomorrow. When you locate your aunt's family, you'll find your mother."

Although the drive back to the motel covered little more than a mile, it seemed to Frieda that hours elapsed. She wanted to phone her adoptive sisters to ask what they knew, and she also wanted to get back to Baltimore to begin her search in earnest.

One thing is certain: nothing would stop her now. *I'll do whatever it takes,* she promised herself, *and I will find her.*

Neither Coreen nor Bates could have imagined that somewhere, a few hundred miles away that Sunday night, events were being set in motion that could change their lives. Coreen had gradually dismissed from her thoughts worries that her high-profile job would bring unwanted recognition, and focused on the international conference and the prominence she hoped to gain there.

"Why are you buying all these clothes," Bates asked her while sitting on the side of their bed after supper watching her try on her new suits, dresses, and shoes. "Nobody in Brussels, Belgium, has seen the suit you bought a month ago or any of your other clothes."

"I'll feel better if I know I look just right."

"And another thing. It'll be cold over there. It's right on the North Sea, and the sun shines so seldom that everybody runs out to stare at it when it does pop out."

"Our conference brochure doesn't say that."

"Go ahead and do what you want. I run a travel agency, remember? It's my business to know the weather in the main tourist places, and Belgium is one of them. Besides, my butt practically froze off when I was there once at the end of July." He shrugged. "But you know best."

Coreen remembered her resolve to draw her husband and sons more closely to her, to make family her priority, and she knew that meant giving her husband credit when and wherever he deserved it.

"I guess I got carried away, hon," she said. "I never dreamed this would be happening to me. You think I should take some winter clothes?"

He didn't answer immediately, and she knew he'd begun to draw into himself. "At least one winter suit and a sweater," he said, but she got the sense that her brush-off hurt his feelings and he no longer cared about it. She was certain of it when, at eleven o'clock that night, he opened a bag of peanuts, turned on the television, and told her good night without glancing her way.

Bates didn't like being trumped, and especially not by his wife. Coreen had two degrees to his one, but that didn't mean she knew more than he did about every subject, or that she was any smarter. Lately, she didn't hesitate to tell him, in so many words, that he didn't know what he was talking about. When they married, she needed him, ran to him for everything, made him feel that he was important to her. She'd been a good mother, all right, and until she got it in her head to be president of the world, she'd been a good wife. Hell, that wasn't really fair. He shook his head as if to erase the thought.

Somewhere, something started going wrong, and I don't know how to fix it. Looks like we're against each other all the time. He couldn't get used to the feeling of isolation that the unarticulated breach with his wife created in him.

He ate the peanuts without tasting them and watched the television without seeing the screen. He didn't envy her the success she was having; to his mind, she'd earned it. But he couldn't stand the thought of being dragged along behind her, a weight that was too heavy for her to carry. He wanted to go to bed, but he didn't feel friendly, so he ate peanuts he didn't taste and watched a television program he didn't see.

"You coming to bed?" Coreen called down to him.

He looked at his watch. Ten after one in the morning. "Yeah. When the movie goes off. Good night."

Coreen knew the movies ended at one, so he got up to secure the doors and turn out the lights. Maybe if he went to bed that would prompt her to ask him if anything was wrong. If she did, he'd tell her. But she didn't ask, and he didn't open the subject.

"You going to do any sight-seeing after your conference?" Bates asked Coreen the next morning as they lay in bed, mostly to break the silence. During the last few months, they didn't talk as they once had. He didn't think the fault lay entirely with Coreen; he just didn't have much to say to her, and if she minded their silence, she didn't try very hard to bridge it.

"I'd love to," she said, "but I'd rather do that when you and I can knock around Europe together. I'm coming straight back."

"You know I wanted us to plan a vacation. What do you say I plan us something for New Year's? Maybe in the Caribbean? Huh?"

She rolled over closer and rested her hand on his shoulder. "All right. I . . . I need some respite from all these things in my head and on my mind. When we go, I'm taking an empty head."

He had to laugh at that, because he considered it idle talk. "At least you won't be able to work over there. By the way, did you ever find out who trashed your office?" She hadn't mentioned it since it happened, and he knew that was because he hadn't shown concern.

"Not yet. The police detectives think it's someone on my staff. There wasn't any evidence of a break-in or even an attempt, and the criminal apparently didn't disturb any office but mine."

"Then it's someone working close to you and close to your level. Nobody else would consider doing that."

She sat up in the bed and stared at him. "That's scary."

When he looked up at her, his gaze drifted to her breasts jutting out against her sheer gown and their dark brown nipples winking at him, begging him to suck them. He swallowed the moisture that accumulated in his mouth and told himself not to jump at the opportunity. But when she saw where his gaze rested, she let the gown fall from her left shoulder, cupped her left breast, and offered it to him.

He looked at her face, saw her tongue moistening the rim of her lips and the slow descent of her lids over her eyes. Damn her! She knew what he loved to do to her. He stopped thinking, grabbed her, and sucked the nipple deep into his mouth. She fell over on her back and brought him with her. Hell, he'd never been able to figure out why he loved it so much. He sucked it until she began to twist and wiggle, but he meant to see that she asked for what she wanted. He pulled the gown down to her waist, rimmed her right nipple with his tongue, and then sucked it into his mouth as his left hand eased down over her belly and into the folds between her thighs.

His fingers danced in and out of her until she tried to force his entry, but he managed to resist.

"Get in me," she begged. "Why don't you get in me?"

"I'm not ready. This time, I'm going to get just what I want."

He slid down, hooked her legs over his shoulder, plunged his tongue into her, and ignoring her coos and pleas, licked and sucked until he could feel her tighten and her tremors begin.

"Don't you leave me like this," she screamed when he moved away from her. "I need relief."

"It hasn't occurred to me," he said, and positioned himself and drove into her still pulsating vagina. She raised herself up to him, almost pitching him from her. Within minutes, she convulsed beneath him and he shouted his release.

Recovery came slowly, and when he could breathe effortlessly, he looked down into her face and asked her, "What did you expect to gain by that? You didn't want to discuss your office problems with me? Or what?"

"For goodness sake, empty that out of your mind," she said, staring him in the eye. "You should have seen the expression on your face when you looked at my breasts. I wouldn't have passed that up unless somebody held a gun to my head."

"All right." He squeezed her right nipple. "The Lord sure knew what he was doing when he put them there. Best friends a man ever had." He rolled off her, got up, winked at her, and said, "That was damned good. We'd better hurry. I'll use the guest bathroom, and you can use ours. Breakfast will be ready in twenty minutes."

A few minutes later he ran down the stairs, whistling, and stopped at the last step. *I can't remember the last time I whistled a song. And 'Sunny Side Of The Street,' at that. I didn't even know I remembered it. That woman really gets to me.* He walked into the kitchen and selected the pans he would use. "If only she'd pay me more attention," he said to himself, "give me a little credit, I'd—*we* could get back to where we were."

Not likely, his conscience nagged. *You need total control, and you want things done your way. If your relationship with her isn't what it was, it's as much your fault as hers. What are you going to do about that?*

Twenty minutes after Coreen sat down at her desk the next morning, she answered the telephone and recognized her sister-in-law's voice.

"Coreen, a TV producer just handed me a super deal. He'll do a shot of me doing your hair in my shop, a . . . uh . . . kind of commercial for my beauty parlor, then he would interview you and the TV station would run both as a part of its community awareness week. He wants to kick it off next week on his ten P.M. show. Honey, please don't say no. These are lean times, you know, and I can use the publicity."

She liked her sister-in-law, but the thought of more television exposure brought with it the fear she had managed to banish from her consciousness. If she lent herself to that kind of publicity, eventually someone would recognize her or see a resemblance to herself or himself and seek her out. She couldn't do it, not even for Lizette. If Bates knew she'd had a child, it would be the end of their marriage, because he would ridicule her, and she couldn't stand that.

"Sounds great, Lizette, but I don't know. The media usually has an ax to grind, and in my position, I can't risk letting someone make a fool of me on television. Why does that producer want to interview *me*?"

"Gee, Coreen, I don't think he'd do anything you didn't like. His wife is my customer, and, well . . . you know I'm always boasting I know you, so I guess—"

She interrupted her. "I can't do it now anyway, Lizette. I'll be in Europe for two weeks, and I don't have time before I leave. I'm sorry."

"Well, I could dream, couldn't I?"

She'd slipped down a few notches in Lizette's esteem, but she couldn't help it. *Nobody knows what I've been through to get where I am. Nobody. And I'm going to the top, whatever it takes.* She said the words aloud, whispering them as if they were a sacred mantra. "I've been dumped on, abused, and kicked around, and I deserve my place in the sun. The presidency of that international union is going to be mine. I owe it to myself."

Ten days later, Coreen stepped down from the rostrum to a standing ovation and thunderous applause. She couldn't believe the warm reception she was receiving for her first address before the ISSWA. She had worked hard on the speech, and during the flight from Raleigh to Brussels had practiced delivering it.

"Treadwell's a rising star," she heard a Dutch woman say, as she mingled in the crowd at the meeting's close.

"Yeah. Just elected head of her national society and already bucking to be president of the international. That's what I call ambitious."

"There's no law against it. Anyway, she hasn't been nominated, so you needn't put up your fists yet," the Dutch woman replied.

"What's to stop her from nominating herself? These Americans are so strident, and what surprises me is that the black ones are just like the white ones."

Coreen couldn't see the name badge of her detractor, shrugged, and moved on through the assemblage of women, who came from over one hundred countries, acknowledging congratulations as she went.

"This is for me," Coreen said to herself at the end of what she considered the most successful day of her career.

She sat up in bed watching an international cable news station and remembered that she hadn't called Bates. *Something's wrong,* she thought, *if I don't feel a need to tell my husband how it went with me this morning.* She stayed up until one o'clock the next morning, when it would be seven o'clock in Bakerville, and telephoned Bates.

"How does it feel being out of the country?" he asked her after their greetings.

"Strange. Seeing the black, yellow, and red Belgian flag flying everywhere was sobering, a reminder that I wasn't home."

"Glen phoned me last night. He saw a clip of your speech on CNN International, and he said you were good. Wish I'd seen it."

They spoke for about ten minutes, and after signing off, she wondered when they stopped saying "I love you." Brooding over it wouldn't help. She set the alarm, switched off the light, and went to sleep. But the next morning, as she dressed to leave the hotel, still exhilarated by the previous day's success, the possibility of detection and exposure dawned on her, once more shrouding her in fear. If CNN carried excerpts of the conference, anyone anywhere could have seen her.

She sucked her teeth and shook her head. "If only I knew who could be looking for me, or if anyone is interesting in finding me." Casting her gaze toward the ceiling, she spoke to herself. "I'm getting paranoid. Maybe nobody gives a damn about me, and I'm worried for no reason." She inhaled deeply and exhaled several times, stoking her courage. Nothing, not even the possibility of exposure, was going to cheat her of her goal.

She wore a red wool crepe suit, because she knew she looked great in red, and entered the dinning room for breakfast exuding confidence. Almost at once, a group of African and Scandinavian women surrounded her, asking if she would agree to their nominating her for international president.

"Well . . . if you feel that I can be of service in that capacity," she said with genuine modesty, even as the challenge half frightened her.

"Then you're our nominee," Nana Kuti of Nigeria assured her.

She thanked the women and hoped the uncertainty she felt wasn't reflected in her voice and demeanor. Later that afternoon, she phoned Bates.

"Looks as if I'll be nominated for international president. I didn't even dream it could happen so soon."

"As long as you don't have to live over there, it can't hurt," he said, "though I don't know where you're going to get the time for all that."

"I get secretarial and clerical help, so it's not a great burden. You know, I had hoped to find something for Glen's birthday, but I don't see a thing here but linens, crystal, and diamonds. What are we going to give him? It's his twenty-fifth birthday."

"I'd like to give him a boot in his behind, but I don't suppose you can wrap that up in a fancy package. Glen needs to take hold of his life and try to succeed at something. He's got a brilliant mind that he uses to avoid doing what he obligates himself to do. Hell, he can't smile his way through life unless he's prepared to panhandle on the street."

"Now, honey, you're always down on Glen. He's a good boy, but he's young. Give him a chance to find himself."

"You kidding? He's twenty-five, and as long as he can run to mama and get what he wants, he won't find his place in life."

"He's doing well now, and he's going to make us proud. You wait."

"Yeah. I hope to live that long. Working at a college cable TV station. You call that doing well? I don't."

At the duty-free shop in the Brussels airport, she bought Glen a black Moroccan leather jacket, two Scottish cashmere sweaters, and a bottle of Ralph Lauren cologne. She knew she spoiled Glen, but the boy was her heart and had been since he was two years old, his age when she married his father. Because his mother died weeks after his birth, he hadn't known a mother's love, and from the day she met him, he reached out to her for affection, exulting in the warmth, love, and attention that she lavished on him.

She loved Glen as much as if he'd come from her own body, and over the years she managed to communicate that to him. She would have to tolerate her husband's complaints about the purchases, but at least Glen would be happy.

Bates awaited her when she passed through customs at Raleigh-Durham International Airport, bussed her briefly on the mouth, and took her luggage. "What did you buy him?" were his first words.

She told him, and added, "We don't give him presents except at Christmas and birthdays. It isn't much."

"It's a good thing Eric isn't jealous of him. I used to wonder about that," Bates said.

She didn't want them to argue about the boys, a source of contention between them, and she sought to diffuse the rising tension. "Eric spoils him, too. After all, Glen's the baby."

"Well, they'll both be here for Glen's birthday. Bright Star, too. I hope Glen doesn't spring one of his women on me. He's twenty-five and doesn't know the difference between a moonlit walk by the ocean and a romp in bed."

"Aw, honey, how old were you when you learned the difference?"

He chuckled in amusement. "Fourteen, with some considerable help from my father's belt and tongue-lashing, and I haven't been confused since. If I had punished Glen every time he needed it, you'd have had me arrested."

"Not so," she said as they began the drive to Bakerville.

"You would have, Coreen, and one of these days, Glen is going to make you shed tears. Mark my word."

"What on earth am I thinking about?" Frieda said to herself as she drove away from the Reverend Harper's house. "I'm staying right here in Pick-Up till I find somebody who knew Agatha Monroe."

Around seven-thirty the next morning, she began retracing the steps she took the previous day, more confident and more determined, for she now had a name.

"Did you know Agatha Monroe?" she asked an old woman who sat on her front porch, rocking, stringing beans, and humming a Baptist hymn in the early morning breeze.

"Sure did. She passed on not long ago."

Frieda did her best to control her excitement as she recited the story she'd told so many times during the last three days. "I've got to find her," she added. "It's urgent."

The woman's gnarled fingers, their red nails standing out against the wrinkled black skin, strung and snapped the beans rhythmically, as if she were tickling the strings of a jazz guitar. Frieda couldn't help admiring the peaceful aura the woman exuded in spite of her unpainted house, sagging windows, and tumbling front steps, all testaments to her humble existence.

"Well, I always thought of Agatha as a bitter, unhappy woman. She had a young girl staying with her one summer a long time ago, or so I was told. She could be the woman you're looking for. I never saw the girl and don't know anybody who did see her. It couldn't have been a happy time for that girl, what with Agatha always crying poor mouth and pinching every penny till it hurt."

Frieda gasped for the breath that caught in her throat. "Who said a girl was with her?"

The woman stopped rocking and peered at her visitor, her reddened eyes narrowed in a squint. "Old Miss Maybell. She used to buy home-canned fruits and vegetables from Agatha, and according to her, the girl was there. But Miss Maybell's been dead for years, so she can't tell you nothing."

"I see." Frieda thanked the woman, went back to the motel, checked out, and headed for Baltimore.

She waited three days for the Reverend Harper's letter, and the shaking of her hands like brown leaves in an autumn wind prolonged her torture as she waited to see what the letter would reveal. Finally, she sat down, numb with excitement, and with perspiration soaking her blouse, placed the letter on the sofa beside her and prayed.

"Lord, please let this be it. Please. Only you and I know how much I suffered. Please let it be in here."

After drinking a glass of cold water to calm herself, she managed to open the letter, and there in her hands lay a copy of Agatha Monroe's death certificate. She folded the paper to her breast, threw her head back, and laughed aloud. Laughed and laughed. Laughed until she bawled aloud with tears streaming down her face and clouding her vision. Laughed until she gagged, struggled to the kitchen, opened the tap, filled her two hands with water, and drank from them.

Two hours later, as darkness settled in, Frieda still sat on her living room sofa holding the death certificate in her right hand, a catatonic-like figure suspended between reality and dreams. The ringing telephone shook her out of her trance.

She struggled to get up and get to her bedroom before the phone stopped ringing and she missed the call. "Hello?"

"Hello, sis. Where in the world have you been?" her sister Julie screeched. "Portia and I have been out of our minds."

She clutched her belly, anticipating bad news. "What is it? What's the matter?"

"The matter? We both happened to call you a dozen times over the weekend, that's the matter. Are you all right?"

"Girl, you scared me to death. I'm fine. This is my vacation time, and I just took off."

"Why didn't you come down here?" Julie asked her. "We'd love to see you. We sold the old house and land for forty-five thousand, and I tell you I was glad we could get that. Nobody wants to live down there. A developer bought it. I'll send you a copy of the bill of sale and your fifteen thousand."

"You did good, Julie. I'd begun to think we'd have to forget about selling it. By the way, did Mama or Papa ever mention a place called Pick-Up, North Carolina?"

"Uh . . . not to me. Why?"

"I was just—"

"Now, Frieda, let sleeping dogs lie. I know exactly what you're doing. Is that where you were this past weekend?"

"Uh huh."

"Do you remember how you used to tell us you were going to find your birth mother, and you'd make us swear not to tell? Don't do it. You could make yourself miserable."

"Maybe, but not as miserable as I'd make her. How did you guess?"

" 'Cause Mama told Portia and me to discourage you if you ever mentioned looking for her. She said she didn't know and that you would be better off not knowing. That's all she told us."

"I have to tell her what my life has been like, but I'm also trying to understand why Papa treated me the way he did. At first I thought it was because I was adopted, I'm so dark, and the rest of the family was light-skinned. But if he did the same to you and Portia, his own biological daughters, those weren't the reasons."

"The reason," Julie said with more vehemence than was usually her wont, "is because he was a domineering, possessive, and unprincipled man. It didn't have anything to do with us. Trust me, Frieda, it was just *him*."

"I'll never stop despising him for what he did to me. I can't have a normal relationship with a man, and I can't make myself trust them enough to . . . to . . . Oh, what the heck."

"Portia and I are trying to put the hurt behind us. We ought to be even angrier at him than you are. Portia said she's going to take fifty dollars of the money from the house sale, buy some great champagne, go to the cemetery, and stand on his grave and drink it."

"*What?* Child, you go 'way from here."

"Right. I told her she was crazy, and she said after she drinks it, she's going to dance on his grave. Then she'll consign him to the past."

"Lord forgive me," Frieda said, "but I sure would love to be there when she does it. I remember the time when I could wind up a storm."

"Both of you ought to be ashamed of yourselves," Julie said. "It would have hurt Mama if she had ever heard you two talk like that."

"Humph! Nobody's gonna make me believe Mama didn't know what Papa was doing to us. She was scared of him. Oh well, no point in continuing to stir up that old manure."

"Does that mean you're going to stop looking for your birth mother? If you find her, you may wish you hadn't."

"I don't want a thing from her but fifteen minutes of her time, and I hope she's not deaf."

"Well, Mama said you were always hardheaded, and that you'd do this. I can't stop you, but if you need me, hon, I'm here for you."

* * *

The next morning, after a restless and sleepless night, Frieda called the hospital and reported herself ill. Then she dressed and drove to Kinko's without eating breakfast or even drinking one cup of her beloved coffee.

"I don't use the computer," she told a clerk, "but I need this information from the Bureau of the Census in Washington. It's very urgent. Can you help me?"

When told of the cost, she said, "I don't care. I need the information desperately, and if you get it for me that's all I'm interested in. Get me the names of everybody who lived in the house with my aunt at each of the last six censuses and their relationship to my aunt."

After half an hour at the computer, he told her, "The charge for the search is fifty dollars, and I need your name, credit card, and address."

Frieda gave the man what he asked her for. "When can I get it?"

"It should be ready day after tomorrow."

She didn't want to wait that long, but if she rushed him, he might not do a thorough job. "All right. I'll come for it Thursday around five-thirty."

She left wondering what she would do with those names when she got them, and vowed to figure it out even if she had to get an expert to help her. It would cost her, another dip into the pennies she struggled so hard to save in order to have a little house, something to call her own. She went to the library to look for information on Pick-Up, North Carolina, around the time of her birth. Perhaps Sarasota or Walstonburg, the nearest towns, had a weekly or bi-weekly newspaper. Maybe she wouldn't find anything, but she had to look.

After several hours and the help of the librarians, she had found nothing that pointed to Agatha Monroe.

"You must be tired by now," one of the librarians said to Frieda as she handed her another envelope of microfiche.

"No, ma'am. My problem is I'm not finding anything. I think I'll quit now and get back to it another time. I can use some fresh air."

The following afternoon, Frieda collected a large envelope from Kinko's. On her way home, she stopped at Jack's Jerked Chicken, a fast-food takeout, bought her dinner, and hurried to her apartment. Inside, she locked the door, dropped the bag of food, her pocketbook, and coat in the chair that faced the sofa and sat down to examine her treasure.

She pored over household questionnaires from census tracts in Charlotte, North Carolina, its suburbs, and in Pick-Up, and realized that her birth mother may have lived in or near Charlotte. Darkness settled and her eyes could no longer adjust to the dimness in which she tried to read the scribbled handwriting of the census takers. She rubbed her eyes and was suddenly aware of pangs that gnawed at her belly.

Frieda vowed to let nothing discourage her, not even the nearly unreadable handwriting on the census schedules. She warmed and ate her dinner, took a shower, said her prayers, and got in bed. But after turning out the light and closing her eyes, she suddenly bolted upright. The name Joshua Manners had appeared on the 1960 and 1970 censuses as household head. She jumped out of bed, got the schedules for those censuses, and scrutinized them as best she could without a magnifying glass. Finally, she decided in triumph that the barely legible name was not Manners, but Monroe.

"Thank you, Lord," she said. "Thank you. Thank you."

Frieda didn't go back to bed. She slipped on a robe, got a cup of coffee, and began searching again with different eyes. Now she knew that what she saw need not be the fact, that she had to use her imagination. By daybreak, she had the names of individuals enumerated with Agatha Monroe at consecutive censuses, and she was about to call a halt to it when she noticed that she had skipped a census. She shifted through the pages for twenty minutes before seeing a tract for Wilson County, peered at the smaller print, and saw Pick-Up, Wilson County, North Carolina.

She grabbed her chest, symbolically slowing her heartbeat, but couldn't control her emotions sufficiently to read the clear handwriting on the page. With the paper held tightly against her breasts, Frieda paced to her tiny kitchen and from there to her bathroom and back to the living room, where she placed the paper on the sofa and dropped to her knees.

"I hope you're going to forgive me, Lord," she prayed, "'cause if her name is here, I'm going to find her. I can't stop now. I just can't."

She got to her feet, sat on the sofa, picked up the paper, and barely breathed as her eyes skimmed the sheet. Then she saw: "Head of household—Agatha Monroe, female, age 41. Other occupant—Coreen Holmes, female, age 17; relationship to household head, niece."

After staring at the name for some minutes with perspiration dripping down the sides of her face and her breath coming in short pants, she calmed herself and sucked air through her front teeth.

"You bitch."

Larry had to know that if he received a telephone call from her, it was because she wanted something, Frieda told herself as she drove to work the next morning. He'd want something in return, too, she figured, but he wouldn't get it. She called him on her lunch hour.

"Well, well," he said when he detected her voice. "It sure is good to hear from you, honey. That tip you gave me didn't work out; Rose doesn't know the difference between a man and a flagpole. She run on and on about that the pastor—you know, Reverend Hall—like he was the angel Gabriel or something. I ain't got no time for that kind of woman. Now you. You know how to make a man feel *reeeeal* good."

"You didn't go about it right, Larry. I know you, and you can sure get it on when you want to." She didn't want to give him a chance to get on his favorite topic—her, and when could he see her—so she said. "Larry, you always have good answers to things. How do you find somebody if you only know their name and age?"

"I hope it's not a man you looking for."

"If I was, would I ask you?"

"I don't know. Try schools she might have attended. If you're flushed, get one of these fellows who promises to find anybody anywhere for fifty bucks. Frieda, you gotta get a computer; you could find her through the Internet in a couple of hours. Want me to do it for you?"

Frieda wasn't impressed. Larry liked to exaggerate. Besides, she couldn't trust him or anybody with her secret; if he gossiped about it, he could ruin her chances of finding and confronting Coreen Holmes.

"I'll appreciate it if you'll just give me the names of a couple of people who look up lost relatives." She added the latter to allay his suspicions.

"All right. Call me when you get home."

"You saying you'll have the information for me?"

"Sure. You know me. I got all kinds of people in my pocket."

He certainly did, she mused, and that was one reason she didn't intend to let him get too close. She'd always suspected that he had a devious side, but if he found the person who would locate Coreen Holmes for her, she would gladly forgive his deviousness.

Chapter Six

Three days later, armed with the name and address of a man she didn't doubt was a scoundrel, Frieda drove down Franklin to Post Street, shaking her head in disgust as she went. She wanted to close her eyes, to avoid the sight of boarded-up buildings, broken windows, and piles of refuse. Several times, she swerved to avoid the pieces of furniture that littered the streets. Fumes from chop suey carry-out shops assaulted her nostrils, and she drove with one hand, using the other one to cover her nose. She found the address in the seven hundred block and pulled up to the curb, risking her tires in a sea of broken glass as she did so.

"I'm looking for Gabe," she called out to three men who leaned against a building that adjoined the address Larry gave her. It didn't occur to her to chance getting out of her car in that neighborhood.

"I'm Gabe." The man sauntered over to her. "Who's looking for me?"

She caught her breath, ready to make a run for it if necessary. "Uh . . . Larry told me to look you up. He said you could help me."

"If you got fifty bucks, I sure can. Who you looking for?"

She told him, and gave him her birth mother's name and other information that she had. He held out his hand.

"Like I said. Fifty bucks. I get paid up front. Larry will give you what I find day after tomorrow. If she's in the good old U.S.A., I'll find her."

Frieda stared at him. "Don't you ever get a case you can't solve?"

He shook his head and rolled his eyes toward the sky, giving the impression of a man losing his patience. "With as much information as you've given me, how could I miss? What'll it be? Yes or no."

She rolled up the window, picked her purse up from the floor, counted fifty dollars—wrinkling and squeezing them to make certain she counted accurately—and handed them to him.

"Looks like you don't trust me," he said, referring to the fact that she rolled up the window before opening her purse.

She lifted her right shoulder in a quick shrug. "If you'd met as many louses as I have, Gabe, you wouldn't spread your trust around either. If Larry doesn't have this information for me day after tomorrow, both of you will hear from me."

Gabe let her see his sparkling set of white teeth that a dentist had decorated with two gold incisors. "Right on, sistah. Don't you worry none. I don't have to swindle the sistahs; I make my bread on the Man."

She didn't quite know why, but as she headed home, his last words comforted her. She telephoned Larry as soon as she walked into her apartment.

"Gabe took fifty dollars of my hard-earned money, and he said he'd give you what he finds. I don't want no stuff out of you two, you hear me."

"Don't get upset for nothing. Gabe's as good as the U.S. mint. Would I mislead you?"

Yeah. Sure, she thought. In her experience, getting tough with men rarely netted you much, but as soon as you sounded stupid and helpless like you couldn't brush your teeth by yourself, they'd do just about anything for you.

She changed tactics. "Well, I know you're a gentleman, Larry, but some of these men out here latch on to a woman for nothing but what they can get."

"You know me better'n that, Frieda. So you just relax. You hear?"

She thanked him and hung up, knowing she probably wouldn't relax again until she looked Coreen Holmes in the eye.

Oblivious to the storm clouds headed her way, Coreen arrived at her office that Monday morning in early May bursting over her triumph in Brussels. Her first time attending the conference and addressing the members, and they were offering her a chance at the biggest prize a person in her line of work could capture.

"Good morning, Oscar," she sang in a merry greeting.

" 'Morning, ma'am. Everything's just like you left it."

"Glad to hear it." She rang for the elevator, and while she waited for it, her deputy, Maddie Franks, joined her.

"Good to have you back, Coreen," Maddie said. "Nothing happened in your absence, except those policemen sniffing around here and upsetting everybody."

"They have to find out who trashed my office, Maddie, and I want everyone to cooperate with them."

"They're a nuisance, Coreen. One of them walks in while we're interviewing our clients and doesn't even say excuse me."

"I'll take care of that, but I do not want anyone to discourage the investigators." She made a mental note to circulate a memorandum requiring each staff member to cooperate with the investigating authorities. She couldn't imagine why anyone would refuse.

With one glance at her incoming box and the realization that Maddie hadn't assumed her responsibilities as a deputy, but had merely done her own work as usual, Coreen's ebullience over her success in Brussels fled like a comet shooting through the night.

"I'm going to have to make some adjustments," she said to herself, aware that if she shuffled her staff or, God forbid, fired anybody, her senior aides would think she was carried away with her new status, flexing her muscles. But what was the point in having someone who was supposed to substitute for you in your absence, if that person ignored the responsibility? She buzzed Maddie.

"Could you please come in here for a minute, Maddie?"

"Sorry. I can't right now. I have to prepare for my afternoon clients."

Coreen's lower lips dropped and hung there. Hoping her silence sent Maddie a message, she straightened her shoulders, braced her feet flat on the floor, and said, "Maddie, as a senior caseworker, you should be able to dialogue with your clients off the cuff, so to speak. I want to see you *now.*" *There goes that relationship and, with it, my reputation as a nice guy.* "I've been away a week, and I expect a report, since you've been running the agency in my absence." Maddie hung up without saying a word.

"I didn't think I was supposed to do your work," Maddie said, standing in the doorway, and in effect refusing Coreen's request that she go *into* her boss's office. "I don't get paid to be the director."

Coreen pasted a smile on her face and told herself not to show anger. "That's true, Maddie. You don't. Unfortunately, that's what a deputy does in the absence of the director; she becomes the acting director. And she's paid well for it. But I wouldn't want you to feel as if you're being used, so as of now, you're a senior caseworker. I'm appointing Alice as deputy director. That's all."

"You can't do that. I just bought a new car and I'm—"

Coreen didn't look up from her desk. "I'm sorry, Maddie, but I have to take care of all this stuff in my in-box. Let yourself out."

She heard the door close, sat up, and leaned back in her chair. When had Maddie become so impertinent? She dialed Alice Jergen's number, told her of her promotion, and busied herself doing what Maddie should have done the previous week.

"Coreen Treadwell," she said after answering the phone. "How may I help you?"

"Eric just called to say he and Bright Star will be a little late for Glen's birthday celebration this weekend, but they'll be here

Friday evening for sure. Did Glen ever say when he'll get in and who he's bringing with him?"

She thought for a minute. Bates always assumed that she knew more about Glen and his plans than he did. "No, he didn't," she said. "He's not likely to bring a girl. Glen's not serious about anybody."

"The way he's going, he'll run through women till he's fifty"—Bates snorted—"and then he'll start making a fool of himself with girls half his age."

"Oh, honey," she said."He's going to make us proud yet. You wait."

"This I hope to live to see." He hung up.

She'd better call Bates back. He didn't think it important or appropriate to tell all that transpired in his office, but he demanded to know promptly who ventured into hers and why.

"Bates, honey, when you called a minute ago, I was plenty flustered. I don't know what got into Maddie, but she was rude to me and I had to demote her. Besides, she didn't do her work. She's the last person I would have thought—"

"Maybe you should have fired her."

"But Bates . . . she's helping to take care of her parents and her nieces and nephews. I couldn't do that." If only he would show more compassion for the less fortunate.

"No? They're not your responsibility, or even Maddie's. People shouldn't have children if they can't take care of them. Why should my taxes support the stupidity of some guy who didn't have sense enough to use a condom?"

She knew she'd better get off that subject and quickly. "I've given Alice Jergen the job of deputy, and I probably should have done that earlier. So you don't think Glen's bringing a girl?"

"Probably not, and considering his taste in women, we can be thankful."

She didn't comment on that, not wanting to begin another argument with Bates about their son's shortcomings as a man. He had them, but she didn't want to hear anything of him that wasn't good.

Little did she know that Glen would someday be at the core
of her most dreaded problem.

"I have to stop by Lizette's to get my hair done, so I may not
get home till around seven."

"This is my late night at the shop, so you'll probably get there
before I do. See you later."

She stared at the phone. Nothing. Endearments had long
since been dropped from their discourse. Yet she loved him and
believed he loved her. She shook her head in dismay. Maybe
they were no longer *in love*. She hung up, wrote a memorandum
requiring every person who worked in the building to cooperate
with the authorities' investigation of the ransacking of her office,
and had her secretary distribute it. As the day passed, the sting
of Maddie's disloyalty lessened, but she knew she would never
again like or trust the woman.

It rarely got blistering hot in Bakerville, because the breeze
from the Atlantic Ocean kept the town cool except at midday.
Still, Coreen didn't recall such warm weather in early May, and
especially not late in the afternoon. She removed her linen jacket
and hurried along Rust Street to the beauty shop, propelled by a
giddy high that she couldn't explain. Perhaps success did that to
a person. When she reached the shop, she flung open the shop
door, walked in, and stopped. Only two customers. Lizette's
shop was always full with its own special blended scent of fry-
ing hair and expensive perfumes. Not only was it almost empty,
but it lacked its characteristic buzz.

"Hi, Lizette," she said, walking slowly toward her sister-in-
law, who was wrapping sections of one customer's hair in alu-
minum foil. Coreen controlled a groan. The woman was getting
blond stripes in her hair, an image for which Coreen had not developed an appreciation.

"Hey, girl. How you doing? Would you . . . uh . . . mind coming back tomorrow? I'd like to close up as soon as I finish Janie
over there."

"Well, sure. I'll get here right after work. How's Porgy?"

"He's fine."

Coreen's eyebrows shot up. Not a single sexual innuendo with the mention of Porgy. She wondered at Lizette's subdued manner.

"Give him my love," Coreen said. "See you tomorrow."

"Right," Lizette called after her.

Coreen walked through the parking lot, got in her car, and headed home, driving more slowly than usual as she mused over Lizette's behavior. By the time she got home, she decided that Lizette hadn't forgiven her for not doing the commercial in the beauty shop.

"If I please everybody, I'll never please myself," Coreen said to herself as she parked in front of her house. "Wait a minute. Maybe something's wrong with Porgy." No matter. She didn't intend to ask. It was all she could do to protect her own secrets.

At about that time, Bates walked to the door of his travel agency and stood there as if by doing so he could will someone to come inside and buy a ticket. He hadn't made a sale all day, although he'd talked himself hoarse explaining his special Mediterranean package to half a dozen people. He saw Jessie Holcomb crossing the street, rushed back to his desk, and made himself appear busy.

"How's it going, Bates?" Jessie asked him. "Everybody says business is bad, but with the weather heating up, you ought to be making it."

"You don't see a crowd in here, do you?"

"Uh . . . well, no. I've been trying to figure out what to give Lorna for our twenty-fifth wedding anniversary. What do you think of a cruise?"

"Cruise is fine, but everybody does it. Now, I got a great package, a nice trip to Italy, Spain, and Portugal, a real bargain."

Jessie cocked his head to one side and stared at Bates. "Man, you got the only travel agency within forty miles of Bakerville and you still grubbing for a living. Everybody says they hate to come in here 'cause they ask for one thing, and you try to sell 'em something they don't want. You're your own worse enemy."

"Look—"

Jessie held up his hand, refusing to be interrupted. "Wake up, man. Herbert Wilson is talking about opening a Liberty Travel store over on Tryon Avenue. He was mad as the devil when he left here yesterday. All he wanted was a couple of round-trip tickets to Denver, and you wanted to sell him a Mediterranean tour. He phoned the airline, gave the folks his credit card number, and got the tickets himself. If you weren't so hardheaded and so stubborn, you'd be wealthy."

After the day he'd had, he didn't need Jessie's lecture, but he needed a sale. Any sale. "Where do you want to go on a cruise?"

"Anything going to Alaska?"

Bates's eyes widened, and he stroked his jaw wondering how Jessie could afford such an expensive trip, even for his anniversary. "I got several good ones."

By eight o'clock that evening, he'd made a thousand dollars, his biggest one-day take in months. In spite of his joy about the money he'd made, he envied Jessie's ability to give his wife fine accommodations on a six-week cruise. He closed the shop and walked home, taking a shortcut through the shopping mall.

"How'd it go today?" Coreen yelled from someplace near the kitchen when he entered the house.

"Real good," he called back, the odor of buttermilk biscuits titillating his olfactory senses and whetting his appetite. He loved buttermilk biscuits slathered with fresh butter, and the scent made him lick his lips. "How did things go with you?" he asked Coreen.

He dropped his briefcase on the table in the foyer, started to the kitchen, and stopped. Coreen stood before him wearing nothing but a red-bibbed apron.

"What the—" He began to salivate, and his treacherous body threatened to make a slave of him again. Then he wondered if she was trying to manipulate him or to pull a fast one on him.

"What's that for?" he asked her. "I'm hungry."

When she narrowed her eyes and headed for the kitchen, letting him see her naked buttocks, he knew she'd make him pay for it. At the moment, food was the least of his interests.

"It'll be on the table in two minutes," she said as she walked away. "And after you eat, you can clean the kitchen."

He wondered if Jessie was right, that he heaped misery upon himself. *I really made a mess of things tonight. No matter what I say or do, she's going to turn her back when she gets in that bed. And that won't be the end of it.*

While Bates spent the remainder of the evening trying to understand why Coreen and almost everyone else he knew got vexed with him from time to time and why Jessie considered him stubborn and hardheaded, Frieda plotted to torpedo his marriage.

Larry was due to bring her the information on Coreen Holmes's whereabouts that day, and as of eight that evening she hadn't heard from him. It wasn't only her fifty dollars, though she could hardly afford to lose that, but she had trusted a man—something she had learned at age twelve never to do. She perked a pot of coffee, flipped on the television set, and decided to wait until nine o'clock.

"If Larry isn't here by then," she swore aloud, "I'm sending the cops after him."

A few minutes later, her phone rang. "Hello." She was impatient and sounded that way. "This is Frieda."

"Sorry to be late getting to you, honey, but I had a few fish to fry. You know how it is with a fellow who's hustling to make a living."

At the sound of Larry's voice, her shoulders went back, and she blew out a long breath. "I don't care about that. What do I get for my fifty bucks?"

"Now, now, Frieda. Give a man credit. I told you Gabe would deliver, didn't I? You got a pencil and some paper?"

"Hold on." She ran to the living room, got her tablet and ballpoint pen from the coffee table, and raced back to the phone. "All r-right." Her teeth began to chatter and her fingers shook as if she were an old woman crumbling under the ravishments of a degenerative disease.

"It says right here—"

"Larry," she yelled, "would you please cut the crap and tell me what Gabe said."

"All right. Don't get your dander up. He said you're looking for Coreen Holmes Treadwell, number thirty-eight Queen Street North, Bakerville, North Carolina. He didn't give me the phone number. Said that costs you an extra ten bucks."

Her fingers wouldn't move. "Wha-what did you s-say?"

He repeated it, but her hand seemed to cramp and she couldn't move the pencil. "Bear with me, Larry. This is s-so import-tant to me that I c-can't even write."

"Well, I could bring it to you. I'm pretty needy tonight and I was going somewhere, but you know I'd rather be with you, don't you?"

"You blackmailer," she screamed at him, no longer immobilized. "Tell me again what he said." She wrote her birth mother's name and address on the tablet, thanked Larry, and added, "I appreciate your offer to bring it over, but I don't feel like playing Good Samaritan tonight. Be in touch."

She hung up, reheated the pot of coffee, got her maps of North Carolina, and began searching for Bakerville. When she found it, she drew a red circle around the spot and leaned back against her sofa.

"It didn't have to be like this," she thought as tears streamed down her cheeks, "but she's got it coming, and I'm not backing down now. She should have done better by me."

Coreen had waited anxiously for Friday night when Eric and Glen would arrive. Eric would bring Bright Star, but neither she nor Bates attempted to guess who, if anyone, Glen would bring with him.

"It's his birthday," she told Bates, "so I'm going to welcome whoever Glen brings here."

"You'd welcome her if it wasn't his birthday," Bates muttered.

She turned the roasting fresh ham on the spit in their new oven and checked the leek soup. The dinner she'd planned consisted of foods that Glen loved; she paid little attention to whether they complemented each other. The doorbell rang in rapid succession, and she rushed to open the door.

"Glen! Happy birthday, Son. How are you?" she asked him, opening her arms to hug him.

"Great. And how's my celebrity mom?"

"I haven't changed. I'm still just your mom."

He hugged her again. "Yeah, right. Where's Dad?"

"In the kitchen stirring some kind of sauce. Go on back there and let him know you're here."

Half an hour later, Eric and Bright Star arrived, and Bates's dash to open the door when he heard the doorbell amused Coreen. Bates was proud of his elder son, but considered Glen a failure and seemed to hold a grudge against him because of it. If Glen noticed, he didn't make it obvious.

Coreen didn't know when she'd had such a happy time with her family. She had promised herself that she would be tolerant with Bright Star, but found that she liked the woman.

"Man, you sure know how to pick them," Glen said to Eric during dinner.

"Don't give me the credit," Eric replied. "I looked up and there she was. Man, I didn't choreograph this dance. Someone somewhere else had a hand in it."

"Well, at least you had sense enough to latch on," Bates said.

Bright Star, who asked to be called Star, looked at Coreen with a twinkle in her eyes. "He's not the only one who latched on. After I figured out what was happening to me, I went for it."

"I like a woman who goes after what she wants," Bates said. "A man likes to know his woman wants him."

Coreen leaned back in her chair, weighed the consequences of voicing her thoughts and decided against it. Instead, she said, "Right. And a smart man teaches himself to understand his woman's moves. If he's not careful, subtle gestures can pass right by him." She allowed herself what would seem to the others present a hearty and friendly laugh. "Remember that red apron, honey? Wasn't that a gas?"

"When are you going to bring a nice girl home to your parents, Glen?" Bates asked with a hint of hostility in his voice and ignoring Coreen's jab.

"Don't get uptight, Dad. I just got to be twenty-five today. Nice girls like to settle down, and I'm not ready to do that."

The evening passed without anger or recriminations, as if Bates had programmed himself not to criticize Glen so as to maintain a peaceful, pleasant atmosphere. To Coreen's amazement, Eric didn't mention her speech in Brussels, and she was grateful for it. If he'd forgotten about it, perhaps the event hadn't made a lasting impression on anyone who could be looking for her. It pleased her, too, that Eric didn't seem to think her gifts to Glen were excessive, although Bates expressed his displeasure by not commenting on the sweaters and leather jacket.

She crawled into bed around midnight, thankful for her blessings, clicked off the light, and before Bates finished his shower, assumed the posture of one sound asleep. Her libido had begun to trouble her, but not to the extent that she was ready to forgive Bates for his offensive reaction to her red-bibbed apron.

The next morning around seven-thirty, Bates opened the front door and reached for the weekend edition of *The Bakerville Star Ledger*. As he straightened up, he grabbed his back and leaned against the doorjamb.

"Looks like I'm finally feeling my age," he said to himself, glanced across the street at his neighbor's house, went inside, and closed the door.

"Maybe you ought to see a doctor, Dad," Eric said. "Bad backs only get worse."

"This morning was the first time it bothered me, but maybe I'd better do that." He made a mental note to see the family doctor the following Monday. "Too bad you can't stay longer, Eric."

"Wish I could, Dad, but I'm working on an experiment and I have to water my seedlings."

"I understand, son," Bates said, "and I'm proud of you."

The family stood at the front door, biding Eric and Star goodbye, and watched them until they drove away.

"Gotta be going, too," Glen said. "Thanks for a great birthday dinner, Mom, and for those fabulous presents. Call you when I get home."

Bates couldn't help being peeved at Coreen when she handed Glen a package of food for his trip home—something she hadn't thought to do for Eric. And as he knew she would, she followed Glen to his car, embraced him warmly, and stood in the driveway watching his sleek red Mercury Cougar fade from sight.

"If that boy ever amounts to anything, it won't be your fault," he said to Coreen when she walked up the steps to where he stood. "Say, that car was parked over there this morning when I took the paper in." He watched the blue 1995 Plymouth as it headed out Queen Street in the direction of Raleigh. "That's a Maryland license plate." He shook his head as if perplexed. "The Robinsons must have weekend guests, because that car doesn't belong to anybody here in Bakerville."

His next thought was that one of Glen's girlfriends was spying on him. After all, Glen produced programs for a cable radio station at Baltimore Community College and encountered all kinds of women on a daily basis. He shrugged it off as a fanciful notion, but he noticed that Coreen had withdrawn, her ebullience of half an hour earlier no longer evident.

"We can't keep the boys with us always, Coreen," he said in an attempt to soothe her. "We have to turn them loose to be their own men."

Immediately, her countenance brightened almost as if the sun suddenly shone on her. "I guess you're right."

He had the feeling that he'd thrown her a lifeline, and that she'd grabbed at it as if it were her salvation. *She's faking something,* he thought, *and I gave her an out.*

He maneuvered himself into a position from which he could look directly into her eyes, and what he saw stunned him. Coreen's always expressive eyes, her best features among several fine ones, had a vacant and troubled look, an expression of hopelessness. He caught himself as he was about to shake her, to stir up some life in her.

"You all right?" he asked her.

Again, her face radiated a smile. "Me? I'm fine."

If she said it a dozen times, he wouldn't believe her, and for the first time since he married Coreen, Bates didn't trust her. A person's word was his bond, and Coreen had elected to lie to him.

Murder will out, he said to himself, *so I'm not about to stress over whatever it is. Can't be too serious anyway.*

However, what Frieda had in mind was indeed serious, and with the knowledge she acquired during the weekend, Frieda Davis held all the cards. She got back to Baltimore late Saturday afternoon, did some grocery shopping at the Lexington Market, and drove on home. While her pot of fresh spareribs, sauerkraut, and potatoes cooked, she sat down with her tablet and outlined her plan of attack. But when she went to the bathroom to brush her teeth, what she saw in the mirror depressed her.

She telephoned her friend, Thelma. "You heard of those make-overs, you know the ones that make you look like a glamour girl? How much does one of them cost?" she asked Thelma after greeting her.

"Girl, you off your rocker if you thinking about going to one of those spas. It'll cost more than you make in a month. All you need is a good hairdresser and some clothes that fit and that aren't black, brown, gray, or some other mud color. Go to Dillards or some such place and let one of those women selling Fashion Fair cosmetics give you a makeup job. It's free. If I was half as good-looking as you, I wouldn't go around looking like you do."

"I'm saving my little change to buy a house. When it comes to clothes, I buy whatever is on sale."

"Oh yeah? Let me go shopping with you. You bet I can find you something on sale that looks decent. What you sprucing up for? You met a man?"

"No, but I'm going to."

"Well 'scuse me. You been to see old lady Jewel over on Franklin Street? That old woman makes a living lying to people and making them believe her. Claiming to be clairvoyant. She can't even spell the word."

"What do you take me for, Thelma? I got other things on my mind. Want to go shopping with me next Saturday?"

"Like I said, must have something to do with a man. 'Course, I know you're gonna be tight-tongued about it as usual."

Thelma and Frieda spent the following Saturday afternoon shopping, getting their hair done, and enjoying a free makeover at the Fashion Fair cosmetics counter.

"Girl, if I met you on the street, I wouldn't recognize you," Thelma said to Frieda. "The Lord gave you these good looks, and you waste them looking dowdy."

"Look at *you*. I could say the same about you," Frieda said to Thelma. She could hardly contain her joy, certain now that she had things going her way.

At work the following Monday morning, Frieda considered the wisdom of asking Larry or Gabe to find out who owned the car with the license plate number she had. Not only had she copied down the number, but she had imprinted it on her brain, a number she would remember until she died. That car belonged to someone who Coreen Holmes Treadwell loved, maybe her son, for Coreen had stood at the curb watching the car for as long as she could see it after its owner drove off.

A mistake at this stage could ruin her plans. "I can't trust Larry as far as I can throw him," Frieda said as she pulled sheets from the linen closet on the general surgery ward and prepared to change beds. "And I wouldn't believe a hustler like Gabe would keep a secret if he swore to it and his tongue was notarized." She'd have to do it herself, and that meant going to the police station.

On her lunch hour, she bought a small calculator for nine dollars and headed for the police station about five blocks from the hospital. She threaded her way among the dozen or so squad cars parked on the street and the sidewalk, tripped up the steps—mainly to show that she had no reluctance about entering a police station—and pushed open the heavy door. The scent of stale perking coffee assaulted her nostrils along with the smell of Chinese food, which reminded her that she hadn't eaten since breakfast.

If the officers had eaten lunch, so much the better. You couldn't expect benevolence from a hungry man. She approached the policeman at the information desk and asked how she could locate the owner of the car with that tag number.

"Did he commit a crime?" the officer asked her.

"No, sir. I want to give him this solar calculator." She showed the officer the calculator that she bought minutes earlier, knowing what the policeman would assume.

The officer sipped from the cup in front of him and wiped his mouth with the back of his hand. "This stuff is cold," he said. "Let's see now. Not many people would go to this much trouble to return something they found. We need more honest citizens like you. Have a seat."

"Well, Lord, you must be working in my favor today," Frieda sang out as she marched down the steps of the police station. "Glen Treadwell, and he lives right here in Baltimore." She clutched the paper on which the officer wrote Glen's name and address, folded it, and tucked it inside her blouse, as if she feared it might vanish.

The next morning she drove to the apartment building in which Glen lived, parked a few lengths behind his car, and followed him to the community college. After waiting about half an hour, she went inside, got a catalogue, and prepared for her next move. She arrived at work one hour late, and it was her ill fortune that she bumped into her supervisor and sent the woman sprawling across the floor.

"I'm so sorry, ma'am," she said to the startled woman. "I was rushing to my station." She helped the supervisor, a heavyset and now angry woman, to her feet. "You know I never come to work late, but this morning I got into a traffic jam." *Lord*, Frieda said in silent communion, *you know how I hate to lie and it looks like lately that's all I do.*

"I guess I ought to be grateful that you don't weigh a ton. Be careful how you charge around these corners. You'd have killed a post-op patient. Get those beds made and the rooms tidied before lunchtime."

"Yes, ma'am. I hope you're all right, ma'am."

Later, on her lunch hour and at home after work, Frieda

pored over the catalogue, trying without success to find Glen's connection to the college. From a distance, he had seemed too old to be a student; if he was one, she would have to try a different tactic.

Frustrated, she phoned information in Bakerville and obtained Coreen's home telephone number. "If I can't sleep, neither will she," Frieda vowed. Almost immediately, she remembered caller ID and discarded the idea of harassing Coreen. Besides, she had never stooped to anything that low and she wasn't going to start. What was wrong with her? And what would Reverend Hall say if he knew what she was up to? She shrugged. Reverend Hall probably hadn't experienced anything like what she went through with Claude Davis.

The next morning on her first break, she phoned the college. "May I please speak with Glen Treadwell?" If he wasn't a student, the operator should be able to locate him.

"Just a minute," the operator said.

The bottom seemed to plunge from her stomach as she waited in anticipation while the phone rang repeatedly. At last a deep masculine voice reached her ears, immobilizing her.

"WBCC, the Voice of Learning in Baltimore. Treadwell speaking."

She grabbed at the wall above the pay phone and steadied herself. No point in being scared. She'd come too far to think of backing away. "Uh . . . Mr. Treadwell, my name is Frieda Davis, and I'm looking for role models for the teens in my church. Would you talk to them about what you do? These kids need encouragement."

At least she wasn't lying this time. She had promised to find a guest for the teen venture the following Sunday, and until today, no friend having been unearthed who could pass for a celebrity, she had planned to talk to the youth herself about nursing.

"When does the group meet, Miss . . . uh . . ."

"Davis. I hope you can meet with us this coming Sunday afternoon at two. I know it's short notice, but it's taken me a long time to get up the nerve to ask you. We're at Mt. Zion AME Church on Carey Street a block below Franklin. The children will be excited to meet a distinguished radio . . . uh . . . personality."

"Why, thank you. I'm surprised anyone remembers my work as a disk jockey. I've been a producer for the past year. It will be my pleasure to speak with them. You might ask my stepmother, Coreen Treadwell, to talk with them sometime. She has a very interesting, very exciting career. I'll be glad to arrange it for you if you like."

Stepmother? *"Did you say stepmother?"*

"Why, yes," he said. "You seem surprised."

She told herself to watch it. One slip could ruin everything. "You spoke of her affectionately," Frieda said, retrieving her aplomb. "Stepmoms aren't usually so popular."

"Mine's the best," he said, his deep vibrato sending more shivers through her.

Now there's a man, she said to herself. To him, she said, "I'll be waiting for you at the front door at two o'clock. Okay? And I'll be wearing a red suit."

"Cool. I like to see the sistahs in colors. I'll be there."

She hung up with the feeling that she'd had the wind knocked out of her and let the wall take her weight. So he wasn't Coreen Treadwell's biological child. A new plan, and a dangerous one, she realized, began to take shape in her thoughts.

Glen Treadwell sounded like a man of the world, but he wouldn't be the first one of them to fall for a woman like her. With her new look, she could attract any man from seventeen to seventy.

"Hey, girl," a coworker greeted her as she began finishing her day's work with slower than usual movements. "You musta had a big night."

"Don't I wish," Frieda said and forced herself to liven her steps.

She made a mental note to get her hair and nails done before the weekend and to take her black patent shoes to the shoe repair shop for new heels and soles. Opportunity seldom knocked twice and she meant to make good use of that one.

"Oh my goodness," she said aloud as she left work. Suppose she looked like Coreen Treadwell. She hadn't been able to see that from a distance the morning she saw Coreen with Glen. "I'd better get myself a pair of tinted glasses. Lord, this is costing me my good hard-earned money, but it's gonna be worth it."

Chapter Seven

Bates stood in the kitchen doorway with his arms stretched above his head and his hands braced against the sides of the doorjamb. She thought he looked unusually large, even menacing, and stopped before she reached him.

"What is it, Bates? What's the matter?"

"You think something's the matter? You should have seen yourself out there with Glen, hanging on to him. When the boys were growing up, I was busy trying to make a living and so glad I'd found a woman who was kind and loving to them as well as to me that I didn't notice you made such a difference between them. It wasn't right, Coreen."

"I didn't do that. I love Eric and he knows it, but he never seemed to need me as much as Glen did."

He threw up his hands. "All right. You go ahead. That boy's going to make you cry one of these days." He turned as if to go into the living room, stopped, and looked back at her. "Let him go, Coreen. Let him be a man. He can't make up for whatever it is that bothers you all the time."

Bates had an uncanny habit sometimes of digging into her psyche and yanking at the part of herself that was hers, that she didn't share with any living soul. When she gasped, he said, "That's right. You don't tell me what ails you, but plenty of times I catch you with a faraway look in your eyes. And sometimes you act strange, like you're scared of something. I'm your husband; you can't hide much from me."

What could she say to that? "If that's what you think, nothing I say will change your mind." It was a cop-out, and he had to know it.

She sat on the steps, and the sun—strong for early May—seemed to beat down on her head. She shaded her face with her hands and closed her eyes. Lawn mowers hummed across several neighbors' lawns, as the men treated themselves to their once-weekly exercise. The smell of freshly cut grass mingled with the scent of roses and hyacinths, and a breeze finally stirred, bringing with it the cleansing air from off the Atlantic. Normally, she would have thought it a pleasant, invigorating morning, but on that occasion, none of it could banish the weight inside of her.

"How y'all doing this morning," her next-door neighbor Cee Cee called, as she stood at her car with the obvious intention of going to the market. "Want to come along? It's such a nice day."

"I'd love to, but we shopped yesterday. I'm just sitting here taking in the weather."

Coreen let her gaze roam over her upscale neighborhood with its manicured lawns, six-figure individually designed homes, two- and three-car garages, and expensive cars. Bates had bought their home thirty years earlier for one third of the current price or they wouldn't have been able to afford living there. Even if they lived back of the tracks in Bakerville, she would be in heaven compared to the life she had growing up.

In her mind's eye, she could see the tilted, shingled house in the tiny hamlet of working-class people on the outskirts of Charlotte, North Carolina. The house in which she lived the first seventeen years of her life. Poor, but honest and proud, they said. Even as a child, she didn't see poverty as a reason for pride. And then those dreadful five months with her aunt Agatha. Months of agony during which she often prayed to die.

"You gonna sit out there in that hot sun all day? You want heat stroke?"

Bates's voice brought her out of the past, and she rose slowly and started into the house. At the door, he slung an arm around her shoulder, closed the door, and turned her to face him.

"I'd be here for you, if you'd let me."

And he would, she knew, if baring her soul only made her shine brighter in his eyes. But if what he saw was a woman from a lower-class family who dragged herself up by toughness and an unswerving will to succeed, to put the ugliness behind her, would he still wrap her in his protective arms? She doubted it. And certainly not if he knew the hell she'd lived in for five long months, and that she had a child somewhere who didn't know her. Maybe she misjudged him. She couldn't risk it.

"I know, love," she said. "I know." She had to escape before Bates began the interrogation for which he seemed primed. "I need to get my hair done. Lizette was too busy last time I went."

"Probably busy running her mouth. How's she doing?"

"She's looking good." It occurred to her that Bates seldom mentioned his sister, who, as far as she knew, was his only living relative other than his sons. She knew he didn't approve of Lizette's common-law marriage with Porgy, but she figured that after twelve years he should have accommodated himself to it.

"I ought to be out of there around three or four. Want me to come by the shop and help out?"

He shrugged. "I close up at five on Saturdays, but you can come by if you want to."

She walked down the hallway a few paces and stopped. With a glance, she could see the brown patches of skin shining through his rapidly decreasing strands of hair. And though he still stood tall with a commanding presence, the hard biceps and washboard belly she'd loved, as well as his days of youthful verve, were behind him. The fact that he could still make her holler in bed didn't entitle him to the presumption that he was indispensable, or that she would wag her little tail and start panting if he enthused over the prospect of her stopping by his shop.

"Maybe I'll just see you when you get home," she said. She got her pocketbook, car keys, and sunglasses, kissed him on the cheek as she passed him, and headed for Lizette's shop.

Coreen pushed open the door of the beauty parlor and nearly staggered from the fumes of Lydia Felton's perfume. "It's not that the scent's bad," Lizette explained when Coreen complained about it. "The problem is that she douses herself and her clothes with it. I expect it costs her a lot to keep herself supplied with perfume."

"How's Porgy?"

"He's . . . uh . . . fine."

Coreen's ears perked up. For the second time, mention of Porgy didn't bring a testimonial from Lizette as to his male prowess. Something had to be wrong, but she didn't think it proper to pry. Lydia saved her the trouble.

"Ain't seen Porgy around lately, Lizette. He out of town?"

"Guess that's because your schedule's different from his," Lizette said, though without her usual bravado.

"Well," Lydia persisted, "he usually comes to eleven o'clock service at church on Sunday morning. That's when we all on the same schedule. 'Course, if you don't want to say, ain't no skin off my teeth. I was just being friendly."

"Yeah," Coreen heard Lizette mutter under her breath, "with friends like you, I don't need enemies."

"You're next," Lizette said to Coreen, after putting a customer under the dryer. She oiled Coreen's scalp and prepared to give her a relaxer. "Girl, business is so slow and I'm getting all these bills. Maybe if you'd do that spot here in my shop for the TV producer I told you about, more people would come in here. A lot of these white girls have started wearing braids, and I want to advertise that we specialize in braids, but I can't afford it."

Coreen could see that, for a Saturday, the shop was practically empty. "Don't people get their hair done anymore?"

"Yeah, but they come every three weeks now, instead of weekly or every other week. If you could find the time . . ."

How could she refuse? Yet, she didn't want the exposure. So far, her luck had held, and no one had contacted her in respect to her past or tried to blackmail her. There was no telling what Lizette would think if she refused a second time.

"Well, all right. I'll think about it and let you know tomorrow. I guess it can't hurt either one of us."

White paste from the tongue depressor that Lizette used to apply the relaxer dripped on Coreen's green silk dress as Lizette stared down at her.

"You're going to give it serious thought? Is that what you said?"

Coreen nodded. "He'd have to keep it local, Lizette. I . . . uh . . . might want to strike up a . . . uh . . . national endorsement of some kind. You never can tell. So, if I do agree . . ." She had to get out of it. She just *had* to.

"Of course it'll be local. Nobody in Raleigh is coming all the way to Bakerville to get their hair done in my shop." Lizette said. "But what did you mean, 'it can't hurt either one of us'? Seems to me it can only help."

Coreen squeezed her eyes tight and cautioned herself not to get loose-tongued. After thirty years of averting suspicion from herself, she'd better not get careless. "That ought to be clear," she bluffed. "I meant it can only help both of us. Right?"

"I'll say, and I'm praying to the good Lord that you'll help me. Coreen, honey, things aren't so good with me right now, but the Lord will see me through."

Coreen reflected that Lizette had mentioned the Lord's name as often in the past twenty minutes as in the twenty years she'd known her. Something was wrong. "Sure thing," she said to Lizette.

"I'll call Fred and let him know you're considering doing that TV spot. He said it would be great for his show. You know, having a conversation with our local celebrity."

By the time Coreen left the beauty parlor, she had developed shortness of breath and could barely manage to walk to her car. She recognized her condition as a panic attack, and when she got into her car, she took deep, slow breaths until she could calm herself. Not until after she had almost agreed to the taping had she remembered that the show's broadcast range extended all the way north to Elizabeth City and as far south as New Bern.

"I can't back out this time," she said aloud. "It wouldn't be fair to Lizette, and especially since I know she's in trouble."

Coreen was no stranger to problems; time and again, she had sailed over some choppy seas and reached shore safely with barely a scratch. Consoling herself with the thought that her national appearance before the Senate committee hadn't caused her any problems, she drove on home, parked, and took her time going into the empty house.

She answered her cellular phone, knowing that it wouldn't be her husband, who preferred to ignore the existence of cell phones. "Hello. This is Coreen."

"I need to talk with you," Lizette said. "I should have said something when you were here, but I just couldn't bring myself to do it. We could meet someplace if you don't want to come back to the shop. I'm closing in about half an hour, soon as I get Lydia Felton out of here. I did her hair and her nails, and now she wants her damned toes done. I think she asks for that service just to humiliate me."

Coreen laughed, though she knew Lizette didn't think the matter amusing. "Get even with her. Ask her not to wear that perfume when she comes in the shop. Tell her your customers have complained about it."

"I thought about that, but she's the one who would ask who complained. Where can we meet?"

"I'll go back to the shop."

She dreaded the conversation she would have with her sister-in-law, because her instincts told her that Lizette wanted to talk about Porgy. If she had wanted to boast, she would have done that in the shop where her customers could hear her.

If she spills her insides, Coreen thought, *her attitude toward me will change and not for the good. People don't like being around you if you know their weaknesses.* She left Bates a note saying she'd gone back to the beauty parlor to have tea with Lizette and that she'd call him.

She followed Lizette through the beauty parlor to the room in back that Lizette regarded as her sanctuary.

"You can have tea if you want it, but I'm having a beer. Porgy ain't here to raise a stink about it, so I'm doing as I please."

Coreen paused in the act of sitting down, and both of her eyebrows shot up. That didn't sound like a woman who flaunted her independence; indeed, those words had the mark of what passed for equality between her and Bates.

"Where *is* Porgy, Lizette? What's going on between you and him?"

Lizette leaned back in the chair, closed her eyes, and exhaled a long breath. "Nothing. Not one damned thing. And that's the problem. I don't know where he is."

"What did you say? What happened?"

"I don't know. He'd been acting odd, like his mind wasn't on me at all. Didn't talk much, went to bed after I was asleep, and got up before I woke up. And one day he just didn't bother to come home from work."

"Did you call the school?"

"Coreen, school's out. You know that. Most of the teachers are scattered halfway around the world by now. I can't help wondering if I've been wrong all these years. I know Porgy wanted to get married, but maybe he wanted a family, too, and I just wasn't listening. He asked me to marry him just about every day, and I always told him no without thinking about it."

"Did he take his clothes?"

"I think he'd been slipping out a few things at a time." Her voice dropped and Coreen could hear in her words the sound of unreleased tears. "I didn't notice. I was too sure of him, and I guess he showed me how stupid I've been."

"How long since you've seen him?"

"He's been gone four weeks tomorrow. Worse month of my life. And with the mortgage, car payments, and bills on this shop coming due, I'm headed out of my mind."

"I can help you out this month," Coreen said. "You planning to share this with Bates?"

Lizette shook her head. "I'll take any help I can get, and you know I thank you. Bates has never hidden his feeling about me living with Porgy and not married to him. He'll probably enjoy this."

Coreen agreed with her, but didn't say so. "He certainly won't miss the opportunity to lecture you about it. I won't mention it to him, but if he finds out that I knew and didn't tell him, he'll be unbearable."

"I know. I wish my brother had more feeling for ordinary people. Anybody would think he was born in Windsor Castle."

Coreen stored that remark in her mind for future reference and tried to concentrate on Lizette's problem, and how she could help her. Little by little, she was becoming a fatalist. Or so it seemed. Every step she took and every decision she made pointed toward her exposure, malignant arrows headed for the bull's eye. With a deep breath signaling her resignation, she bit the bullet. "All right, Lizette, call that TV producer and tell him I'll do the spot."

Lizette gaped, staring at Coreen above the rim of her beer glass. "Did you say? I mean, are you really going to do it? You won't change your mind?"

"If I say I'll do it, I'll do it," Coreen replied, though she didn't sound convincing even to herself. "I hope he can do the taping on a Saturday morning."

Lizette rested the glass on the table beside her chair. "That's no problem." Then she looked toward the ceiling and raised her glass as if in a toast. "Lord, I do thank you. I sure do." She got up and hugged Coreen. "If you ever need me, just let me know. I don't care where or when, I'll be there for you."

"That's the way it should be with sisters, Lizette," Coreen said. "But I don't ask for thanks; I just want you to get your life back together."

"Me, too, but I don't know how I'm going to do that without Porgy." A cloudy glaze covered her eyes, and she quickly closed them. "Coreen, do you think Porgy doesn't know I love him, that he's the air I breathe?"

"He knows it, Lizette. Maybe he's making certain that *you* know it. I can't believe he won't come back."

"I can, 'cause Porgy's not a man to make threats. Whatever he's gonna do, he does it with no fanfare. He's gone."

Coreen left the shop and found herself walking down Cord Street in the direction of the Sound. She had promised Lizette not to tell Bates about Porgy's disappearance, and with all the questions filling her thoughts, she didn't want to face him.

Lizette Treadwell had every right to confidence that she could keep her man. Tall and statuesque, Lizette had the figure of a twenty-year-old, and no lines marred her face. Her long-lashed brown eyes and chiseled features in a smooth-skinned, dark brown face surely made many a young man take a second look at her. At age thirty-six, when she met Porgy, Lizette was considered one of the town's beauties, and at forty-eight she could still lay claim to the title.

Coreen approached a slab bench facing the water, and sat down to rest and ruminate. Almost at once, she recalled how she had envied Lizette her freedom and independence and dreamed of experiencing the sexual feasts that Lizette related with such relish.

This will teach me a lesson, she acknowledged to herself. *I may have what Lizette calls boring sex lying flat on my back, but Bates is still with me.* She got up and headed for her car. *If I can just get through this TV showing without anybody locating me, I won't tempt fate again.*

However, another trial faced Coreen, one that she might have anticipated had she taken more seriously the relationship between Eric and Bright Star.

"Eric just phoned," Bates told Coreen the minute she stepped into the house. "He had good news, too. That boy's everything smart women should look for in a man. He and Star have decided to marry, and he wants our blessing."

Coreen found a chair and sat down. "But we don't know anything about her or her family. She'll be the mother of our grandchildren, and who knows what kind of genes they'll have?" She said the wrong thing and knew it; indeed, she didn't believe what her remark implied.

Both of Bates's hands went to his hips in knotted fists. She knew he wouldn't consider hitting her, but the force with which he knocked his hips let her know he'd used his body as an outlet for his frustration.

"You listen to me, woman. Eric needs our support, and we're going to give it to him."

"I didn't say—"

He cut her off. "You'd be happier if he was just like Glen, exploiting women for the fun of it, wouldn't you? You claim you love him. Well, act like it." He slapped his left fist in his right palm and walked to the other end of the living room. "They're having a formal wedding, and we"—he poked his chest with his left thumb—"are giving the dinner for the bridal party."

She searched for the right words, words that could convince him. Star was an adopted child. What if her father was a ruffian like Leon Farrell, who violated innocent women with no thought as to the consequences? *Adopted!* Every time she looked at her daughter-in-law and her grandchildren, she would think of that other child—born to her nearly thirty years earlier—and the conditions surrounding its birth. She didn't think she could handle it.

"I'm not against her," she said, hearing the feebleness of her words. "What if her children should have a rare blood type and need—"

He stood over her, his face the picture of rage. "I want you to think about what you're saying, Coreen. The first time Star came here, you made up your mind to dislike her. Well, my son is going to marry the woman of his choice with or without your blessings. Big-time social worker, and not a hint of compassion where your own stepson is concerned."

"My son . . . your own stepson." Not in the twenty years of her marriage to Bates had he made such a distinction. He had always referred to the boys as "our sons," or in jest, "your son."

In defense of her error, she struck back at him. "So this is the thanks I get for being their mother, for loving them and taking care of them when they couldn't take care of themselves." Knowing that her position was untenable, she walked up the stairs and left Bates to contemplate her words.

One of them had to cook dinner, and she didn't need a clairvoyant to tell her that Bates was too angry to consider it. She sat on the edge of their bed to pull off her stockings, and as she reached down, the sight of her belly dragging along Agatha Monroe's rows of spring lettuce filled her mind's eye. She gasped, and a cry nearly surged out of her.

Suppose another woman somewhere is denying her son the right to marry your daughter because she was adopted, or a man is telling his daughter that she can't marry your bastard son. What right do you have to judge Star? She fell across the bed and let the tears have their way.

"Why on earth are you crying?"

She jerked up, grabbed the bedspread, and dabbed at her eyes. "Sometimes life is hard," she said, went into the bathroom, and washed her face. She didn't want to overplay her hand, as Lizette had done, because that could have disastrous results.

As she expected, when she came out, he remained where she left him. "You all right?" he asked her.

"I'm fi—not really," she said, deciding not to lie.

His arm draped around her shoulder and tugged her to his body. "Eric is lucky to find a girl like Star, Coreen. They can work together, share a dream, build a future together. They complement each other. And I like her a lot," he added. "She'll be a good, loving daughter to us. I wish you would welcome her with your arms wide open."

He was offering her a chance to make amends, and she grabbed at it. "No mother wants to see her sons leave home for good. I've always been first in his life, but she's number one now. Silly, aren't I?"

To her amazement, he laughed. "You sure are. Don't you remember that my mother practically shifted her devotion from me to you? Anybody would have thought you were her child. Let's go downstairs and cook dinner. I'm hungry."

They walked down the stairs together, but how long would it be, she wondered, before the fruits of her past exploded in her face and left her with nothing?

"There's that strange car parked across the street again," Bates said when he walked into the kitchen.

She dashed to the dinning room window and looked out. "That's a different car," she said, and let herself breathe.

"Maybe, but it doesn't belong to anybody in this neighborhood."

Frieda returned the rental car to the agency and took a bus to within a block from her apartment building. Though it was well after midnight, she didn't want to spend the money for a taxi. She had left Baltimore around three o'clock Saturday morning and spent the day in Bakerville tracing Coreen's steps and making notes. If her plan with Glen didn't work, she needed an alternative. She knew where Coreen lived, got her hair done, and shopped, and she intended to find out where she worked. Coreen Holmes Treadwell was going to deal with her.

She climbed the steps to her apartment, went in, and closed the door with one thought in mind: dropping herself into bed after a warm bath.

Now who could that be? she thought when she saw the red light blinking on her answering machine. After checking, she sat down and phoned her sister Julie.

"Sorry to call so late, but I just got in."

"Just got in?" Julie asked her. "In from where? Honey, are you still looking for your birth mother?"

"You know I do a lot of things for my church. We have a wonderful program for our teenagers, and I've been busy rounding up speakers and planning programs for them."

"I notice you didn't answer my question. When you coming this way? You should see the apartment Portia's buying. She used her share of money from the old homestead as a down payment. It's beautiful."

"I'm glad for her, Julie. I'm saving my little money to buy a house somewhere near the water or the mountains. I want to be in a quiet and beautiful place."

"And you will. But you stop that witch hunt. If you don't, you'll be sorry. Come see me, now."

Frieda hung up. Every time she went looking for Coreen, Julie seemed to sense it and caution her against that course. She wondered if her mama was speaking to her through Julie.

"Too bad if she is." She looked toward the ceiling. "Lord, you forgive me, please, but I'm going to have my day with that woman, even if I have to suffer for it."

The next morning, Sunday, Frieda dressed in her red, short-sleeved piqué suit, white blouse, and earrings, black patent leather shoes and pocketbook, and left for church. She had the feeling that her nerves were rearranging themselves throughout her body, and with her knees shaking and her fingers moving like trembling leaves, she leaned against the building in which she lived in an effort to gain some composure.

After calming herself, she walked as fast as she could, because she hated entering the sanctuary after the choir marched in. She took a seat on the aisle midway into the church and tried to concentrate on the proceedings, but to no avail. At last the long, seemingly interminable service ended, and she made her way to the front door of the church to wait for Glen Treadwell and her fate.

It hadn't occurred to her that he would arrive early, but at a quarter of two he hopped out of a taxi, strode up the steps, and stopped less than a foot from her. At five feet seven and a half inches, she considered herself a tall woman, but he dwarfed her. His white teeth glistened in his dark face as he treated her to a sample of his charismatic personality.

"Don't tell me you're Frieda. How'd I get so lucky?" He held out his hand and simultaneously leaned forward and kissed her cheek. "My. If I'd known church was like this, I'd have been attending regularly."

"Hi, Glen," she managed to say. "Thanks so much for coming. You look just like you sound." And he did. Gray suit, white shirt, and a yellow tie with a thin gray stripe. Perfect.

His left eyebrow shot up. "Really. I'll have to listen to myself."

He's full of it, she said to herself, *but he sure is a looker. Head to foot, this man is hot stuff.*

To her surprise, he took his lecture to the teenagers seriously, and their delight in meeting and talking with him far exceeded what she had hoped for. The discussion extended beyond the usual one hour, and eventually Reverend Hall arrived, introduced himself to Glen, and asked the children to let him go.

A sense of guilt pervaded Frieda when the children and the minister thanked her profusely for inviting Glen to talk with them, for her motive in inviting him had been unscrupulous and treacherous.

With the children crowded around them, he took her arm, gazed down at her, and smiled, poleaxing her. "I'm starved. Let's go pick up a burger or something."

She wondered why he arrived in a taxi. "Didn't you drive?"

"Nah. Finding a parking space over here is about as easy as finding a diamond. I never attempt the impossible; it's a waste of time.

"Why don't we walk over to Franklin?" he said, resting his hand easily at her lower back as if he had special permission to do so. At Fannie's Barbecue Shop, he gripped her waist. "Wanna stop in here? Fannie's barbecue is great."

She knew that. She also knew she had acquiesced to each of his suggestions, and that he had expected her to do so. But like a lemming headed for water, she didn't seem able to alter the course.

"I think I'll have the barbecue," he said as he seated her at the marble-top table with all the flourish of one about to dine at La Tour D'Argent in Paris. "It's already cooked, and like I said, I'm starving. What're you having?"

Frieda ate in restaurants so infrequently that the plethora of choices along with the mesmerizing effect of Glen Treadwell's stare addled her. He had the upper hand, she thought, and she didn't plan to let him keep it. Doggedly, she continued to look at the menu. Then she put it on the table, smiled at him, and said, "Sorry, but I think I'll stick with the burger."

When his eyes narrowed slightly, she knew he expected her to order what he ordered. Well, she loved barbecued beef, but allowing him to lead her as a ram leads sheep would guarantee that she wouldn't reach her goal. She couldn't let herself forget that Coreen was her reason for being with him.

"I'll finish before you start," he said.

"I know, and I'm sorry. Eat one now, and order another one when my burger's ready."

"You're a hard woman, Frieda. I can't eat while you're sitting there looking at me." He gave their orders and drank the water that the waitress placed before him.

"Tell me about yourself, Frieda. I'm not an air jock, I'm a producer. So how'd you happen to decide you wanted me to talk to your group?"

"I went through the college catalogue and checked out all the departments. Then I called the switchboard and asked for the morning radio show producer. I wanted the kids to know that the producer creates the show and that it takes people with different skills to get a program on the air."

"Right. What do you do from nine to five?"

She leaned back in her chair and looked him in the eye. Her work didn't require a Ph.D., but she took pride in it, and the hospital couldn't operate efficiently without workers like her.

"I'm a nurse's aide, Glen. I work at Maryland General."

He looked at her for what seemed like ages before he said, "If I were sick, I wouldn't mind waking up and looking at you. You're a beautiful woman. Are you married, or living with someone?"

"I'm not married, and playing house with a guy who won't commit to me is definitely not in my DNA."

He laughed at that, then leaned forward. "But all you have to do is snap your fingers, and—"

She cut him off. "Glen, I'm particular about who I spend my time with, and that goes for girlfriends as well as men. I don't let myself get involved with a man just because *he* wants *me*. I don't see the sense in that."

She could see that she'd piqued his interest when sparks began to dance in his eyes. "So the man who wants you has his job cut out for him. Right?"

When it came to men, she wanted plain talk, not riddles. "What do you mean?"

"I mean he's got to make you want him."

Frieda strummed her fingers on the marbled bistro table before brushing away a few crumbs, then moved her hand to her lap as their food arrived. "I thought it had been that way since before the time of Christ, but maybe I've been missing something," she said.

"Touché." He took a bite of barbecue. "Want a tour of the studio?" She nodded. "Oh, yes. I've got some free tickets for a harbor cruise. Ever been on one of those?"

She wasn't stupid. She'd slow down for him eventually, but not because he offered her entertainment that he didn't have to pay for. Even Larry paid for the movie tickets.

"I think I'll skip the cruise," she said, "but the studio tour sounds good."

As they left Fannie's modest shop, he locked arms with her and asked, "What are you going to do with the rest of my day?"

Lord, if only he wasn't so . . . if I didn't want to cuddle up with him. How am I going to resist this man long enough to lead him where I want him to go? If I'm smart, I can make her cry a river.

She stopped walking. "Glen, I confess you're sweet as sugar, but I have to run along now. Maybe I can see the studio one evening next week or on the weekend. How's that?"

His mouth curled into an inviting grin. "I'll take any crumb you're willing to give me."

Yeah, she thought. *I'll bet you will.* "Here's my phone number at home, so I'll expect to hear from you sometime next week," she said to make certain that he saw her as an equal.

She turned to walk off, but he grasped her shoulders, bent down, and pressed his mouth to hers, twirling and flickering his tongue over her lips as he did so. She stared up at him, shocked, as her blood plowed toward her loins.

"That's what I want from you," he said. "See you." With that, he hailed an approaching taxi, got in, and rode off.

Frieda walked with slow and plodding steps the dozen blocks to her apartment, hardly aware of the time that passed or the energy she used to get home. Pressing on her mind was the possibility that her scheme could entrap her, that Glen Treadwell was a worldly man skilled in getting what he wanted from women. Resisting him would require as much strength as she possessed.

With all I've been through, I'm not letting him get the better of me, she vowed. *He's just a stepping stone to what I'm after. All in all, I've had a banner day.*

She walked into her apartment, kicked off her shoes, pulled off her suit, shook it, and hung it on the closet door. The electric window fan cooled her body and enlivened the scent of Evening in Paris perfume, her favorite and one of her few extravagances. With the demise of five and ten cent stores, she had difficulty finding it, so she treasured every drop.

After flipping on the television and resting her feet on the coffee table, she took her notepad and wrote what she recalled of the meeting with Glen, recording that he drank water, didn't put salt or pepper on his barbecue, and didn't order coffee or anything sweet. She meant to learn as much about him as she could, and especially his likes and dislikes. A woman could more easily control a man if she knew his weaknesses and strengths.

She put string beans, candied sweet potatoes, and two fried chicken legs in a pan to warm for her dinner and ran to her bedroom to answer the telephone.

"Girl, you must be feeling like Miss It," Lacy said after they greeted each other. "Strutting off from church with that fantastic brother. Who was he?"

"He was today's speaker for Teen Venture."

"You gotta be kidding. That guy's a forty-carat stud. Girl, you better watch it."

Didn't she know it! "Lacy, you're getting to be as bad as Thelma, plus your mind's always on sex. The man didn't know me from Adam until two o'clock this afternoon."

"Hmmm. Is that why he laid that kiss on you right there on Franklin Avenue? You looked like you'd been hit by a freight train. Not that I blame you. If I live to be ninety, I don't expect to get a kiss from a man like that one. If you're smart, girl, you'll keep your dress down." Lacy laughed. "Listen to me. I'd a followed him right into that taxi, and I wouldn't a kept my dress down either."

"Girl, stop talking foolishness," Frieda said. "Not even a dog wants food that you throw at him. If you get your mind off food and sex, you'll lose weight and give your man a chance to salivate once in a while."

"You going to see that fellow again?"

"I don't know," she said, as if it didn't matter. "I told him to call me."

"Oh yeah? Well, good as you look these days, I guess you can afford to be casual about him, but you may regret it. That one is choice."

"How come you know so much about it, anyway? We went to get a hamburger, and we separated right in front of Fannie's. Where were you?"

"In my car about ten feet from you. You were so busy staring into the guy's eyes you didn't see Mack come out of Fannie's with a bag of barbecue sandwiches. If I was you, I'd watch it, girl."

"You always give great advice about men," Frieda said, "but I never knew you to take it. I gotta eat my dinner."

"Okay. If Thelma calls you, tell her to give me a ring."

"I will, so you two can gossip about me. Talk to you later."

She put the phone down a split second before it rang again. "Hello, Frieda. This is Glen Treadwell. Do you have company?"

She grabbed her chest as if to steady herself and nearly slipped to the floor instead of the side of the bed where she had planned to sit.

"Hello, Glen. Now, this is a surprise."

"Why? You knew I'd call you. Who were you talking to a minute ago?"

"My girlfriend. She goes to my church."

"Let's not talk about her. I want to talk about *you*. When am I going to see you again?"

Shivers raced through her at the prospect of striking up a friendship with him. "I don't usually go out during weeknights. Early to bed and early to rise. That's me."

"Then we won't go out. Nothing I'd rather do than stay in with you." His voice dropped several decibels. Deep, mellifluous, and seductive. "What do you say?"

"I say let's plan something for the weekend . . . unless, of course, you're all tied up. I'm supposed to get a tour of the TV station. Remember?"

The playfulness she heard in his laughter excited her, and in her mind's eye she could see herself curled around his long hard frame. "Remember?" she repeated.

"Of course I do. And after that, we'll go to the Inner Harbor and eat some Maryland crab cakes. What do you say?"

"Which day are we talking here?"

"Saturday afternoon. I know you'll be in church Sunday."

"Fine," she said. After he hung up, she recalled he'd said Saturday afternoon. Wasn't she good enough for Saturday night?

Chapter Eight

Coreen dragged herself to her office the following Monday morning, her usual enthusiasm for her work lacking. She had wanted to ask her neighbor whether she had out-of-town guests, but hadn't gotten the courage to do so. She couldn't shake the notion, a haunting instinct, that the car parked across the street from her house had something to do with her. A rented car and its driver the sole occupant. Anybody in Bakerville who didn't own a car couldn't afford to rent one.

" 'Morning, ma'am," Oscar said, opening the door for her. "The officers are waiting for you in the reception room." She didn't bother to ask him which officers, because she didn't want to wait ten minutes while he collected his thoughts sufficiently to remember what the officers told him.

"Thanks, Oscar. I hope they have some news for us."

"Yes, ma'am."

In the reception room, she found two police sergeants and the police lieutenant in charge of investigating the ransacking of her office.

"This was an inside job, ma'am," the lieutenant said. "Did Miss Franks use your office sometime during your absence?"

She sat down and dropped her briefcase on the floor at her feet. "Why, I don't know. I've never given anyone permission to use my office. Maddie Franks has a very nice office just down the hall from mine."

"I know," he said. "Are you aware that Becky Smith's friend, Rudolph, is Maddie Franks's nephew?"

Her eyes widened and she gripped the arms of her chair. "What did you say?"

He repeated it.

"But . . . but that's unethical. I mean, I gave her responsibility for Becky, and they didn't get along. She should have told me."

"I'm sure you'll take care of that. Who has keys to this building?"

"Oscar, the janitorial service, Ms. Franks, and me."

He made notes on a writing pad. "We're taking Rudolph in for questioning."

"I see," she said. "Lieutenant, I'd be surprised if Rudolph had anything to do with it. He's been in trouble, but he's honest."

"What kind of trouble was he in?"

"Rabble-rousing and intimidating a group of workers picketing down at the bus station. I'm told he and his friends were paid to do it. He received one year probation."

"That was foolish of him. This is a union town. He's the only male who might have been in here when you were away. We've interviewed the employees of your janitorial service. Nothing there, and Oscar lacks the imagination to do something like that. We'll check Rudolph out; if he's clean, we'll be glad to know it."

"I'm going to have a talk with Ms. Franks."

The officer asked her to delay the talk until he had a chance to interrogate Rudolph.

"All right," she said, anxious to get on to her office. "I assume I'll be hearing from you."

"You bet. Probably late this afternoon."

As soon as she sat at her desk, she dialed Weeks Halfway House. "How are you, Mona? How's Becky Smith getting along?"

"Too docile. The girl accepts whatever happens to her as if she were watching it happen to someone else. We told her she has to keep the baby a week before giving it up, but she swears she's not even going to look at it, that she doesn't care whether the child is a girl or boy."

"That shouldn't surprise you since she's a victim of rape."

"Nothing surprises me in this place."

"Let me speak with her, please."

Coreen could hardly believe the lackluster, faraway sound that was Becky's voice. "Hi you, Miss Treadwell. I thought you'd forgotten about me. The doctor said the baby's due day after tomorrow, and they're trying to make me keep it."

"Only for a week."

"I won't do it, Miss Treadwell. You tell them I'll . . . I'll do something awful before I'll have anything to do with that child."

Coreen rested her left elbow on the desk and clasped her left hand over her forehead. *That child*, as if it weren't hers. "What do you mean by 'awful,' Becky? Be careful. If you commit a crime, you may spend the rest of your life in jail. I'll speak to your caseworker and ask that the one-week rule be waived for you, but you'd better not hurt that child. Do you hear me?" She remembered her own wish to die, her prayers that the child would be stillborn, and her refusal to look at or to know anything about the baby to whom she gave life, including its gender.

"I know this is difficult for you, Becky, and I'll do what I can to help you."

"Where am I going when I leave here, Miss Treadwell? I don't want to go back to my parents."

"We'll take care of that, but not if you break the law."

"I won't, Miss Treadwell." A lengthy silence elapsed, and then she said, "I wish I knew you before I got into this trouble. Everything would have been so different. Maybe I'd a gone to college. Your children are lucky. Well, thanks for . . . for calling to see about me."

"Good luck day after tomorrow, Becky." It was all she could say, and she had to push those few words out with force. She couldn't walk away from Becky as a defense against the reminders of the harshness of her own life. If she didn't help Becky, the girl would go down the drain like sand in an hourglass. Back to the post office steps with her hand out, and eventually to pounding the pavement in search of tricks.

Coreen pushed the thought from her mind, though with a struggle, and started plowing through the list of people in her profession who owed her favors. After several hours, she found the telephone number of Elizabeth Church, manager of a senior center and retirement home in Hampton, Virginia. Half an hour after that, she had a job for Becky and a place for her to stay.

"I hope somebody somewhere did as much for my child." She heard the words that could only have come from her own mouth, slapped her forehead so hard that it hurt, and flopped down in her desk chair. Stunned. Yes, and frightened. If only she could shake the guilt and forget about that era of her life. She had done nothing to deserve the hell she had lived through for nearly thirty years—scared of being discovered, living a lie, unable to deal honestly with her husband, trapped inside of herself, and longing to open up and pour out her soul to someone. It was as if she were serving a life sentence, and all because Leon Farrell took what he wanted when he couldn't get it by asking.

She tried without success to get Becky out of her thoughts. She'd done her best for the girl and hoped Becky would seize the chance for a better life. A person who, from childhood onward, had yearned for parental caring and never gotten it was likely to idolize anyone who treated her kindly and offered her an escape from destitution.

Coreen suspected it was that way with Becky, but she didn't want to be worshipped or even admired. "I'm only doing my job," she said aloud, though unconvinced of it. Knowing it wasn't true. Forcing herself to look squarely at the facts, she admitted she didn't want Becky's admiration because the girl reminded her of her past and perpetuated the sense of guilt that she seemed unable to banish. She wanted Becky out of her life, but the girl needed her. She didn't want to look back years from now and know she'd had it within her power to prevent a person from falling through the cracks and hadn't done it.

"I'm cutting my own throat," she said as she made a note on her calendar to visit Becky the following week.

Hoping to erase all thoughts of Becky from her mind right then, she telephoned Lizette and immediately regretted it.

"I still haven't heard from Porgy," were Lizette's first words and a reminder to Coreen of her sister-in-law's problems.

"How's business so far today?" Coreen asked her.

"Better than I expected. Imagine me working on a Monday, but I gotta deal with these bills."

"Stop worrying about the bills, sis. Didn't I tell you I'd help you this month?"

"I know, and I thank you, Coreen, but I'm used to standing on my own two feet. If I ever get my hands on that man, I'm gonna—"

Coreen laughed. She couldn't help it. "You'll probably drag him to bed by the seat of his pants." The light flashed on her phone indicating a call waiting. "I'd better get to work."

She hung up and took the other call. "Coreen Treadwell speaking. How may I help you?"

"Ms. Treadwell, this is Nana Kuti in Nigeria. The board has approved your candidacy for president. If we have your agreement, we'll print the ballots and mail them at the end of the week. If you win, you'll be president elect until the next meeting, after which you'll be president for two years. We want you to serve."

It was happening so fast, a stone barreling down a mountainside. A tide rushing toward shore, and she was being caught up in its swirling waters. For every episode of flagrant injustice to girls or women anywhere in the world, the media would want her views on it. Her face would be as familiar as a rap star's. The shudders of fear that raced through her did nothing to prevent her hurdle toward the international limelight. Like a moth flirting with an open flame, she savored the thought of international prominence, and in a voice so calm that it startled her, she said, "I don't know what I've done to deserve this honor, but if I'm elected, I'll be proud to serve."

"Thank you. We're all so proud to have you with us, Coreen. You'll bring new life into the organization. October thirty-first is the deadline for receipt of ballots. I'll be in touch."

Coreen wanted to tell Bates, but his line produced a busy signal, so she phoned Lizette.

"Guess what, girl. I was just going to call you," Lizette said, her voice bubbling with an enthusiasm Coreen hadn't witnessed in Lizette for at least a month.

"I called the bank to ask for a short-term loan, and the clerk told me Porgy deposited three thousand dollars in the account day before yesterday. I guess he's not going to let me go under. That takes care of all the house bills and the car payment. Lord, I'm so happy. But Coreen, I still don't know where that bugger is."

"I'm glad for you, Lizette. I guess my news is sort of pale by comparison. I'm on the ballot for president of my international professional organization."

"What? Get outta here, girl! Good thing the taping's this weekend. Before long, you won't give this place a second glance. I hope business will pick up after your interview airs."

Coreen nearly slammed down the phone at the mention of the word Pick-Up, a place whose name she tried to bury in her subconscious. After that, she had to force herself to listen to Lizette's words.

"The cameraman said be here at eight so you can get made up and I can set your hair before the shop opens at nine." She paused. "I sure wish Porgy could be here for the taping. He loves celebrity."

Even with the knowledge that Porgy had taken care of his financial obligations and hadn't left her to deal with them as best she could, Lizette spoke with the vigor of a much bedraggled woman, one whose castle had shattered in debris around her feet. Gone was the modern female known for espousing the glory of independence and living it to the hilt.

Suddenly, Coreen didn't feel as if she was missing anything with Bates either in bed or out of it, and she didn't want to exchange places with her sister-in-law to find how many different ways human beings could make love. She was, in fact, losing patience with Lizette.

"Lizette," she said, "I know you love Porgy, and you think the sun rises just to shine on him. But it doesn't. It shines on a lot of men, and if Porgy's acting out, do a little dance yourself. Get some attitude, girl, and let Porgy's friends know about it."

"You're saying I should be unfaithful?"

Coreen pulled air through her front teeth. "I didn't say you should go to bed with another man, but you're not legally married, so you can see a movie or walk with a guy along the beach.

You've got a great figure. Why don't you put on a bikini and loll around in the sand?"

"I don't know. It might backfire."

"I know you think I'm old-fashioned about sex and men, but there's more to life than making Porgy crow in bed."

"Like what?"

"Like sticking up your nose, laying back your shoulders, and reminding these people here in Bakerville that you're somebody. You don't want people shaking their heads and saying 'Poor Lizette,' do you?"

"But this is all my fault, Coreen. If I had married Porgy, he'd still be here."

Coreen was getting tired of Lizette's suddenly drooping persona, a different woman, minus her devil-may-care attitude, independent mien, and blatant femininity. A new and far less attractive demeanor.

Coreen didn't mince words. "But he isn't there. Girl, show that man what you think of his disgusting behavior. Let him know he can be replaced, and I'll bet he'll come charging back here in a hurry. And for goodness sake, stop moping. You don't care. Understand? Show him and everybody in Bakerville that you don't care."

"But I do care. Besides, how will Porgy know what I do?"

"His friends will tell him."

"We'll see. You gonna get here by eight Saturday morning?"

"I said I would, didn't I?"

Coreen hung up, walked over to the window, and gazed down at the stragglers along Poplar Neck Road, weathering the blistering heat for a swim in the Sound. What she wouldn't give for a carefree swim, for one hour free of worry about the destruction of her marriage or her career because of something that happened long ago. Didn't she deserve to enjoy the success she had worked so hard to achieve? She trudged back to her desk, unable to see a choice but to go through with the interview, to let Lizette have her hour of glory, and take whatever came as a result.

* * *

The following Monday morning, Bates sat on the side of the bed he shared with his wife, holding her hand and drinking warmed-over coffee. "You looked great on TV," he said. "I never saw you wearing that much makeup."

"Lizette fixed my hair and did the makeup. She's really good at what she does."

"Yeah, but she ought to have more self-respect. Everybody knows Porgy Jenkins walked out on her. She should have made him marry her. I told her he'd do it. Now, she's moping around looking like she's the last person alive on this earth. I say good riddance to him."

How had he found out, she wondered, before recalling that no secret remained one for long in Bakerville, a thought that gave her no comfort; indeed, it exacerbated her concern, a concern that she knew was rapidly slipping into paranoia. She made herself focus on her husband.

"Oh, Bates. I don't like to hear you speak this way of Lizette. She's been a real friend to me."

"Yeah? She fills your head with a lot of stuff, and don't tell me she doesn't. I know my sister. From the time she was twelve, she hasn't been able to think about anything but men. And look what she ended up with. I don't—" He stopped in midsentence. "Why didn't you tell that interviewer it's none of her business why you never had children of your own, instead of looking as if she shot you? These TV airheads give me a pain."

The question had caught her off guard, and she had tried to finesse it, but looking at the tape later, she realized she had merely seemed embarrassed.

"You're a natural," he said. "That man's camera sure loved you."

She thanked him. "What do you think of the shop? Lizette had the floor so clean you could eat off it."

"Her business will pick up if that's what she's after with this program. No doubt about that."

There it was again. *Pick-Up.* The word triggered in her a sense of desperation. She rolled off the other side of the bed, put on her robe, and headed for the bathroom. Half an hour later, having lectured herself on the futility of panicking, she strolled into the kitchen, took her place at the table, and waited for Bates to serve her breakfast.

"Uh . . . I meant to tell you that Nana Kuti called me from Nigeria Friday morning with the news that the board approved my nomination for president of ISSWA. I probably won't win, but a nomination to that position means I've accomplished something."

In the process of putting flapjacks on her plate, Bates suddenly stood motionless, staring at her. "This happened Friday morning? I suppose you forgot about it till now."

She *had* forgotten, and she prepared herself for a tongue-lashing, a dose of Bates's bitterness.

"I called you as soon as she phoned me, but your line was busy."

He raised the chair and set it down hard, as if he would like to break it. "You slept in the bed with me three nights since then, ate breakfast and dinner with me three times, too. Like you forgot to tell me somebody trashed your office. You're full of crap. I don't matter a damn to you."

"Bates, please. You don't mean that."

"Don't I? All you want from me is a hard penis once in a while, and even then you want to dictate the terms. Half the time, when you finish with me, I feel as if I've been used."

A few more minutes of this, and she would be as angry as he. She knew she had wronged him, so she struggled to control her reaction to his harsh words.

"How can you say such a thing?"

He put a batch of flapjacks on the table, sat down, and served himself. "How? Easily. If I want it and you don't, you say good night and go to sleep without giving me that much of a chance"—he flicked his finger—"to get you interested. But if you want it, you go for the jugular."

She rolled her eyes and expelled a long breath. "What do you expect? Men are more vulnerable than women."

"Than *some* women. I gotta get to work. This too shall pass, and if you're smart, you won't forget this conversation." His lips brushed her forehead. "See you this evening."

He could make her feel inferior with a few cutting words, but then Bates seemed superior to practically everybody. He wore about himself an air, one as distinctive as a matador's cape. It was in his bearing, his walk, his grudging smiles, and his refusal to show deference to anyone. He and Lizette resembled each other physically, but they shared no other similarities, for Lizette was by any gauge earthy. She wondered, not for the first time, how much of Bates's behavior was affected. Was he being himself or his estimation of himself?

What a way to start a week. She straightened the kitchen, finished dressing, and left for work. After parking behind the agency in the spot reserved for the director, she walked rapidly toward the building's entrance and stopped, nearly tripping over her feet, stumbled forward, tightened her hold on her briefcase and her sanity, and rushed into the building. She didn't run, but she used all the willpower she possessed to resist doing so. Inside, she didn't take time to return Oscar's greeting, got into the elevator as quickly as she could, and leaned against one of its walls.

The car parked across the street from the agency was the one she saw opposite her house two days earlier. A blue Plymouth with Maryland plates and a single passenger who looked straight ahead as if to avoid being recognized. She flopped into her desk chair and leaned back, her perspiration-dampened blouse sticking to her body. In her mind's eye, she saw Bates towering over her in mockery, deriding her about her past. Maybe she should phone Nana Kuti and tell her she couldn't accept the nomination, for if she won, the publicity would guarantee her exposure and downfall.

Coreen checked the time and determined that it was afternoon in Nigeria. The phone rang as she reached for it.

"Hi, Mom. I was talking with Dad a minute ago, and he said you've been nominated for president of the international. Wow! You're on a roll. Congratulations!"

"Oh, Glen. Darling, it's sweet of you to call and congratulate me, but I haven't won yet."

His voice had the cocky certainty of youth when he said, "But you will. Want me to be your campaign manager? I could sell beef to a vegetarian Brahman."

Coreen laughed, her fear of exposure momentarily forgotten. "I'll bet you could. I haven't been in that international crowd long enough to make enemies, so I stand a good chance."

"My mama's a real big shot. Say, how'd you like me to interview you on my radio station? I have a big audience, and I'm always looking for celebrity guests. Let me know when you can do it. See you in a couple of weeks."

They talked for a few minutes longer. When Coreen hung up, she lay her head on her desk, cradling it with her arms, and told herself to keep on breathing. She had paid many times over for Leon Farrell's violation of her body and soul, and it looked as if, with all that fate had piled on her, it had just begun to collect. She didn't know if she could stand it. She couldn't even accept her stepson's offer to interview her on the radio station at which he worked.

For a few minutes, she remained with her head down. Then anger lifted her mood. She sat up and banged the desk with her right fist. "I'm damned if I'll cry," she said and telephoned Weeks Halfway House.

Frieda's resolve to confront Coreen and to heap upon her as much misery as possible was no less powerful than Coreen's determination to avoid disclosure while enjoying the trappings of success. Minutes after frightening Coreen nearly senseless, she turned the key in the ignition of her blue Plymouth and headed home for Baltimore. Finding where Coreen worked had been a simple matter of following her from home that morning. Satisfied that her birth mother knew she was being watched and feared the consequences, Frieda knew that if she *never* faced the woman she should have called Mother, at least she had that one small victory.

"I owe her one for every time Claude Davis pounded into me," she said to herself, "using me whenever it suited him. Like I didn't have feelings. Like I wasn't human."

When she heard herself speak those words aloud, anger coursed through her. *Oh, yes. Coreen Treadwell will never be safe from me. I know her name, where she lives and works, and I have a good idea what she looks like. She'll hear from me, but not till I can turn the screw real tight. Lord, you please forgive me. I know I'm wrong, but I can't seem to want to stop myself.*

Frieda didn't worry about skipping work that Monday; experienced nurse's aides weren't easily come by. Besides, she had called in and given a good excuse. She reached home around three o'clock that afternoon, and her heart began thumping when she saw the note sticking to her door. She didn't forget her date with Glen the previous Saturday afternoon—but when he didn't call her all week long, she decided he needed taming, that he was used to having his way with women. But not with her. She stood him up. He was a part of her larger plan, and that meant she had to hold the trump card.

Her fingers trembled as she took the note off the door. She went inside, threw her pocketbook on the living room sofa, and sat down to read what she hoped would be a loving note from Glen. She slumped into the sofa when she saw Julie's bold strokes.

> *Girl, you gotta stop sneaking away for days at a time and not telling anybody where you're going. Suppose Portia got sick; I wouldn't know how to reach you. Where were you? Didn't you remember that I'd be in Baltimore today? And didn't you remember what I told you Mama said?*

She phoned her sister, who repeated what she'd written.

"Gosh, I forgot. I . . . uh . . . had a little mission to—"

"You'd better stop it, Frieda. Portia said she dreamed Mama was shaking her finger at you. Don't you remember my saying Mama told us to tell you not to look for your birth mother? Please, Frieda. Let it go."

"What he did! What he did to me! Only the Lord knows what I suffered trying to keep my head above the water after I ran away from home. Julie, I left there wearing a thin dress and Mama's bathrobe in the middle of winter. I didn't take time to find a coat, because I didn't want him to catch me. And to this day, I can't relate to a man in no decent fashion. When you've walked in my shoes, Julie, you can tell me to drop it. He's dead, but she's alive, and I won't rest till I confront her."

"I feel with you sis, but this is wrong. Still, I know nothing I can say or do will stop you. Have you found her?"

"I know who she is and where she is, and I've seen her several times, though not close enough to make a positive identification. When I get good and ready, I'll let her see me."

"I wish you'd back off, honey. You don't know what you'll get into. Please be careful."

Frieda passed her hand over her face as if to erase the effect of her adoptive sister's words. "I know you mean well, Julie. Papa raped you and Portia just like he violated me, but if that woman hadn't given me away, it wouldn't have happened to me."

Julie's tired and helpless sigh reached her through the wires. "You don't know what her circumstances were, so how can you judge her? I hope you don't regret this."

"I'm willing to take my medicine. It can't be worse than the stuff I've already swallowed."

Julie had a way of letting silence speak for her. After a long while, she said, "Remember Portia's birthday is coming up right after Labor Day. Let's plan a nice party for her."

"Fine. I'll go down that weekend. Charlotte's nice in late summer." They spoke for a few minutes longer, and although Frieda loved Julie, she wanted the conversation to end so she could check her answering machine. She had to find out whether Glen Treadwell had called her.

She turned on the machine and the deep, rich voice of Glen Treadwell filled the room. "Woman, you scored a first. Do you realize you've stood me up? Did I make such a poor impression on you that you forgot about me in less than a week? My heart's bleeding. Call me."

She made coffee, kicked off her shoes, sat on the edge of her bed, and telephoned Glen. "I'm surprised that you're home today," she said after greeting him. "I got your message."

"And what do you have to say for yourself? I waited half an hour for you."

She stretched out on the bed. "Now, Glen, you said you'd call, and when I didn't hear from you again, I thought, that brother's trying to do a snow job on me. I don't let nobody dupe me, honey."

"How could you even think it?" He dropped his voice to a lower register. "Didn't I let you know I wanted you? Now, you listen to this. I intend to get you. The next time you make a date with me, you keep it."

She rolled over on her stomach to steady herself. "And the next time you tell me you're going to call, see that you do it. Glen, I don't sit around waiting for no man's telephone call and no man's visit. I also don't weep over no man."

"You and I are going to make quite a pair. Do you remember the biblical passage, 'And they came to a place where two seas met'? I don't remember what happened, but I believe the boat broke in two."

Her laughter was more the release of tension than evidence of mirth. "All right. All right. Am I forgiven?"

"Absolutely. Want to see a movie?"

"When? I don't go to matinees."

"Friday or Saturday night."

She flipped over and sat upright on the bed. "Uh, what's your girlfriend going to say about that? And don't tell me no woman has a claim on you."

"No woman has a claim on me, as you phrased it. Make it Friday night. I'll come by for you at about six-thirty."

She had intended to meet Glen at the theater so that he wouldn't see her modest apartment. She said the first thing that came to her mind. "Not so fast. I don't tell a man where I live till I know him well enough to trust him."

"*What?* What did you say?"

Her extemporaneous reply pleased her, so she didn't retract it. "You heard me. You don't know what these men are like. I've learned from experience to be careful."

"All right, but I don't like your dumping me into a bag with a bunch of bad-mannered, nameless Joes with no style. Meet me at the Century. They're having a sneak preview Friday night and the popcorn's the best. How about it?"

"Okay. Don't forget to call and confirm it."

"You think I'd make the same mistake twice?" he asked. "You fascinate me, and I intend to find out what makes you tick."

She cautioned herself not to be taken in by his easy manners and smooth tongue, to remember her goal. She shocked herself when she said, "If you want to know what drives my engine, baby, just ask me."

His sharp whistle excited her. "Whew. You're a body of still water, babe, and I'm told that stuff runs deep. When you get ready to loosen up and shake it out, I'll be right here waiting for you."

She attempted to repair the damage. "Glen, I've got one of those mouths that runs off like that. There's not a thing to back it up."

"Don't hand me that. You knew exactly what you were saying. If you want to play games, fine; I can use a different kind of exercise. But you mean business, babe, and I do, too. Let's get that straight right now."

She slid off the bed and stood beside it, hoping to raise the level of her thinking. "Trying to read my mind won't do you a bit of good, Glen, 'cause I changed it twice since we've been talking. I hate plotting and planning when it comes to people, so why don't we just go to the movies and then see where we are."

"Fine with me. But what I said back there a second ago still goes. Sleep well, and I mean sleep by yourself. See you Friday at seven at the Century, but I'll call you."

"You sleep well, too. Good night."

An hour later, Frieda gazed out of her window as darkness enveloped the sky and thunder roared and howled in the distance. The inclement weather loomed as a threat to her physical and mental safety, for she couldn't separate the distant bellowing from the turmoil in which her mind had become embroiled. She wasn't in Glen Treadwell's league and she knew it, but he behaved as if they were equals. She intended to use him for her purpose, but if she played his game, would she entrap herself, caught like a crustacean in a fisherman's net?

A flash of lightning brightened her surroundings and the

crack of thunder that followed riddled her nervous system. *It's an omen,* she thought, *and a bad one. Maybe Mama was right, and I should leave that woman alone. But I can't.* She got in bed, huddled beneath the covers, and tried to exorcise the fear plowing through her with words of prayer.

The Lord's not going to help me with this, she said to herself and stopped praying, for her pastor preached that vengeance belonged to the Lord, and even as she sensed that the route she'd chosen might exact a heavy price, it did not occur to her to change her course. She had lived so long with the hatred that she didn't know how to exist without it.

As the thunder and lightning gave way to rain, her gaze captured the bag of knitting wool in the corner of the room, reminding her that she had promised to meet with Thelma and Lacy that evening to knit caps, scarves, and socks for homeless children. They had each pledged to knit a dozen sets by Christmas.

"I don't need to feel sorry for myself," she said aloud, "considering what those kids go through." She washed her face and phoned Thelma.

"I can make some macaroni and cheese and fry some chicken wings. I already got a pot of turnip greens and a pan of cornbread. Why don't you and Lacy come over here. It's just about stopped raining."

"Fine with me," Thelma said, "although I was going to suggest y'all come over here. I'll call Lacy. We ought to be over there in about an hour. The pastor's going to be real proud of us."

"He sure will. This is his pet project." She didn't say it would take a load off her pocketbook if the pastor would buy the knitting wool.

By the time the women arrived, Frieda had finished cooking. They ate before knitting.

"Girl, you sure know what to do with chicken," Thelma said. "If I ate at your house, I'd soon be wearing Lacy's clothes."

Lacy sucked air through her front teeth. "Y'all mind your own business, and let's get to knitting."

"One thing I like about Mt. Zion church," Thelma said as she wrapped knitting yarn around a piece of cardboard, "Reverend Hall believes in helping people that can't help themselves."

"He sure does," Frieda said, "and amen to that."

"Humph," Lacy muttered. "I would admire him for it, if he helped people with *his* money instead of *mine*. He sure knows how to rake it in from the members, and half of 'em poor as Job's turkey. I don't think it's got a thing to do with the Lord. Just Hall's ego."

"Shame on you. Always grumbling about something," Frieda said to Lacy. "Where's Mack this evening?"

"He's at his father's house. Where's that hunk you went off with last Sunday?" Lacy shot back. "Lord, if I had that brother, I'd spend my life supine. Or try."

Thelma treated them to a lusty laugh. "Wonder where he'd be while you were lying there waiting for him to show up. Girl, if I was you, I'd exchange my mind for something better."

"I don't care if all our charity work does massage Reverend Hall's ego so he can boast at the ministers' conference," Frieda said. "I feel good helping people who can't help themselves. Besides, that's what the Lord wants us to do."

Thelma held up the toe of a red sock through which purple thread crisscrossed, and began to unravel it and start again. "I gotta get some glasses. Can't tell red from purple sometimes." She squinted at Frieda. "You talking mighty devout, Frieda. You sure you don't have something to pray about?"

Frieda stopped knitting and looked at Thelma. "What do you mean?"

"She means it ain't like you to be so sanctimonious," Lacy said. "So you must've been doing some sinning. Sure you didn't spread out for that good-looking hunk? What's his name?"

Frieda didn't look up from her knitting lest she indict herself. Sin hardly described the morass in which she had begun to embroil herself. She gripped the knitting needles with trembling fingers as Lacy's words found their mark. She couldn't fake her actions with her friends, because they knew her.

"Y'all full of it," she said, escaped to the kitchen, and let her nerves settle while a kettle of water boiled. She made a pot of tea and took it to the living room along with three mugs.

"Thanks," Lacy said. "Bet you don't give what's-his-name no tea."

"He's never been here," Frieda said, glad that she could tell an unexpurgated truth. "Y'all get off my case."

She nearly jumped from her chair when the telephone rang, her first thought being that Glen had decided to play games with her. "Hello," she said, and the impatience with which she spoke caused both Lacy and Thelma to stop knitting and look toward Frieda's bedroom.

"You musta had razor soup for supper," Larry said. "I was just wondering if I could come over and we could talk awhile. I'm not seeing anybody right now and I thought—"

She inhaled deeply, partly in relief and partly in annoyance. "Didn't we agree that you're gonna look elsewhere?" she said. "Larry, I'm telling you you're wasting your breath and my time. Besides, I'm busy right now doing the Lord's work."

His laughter infuriated her, though she knew her anger was aimed partly at herself. "The Lord's work, huh? Is that what they call it nowadays? All right, if that's the way you wanna act. Be seeing you."

"It's funny with men," Lacy said when Frieda walked back into the living room. "When they hot after us, we play it cool, but soon as they lose interest, we go crazy about 'em. Larry's a good man, Frieda. Why don't you want him?"

"It would take me a year to list all the reasons why I can't take much of Larry."

"I hope it doesn't take you that long to figure out you playing with fire when you messing with that hunk," Thelma said. "I'd think twice before I started anything with that brother."

Frieda didn't like the way the conversation was going. She well knew the danger of consorting with Glen Treadwell, but she had convinced herself that she was willing to pay the price.

"I wasn't born this morning," Frieda said, "so give me some credit." She wished she was as self-assured as she sounded.

Chapter Nine

Coreen fished around in her mind for the best way to tell Bates that she had to go to Brussels for a meeting. No matter how she coated the announcement, he wasn't going to like it. The best travel season was behind him and his business had shown very little improvement, so she didn't expect him to be supportive of her career moves. She telephoned Lizette and confided her problem.

"If he wasn't so pigheaded," Lizette said, "he'd be wealthy. But no, Mr. High and Mighty has to tell the people where they should travel and how to get there. Never mind that they may have a reason for doing something else. Big brother has to show them how stupid they are, 'cause he knows best."

"This is not helping me, Lizette."

"You can always get in bed with him and rock him senseless. Then you can tell him just about anything. He'll be so besotted, he won't know what side is up."

Frustrated, Coreen rolled her eyes toward the ceiling. "We're not talking about the same Bates, Lizette."

She imagined that Lizette made a show of exasperation. "Oh yes we are. The trouble is that you and I are looking at this with different eyes and, honey, your husband's got the same weakness that every other man's got. All that highfalutin' stuff he hands out don't cut no ice with me."

"I'll try it," Coreen said, though she held little hope of seducing Bates to such a degree. "Thanks, sis."

After dinner that evening, Coreen took a leisurely bubble bath that filled the bathroom with the odor of Dior perfume, put on a red lace teddy and negligee, and called downstairs to Bates.

"Come on, honey; it's time to go to bed."

"I'll be up after a while. I'm watching Halle Berry," he yelled back.

Which forty-six-year-old woman could compete with that? To make her point, she walked down to the foot of the stairs where he could see her. "How long do you think you'll be?"

He glanced toward her, though she would have sworn that he kept the gaze of one eye on the television screen. "Shouldn't be too long. An hour maybe." He did a double take. "Say, what's this? What are you up to?"

The man was about as romantic as a porcupine, unless he was after what *he* wanted. Seconds before she headed for a seat in his lap, determined to seduce him, she remembered his accusation a few days earlier that when she wanted to make love she went for the jugular, but that she ignored him when he wanted it and she didn't.

"As you can see," she said, changing tactics, "I'm out for the jugular."

He let his gaze sweep her from head to foot several times before a grin spread over his face. "Oh, what the hell. I can tape Halle and look at her some other time." He flipped on the VCR, grabbed his wife's hand, and took her to bed.

Later, Coreen lay awake for hours, listening to Bates snore and berating herself for not having the courage to tell him she had to leave for Brussels two days later. The next morning, leaning on her left elbow and sipping the coffee that Bates brought to her in bed, guilt hooked into her the way a hot knife slices through butter. It hurt to realize that she'd used him.

She put the coffee on the night table and took his hand. "You were right last night. I was up to something, and I can't figure out how to tell you."

He inhaled a long breath and let it out slowly. "Well, let me make it easy for you. What kind of prize did you win, and where and when are you going?"

She told him. He dropped her hand and sat there on the edge

of the bed for a long time not speaking, and as best she could see, barely breathing.

"The way you made me feel last night . . . no words can describe it. I was feeling like a king. I know I haven't succeeded big like I always dreamed I would with a chain of travel agencies all over the country, but I make a passable living with the store. My sons respect me, and they're loyal to me. And after twenty years, my wife still desires me and makes love to me like it was the first time, rocking me clear out of my senses.

"That's what was going through my head when you wrung the insides out of me, reducing me to putty. Thank you for not making a fool of me. If you'd told me about your trip right after what you did to me, I don't think I would ever have forgiven you."

She didn't know what to say. True, she had lost herself in him and in their lovemaking, partly—she knew—because he had exposed his vulnerability to her in ways he hadn't previously done. He hadn't communicated want or desire, but naked need, and she had responded to that. For once, he chucked his pride and let her know what he was feeling.

She tried without success to push back the ugly thoughts that popped into her mind. Were they living a lie? Was he keeping secrets from her as she was from him, secrets that had bearing on the integrity of their marriage?

"Don't you have anything to say?" Bates asked her in a tone more subdued than was his wont.

Coreen sipped coffee and cleared her throat. Bates had spoken from his heart, and she owed him honesty, as well. "I'm ashamed to admit that I had planned to tell you about Brussels right after we made love. Lizette said that was when a man would accept most anything you told him and do whatever you asked. But I didn't want to trivialize what I'd just experienced with you."

He turned to stare at her with a sadness in his long-lashed brown eyes that pained her. "Lizette? If my sister used her philosophy about men on Porgy, you can see how reliable it is. How long will you be in Brussels?"

Did that mean he wouldn't complain? "Two days."

He asked her how often she would be required to travel to Europe, and she thought he held his breath while awaiting her answer. Did her being at home with him really mean that much to him? She answered as truthfully as she could. "I don't know, but I suspect it won't be too often."

He took the cup from her hand, placed it on the tray that lay on the floor at his feet, and stood beside the bed. "It isn't home when you're not here," he said, picked up the tray, and went downstairs to the kitchen.

If he had told her he was going off to climb Mt. Everest, she wouldn't have been more surprised. For several minutes, she ruminated about that comment, another revelation of the man probably as he really was, not as he had designed himself. Did she know him at all? And if she didn't, would she like his genuine self? She shook her head, confused, and began to get ready for work. *Two adults playing make-believe, shadowboxing in the dark.* She went down to the kitchen where Bates sat before a stack of pancakes and a dish of bacon, waiting for her to join him. As they ate, the silence seemed to scream at her. She took her dishes to the sink and kissed him on the forehead, got in her car, and headed for work. For once, she didn't look forward to it.

"I'm the new man on this case," a uniformed officer said to Coreen when she entered the building. "May I see some identification, please?"

She handed him her driver's license. "I'm Coreen Treadwell, director of this agency. Who are you?"

He examined the driver's license. "Mitchell. We've spent enough time and money on this case. I'm fingerprinting everybody in this building today, and any man closely associated with the women who work here. We have to wrap up this thing."

She dropped her briefcase on the table used for displaying literature on the agency's work and looked him in the eye. "Everybody who works here has been interviewed."

"Right. And nobody knows a thing, which means somebody's lying."

"Do what you have to do, Mitchell," she said. "The sooner

you find the culprit, the sooner this agency gets back to normal and the happier I'll be."

He raised an eyebrow, shrugged his left shoulder, and turned to the next person who walked in the door.

In her office, Coreen told herself not to procrastinate, that she had swallowed pills more bitter. Still, she cringed as her fingers dialed Weeks Halfway House.

"How's Becky doing?" she asked the receptionist.

"Fine, ma'am. You must be Ms. Treadwell, since nobody else calls here about Becky and she's never had a visitor. She's all right, though."

"I'm glad she's getting on well," Coreen said, and was equally glad to terminate the conversation. The thought of going to a home for unwed expectant mothers sent chills scampering through her body. Her stomach rolled, and the picture on the wall moved from side to side. She grabbed her desk for support.

"I hope I'm not getting vertigo," she said to herself, though she knew the problem was not physical but psychological. Walking into that building represented a trial, but she didn't consider turning back.

She parked in the small parking lot beside Weeks Halfway House, a sand-colored stucco Tudor-style house that was reminiscent of the huge dwellings built in the halcyon days of the robber barons. Indeed, the heirs of Wilbur Weeks, a turn-of-the-century entrepreneur, donated the mansion to the Weeks Foundation.

Coreen didn't want to walk into that place and back into her past, back to that era of her life that she would give anything to blot from her memory. Cowardice had never been one of her attributes, but as she walked up the few steps leading to the front door, she had an urge to turn back. Remembering her promise to Becky, she forced her fingers to ring the doorbell.

As she waited in the reception room, she pushed aside magazines that featured information on parenting and child care in search of something to read that would distract her. After about twenty minutes, Becky appeared, slipping into the room like a frightened child, yet a different girl from the person she last saw.

"Hi, Miss Treadwell. I wanted to look nice when you came,

so I got my hair done and dressed up. One of the volunteers gave me this suit. I never had anything this nice before." She caressed the sides of the jacket as if she enjoyed the feel of its fabric. "I hope you like how I look."

Coreen let her gaze travel over the girl. Attractive. Even elegant. The transition brought a genuine smile to her face. "You look beautiful. You *are* beautiful, Becky."

She realized that Becky wouldn't broach the subject, so she asked her, "What about the baby?"

The girl seemed to shrink the way a puncture deflates a balloon, her self-confidence eroded. She looked down as if unwilling or unable to meet Coreen's gaze.

"I don't know. I signed the papers and that's all I know."

What could she say? Hadn't she done the same? "Hold your head up, Becky. You'll have a new life now, a good job, and a rent-free place to stay. You can get your General Education Diploma, which won't take more than a year. Save your money and go to college. The center at which you'll be working is walking distance from Hampton University."

Becky's hands moved from her sides seemingly voluntarily, as if to reach out, but dropped back. "I don't know how to thank you, Miss Treadwell. I've got a chance now, and I'm gonna make good. You'll see."

Coreen walked over to the girl and looked her in the eye. "Take my advice and don't look back. If you do, you'll always be crippled. Five years from now, you ought to have a college degree. I wish you well."

She had to get out of there before she broke down, for looking at Becky, she saw herself. The girl took a step forward and wrapped her arms around Coreen, startling her. As she returned the embrace, her heart seemed to constrict. What she wouldn't have done for a little affection at that time in her life!

She released Becky slowly and gently, for she understood what it meant to feel raw and exposed. Nonetheless, she stepped back. "I've arranged everything for you," she told the girl, "and from now on you're on your own. You're strong enough to make a good life for yourself, and a crutch would make you a dependent person. You don't need me."

Tears pooled in the girl's eyes. "You're telling me good-bye, aren't you?"

Coreen nodded, battling her own tears, and forced a smile. "Yes. If I don't, you'll lean on me, and that's not a good thing. I know you'll get along just fine. One thing: be sure you make friends with young people who are trying to get ahead. Stay away from street kids."

"I will. You sure don't have to tell me that. Thanks for everything."

"Your success is all the thanks I need," Coreen said. She got back to her car, opened the door, and slumped into the driver's seat. Not even facing one of Bates's grueling inquisitions had ever demanded so much of her. She sat there for a quarter of an hour before igniting the engine and heading for Route 17.

When I get to Brussels, she promised herself, *I'm going to speak with a therapist. I can't go on like this and I don't dare seek help here.*

Over one hundred miles away in Baltimore, Frieda prepared for the beginning of a venture that would change her forever. Ignoring the June warmth, she dressed with care in her good black linen suit, pink blouse, and Majorca pearls and earrings. Her complexion had no blemishes, so she used makeup sparingly, leaving her beautifully shaped lips natural, but applying mascara to lengthen her lashes. She dabbed her precious Evening in Paris perfume behind her ears and at her wrists.

"That's the best I can do with what God gave me," she said, and as she closed the door, she stopped and prayed.

"Lord, I know what I'm doing is not right. But please don't let it backfire on me. I suffered enough already. And please forgive me."

She didn't drive, because she didn't want Glen to think she was prepared to chauffeur him around. She took the bus.

Frieda took her time approaching the Century Theater, stopped, and looked around for Glen. Immediately, a pair of masculine hands grasped her shoulders from behind and turned her around. The pressure of his lips did nothing to reassure her that she hadn't stepped out of bounds. Beyond her level. He took possession of her with his left arm around her shoulder and his right hand clenching her waist. *Too forward and too self-assured.* She pushed back the thought that he wouldn't caress a girl on his social level so openly and so blatantly in front of a theater.

When his tongue flicked across the seam of her lips, she had a need for fresh air and somewhere to run.

"I like my women to look good," he said, "and you're perfect. A gorgeous face, and a real woman's body. Just what I like. A voluptuous size twelve."

His comment pleased her, but she didn't let him know it. Grasping at one last shred of control, she said, "If you don't stop trying to snow me, I'm leaving here this minute."

In the lobby, the popcorn vendor, a teenaged boy with Elvis Presley sideburns, and pimples that bespoke his age, wore a chef's apron that proclaimed, "Forget gloom, folks; we gotta deal with the doom."

The phrase distracted Frieda, who interpreted it as an indictment of herself. As she stared at the apron, Glen's hand skimmed her waist before sliding down and cupping her buttocks.

"I don't care if he reached adolescence this morning, quit looking at that kid. You're with me."

"Take your hands off my behind," she said, but her heartbeat accelerated, and she knew it was too late to turn back. She had been in his company less than ten minutes and couldn't wait to be with him again.

I'd better talk to myself and get my head straightened out, she thought, but she doubted talking to herself would do much good. She allowed herself a mental shrug, thinking, *He's part of my game plan, and I'm sticking with it.*

Frieda didn't see much of the movie; indeed, she couldn't recall the gist of it. "You've got a pair of octopus hands," she told Glen, referring to the way in which, in the dimly lit theater, they roamed over her body.

"You liked it, and don't tell me you didn't," he said, tucking her left hand in his coat pocket.

His hug and suggestive tone aroused in her as much furor as desire, and her annoyance rippled off her tongue. "I'd like you a lot better if you wasn't so crazy about yourself," she said. "Nothing gets on my nerves more'n a man with a big head." She glanced at him from the corner of her eye and saw his left hand caress his chest.

"Does that mean you don't like me? I'm crushed." He stopped walking and faced her, his face alight with a grin. "Tell me what I can do to make amends."

She wasn't taken in by his sweet-little-boy act. He had just given her a reason why he should tell her good night at her front door.

"Just slow down, and don't assume I'm gonna be like the other women you know."

"All right," he said with no trace of a smile on his face. "I'll play it your way. But get this straight: when I want something as badly as I want you, I get it. I don't miss. So if you take too long, we'll do it my way."

She didn't answer. What was the use? At the building in which she lived, he climbed the stairs with her and walked on to her front door.

"Am I coming in?"

She shook her head. "I didn't think so."

Nothing had prepared her for the onslaught that followed. He didn't spare her. Pressing her against the wall, he applied every sexual technique except the overt sex act itself. When he released her, she slumped against the door.

"Next time, we go to my place, so come prepared. I enjoyed the movie . . . what I saw of it."

She didn't know how she got into her apartment, or how long she stood beside the unlocked door, shaking in the dark.

Frieda Davis did not consider herself foolish; she had succeeded in avoiding serious involvements with men, and in at least one case following that course had demanded every ounce of her resolve. Indeed, she could truthfully say that Claude Davis, her adoptive father, was the last man she trusted. She didn't think she could trust Glen either, and for the first time in her adult memory, she lacked confidence in herself.

Glen oozed charm and could mesmerize a woman with his dreamy-eyed good looks, but she had learned that charm and looks in a man were worth about as much as a bogus check and as comforting as frostbite. Common sense told her the core of the problem, and she shuddered at the thought: Glen Treadwell knew what to do with a woman. He had a technique that fired her up, made her burn for him. No other man could make that claim.

As she leaned against the doorjamb inside her apartment, she had to summon all of her willpower to prevent herself from yelling down the stairs and calling him back.

"I won't get sucked into that man's orbit," she vowed. "It's not him, but his stepmother that I'm after, and I don't intend to forget that."

She undressed in the darkened bedroom and crawled into bed minutes before the phone rang. "Lord," she moaned, "please don't let it be *him*. I can't handle it right now."

She lifted the receiver, hoping to hear the voice of one of her sisters. "Hello."

"Hi, sweetheart. Thinking 'bout me?"

If Frieda had her demons, so did Coreen. The following afternoon as United Airlines Flight 951 out of Brussels headed for Reagan International Airport in Washington, D.C., Coreen rang for the flight attendant.

"Could you please give me something for this headache?" she asked the attendant, though she doubted an aspirin could cure the pain. Her head had throbbed unremittingly from the time the therapist—after listening for two hours to the story of her life—advised her that she would not be a whole person until she went back to Pick-Up, North Carolina.

"You experienced nothing there but unpleasantness and the further corruption of your innocence," he said. "That episode in your life will plague you forever if you don't go back there and slay those ghosts." Before she could calm herself after receiving that bomb, he said, "And then you have to tell your husband who you are. Living a lie is a certain route to the total collapse of one's personality."

When she told him she couldn't tell Bates about her past, his face became the picture of sadness. "Then you will forever be imprisoned, pacing ceaselessly like a wild animal behind a barbed wire fence. It's up to you."

As she rose to leave the man's office, she asked him. "Isn't there any other way? Any other solution?"

He threw up his hands. "No, and you're aware of that. This isn't something you can cure with pills. You're ridden with senseless guilt that has multiplied over the years. Look at your profession, your job. Did you choose them to punish yourself or to absolve yourself? Go back to Pick-Up and start right there to mend your life."

Her seatmate shifted in his seat, bringing her back to the present and her attention to the flight attendant. She accepted the tablets and water, thanked the attendant, and closed her eyes,

"Why not take it now?" the flight attendant asked her.

"Yes. Yes. Thank you," Coreen said, and was barely aware that she swallowed the painkillers. She was seventeen years old again, dragging her heavy belly along the rows of her Aunt Agatha's lettuce patch. A moan slipped from her throat, and to muffle the sound she covered her mouth with one of Bates's handkerchiefs.

"Can I help you?" the man sitting beside her asked. "You seem distressed."

She glanced at him. About fifty-five years old, she thought, with the outward trappings of success and money. He didn't capture her interest, and she shifted her gaze to the clouds among which the big Boeing 767 sped.

When he asked her a second time, she replied, "Thanks. I could have used some help about thirty years ago. I'm fine now. What's done is long done. The deck's been stacked for years and years."

"Don't tell me you're a fatalist," he said in a tone that suggested he had little respect for those who were. "Long ago, I decided to stand up to life. If I make a mistake, I tell myself I'm never doing *that* again and I get on with my life. Life is too short to waste worrying about the past."

The man got her attention when she recognized the relevance of his statement to the problems she faced. "Are you some kind of mystic?" she asked him.

He reclined his seat, leaned back, and locked his hands behind his head, creating an aura of complete self-satisfaction. "Read you right, did I?"

Coreen settled her gaze once more on the clouds. "You don't really care what's going on with me; you couldn't. My concerns would divert you, maybe even amuse you for a few hours, and you would forget about them as soon as this plane landed in Washington, D.C. Just a curiosity for you. But to me, they're too important to be trivialized. They're my life."

"I'm sorry," he said. "Sometimes talking about a problem helps. My motto is do something about it or accept it. Either way, but get on with your life."

A tinge of annoyance surfaced in her, but she attempted nonetheless to parry his remark in a gentle way. "It isn't that simple," she said, "and I've had thirty years to know it. Who do you think will be the U.S. Open tennis champions?" She posed the question to signify her intention to avoid further personal conversation with him.

"One of the Williams women. Among the men, it's a toss-up."

She closed her eyes. "I agree. Would you excuse me, please? I can hardly keep my eyes open."

"Sure thing," he said, and turned to face her. "You know, you remind me of someone who once worked with me. She's almost a dead ringer for you even though—if I guess right—she's a whole generation behind you." He shook his head as if considering the incredulity of the coincidence. "I tell you, nature does some strange things."

The bottom dropped out of her belly, her breath shortened, and she gripped the arm of her seat as fear once more rode through her like a cyclone through grass huts. She didn't want to know any more, yet she realized that she had to respond to his comment, and in a voice that had all the punch of lukewarm, weakened tea, she said, "I had just about decided that you're a successful businessman. What kind of work do you do?"

"Open-heart surgery."

Coreen swallowed a gasp, happy that she could reply truthfully. "I don't know anybody in the medical field." As she said the words, her mind filled with the image of the lone woman sitting behind the steering wheel of a blue Plymouth first in front of her house and then across the street from her agency.

She didn't dare question the man about the woman who looked so much like her, but she desperately wanted to know more. Although pretending to doze off, the dizzying speed with which her mind cast her in the role of a ruined, humiliated woman guaranteed that she wouldn't sleep. In silence, she struggled with the burden of her thoughts. What did that woman want with her? And why did she prefer to stalk rather than confront her?

Her seatmate heaved a heavy sigh. "We'll land in about an hour."

"I imagine you'll be glad to get home," she said, making conversation since he insisted on talking.

"I'm not going home," he replied with what she thought was a catch in his voice. "I'm . . . uh . . . I'm going to bury my mother."

Her right hand clutched his wrist. "I'm so sorry. I'm terribly sorry."

His right shoulder rose and fell in a quick gesture of nonchalance. "It's nothing," he said, shocking her. "She gave birth to me and three days later gave me to my grandmother. The only times I've seen her were at the funerals of her father, sister, and two aunts. About a year ago, I wrote her a letter telling her what I thought of her. She didn't answer, and I don't blame her."

She turned fully to face him. "If you don't care, why are you going?"

"I want to see them throw dirt in her face. When I had the chance, I didn't have the nerve to do it."

Chills raced through her. "My God." She turned away and didn't speak to him again. Somewhere, somebody probably felt that way about her, somebody who could be looking for an opportunity to harm her.

While Frieda had begun to doubt the wisdom of a relationship with Glen even for the sake of revenge against her birth mother, Coreen was developing an obsession about the child she gave up for adoption and the ramifications of that one act.

Sunday, the day after her return from Brussels, while Bates was at church she seized the opportunity to talk with Eric, her elder stepson, and to say some things of which she knew Bates would not approve. To her mind, having Star, an adopted child, as a part of her immediate family would remind her constantly of the child she gave up.

"Listen, son," she said after they greeted each other, "your father wouldn't want me to say this to you, but I have to speak what's on my mind. I just . . . I mean, I wonder if it's wise for you to marry a woman who was adopted almost at birth and who—"

He interrupted her. "What are you talking about? I thought you and Dad liked Star." She heard the controlled anger in his voice, so unlike Eric, and hoped he hadn't gone so far that he couldn't turn back.

"We do, but adoption can . . . well, it can distort people." She recalled the stranger who sat beside her on the flight from Brussels to Washington. "It can make them bitter and . . . and she may have some kind of genetic impairment. You know what I mean."

"No, I don't, Mom. What brought this on, anyway? After Star found her grandmother, she learned everything she needed to know about herself. You know her grandmother would have explained to her about her parents. They drowned in that flood, and the family that raised her, found her, took her in, and adopted her. That's not news to you. Except for her maternal grandmother, her family was wiped out. Why should she be bitter and toward whom?"

Eric was not easily placated, never had been, and she searched her mind for an answer. However, in his impatience, he moved ahead of her in a mild attack. "What's behind this? I have a hunch you have a reason for bringing this up that has nothing to do with the explanation you gave me, and I'd like to know what it is."

Glen would have regarded her comments as concern for him, an element of her usual pampering. She hadn't considered Eric's more mature, more serious bent. Knowing that he would pursue the matter until her answer satisfied him, she quickly backtracked.

"You've always been able to trust your judgment," she told him in an effort to ease the impact of her transgression, "and we do, too. Mothers never want to give their sons over to another woman, and I guess I'm guilty."

"Shame on you, Mom," he said and laughed, but she detected tension in his voice and harshness in his strained laughter.

"While you're rapping wrists," he said without a hint of

amusement, "you'd better get after Glen. I wouldn't be surprised if he had a different woman for every occasion. I've yet to see him with the same woman twice."

To her mind, Glen was smart, with great potential; at twenty-five, he was too young to settle into a serious relationship. She told Eric as much.

"You talk to him," she added. "He can have a great future if he puts himself to it. I want him to be something better than a disc jockey who plays music that other people created."

"He isn't a jock, Mom. He was a producer, but last week he became station manager, and that's a credit to him. WBCC is heard throughout the southern and eastern parts of Maryland and in Northern Virginia. By the time he's fifty, he could be head of NBC. Don't knock it."

She had discounted Glen's work at the college radio station as his killing time while he looked for a real job. Maybe she'd been wrong about that, too. "That's wonderful," she said, and even to her, her voice had the sound of one thoroughly chastened. "Maybe he *will* have a career in broadcasting."

"That's what he intends."

"Well, you talk to him," she insisted. "He needs your support, Eric."

It wasn't like Eric to suck his teeth, she thought, beating back her annoyance. Didn't he understand his brother, and didn't he care what happened to him?

"Glen needs my meddling just like he needs flat tires on that red Mercury Cougar he drives. Mom, Glen is very good at taking care of himself—usually at the expense of another person—and it's time you let him fend for himself. I'd hate for my brother to become a user of women."

She didn't think Glen capable of that and told Eric as much. "He's always needed me, Eric," she insisted. "He was so little when your mother passed."

"He didn't need you one bit more than I did," Eric said in a tone sharper than he had ever used when speaking to her. "The difference was that I was too big to crawl up in your lap, stick my thumb in my mouth, and put my head against your breast. You know what I'm saying?"

Perspiration dampened her forehead and she had a sinking

feeling in her chest. Her salvation was that she wasn't facing him, for Eric was direct and unsparing when he criticized anyone. "Oh, Eric. Are you telling me that I failed you? That I rejected you?" She didn't recognize the voice that came from her throat, shaking and wobbling like that of an aging tenor who had sung too long past his prime.

"I don't think *that*," Eric said. "But whenever I came to you, Glen was already there, and you were taken up with him. I didn't resent him, but there were times when I hurt something awful."

The rapid pounding of her heart frightened her, but she couldn't let him know how badly she felt. "But I always loved you, too."

"I know that, Mom, and I love you. My point is, let Glen make his own way. Give him a chance to prove he's a man." Hadn't Bates said the same thing?

After hanging up, she made coffee and sat at the kitchen table sipping it and pondering Eric's words, words that cradled bitter and not easily forgotten sentiments. She had favored Glen, but she had been able to justify it with what she rationalized as his greater need of her. She had considered herself a good mother to both of her sons, and now . . . Eric said he loved her, and maybe he did, but had he forgiven her?

She didn't feel like going through the papers in her briefcase, cooking, or any of the things she normally did on Sunday mornings while Bates was at church. Restless, she dressed in a lightweight suit, got into her car, and drove out Queen Street to the Albermarle Sound. On Sunday mornings in Bakerville, parking space was easily found anywhere except near a church. The ocean breeze tempered the early June air, invigorating her. She walked out on the Queen Street Pier and was about to sit on the only bench available when her gaze landed on Porgy Jenkins, causing her to stop short. Should she speak or try to pretend she didn't see him?

"Hello there, Coreen. What're you doing out here this time of day?"

"Hi, Porgy. I guess I just needed a change of scene. Where've you been? Lizette's upset about your leaving without a word."

"She's upset about the way I left or the fact that I left? She has her own way of looking at things. Anyway, I'm not going to talk about my business with Lizette. I see you hit the big time. I would have loved to be at that interview in Lizette's shop."

"That's what she said."

"Lizette cared more about that shop and her clients than she did about me and her. I couldn't let my eighty-year-old mother visit me because I was shacking up with a woman. My mother considers that living in sin, and she wouldn't have stayed in that house a single night 'cause she knew I wasn't married. Lizette didn't want to give up her independence, so I let her have it."

Coreen listened to him talk. He said he wouldn't discuss Lizette and their relationship, but he'd done nothing else.

She rested her left hip against the side of the bench but didn't sit down. "You . . . uh . . . think the two of you will get back together?"

He looked up at her, locked his hands behind his head, and leaned back. "Sit down, why don't you? I don't know about getting back together. I haven't changed one bit, and if Lizette told me she had, I'd have a hard time believing her."

She couldn't sit down because any gossiping Bakerville saint who saw them sitting together would damn her with both Bates and Lizette. "Thanks, but you know how these tongues wag. It's none of my business," she said, "but if you talk with her, you may find that you're wrong. She's not foolish enough to value the setting of a solitaire more than the diamond that's in it. Think about that. Be seeing you."

"Yeah. Give Bates the word."

"I will," she said, walking back to her car with her need for peace in the soothing setting of the lapping waves unfulfilled.

She headed back home, crossing Courthouse Square, circling the Wright Brothers statues with the intention of driving up M. L. King Avenue. At the avenue's junction with the square, she thought she saw Bates step into Roy's Hot Grill, slowed down for a second, then shook her head and drove on home. Any man could wear a dark gray suit.

However, the niggling question as to whether she'd really seen her husband persisted, and when he hadn't come home by two-thirty, she began to pace the floor and stare out of the front windows. If she didn't know him any better than he knew her, she could expect most anything. *And after twenty years of marriage!*

She busied herself cooking dinner—or trying to. Biscuits baked without baking powder and dry, overcooked pork chops confirmed that her thoughts were elsewhere. The tongue-lashing—what else could she call it?—that she'd received from her elder son that morning surprised and saddened her, but Bates's behavior was so far out of character that it depressed her. A phone call to her sister-in-law went unanswered, and when she thought of it, she considered herself fortunate that Lizette hadn't been at home.

At about four-thirty she heard the front door open, but she didn't go to greet Bates as she usually did. She was tired of the pretense and game-playing. Yet she knew she was its chief architect. Something had to be done, but she didn't relish the role she would have to play.

"Did you have a special program at church today?" she asked Bates when he walked into the living room where she sat, pretending to read a magazine.

"Nope. We didn't. I ran into Jessie as I was leaving church. Hadn't seen him for a while, so we went to Roy's for some coffee and . . . and just talked. Sometimes things don't look so bad when you can talk about them with somebody."

She felt her lower lip dropping. Bates, the most secretive person in respect to his feelings, needs, and desires, was saying it felt good to talk about them. Suddenly, she didn't believe him. She'd only seen his back going into Roy's Hot Grill; only God knew who stepped in the door in front of him. For the first time in twenty years, she sensed that the bricks of her marriage were crumbling.

I won't challenge him, she said to herself. *My closet has its skeleton, and for all I know he could be squeaky clean.*

"Next time you feel you need to talk," she said, not trying to control the sarcasm in her voice, "try me. I'm still your wife."

"Sure. If you happen to be around when I feel the need."

Chapter Ten

June slipped by, and the East Coast from Maryland to South Carolina sweltered in a monthlong heat wave. Frieda didn't plan to avoid Glen, nor did she want to, but with the hospital crowded with patients suffering various illness associated with the nearly unbearable heat, and with nurses and nurses' aides in short supply, she slept at the hospital and worked twelve-hour shifts.

Even as she worked, her mind didn't stray from Glen and Coreen for very long. *If having to live at the hospital means the Lord is wrecking my plan to confront Coreen Treadwell, I'll have to accept it. But I am not going to help him.* She believed in fate if what it brought to pass made sense. Her relationship with Glen didn't; he seemed hotter after her than ever, if his calls three and four times a day could be considered evidence. Only a serious man would chase a woman in her circumstances, or so she reasoned.

On the last Sunday of July, her first day off in over a month, she went to her apartment, dressed in the stifling heat, and went to church. On the way back home, she bought a copy of *The Baltimore Sun.* Once inside her apartment, she undressed down to her underwear, turned on the electric fan, got a glass of iced tea, and prepared to read the paper. Minutes later, she gasped, nearly gagging on the tea, spilling it on herself, the sofa, and the coffee table. There, before her eyes was a picture of Coreen Treadwell on the first page of the Today section. The woman had been nominated for president of an important international organization, the first American to have that honor. Her heart thumped wildly as if it wanted to tear itself from the confines of her body, and she ground her teeth in anger as she read of her birth mother's honors, her achievements, and the esteem that she enjoyed.

Well, not for long. After I speak with Her Highness, she'll be right down here with the rest of us where she belongs. "I'm gonna pay more attention to Glen," she said to herself, for she regretted not having told him she had a day off. Realizing the danger in her increasingly strong attraction to him, she had used every means in her arsenal of tricks to keep him at bay without squelching his interest. But her efforts seemed only to whet his desire.

Suddenly, she began to stare at Coreen's picture. "Good Lord, it's like looking at myself. If Glen ever sees me without those glasses . . ." She decided to replace her fake glasses with contact lenses that would make her eyes either gray or a lighter brown.

"I called you yesterday afternoon, but got no answer. Where were you?" Glen asked her when he called her at the hospital the next morning.

"Honey, I got in bed and passed out. I never slept so hard in my life."

"I'm not surprised. Working a twelve-hour day for five straight weeks would kill a horse. Break the rules and meet me somewhere. I'm needy as hell."

She wanted to see him, but she was on call even when not on duty, and she wouldn't leave her unit without a backup. "Glen, I wish I could but I'd get fired. Besides, I couldn't do anything so unprofessional. Our time will come."

"I'm going to hold you to that. The first night you're back to normal duty, I'm going to put you in my bed and wear you out."

She heard herself laugh, though she knew it wasn't due to amusement but to unsteady nerves. "Glen, I don't want no man to wear me out. Any man can do that. What I . . . uh . . . want is first-class togetherness."

"And that's what you'll get. This has dragged on for almost three months, which means you've set a record. I told you that when I got tired of fooling around, we'd do it my way. From now on, that's it."

"You dictating to me?" she asked with one last grab at a pretense of indifference.

"You got it, babe. Let me know when you're going to have a free evening and I'll pick you up at the hospital. And come prepared."

"Glen—"

"Don't bother to put up fences. You want me and I definitely want you. Come prepared. Talk to you later."

A week later, fate intervened on Glen's behalf. It was a morning in which three of the patients in Frieda's unit expired, devastating her. One of the women, a single parent, left four young children.

"You'd better take the rest of the day off," the supervisor told Frieda. "This is rough on all of us, but you were close to her. We're collecting money for the woman's funeral and burial, so if you'd like to contribute . . ."

"Yes, ma'am, I sure do, and I thank you for understanding. I talked to that woman this morning and she seemed . . . Well, the Lord don't tell you when he's coming. I hate to think about the future of those poor little kids." She took her wallet from her pocket and gave her supervisor one of her three precious ten-dollar bills.

She sat on her cot in the nurses' quarters pondering the day's events. The doctors, nurses, and she had worked so hard to save that woman, and for what? The poor thing hadn't stood a chance, Frieda thought as she wiped the tears of hopelessness that gushed from her eyes. When the telephone rang, it didn't occur to her that the caller might be Glen, for she wasn't thinking of revenge or of desire for a man, but about the frailty of human life and the limits to man's abilities, awesome though they were.

"Hello," she said without the self-assurance and strength that her voice usually projected.

"This is Glen. You been crying?"

"Huh? Who me?" she asked, reverting to her habit of glossing over problems and showing strength no matter how badly she hurt.

"What's the matter, Frieda?"

"Nothing. I . . . uh . . ." She choked up, unable to suppress the tears.

"Get yourself together. I'll be in front of the hospital in forty-five minutes and I want you to be out there waiting for me. You're in no shape to work, so sign out. You hear me?"

"I've be-been excused for the rest of the day, so I'll m-meet you out front."

She dressed as quickly as she could, rushed across the street to the optometrist, and got fitted with brownish-gray contact lenses. "Thank the Lord I remembered the contact lenses," she said to herself as she hurried back to the hospital.

She waited only a minute before Glen's red Mercury Cougar rolled into view, and her heart began to thump like a locomotive out of control. To her surprise, he got out of the car, embraced her, opened the door to the front passenger's seat, helped her into the car, and fastened her seat belt. She had no familiarity with that kind of almost imperceptible seduction, just as she hadn't previously known a man who practiced it, and she admitted to herself that it undermined her defenses.

"Do you need to go home first?"

"I just need to go home. Period," she said, bluffing.

As if he hadn't heard her, he replied, "I'll wait for you in the car while you get what you need. What happened?"

She told him, adding, "I know I'm not supposed to get emotionally involved with the patients, but she was so pleasant. With all the pain she endured, I never heard her complain or even groan, and she always smiled when I came into her room."

He turned off M. L. King Avenue and headed toward Franklin. "Bitterness never bought anybody anything, and I've had opportunities to know it. My dad prefers my older brother to me, because Eric is so damned perfect, and he resents the fact that our stepmom dotes on me. I want my dad to be proud of me, but I am not going to suck up to every Tom, Dick, and Harry who offers me a dead-end, chickenshit job just so dad can boast about me."

Frieda turned to face the man beside her, aware that he had told her something of importance about himself. Something meaningful, as if she were his companion, his equal.

"I'm sorry to hear that, Glen. It never occurred to me that your life wasn't perfect."

He slowed down, parked before the building in which she

lived, slung his right arm across her shoulder, and gazed down at her. "You're kidding. I hurt like hell sometimes, but I am not bitter. I refuse to do that to myself. Bitterness and hatred go hand in hand; if you hate a guy, you think about him all the time. You're miserable, and he doesn't remember you exist. So who're you hurting but yourself?"

She swallowed hard and tried without success to shift her gaze from his lest he see the guilt that she knew she revealed. "I'll be right back," she said, glad that she could flee into the building.

"If you're not back in half an hour, I'm coming after you." He grabbed her shoulders, pressed his lips to hers, and flicked his tongue across their seam. "And if I go up there, I'm not leaving until you know who I am. You got that?"

Frieda jumped out of the car without answering him, and prayed that her knees wouldn't buckle before she managed to get inside the front door.

Glen kept the motor running in order to enjoy the comfort of the air-conditioning. He punched the button on the CD player and relaxed to Duke Ellington's "Satin Doll," letting the melody roll over him like soft clouds over a southern summer moon. He often said that he wanted the last thing he heard before dying to be classic Ellington music. He glanced at his watch. Only ten minutes had passed.

"Why am I doing this?" he asked himself, sniffing the scent of Evening in Paris perfume and liking it. "I've seen a lot of women I wanted, and ninety percent of the time I didn't do anything about it. Why am I hell bent on bedding this woman, and what will I do if she goes mushy on me and gets serious?"

His fingers traced the buttery leather on the seat beside him. *Not one bit like a woman's warm and yielding flesh,* he thought, and shrugged. *This is a game, and she ought to know it.*

Frieda knew it was a game to Glen, just as it was a ruse for her. What she didn't know was the cost. She had told herself many times that she would willingly give whatever it took and reminded herself of it when she hesitated. As Glen had done, she lifted her left shoulder in a shrug, banishing indecision. "I'm on my way," she said as she stepped out of her apartment, closed the door, and turned the key in the lock. "He can't do any more to me than I can do to him."

She realized that Glen intended by his courteousness to put her at ease and make her feel that she was special and that he cared about her. Instead, it made her nervous, like a neighing horse afraid of an approaching storm.

"I don't bite, sweetheart," he said after buckling her seat belt. "At least not so it will hurt. I'm a real pussycat."

"Sure. And I'm a millionaire."

"Come on, now. I love women, and the last thing I'd do is harm one. Just trust me."

For reasons she couldn't fathom, she got a mental picture of a snake charmer seducing his venomous ally with the strains of a flute. However, she glanced toward him at the moment when he looked her way, and his eyes betrayed a wistfulness that she knew could not be feigned. She clasped her hands tightly over her belly and crossed her knees, symbolically protecting herself from herself.

"It's no use, Frieda," he said with his gaze straight ahead, "so don't punish yourself. Nothing's going to happen that we won't both enjoy."

His apartment wasn't posh, but it had a stylish aura that suited him. *Miles past mine,* she thought, gazing around at the reproductions of Doris Price and James Beardon paintings, Italian leather chairs and sofas, Persian carpets, and Drexel Heritage appointments. And when did men have fresh flowers in their apartments, she wondered as her gaze rested on a vase of lavender and cream flowers.

"What are those?" She pointed to the vase.

"They're called calla lilies. Do you like them?"

She nodded. "They're beautiful like everything else here."

"Thanks. Have a seat somewhere. Want some lemonade? Or would you rather have something stronger?"

"Lemonade, please." She sat down, crossed her knees, and leaned back. "If I drank, and I don't, I wouldn't start this time of day. It's just quarter to twelve."

He let a smile suffice for a reaction and headed for what she supposed was the kitchen. The man seemed so much bigger in that room and so much farther beyond her reach.

She closed her eyes and visualized the picture of Coreen Treadwell in the *Baltimore Sun*. *Keep your eyes on the prize, girl*, she admonished herself, paraphrasing something she had heard.

Glen returned with two glasses of lemonade and two paper napkins. "I ordered lunch for us, and it ought to be here in about twenty-five minutes. Tell me about yourself."

He looked at her with turbulent eyes, dark and intense, precursors of a storm. She flinched. Did he know, or was he guessing? She wanted to leave, but he must have recognized her discomfort, for he immediately electrified her with a dizzying smile. What *was* he? Serious and brooding or a charming woman-chaser?

"Glen, you're confusing me. I don't care if you want to be serious, but you've always been so . . . so easygoing. You're making me nervous. You looked so . . . so almost troubled. I—"

"I'm not easygoing, Frieda, but I don't wear my life like the tie around my neck. Haven't you thought about the consequences of a relationship with me? I was considering that a moment ago."

She could feel her eyes widen and her heartbeat accelerate as shock jangled her nerves. "Sure I have," she replied, her voice lacking its normal verve.

"What do you do besides work, see a movie with girlfriends, and go to church? Ever loved anybody? I don't mean your parents; I mean a man."

"I learned long ago that that doesn't pay."

She wondered why he seemed so relieved, but the doorbell rang and he went to answer it. When he returned with their food, the moment had passed and she didn't question him.

"Let's eat in the dinning room. I set the table earlier."

After a lunch of crab cakes, hot rolls, mesclun salad, and apple tarts, Glen cleared the dining room table, put their dishes in the dishwasher, looked at her, and winked.

"I hope you like Duke Ellington." He put several CDs on the player and turned it on. "'Scuse me for a minute. Oh, by the way, would you like a toothbrush?"

She couldn't help laughing. "I brought my own. Thanks for not asking me if I wanted a bar of soap." She went into the guest bathroom, closed the door, and prayed that she wouldn't have to suffer too much for what she was about to do. "Lord, you know I never been dishonest, and this don't feel right. Just please forgive me." She brushed her teeth and washed her hands. She liked her hands. Their long lean fingers had perfect nail beds, and although she washed them many times a day at work, they were soft and youthful.

Frieda stepped out of the bathroom and into Glen Treadwell's arms. He gave her no time to think or to prepare herself, but captured her mouth with his own while his tongue searched for its place inside. Unprepared for the surge of desire within her, she opened to him. In a wild frenzy, his hands moved over her breasts, belly, and buttocks before gripping the V between her legs. He went at her like a ravenous animal, worshiping every spot he touched, drugging her.

She wanted to stop him, and she wanted to scream at him to get inside of her and give her what she had never had, loving with a man who knew how to fulfill a woman. How to make her explode in passion. She rubbed her sides in frustration, and when she could bear the tension no longer, she rubbed her nipples, unconsciously telling him she needed relief. He let her know that in the ways of loving, he was no slouch, when he eased her blouse off her shoulders and fastened his lips to her left breast. There was no controlling the moans that erupted from her throat, and when he unzipped her skirt and slid his hand inside her bikini while he tugged at her nipple, she let out a keening cry.

"Why don't you take me to bed and finish it? I can't stand this."

As if he had been waiting for that cue, he carried her to his bed. Ten minutes later, her screams filled his bedroom as, for the first time in her life, she erupted in an orgasm, so wrapped up in her own climax that she didn't hear his avowal of satisfaction.

I made a big mistake, she thought even before he separated them. *After the way I acted, he knows he can have me whenever he likes. I should never have done it.*

"Everything all right with you?" he asked her, lying flat on his back with his hands locked behind his head.

Still struggling with the agony and sweetness of her tortured release, she replied in what was barely a whisper, "Lord, yes!" But almost at once, an unanticipated emptiness replaced the joy of release as her vaginal canal throbbed and pulsated like mild tremors after an earthquake.

She longed to be closer to him, to put her arms around him and hold him within her. She reached out to clasp him to her, but his foot hit the floor. Shocked, she heaved herself from the abyss of her orgasm and sat up. "You coming back?"

He headed for the bedroom door. "You mean back to bed? Of course not. I'm going to take a shower and get back to work. I can drop you off, if you want me to."

Startled and embarrassed, she wrapped herself in the top sheet and went to the guest bathroom to recover her pride and put on her clothes.

Glen went into the master bathroom, closed the door, and leaned against it. He had been sexually active since the day after his thirteenth birthday—thanks to a neighbor—but he had never experienced a wallop such as that one. She must have been starving, because he had never had such a wild, uninhibited ride with a woman, or one that stripped his insides and left him vulnerable to anything she wanted.

What in hell was I thinking about? he asked himself. *I should have known that once with her wouldn't be enough, because all I ever had to do was touch her and she blazed up like a house afire.*

He turned on the shower, stepped beneath the stream of warm water, and laughed at himself when he realized his attempt to wash away all vestiges of the best sex he'd ever had.

I'm not getting sucked into her cocoon. She'll want permanency, marriage, but I am not going there, and especially not with her.

He rubbed the thick terry towel over his body with more vigor and for a longer time than necessary as he pondered his next move. He had to avoid a serious entanglement, and he needed to get away from her in a few minutes without causing

her to feel as if he'd used her. He went to the closet that faced the
bathroom, slipped on a shirt and a pair of pants, got a tie from
the wall rack and tied it. Safe from the likelihood of being lured
back to bed with her, he walked back to the bedroom. But she
met him halfway, fully dressed, relaxed, friendly, and not the
least bit possessive. More relieved than he would have imagined
possible, he kissed her cheek.

"Thanks for being understanding. I'll drop you home."

She spoke little as he drove to her address on Franklin Street,
but her silence didn't bother him. She wasn't raising hell and
making demands or threats, and he was too thankful to concern
himself with much else.

"I'll be in touch," he said, and in view of his solicitous behavior when he was taking her to his apartment, even *he* thought it
impolite of him not to get out of the car.

He examined her smile and decided that it was genuine. "I'll
be looking forward to seeing you," she replied, as casually as if
they had met five minutes earlier.

He didn't know what to make of it. If she noticed that he sat
there while she let herself out of the car, she didn't indicate it,
and he was grateful for that, too. But when he drove off, his
mind returned to that moment when he released himself inside
of her, and he cursed aloud at his full erection.

Frieda managed to get into her apartment, close the door,
and walk into her living room where she crumbled, in a heap on
her sofa.

"He'll be seeing me—the bastard. Shake me up and turn me
inside out, and all he can say is he'll be seeing me."

She sat upright and pounded the sofa with her right fist. No
man had ever done to her what he did or made her feel the way
he did. "I'm no fool," she said to herself. "I tied him in knots just
like he did me. And when his furnace starts roaring, he'll call. I
just hope I have the strength to tell him to go to hell."

"Want to go see that Denzel Washington movie?" Thelma
asked Frieda the following Friday evening.

"Girl, I can't. I'm sorry. You know I'd go if I could, 'cause I do love Denzel."

"You on call tonight?"

"Uh . . . no," Frieda said, "but I haven't had time to do any knitting on these sweaters Reverend Hall wants us to make for the homeless children."

"You can find a better excuse than that; Christmas is months away, and fast as you knit, you can finish those things in a few weeks. Come on. I hate to go to a movie by myself."

"Why don't you ask Lacy?" Frieda said. She hoped her friend wouldn't plead with her.

"Lacy's hanging out with Mack. Okay, I'll go Saturday afternoon. I haven't sunk to the point where I'll go to a movie at night alone. I'll bet that hunk's got something to do with this. You're not fooling me. See you."

At midnight, she put the knitting away, got ready for bed, and crawled in. Four days had passed, and he hadn't called once. Until Monday, when she slowed down and let him catch her, he had phoned her three and four times a day. For the first time in her life, she had spent an evening beside a phone waiting for a man's call. As she struggled with insomnia, she remembered her vow to confront her birth mother while holding Glen's hand.

Do I stand a better chance with him if I call him or if I wait until he calls? She decided on the latter and turned out the light. Saturday morning, she awakened to the sound of the telephone.

"Hello?"

"Hi. What time do you get off today?"

"Uh . . . five o'clock. W-why?" She hated the unsteadiness in her voice.

"What about I pick you up in front of the hospital? Huh? Bring whatever you're going to wear to church Sunday morning."

She stared at the receiver. *Don't do it. Nothing is worth the humiliation. He isn't even pretending to care.* She wanted to swear at him, but her body remembered what it was like to writhe beneath him. She swallowed the liquid that accumulated in her mouth and told herself to hang up.

"Don't you remember how you felt when I was rocking you

out of your senses? I can make you feel better than that if you let me do what I want to do. I'll pick you up at five-fifteen."

"Uh . . . okay." She hung up, wrapped her arms across her belly, and let the tears fall. What had she done to herself?

The August heat bore down on Coreen as she walked along the beach just before sundown that Monday afternoon. She shunned the comfort of her air-conditioned home because she couldn't conquer her restlessness, the manifestations of which would not escape Bates's attention and comment. She tried to explain to herself her loss of enthusiasm for the environment in which she worked and for the job itself. Until recently, work had been her consuming passion, and the status that it accorded her among the people of Bakerville had eased the burden of her most onerous tasks.

She walked with slow, plodding movements back to the agency's parking lot, turned on the ignition and air-conditioning in her car, and stood beside it while the interior cooled. Pictures of herself getting off the bus in Pick-Up and staring into the un-smiling face of Agatha Monroe flashed through her mind.

"If you came here to get rid of it, think again," her aunt had said without offering a simple greeting. "You let that boy have his way with you, and you're going through with it."

Coreen had only wanted shelter and privacy during the pregnancy, and help in placing the child for adoption so that she could get on with her life. But she didn't explain that to her aunt, whose pursed lips and what looked like a congenital frown did not invite confidences. She dragged her thoughts to the present, got into the car, and sat there enjoying the cool comfort. Maybe if she took a leave of absence from work or if she and Bates went away as he suggested months earlier. . . .

Pulling herself out of her mental stupor, she suddenly snapped her fingers. "How dense can I get!" Like a flower opening to re-veal its stamen, there flashed through her mind's eye the face of the psychoanalyst in Brussels when she asked him if she had a choice other than to return to Pick-Up. From that time, she had moved through the days almost listlessly. If revisiting her past was her only salvation, the only cure for her paranoia about being found, exposed, and disgraced, what was she to do?

I can't go back there. I just can't.

She entered the agency the following morning and immediately sensed a change in the atmosphere when Oscar greeted her without his usual pomp. She stopped and walked back to him.

"What's wrong, Oscar?"

He scratched the side of his head and looked past her left shoulder. "Nothing, ma'am, at least not as far as I can tell."

When she reached the elevator, Lieutenant Mitchell stood beside it as if he had been waiting for her. She spoke to him and got on the elevator, and it didn't surprise her that he followed her. Inside her office, he took a seat beside her desk.

"You can always trace these things to some girl's trifling man," he began. "It seems Marsha Ward, Oscar's niece, put her baby up for adoption against her boyfriend's wishes. They had a brawl, and she told him your agency advised her to do it, that it was the best for the baby. He knocked her around, did the same to Oscar, took his keys, and you know the rest. We don't blame Oscar for the crime, only for lying when we interviewed him."

She shook her head in amazement. "Poor Oscar. He flies with one wing. I hope you're not planning to do anything to him."

Mitchell stretched his long legs out in front of him. "Well, he wasn't intentionally obstructing justice, he was just scared to tell. That fellow banged him up rather thoroughly. A real bully."

"Let's get this straight, Lieutenant. This agency did not advise that girl to do anything; it was her idea. We helped her place the child. Where is Marsha's boyfriend?"

The officer wrote something in a small pocket notebook. "In custody awaiting trial. He has a long record, so he'll probably be away for a while. We've done our job here."

She thanked him, and as soon as he closed the door, she telephoned Maddie Franks. "Marsha Ward was your client. What was the resolution of her case?"

"She said she wanted to have the baby adopted, and I helped her arrange it. Any problems?"

Just as she had thought. "No, none at all. Thanks." In due course, she would speak with Oscar. She walked over to the window and gazed down on Poplar Neck Road at the scene she had loved ever since she'd been head of the agency. Looking down at the people, the trees, and the Sound had always given her a sense of accomplishment. Yes, and of power.

If I could only drum up my normal enthusiasm, she said to herself when the wonder of the Albermarle with its slashing waves and changing tides failed to engage her interest. "I'm not going to Pick-Up," she said aloud, and began to form in her mind doubt as to the analyst's credentials for counseling her.

"I'll see another analyst, one who understands African Americans." But even as her mind produced the idea, she knew she was procrastinating, that she had to go back to Pick-Up. If only she could talk with someone who would understand.

"Let's invite Lizette over for dinner tonight," Coreen said to Bates as they spoke on the phone that afternoon. "She's all alone and she needs our support." With Lizette present, Coreen hoped her sister-in-law, and not she, would be the focus of Bates's attention.

"If she's alone, whose fault is it?" he asked. "Nobody told her to shame herself living with Porgy Jenkins, and everybody in town knows it. Decent people ignore her, so the only friends she's got are the women who pay her to do their hair."

"But, Bates, can't we ask her to have dinner with us?"

After what seemed like an eternal silence, he said, "Yeah, if you want to, but she knows how I feel about her behavior. Decent people get married; they don't shack up for twelve years and then split."

She wished she hadn't thought of it, for the evening would pass with Bates reprimanding his sister for what he considered "her low-class ways," depressing her.

However, Lizette came to dinner well dressed and in an apparently cheerful mood. "Don't tell me Porgy's back," Bates said, letting his gaze travel over his sister. "Nothing else could make you look like this."

Lizette greeted Coreen and her brother and walked on into the living room. "If he's back, nobody told *me*," she said, and took a seat on the far end of the avocado green velvet sofa. "That doesn't mean I'm gonna fold up and die." She looked at Coreen. "Isn't brother dear treating you well? Honey, you look down. *Way* down."

Coreen cringed. Unwittingly, Lizette was the instigator of exactly what she sought to avoid in inviting her.

"Which proves I'm still in my right mind," Bates said. "She's been looking just like this for days, like she didn't win that election. I didn't say anything, 'cause she's been doing her best to pretend everything's all right. But she can't fool me."

Lizette looked at Coreen. "I could bite my tongue. Nothing makes Bates happier than to have a reason to castigate somebody."

"What man wants to see his wife dragging around looking as if she just got bad news from her doctor? This isn't like Coreen, and I want to know the reason for it."

"Before you take off on Coreen, could you help me out with a little advice?" Lizette asked Bates.

His eyes widened. "If I thought you meant to be serious, I'd try."

She looked him in the eye. "Where should I look for Porgy?"

Bates's lower lip dropped. "Don't look for him. Go out with a good-looking man, and if Porgy's ever planning to come back, you'll see him pretty soon. The man's got a good job teaching, and if he wasn't shacking up with a woman he's not married to, he'd be highly respected here in Bakerville."

"His status is fine with me," Lizette said.

He threw up his hands. "Do what you want to do, Lizette. Never could tell you a thing anyhow." Perhaps to his mind he'd acquiesced, but Coreen couldn't have mistaken the note of triumph in his voice, the smugness that never failed to appear when he had occasion to feel superior.

"I'm serving dinner," Coreen said, " and I don't want to hear a word about Porgy or what I look like." The telephone rang. "Would you get that please, honey?" she asked Bates.

He walked into the kitchen several minutes later. "Whoever it was didn't want to talk with me."

She whirled around from the stove and stared at him. "What do you mean?"

"I mean somebody was on the line, but she or he didn't say a word. After a while, they hung up."

"Who could it have been? I can't imagine anybody in this town . . . deliberately doing a thing like that."

"Sure you don't have an idea?" he asked, letting her know he caught her pause when it occurred to her that it might have been the woman who drove the blue Plymouth.

"If I did," she bluffed, "I'd call them up and chew them out. That's disgusting."

"Yeah," he said, and went back to the living room where Lizette sat alone.

Coreen put the food on the dining room table, pasted a pleasant expression on her face, and called her husband and sister-in-law to supper.

"Lord, we thank you for this food and for each other," Bates said for grace and helped himself to the veal cutlet just as the phone rang.

"Ignore it," Coreen said, and could have kicked herself when it occurred to her that she had probably aroused Bates's suspicion.

Bates stared at her for a second. "Not on your life," he said, and jumped up from the table chewing veal as he sprinted to the phone. She didn't look up when he returned, but busied herself cutting a piece of the cutlet.

"Must have been your buddy again," he said, sat down, and continued his meal as if nothing untoward had occurred. However, she knew she would hear more about it, that he wouldn't resist the opportunity to express his displeasure.

By tomorrow night, I'll have caller ID on two of these phones, she promised herself, *and whoever is doing this will pay.* Immediately, though, she remembered that if the anonymous caller was who she suspected, that person had the advantage, and because she feared exposure, she would do nothing about it.

She glanced up from her plate to see that both Bates and Lizette had stopped eating and focused on her. Remembering that she had not replied to Bates's caustic comment, she said to him, "If you're waiting for me to answer your smart remark, don't hold your breath."

"Y'all just about as chummy as a fox and a chicken," Lizette said. "What you guys need is an old-fashioned roll in the hay."

Bates glared at his sister. "I knew you couldn't spend an evening without mentioning sex."

"I didn't say the word, but now that *you* mentioned it, more of that and less bickering would smooth out some wrinkles in this relationship."

"So you're an expert," Bates said, "a woman who lived with a man for twelve or thirteen years—"

"Twelve."

"—and couldn't get him to marry her."

"For your information, brother dear, Porgy begged me to marry him every single solitary day we were together, but I said no."

"You expect me to believe—"

"I don't care whether you believe it or not. I didn't want to swap our life together, my independence, and the mind-blowing way he made love to me for the kind of staid, boring relationship you two have. I guess he wanted to get married or split. So he walked out. It hurts, but I haven't cried yet."

Bates stopped eating and regarded his sister carefully. "And you think marriage would change that?"

"Yeah. Because he wasn't sure of me, he concentrated on keeping me happy. From the time I walked in this house, at least, Coreen's happiness couldn't have been further from your mind."

Coreen tuned out, shutting off the noise that came from their throats. She no longer worried about happiness, neither in her marriage nor in other areas of her life. First, the woman found her address, then her place of business, and finally her telephone number. How long would it be before that woman rang her doorbell?

Coreen also filled Frieda's thoughts, for she saw herself sliding farther from her goal. That night, she lay beneath Glen in his

king-size bed drenched with sweat and depleted of energy. He
had made love to her every way a man could make love to a
woman, bringing her to orgasm time after time until she begged
him to stop. Pleasing her, shocking her, and sometimes hurting
her. He stared down into her face.

"You're one hell of a woman."

Unbearable hurt gripped her in the region of her heart, for
not once had he kissed her mouth, although his own mouth and
tongue had been all over her and in every crevice of her body.

"You've been using me to act out all those things you conjure
up in your wet dreams," she whispered, knowing that as long as
he was on top of her, he held the advantage.

"And yours, too." He ran his left hand beneath her hips and
stroked her. "I hope I didn't hurt you."

She didn't answer, remembering how she had struggled to
hold back the tears and how, minutes later, he had flung her into
ecstasy. She didn't want any more of it, yet she knew that if he
called her, she would go to him.

"I'm going home, Glen."

He squeezed her left breast. "I'm not ready for you to go.
Don't tell me you didn't enjoy it, because you did."

"I said I want to go home. So would you please let me up?"

He smiled in that way she knew had no depth and no meaning. "You walking out on me? Come on, babe. We just got
started."

She squeezed her eyes tight. "A gentleman always respects a
woman's wishes, and I know a man of your class learned that at
home."

He raised up and braced himself on his hands. "Come on,
now. Don't get so serious."

"I'm serious because I hurt, so let me up, please."

He rolled off her and sat on the side of the bed. "All right, but
you're making me feel dreadful."

Why not? Wasn't that how she felt? Didn't she feel as if her
soul had been hollowed out? He hadn't pretended that he felt
anything for her, and yet she was besotted with him. She got off
the other side of the bed, took her clothes from the chair, the
dresser, and the floor where he pitched them in his rush to plunge

into her. The warm shower didn't ease her pain or remove her humiliation, but to her mind, it cleansed her of him.

"Look, I'll call you," he said when she returned dressed to leave.

She nodded. "See you," she said and walked out into the summer night.

Chapter Eleven

Frieda didn't go to church the Sunday after her humiliating tryst with Glen; a sense of guilt and the feeling that she wasn't good enough to associate with respectable people bore heavily on her. She wanted to go where no one knew her. Not since she ran away from home at age seventeen had she done anything for which she was ashamed. Not until she allowed Glen to use her as he chose, when she couldn't summon the will or the desire to reject his comportment and selfish acts. She accepted that his almost demonic behavior and her seemingly unquenchable desire for him were God's way of telling her not to use Glen in revenge against her birth mother.

If this is the price, I'll just stiffen my back and pay it, she said to herself. *That woman owes me.*

She knew she hadn't seen the last of Glen, that as soon as his libido got the better of him, he would call her. If she submitted to him, he would have that much more control over her, for she sank more deeply into his clutches and became more firmly entwined in his net each time he touched her. And if she managed to reject his advances, she would lose him and a chance to heap pain and humiliation on Coreen Treadwell. Shaking her head, she thought, *If I was a betting woman, I'd bet against myself.*

She was soon put to the test, for around two o'clock that afternoon, a loud knock on her apartment door sent her scampering for a robe and slippers. She opened the door.

"Glen!"

His effusive smile rocked her on her heels, evidence that his charm was back in place. He handed her a bunch of pastel camellias and lilies, exquisite by any measure. "Aren't you going to ask me in?"

She thought of her unmade bed and the likelihood that he would want to spend the remainder of the day in it. And she thought of her shame when she walked out of his apartment and into the hot midnight alone a little less than seventy-two hours earlier.

"Sorry," she said. "I don't think that's a good idea."

He raised an eyebrow, and when he frowned, she knew he was on the verge of anger. "I was going to take us to the Great Blacks in Wax Museum."

She didn't believe him. "Thanks, but I've been there a dozen times. It's only about four blocks from here." When he looked disappointed, she gained the strength to get some of her own. "Another time, Glen. I'm not feeling so hot today. If you had called, I'd have saved you the trouble of coming all the way over here."

"No problem," he said, saving face. "Sure there isn't something I can do for you?"

She thanked him. "Not a thing." He had allowed her to go home alone late on that hot night, when he knew men would be roaming the streets, but he would drive to her place in the afternoon bringing flowers. "I'm just fine," she said. "I don't need a thing."

His smile glittered. "You sure?"

Without warning, she bristled as anger replaced susceptibility. "I certainly don't need any more of your gentlemanly behavior. Does having everything you wanted all your life entitle you to treat a woman as if she's nothing? Does it give you the right to be so self-centered, so lacking in compassion? Does it?"

His cocky grin vanished into the shadow of a frown. "Now look here. I came to bring you some flowers, to let you know that—"

She didn't let him finish it. "Shove it, Glen. Like I said, I don't need a single, solitary thing. Thank the Lord."

He appeared contemplative, and then his countenance darkened. She expected a show of charisma, or at the least the little-boy innocence that he affected with such perfection. But he disappointed her. Leaning his head to one side, he scrutinized her.

"Sorry I got you out of bed. Next time."

If there was a next time, she hoped she could handle it. She closed the door and said a word of prayerful thanks that she hadn't weakened and let him seduce her.

The following Wednesday he tested her again, calling her at work. "Look, sweetheart, I've got some kids coming into the studio this afternoon on a kind of field trip, you know, learning about broadcasting. How about coming over and giving me a hand? I'll be good. I swear it."

She didn't doubt that he used the occasion as a opportunity to inveigle her into joining him for another sexual romp, and her head told her to say no.

"What time?" she asked as thoughts of what he offered sent her blood rushing through her body. "Uh . . . I don't get off today till five."

"Plead a headache and check out of there at three. Okay?"

At twenty minutes past three, she opened the door and entered WBCC studio. "Where are the children?" she asked, standing at his office door.

With his face wreathed in smiles, he said, "They just left. Woman, you are a sight for sore eyes."

"What are you doing?" she asked when he walked to the desk, picked up a camera, and snapped her picture several times.

"This will go in our next newsletter." He stepped behind her, closed the door, and locked it. "I can't stop thinking about you. You keep me awake at night and interfere with my work. No other woman can claim that." His eyes closed as he reached for her.

"I can't wait to get to you." With those words, he began to strip her.

She tried to make herself tell him to stop, but the words wouldn't come. And in that air-conditioned office, she shivered in her nakedness as he mounted her with only the parquet floor beneath her back.

* * *

Weeks had passed, and Coreen hadn't told Lizette that she saw Porgy on the Albermarle Pier. She didn't like feeling guilty, so she struck out for the beauty parlor on a Saturday morning thinking that she would tell Lizette to walk down to the beach just before sunset.

"Hey, girl," Lizette said when Coreen walked into the beauty shop. "I thought you were due here next Tuesday after work."

"I am, but I . . . er . . . thought I'd drop by for a few minutes."

"Business picked up after the station started running your interview."

Coreen calmed herself. Maybe she had misunderstood. "You mean they ran it more than once?"

"At least a dozen times to my knowledge," Lizette said with such pride in her voice as a parent has for a beautiful and successful child. "And different times of the day, too. Honey, you ought to be proud. Everybody that comes in here praises that interview, the way you handle yourself and the way you look."

Coreen sat down as, once more, fear began to corrode her nerves. She tried to hide her hands so that Lizette and the woman whose hair Lizette was pressing wouldn't see how her fingers trembled.

"I see you have a full shop," Coreen said. "Maybe I'll stop by later on, and we can have a cup of coffee. 'Bye, everyone."

She left hurriedly, shaken when the chorus of voices sang out, "Good-bye, Miss Treadwell."

Outside, she leaned against her car, certain that the interview had helped her stalker find her agency and her telephone number. Forgotten was her intention to help Lizette by guiding her to Porgy. As she drove home, she couldn't help wondering if going back to Pick-Up would be worse than suffering interminable fear.

She drove out Rust Street through Courthouse Square to Tryon Avenue and parked in the lot behind the shopping mall. She didn't want to buy anything, but she needed to kill time before going to Bates's travel agency, which joined the mall. Time to settle down and drape herself in a facade of contentment. She selected a bag of dried cranberries and walked around munching them.

At the feel of pressure on her arm, she turned to face the

smile of a woman she didn't know. "Miss Treadwell, I just want you to know how proud we are of you. You are a treasure, a role model for every young girl. Could I please have your autograph?" The woman produced a pocket-sized "Week At A Glance" and a pen.

Coreen's heartbeat returned to normal. She thanked the woman, wrote a few words of encouragement, and signed it. "Good luck to you," she said to the woman.

The thrill of giving her first autograph banished her fear and concern about being recognized and she raced out of the mall and into the travel agency.

"Say, you're out of breath," Bates said when she almost stumbled into the shop. "What's this all about?"

She told him, her eyes glistening with the joy she felt.

"Well, damn! I'll bet that brightened you up."

"It was such a funny feeling hearing that from a stranger."

He walked over and kissed the side of her mouth. "With that interview playing endlessly, I expect people from Raleigh to Richmond will recognize you."

He stared at her. "What did I say that got you down so fast? Something is bothering you, and it's not simple. For the last four or five weeks, your moods have been swinging from high to low so fast I can't keep up with 'em. You're not telling what's up, but I'll find out. Trust me."

She stayed until she could leave without further arousing his curiosity. "Want to see a movie tonight?" she asked in the hope of diverting his attention.

"If you insist, but I'd rather rent a movie and watch it at home."

"Well, if you want to. I've got a lot to do, so I'd better run along."

He didn't look up from the ticket he perused. "Yeah. And get your act together."

She didn't respond. *I wish I knew how to do that,* she said to herself. *If I don't figure it out, it's going to cost me a lot.*

Coreen had no way of knowing that the drama in which she was embroiled was nearing its final act. Right then, miles away

in Baltimore, Glen looked at the photo he took of Frieda and felt
his chest broaden. He had seduced what, in his estimation, was
"a real woman," one who could resist him only so long before
returning for what she knew he would give her. He had stopped
worrying about her fits of independence when she would turn
him down with an excuse that he could see through; he could almost time the cycle of her sexual needs, could guess to the day
when she wouldn't have the strength to tell him no. *And when
she finally does say no and mean it, then what?* He tried to shrug, but
it didn't come off. On a hunch, he scanned the photo and inserted it in an e-mail to Eric: "Man, how do you like this! Glen."

He didn't wait long for his brother's reaction. Eric contacted
him just prior to the end of the working day. "Got your e-mail.
Who's this?"

"My woman, man. She hasn't told me so, but I'm sure she's
older than I am, and I've laid the business on her so thoroughly
that she can't resist me. Oh, she tries, but when I call, she comes.
How do you like them apples? Baby brother knows how to light
a fire."

A few minutes later, he received Eric's reply. "The picture
didn't come through clearly. Put the photo in the mail today. I'll
send it right back to you."

Glen put the photo in an envelope, addressed and stamped
it, dropped it in a mailbox when he left the station, and forgot
about it. He didn't think he led Eric to believe Frieda was special
to him, and she wasn't. He had merely boasted of his ability to
bed and keep a good-looking, voluptuous, and mature woman
some years his senior.

So Eric's phone call two evenings later surprised him. "I'm in
Baltimore. You had dinner?"

"Uh . . . no. Why didn't you let me know you planned to
drive over?"

"I didn't plan to," Eric said. "I was thinking about this, and
half an hour ago, I got in my car and headed here. Meet me at
Mo's in the Inner Harbor, and let's pig out on some good
seafood."

"Where are you now?"

"Albermarle and Banks, a couple of blocks from Mo's. You

should be able to make it in half an hour, which is as much time as I needed to get here from the University of Maryland."

"I'll be there," Glen said, wondering what had prompted Eric—a man who did nothing on the spur of the moment—to behave so far out of character.

When Glen arrived at Mo's, he saw that Eric had taken a table that afforded a view of the harbor. His brother stood and came to greet him, draping an arm around his shoulder.

"You're looking great," Eric said. "Gained some weight, too."

Much as Glen liked compliments, he ignored those, because his thoughts were centered on Eric's reason for rushing to Baltimore and leaving Star behind.

"Thanks," he said with as much enthusiasm as he could manage. "You don't look so bad yourself." He knew he would have to wait until Eric ordered his food; his brother placed everything in its proper order, and in a restaurant, food came first.

At last, Eric took Frieda's photograph from the breast pocket of his jacket and placed it on the table. So that was it. Frieda.

Eric leaned back and tapped the table with the pads of his fingers. "Glen, haven't you noticed that this woman is the spitting image of Mom? She's—"

Glen grabbed the picture and stared at the image of Frieda's face. "No . . . I . . . Once or twice I had the feeling that she reminded me of somebody. Her voice and . . . Good grief, you're right. She does look like Mom. But she usually wears glasses, and her eyes are a grayish brown. Mom has dark brown eyes. I guess that's why I didn't notice the similarity."

"They look so much alike that it's eerie. Are you serious about this gal or what?" Eric asked in a tone that said he was within his rights.

Both of Glen's eyebrows shot up. "Serious? Me? Come on, man. If I were serious, I wouldn't have sent you that kind of e-mail about her. She's okay but . . . man, I'm just having a good time."

"I hope she knows that. When a woman gets deeply involved with a man, as this one is with you, she wants permanency, the whole nine yards. You watch it."

"She's not stupid."

"What do you know about her? How'd you meet her?" Eric asked him.

Glen told him. "She's a churchgoing, God-fearing woman, hardly sophisticated. But man, she's a ball of fire in bed."

"Hmm. Be sure you keep it between the lines, Glen. This is strange. Maybe you're attracted to her because she looks like Mom. It's happened, you know."

"Naah. I wanted her at first because she was hard to get, and after I got her, I wanted her because she lets me play out every fantasy I ever had. When I get tired of that, I'll move on."

"Not if she gets pregnant."

"Man, what do you take me to be?"

"All right. But be careful. I don't like this," Eric said, and picked up the photograph and put it back in his pocket.

"How's Star?"

"Great. We're shopping for a house. She's having a good time, and I'm going crazy. Why can't women say, Yes, I'll marry you tomorrow? No. They need months and months to try on dresses and shoes, get fitted for this and that, worry about their hairstyle, and pick out everything they will ever use from the day they marry until they're ninety. It's sending me up the wall."

He almost envied his brother the love of such a woman as Star. Beautiful, feminine, strong, and independent. An intelligent and well-educated woman who would be his true partner in his life.

"You and Star are fortunate," Glen said. "So much in common. You belong together. I'm happy for you, man."

"Thanks. Do I detect a note of wistfulness?"

Glen lifted his left shoulder in a shrug. "Not yet, though I confess I'm beginning to see that finding that one girl has merit."

"Like I said, watch it, Glen."

In his apartment later that night, Glen studied the photographs he took of Frieda. Why hadn't he noticed her similarity to his mom? Not that it mattered so much, but he intended to scrutinize her thoroughly in the daylight first chance he got. However, if she ever discovered that she looked like his stepmother, the information wouldn't come from him. He wouldn't give any woman that much ammunition.

He telephoned Frieda the next morning as soon as he got to work. "The station's doing some people-on-the-street interviews this afternoon not too far from Druid Hill Park. You're good with people. How about coming along in case some people have to be enticed? Oh, yes. Drive, because I won't be able to give you a lift. We have to edit these tapes tonight." He knew that would get her. She would be useful, and she wouldn't think he plotted to seduce her. He wanted some senior citizens in the shots, and Frieda could get them to cooperate. She took considerable time answering.

"Glen, you got me on the floor in your office, but if you've got any fantasies about the grass in Druid Hill Park, forget it. In fact, don't think it."

He couldn't help laughing. "Have I ever got a bad reputation! Frieda, four of my staff and some high-powered cameras will be there. Trust me not to make headlines for *Star* magazine. Can you come right after work? My guys will save a parking space on Sequoia at Reistertown, and one of them will walk with you to our site. Okay?"

"I'll come, because I'd like to see you when you're working at something other than sex."

He slapped his right hand against the side of his head as if horrified, remembered that she couldn't see him, and smothered a laugh. "If I answer that, you'll never forgive me. See you shortly after five."

He waited while she seemed to weigh the pros and cons of joining him in the park. "All right, but I'm not in the mood to let you make a fool out of me. You understand?"

He dragged out his charm. "Honey, that hurts. If that's what you think of me, I see I've got a big job of mending ahead of me."

"It is, and you have. See you later."

Let her protest. He would examine her thoroughly beneath the light of the sun to see how much she resembled his mom. Already, a premonition of dread had begun to displace his sense that his world finally stood upright. He hadn't done anything wrong. Yet a niggling feeling warned him that that made no difference.

*   *   *

Sometimes I wish I was a churchgoing person, Coreen thought the following Saturday morning as she wheeled her shopping cart toward Grant Supermarket's produce section. *Ministers and priests are not supposed to tell your business, and I could talk with mine, if I had one.* So focused was she on the punishment that a return to Pick-Up represented for her that she pushed her cart against a person's leg, looked up, and saw Porgy.

"Sorry. I'm—Goodness, Porgy, I would never have expected to meet you here."

"Why not? It's a free country."

"But you don't . . . Say, were you hoping Lizette might do her marketing this morning?"

A scowl blanketed his face. "She's in the shop on Saturdays. You know that. I see you didn't tell her you saw me on the beach."

She put her left hand on her hip and glared at him. "You said nothing had changed, so I didn't see the point."

"I never could figure out why women take everything so literally," he said, and walked away.

"That settles it," she called after him, and took out her cell phone. "Lizette, this is Coreen. I just ran into Porgy in Grant's. Right. Good luck." She hung up. Lizette would get her Porgy and a chance to correct her mistake. Now, if only *she* could see a little light in the dark labyrinth her life had become. Secrets, lies, intrigue, and all of her own making.

She finished her shopping and headed home. Time was when the house at 38 Queen Street North was her haven, a nest where she enjoyed refuge from her daily hassles, a feeling of belonging in the warmth of her family and the love of her husband and sons. Perhaps it had all changed when first Eric and then Glen went out on their own, or when she began to earn more than Bates, or was it that the only change had occurred in her?

At home, she raced to answer the phone. "Treadwell residence. Hello." There was no response, and the caller did not hang up.

"What do you want?" she asked, nearly screaming the words. "For God's sake, what do you want?" She heard the click of the receiver and knew that by revealing her frustration, she had gratified the pest. She checked caller ID, saw the words "blocked number," and phoned the telephone company.

"Reject all blocked numbers calling this line," she said. "If callers don't want their number displayed, I don't want to hear from them." She knew that wouldn't stop the harassment; with a little inconvenience, the person would use a pay phone.

After a restful weekend during which she enjoyed unusual camaraderie with her husband—so unusual, in fact, that she had to fight her suspicions—Coreen went to work Monday morning determined to stop worrying about the things she couldn't correct and to enjoy the good things in her life.

"You had a call from WTUS-TV in Raleigh, Ms. Treadwell," her temporary secretary said when Coreen walked past her to enter her own office. "Should I call back?"

"Give me a couple of minutes, Coreen said as excitement coursed through her. People were beginning to regard her as a celebrity. She had never dreamed that—As quickly as her spirits buoyed, they fell, burdened by the prospect that her past would rise to deprive her of all that was important to her.

When her secretary buzzed her, she lifted the receiver with reluctance. "Coreen Treadwell speaking. How may I help you?"

"I'm Ann Springer," the high-pitched Southern voice said. "and I have a TV program, *Women in the News*. I read of your rapid rise to prominence in *The Baltimore Sun*, and I'd like to interview you for our program."

Coreen listened with dispassion while the woman explained the show's aims and format. "Our station is in Raleigh," she added, "and we would pay your expenses, although we don't offer an honorarium."

She should have told Nana Kuti that she couldn't accept the nomination. *If I fall, it will be such a long, hard drop.* "Ms. Springer," she said, stalling for time to think, "I've only been nominated for that presidency. There are three other nominees, all of whom are more prominent in our field than I am. Should we hold this until after that election?"

"I understand your concern, but your winning isn't our primary concern. We haven't had an American in that post, or until now even a nominee for it." Coreen knew that, and felt that by reminding her of it, the woman was being heavy-handed.

"Considering the social and welfare programs that this country conducts or sponsors all over the developing world, it's time we had a recognized leader in this field. I'll call tomorrow morning to see how you feel about it. I do hope you'll agree."

"I appreciate your interest, Ms. Springer, and I'll be expecting your call." She had begun to feel like a criminal on the lam, tired of running but too scared to surrender. For twenty-five years of hard work and dedication to her clients, didn't she deserve recognition? Why should she be forced to choose between accepting her due and paying one more penalty for Leon Farrell's crime? Where was the justice in that?

She pushed the button on her intercom. "No more calls this morning," she said to the secretary. "I have to clear some of these reports off my desk."

At supper that night, for want of something else to talk about, she told Bates of Ann Springer's call.

"What was there to think about?" he asked her. "You can't pay for that kind of publicity; an hour on WTUS with just you and the interviewer. All this celebrity must be going to your head." Coreen explained her reasons. "That's a lot of bunk. If you win that election next month, everybody's going to be after you, so you might as well forget about making excuses and procrastinating like you did with that woman."

"Well, you know I've got a lot on me at work right now, and Eric's marriage is—"

Coreen's head bounced around at the roar that erupted from Bates's throat. He nearly doubled up laughing. "Now I know something's up if you're using that for an excuse. Star is managing her own wedding, and neither she nor Eric has asked one thing of us. Think of something else."

"I ran into Porgy the other day in Grant's. He was buying some vegetables." Bates's fork clattered on the plate as he stared at her, his mouth a gaping hole. "I called Lizette and told her he was there, but I don't know what, if anything, happened after that."

"Well, I'll be danged. He wants her to find him."

"That's the impression I got."

"Well, she'd better marry him," Bates said. "Next time he leaves, he'll stay away." He looked at his watch. "I'd better hurry. Jessie talked me into going to a club meeting tonight."

It was her time to stare. "*You?* At a Democratic Party club meeting?" She pushed back her chair, stood, and headed for the kitchen. "Right. And dinosaurs are skipping rope in Courthouse Square."

"I told him I'd go tonight. Come along if you don't believe me."

She set bowls of low-fat peach ice cream in front of them. "No thanks. Watching you at one of those meetings, I couldn't keep a straight face."

Immediately after Bates left, the telephone rang, but when caller ID displayed a number but not a name, she knew the caller was either at a pay phone or was calling on a cellular phone. She ignored the phone, cleaned the kitchen, and sat down to work on a report.

Was she crazy? Bates knew when he suggested she go that she wouldn't attend a political party meeting with him or anyone else. Her job required that she stay out of politics. She tossed the report on a chair and rubbed her forehead. "Just one more thing to drive me out of my mind." When he got home at quarter past one, he found her sitting in the living room staring at a televised likeness of Cary Grant.

"You still up?"

"I'm not used to being home by myself this time of night," she said, not bothering to hide the bitterness she felt or the animosity her voice projected.

He went to the kitchen and returned with a glass of ginger ale. "We stopped by that place Hutchins just opened up and sat around talking with some of the guys. Time just flew by."

She looked at the glass in his hand and got the feeling that the bottom had dropped out of her belly. "If you just left a bar, why did you need a soft drink?"

He put the glass on the table beside the sofa and sat forward with his elbows braced on his knees. "Are you suggesting that I'm lying?"

"I'm not suggesting anything. But you'll agree that you're acting out of character. You're not overly fond of Jessie, you don't have any respect for political parties, and you don't hang out with the guys. Don't you think you're behaving strangely?"

He got up, took his glass to the kitchen, and came back biting an apple. "Just because I've been glued to this house for twenty years doesn't mean it'll be that way for the rest of my life. You do a lot of things that don't include me. I'm entitled to the same."

"I know I have several activities, but all of them are related to my profession. I've worked hard to get ahead and I deserve the rewards."

"Have I said you didn't? No, and I won't stand in your way. But, baby, you can't have your cake and eat it, too." He bit off a piece of apple and took his time chewing it. Then he said, "If you think you can run all over the world and expect to find me waiting here with bated breath when you get back, forget it. I don't like an empty house any more than you do."

She flicked off the television, went upstairs, and got ready for bed. He didn't offer an apology, not that she expected one, for she had often wondered if he knew how to say he was sorry. Maybe he didn't think his behavior necessitated an apology. She crawled into bed and turned out the light.

After the previous weekend when she and Bates had frolicked—jovial, lighthearted, and on a sexual high—as if they were teenagers falling in love, like an aging lover given a shot of testosterone, how could they come to this so soon? The light came on, and she squeezed her eyes shut, hoping to give the impression that she was asleep.

"You've been a good wife, and as a mother for my children I couldn't have asked for more. But we're no longer your priority. I'm not asking you to choose, but you consider this." She heard him knock his right fist into his left palm. "You're not merely my wife, you're also my closest friend—in fact, my only friend. Unless I'm going to dry up here by myself, I need to make some friends. I should have done that long ago."

She didn't know what to say, but she knew that Bates had come to a decision about something and that he would leave her to guess what that was. She sat up in bed. "Are you saying that you're going your way and I'm going mine? Is that it?"

Bates sat down on the edge of the bed. "They say self-preservation is the first law of nature. You know that. Ten years from now you may be governor of Maryland, or the way you're going, president of the country. More power to you, Coreen, but I can't sit around twiddling my thumbs while you do it."

"You have the travel agency, and you can make it grow."

"Shit, woman. That thing's been growing for twenty-two years, and it's the same size it was when I started it." He threw up his hands. "It's like a mule, just gets slower and slower and more and more stubborn." He walked over to the window, pulled back the curtain, and stared out at the dark. "I'm not fooling myself. It's nothing! Not worth a damned thing!"

Of the many moods she had witnessed in Bates, from arrogance and anger to sweetness and affection, she had never seen him dejected. When his shoulders slumped and he recognized it, he braced his hands against the wall and gazed down at the floor.

She didn't know what to say, so she got out of bed, slipped behind him, and wrapped her arms around his waist. After a while she whispered, "I wish we could start all over again. If we don't do something about this, we're going to lose what we have, and I don't want that."

He whirled around and stared down in her face. "Don't you?"

Without giving her time to respond, he crushed her mouth with a bruising kiss, hugging and squeezing her body as if he wanted to devour her, inciting not passion but discomfort and wariness. The intensity of his ardor slowly ebbed, and he lifted her and carried her to bed. When she awoke the next morning, he had gone from the house, leaving the musky scent of sex as the only evidence of their shaky reconciliation.

He hadn't been an easy lover or an ardent one, but had seemed bent on taking everything she had to give, and she knew he withheld from her the extent of his need, for after twenty years, he couldn't fool her about that.

By the time she got to work that morning, she was leaning toward accepting Ann Springer's invitation for a televised interview. Nonetheless, a second call from Ann Springer caught her off guard, for they had agreed that Coreen would call Springer to indicate whether she accepted the invitation.

"Good morning, Ms. Treadwell. My colleagues at the station

here have shamed me for not treating you as we treat diplomats and celebrities, and I do apologize. If you agree to the interview, we'll send a limousine for you and reserve lodging in Sheraton's VIP suite. I *am* sorry for this unforgivable oversight."

Unused to having anyone make a fuss over her and stunned by the woman's deferential, almost obsequious manner, Coreen spoke without considering the consequences of her reply. "How kind of you. I don't require all that, but I appreciate the offer, and of course I shall be delighted to have an hourlong interview on your station. Let's wrap this up now. When will we tape?"

"The first showing will be live, and we'd like to do it next Sunday night. Of course, we'll rerun it here and on our sister stations throughout the month."

It wasn't until after she spoke with Ann Springer that Coreen remembered her original reticence to sit for the interview had nothing to do with her husband, but with the likelihood that the exposure would help the child she gave up for adoption to find her. She didn't have proof that anyone was looking for her, but enough evidence to make the idea so much a part of her that she accepted it as fact.

Around ten-thirty, she telephoned Bates. "Hi. You okay this morning?"

"Yeah. About as okay as I'm going to be anytime soon."

"I won't ask what that means. I was disappointed when I awoke and discovered you'd left. Will you be home for supper this evening?" She couldn't believe she had asked Bates that question, but for the first time in the twenty years of their marriage, she was unsure of him and his moves.

"Funny you should ask that. Yeah, I'll be there. Forgot to tell you Eric and Star will be here weekend after next. Star wants to see Mt. Airy Baptist Church. I guess she knew how happy it would make me if they married at my church, though she hasn't yet decided whether she wants to have her Christian wedding there or in College Park. They'll have a tribal wedding in Oklahoma sometime late in the autumn."

Somehow, she couldn't separate her future daughter-in-law from her sentiments about adoption; Star's presence confounded her. She forced a smile and said, "Great. Maybe I'll call Eric and suggest they bring some swimming togs, and we can picnic and swim on the beach late Saturday afternoon."

"You think it's still warm enough for that?"

She hoped that it would be, and she would be spared an evening of her sons' knowing looks, for Eric and Glen had always been able to sense the slightest problem in their parents' relationship. "Sure. It was eighty-two degrees today," she told him.

"Well, if the weather holds, we could do that. I know Eric will love it. Why don't you call Glen and tell him to come up?"

Later, as she dialed Glen's number, she marveled that their children behaved in adulthood as they had in early childhood; Eric related most easily to his father and Glen reached out to her. And now, there was Star who would follow Eric and lean toward Bates. An evening picnic was what she needed; no one would be able to discern her feelings or her attitude.

Sunday evening found her at WTUS in Raleigh, facing a sleek, perfectly dressed, and handsome man of about forty years old. His easy smile and jocular manner when they were introduced did not put her at ease, for she sensed that his goal would be the elevation of his status at the station and in the community rather than to draw from her such information as would inform his listeners about the work and responsibilities of a social agency.

If he isn't nice, she told herself, *I'll put him in his place.*

He chatted amiably with her until his producer counted from ten down and pointed his finger. "Ladies and gentlemen, good evening. I'm Reginal Cox and this is *Women in the News.* We have Coreen Treadwell with us, and we're going to see if she can justify being elected president of the most prestigious social organization in the world."

For a minute, she stared at him and didn't care if her annoyance showed. "Good evening everyone," she said. "Let me tell you I have no intention of doing that. I'm not on the witness stand. If I'm given a chance, I hope to tell you what I think is good and what is bad—"

He interrupted her. "And of all the women on this planet who are qualified for the job, why do you think you're the best person for it?"

"I've never said I thought that, and I'm not," she answered, "just as you are not necessarily the best person to conduct this interview. So let's start again and be nice," she said with a smile, "and be friends." To her amazement, the audience of about twenty people, mostly women, applauded.

He grinned. "That's what I like: spunk. Am I forgiven?" he asked in what she knew was an effort at face-saving.

The interview proceeded well after that until he said, "I see you're strong on family and the duties of parents to children. Do you have any children?"

She hadn't expected that question, but pasted a smile on her face and replied, "I have two wonderful stepsons."

"But you never considered having any of your own?"

"My sons fulfilled my need to experience motherhood. God never promised any of us the moon."

She let her tone of voice tell him and their audience that the subject was closed. He arched both eyebrows, as if he were aware that he had pushed her button, but confined the remainder of the interview to banalities.

The return trip from Raleigh to Bakerville in a stretch Lincoln Town Car amused her more than it comforted her. She described it to Bates that night.

"I enjoyed the filet mignon dinner and all that went with it, but I couldn't help wondering if they expected me to drink a whole bottle of champagne. I didn't even open the stuff."

Bates stopped zapping television channels. "You're telling me you left a bottle of champagne in that car for the driver to confiscate?"

Wasn't it like Bates to think of that? The incongruence in her husband's personality and behavior flashed through her mind. An upper- or upper-middle-class man wouldn't get out of that limousine carrying an unwrapped bottle of champagne.

She shrugged. "It didn't occur to me to take it."

He turned off the television, moved to the big brown wing chair, and sat so that he could face her. "Since you're so careful of your image, why didn't you prepare an answer in case that joker asked you why you never had a child of your own? This is the second time you got that question in an interview, and each time you looked as if you wanted to hide. What is so alarming about not having had birth pains? You looked as if you had committed a crime."

"I don't like personal questions in interviews; my personal life is my business."

"Don't hand me that. You told him your age and most of your likes and dislikes." He pulled air through his front teeth and looked toward the ceiling. "Damned if I'm not beginning to think you're hiding something. Either that or you wanted children of your own and didn't have the guts to tell me."

She gave silent thanks that he had redirected the conversation. "I had always thought I would have children of my own, but when we married, Glen filled that void, and I've been satisfied."

He continued to look at her. "A lot of people all over the country will see that interview, because the public TV stations share their programs. You'll be more in demand now than ever. Remember not to let your priorities get all screwed up. Nothing's changed."

She heard him, but she hadn't listened to his words and she was afraid to ask him to repeat what he said. Her stomach tightened. If that program aired all over the country, she could kiss her life as she knew it good-bye.

Chapter Twelve

As Glen promised, a man wearing a T-shirt advertising WBCC stood between two parked cars awaiting Frieda's arrival, and after she parked, he took her to Glen, who sat crosswise on the seat of someone's Harley-Davidson motorcycle. He rarely wore jeans and a leather jacket, but it suited him, and dressing down gave him a sense of freedom. He jumped off the bike and greeted her with a possessive hug. After whispering what he would like her to do, he took his seat on the bike and watched her.

Thoughts that he considered insane raced through his mind: *She's the same height, size, and color as Mom, and if I didn't know better, I'd think she was Mom fifteen or twenty years ago.* He rubbed his forehead and tried to concentrate on his work.

"Get that lady in the green jacket coming this way," he called to Frieda.

"How y'all doing this afternoon, ma'am?" she asked the older woman in a tone suggesting that she had known the woman for years. "I'm with WBCC and we want to ask you a few questions about what you think of things these days. Nothing personal. Would you step right over there, please?"

"Well, I'll be damned," he said to a crew member. "This gal has a way with people."

Each person Frieda stopped agreed to the interview. Fine, but it was getting late in the day and he still hadn't had a chance for a close look at Frieda's eyes in the sunlight. His mom's eyes were her most striking feature, large and dark brown with a greenish cast. On an impulse, he told the reporter to interview Frieda.

"Would you mind removing your glasses?" he asked her, hoping to determine whether they were prescription glasses. "They're reflecting the sunlight." He held out his hand for them, but the ploy fizzled when she put them in her purse. He studied her eyes, face, and facial mannerisms as she talked, unaware that he scrutinized her.

"We working people have a hard time," she said in answer to a question, "but I don't complain long as I can make an honest livin' and pay my bills. I don't owe anybody a red cent."

"Did you grow up here? Where is your home?" the reporter asked.

"I grew up in Rocky Point, but you couldn't call that place home. It was my personal hell—hell like you never experienced, mister—and I ran away from it in the middle of the night when I was seventeen and took care of myself to this day by doing honest work. Ain't no need for people to steal and cheat to make a living."

"Thank you, Ms. Davis, for sharing with us," the reporter said and expelled a long breath, evidently glad to escape what seemed to be the beginning of a confessional.

Frieda couldn't know that her words to the reporter gave Glen his first insight into her as a person with needs and feelings. Until then, he had seen her only as a sex object, a vessel for the release of his desire.

Except for those eyes, he said to himself, *she is the spitting image of Mom. Her voice even has that same husky quality as Mom's. What a coincidence!*

"How'd I do?" she asked him.

When he looked down at her face, so full of expectancy and a need for approval, a tugging at his heart set him aback, shaking him. He forced a grin. "Trust me, you don't have a problem expressing yourself. I expect the producer will air your interview first of the five we put on tonight. You were great."

Seeing the brilliance of her smile, he thought of his reasons for asking her to come out to the park, and shame washed over him, pulling at his conscience the way an ocean wave washes ashore and drags the sand into its clutches.

"You know ... you look a lot like somebody ... er ... I know," he said, and wanted to kick himself for the slip.

"Really? I guess I got one of those faces you see everywhere."

It didn't occur to him until much later that she didn't ask him who was the person she resembled. Maybe that wasn't significant. He let it pass.

A candid interviewee always guaranteed an interesting show, but Frieda's words gnawed at him until he admitted to himself remorse for his merciless and heartless treatment of her. He couldn't understand why she cared at all for him.

Singed with guilt, he took her arm. "The crew's going to stop a couple of blocks from here for drinks. You want to come along?"

She let a few moments pass before shaking her head. "I promised myself I was going to make you stick to your word. I'd love to know what these kind of people talk about, but I'm going home."

"I'll walk you to your car," he said, hating the sound of contrition that colored his voice. "We'll be in touch."

Pain seemed to move across her face like a dark cloud racing over the moon. "Yes. Sure."

"You don't have to put on the dog for Star," Bates told Coreen as she studied recipes for the weekend meals. "She's one of the family."

"Not yet, she isn't," Coreen said without thinking. She would have retracted the words had it been possible, for she knew Bates would accuse her of not liking Eric's bride-to-be. She didn't have to wait for his ire.

"If you don't like her, why don't you just . . . just take a trip to Brussels or somewhere for the weekend. I'm not going to have any unpleasantness. I like her, and I can't wait till she's my daughter. She's young and beautiful as well as talented. If you're jealous, there's no reason for it; besides, that's stupid."

Coreen supposed the shock she felt mirrored itself on her

face. She closed her mouth. "Let's try not to hurt each other, Bates. The Tower of Babel crumbled in an earthquake; compared to that structure, a marriage is a featherweight. If I were you, I'd treat it with a little more care."

"That sounds like a threat."

She thought Bates, at fifty-two years of age, had passed the time of male middle-age angst. Reflecting the confusion she felt, Coreen shook her head from side to side. "Not nearly as much of one as you handed me a couple of weeks ago when you announced I could no longer expect you to be home every night. Believe me, that would have blasted any woman's sense of security."

He got up from the kitchen table where they lingered after dinner and poured a cup of coffee for himself. "Yeah. I guess you're right. This marriage is getting to be like lumpy gravy. Funny thing is, I can't figure out when it started."

"Maybe if we helped each other, did more things together," she said, grabbing at straws.

With the coffee cup suspended midway between the saucer and his gaping mouth, he said, "Don't make jokes. You can answer the phone in my shop, but what the hell can I do in a child welfare agency? Relieve Oscar while he goes to the privy?"

"There are other ways, and you do help me, Bates. Your being here is a tonic that I need."

"Yeah. Like I was a royal consort. You don't need me for a thing. Let's finish straightening up here. I want to watch the hockey game."

Coreen continued to scan the recipe books, though she saw nothing on the pages she turned. She had decided what she would cook, but she didn't feel like interacting with Bates on the superficial level that had become their mental meeting place.

With her elbows on the table and her fists supporting her jaw, she catalogued their problems: their lovemaking no longer held any truth; their disagreements always ended in a standoff; and the patches with which they attempted to mend their torn lives proved as useful as wallpaper in an abandoned outhouse. Nonetheless, she got up, walked over to him, and draped an arm across his shoulder.

"We don't ever solve anything. I just realized that we have

years of misunderstandings and disagreements stacked in our mental closets. Can't we try to . . . to clear up all these things?"

He closed the dishwasher and started the wash. "This may surprise you, Coreen, but I'll bet it's one big thing that sprouts problem after problem. Ever noticed how the branches of a tree keep multiplying on the trunk? Whatever it is causes more and more problems. Check your closet"—he pointed to her head— "and I'll check mine." Before she could respond, he strode out of the kitchen and bounded up the stairs.

Friday morning, Coreen gave silent thanks that she and Bates wouldn't be alone that weekend. She told herself that she knew why their marriage was so troubled: her attention to her job, her rising professional status, and the likelihood that she would go even higher apparently made Bates think of himself as a failure. And especially since he merely marked time in his own work. But in the back of her mind loomed the knowledge that she should attribute the change in their relationship to the way she handled her fear that Bates, her colleagues, and the media would discover she had had a child and given it up for adoption.

"Quit running and turn yourself in" was, in effect, what the analyst had counseled, and she hadn't had the courage to seek advice in the United States where any slip could ruin her. "I'm not going to be my own executioner," she vowed that afternoon as she set the dining room table for five.

Later, she stood at the door and watched Bates greet Eric and Star with hugs and warm smiles as they got out of Eric's car. When Eric looked up and saw her, she went to greet him.

"Glen didn't get here yet?" he asked after they greeted each other.

"No, but I expect him soon. Let me go and greet Star." She walked down the hedge-lined gravel path, and Star rushed to meet her.

"You're more beautiful than I remembered," she told the younger woman. "We're so glad you'll be here for a few days."

She glanced up to see an expression of disbelief on Bates's face, but ignored it, put an arm around Star's waist, and went inside. Glen arrived alone around seven o'clock and they sat down to dinner.

"Look at this, will ya, Mom?" Glen said, and passed the picture to her. "Isn't that the eeriest thing you ever saw? If I didn't know better, I'd think it was you twenty years ago."

Her flesh began to crawl over her bones, and what felt like magnets danced along her nerves, sending electric sparks as they moved. She told herself not to squeeze her eyes shut and pasted a smile on her face as she reached for the photo.

"Looks like *me*? People are always telling me I look familiar, but I didn't know I had a double. Let me see." She made herself look at the picture, widening her eyes as she did so. "Well, I'll be doggoned. Who *is* this imposter?"

"A friend of Glen's. A pretty close one at that," Eric said.

"Don't stretch it, Eric," Glen said. "I wouldn't call her close. I think of Star as being close to you, and nothing like that is happening here."

Glen passed the photo to Star, who soothed the situation for Coreen. "There's a strong resemblance, but not enough to suggest she's a double. Ever see that TV show about look-alikes? One American woman was a dead ringer for actress Vivien Leigh and another one could have passed for Princess Di." Star looked at Coreen. "I imagine it's unsettling to know someone looks this much like you."

"It is," she said, drawing a deep breath, "but there isn't a thing I can do about it."

She had to get out of there before she screamed. "I'll be back in a minute," she said. "Dessert coming up."

Coreen went into the kitchen, allowed the door to close behind her, and leaned against the sink, hyperventilating. However, fearing that Bates might walk in, she gulped a glass of water, took the peach pies from the warming oven, and began to slice them.

"Let me help you with that."

Coreen nearly burst from her skin at the sound of Star's voice. "Where are the pie plates?" She looked directly at her future mother-in-law, and Coreen knew she judged properly that the expression on Star's face, with its faint smile, was one of sympathy. A less discerning person than Coreen would have missed

Star's wavering gesture, as the hand that reached toward her fell back to Star's side.

Coreen pointed to a cupboard and marveled at the harmony in which they worked. "Do you like to cook?" she asked Star, feeling for the first time a kinship with Eric's fiancée.

Star held her head back and let her shining black hair swing away from her face. "Not even water. However, I do know how, and I cook when I have to." She took four plates of pie and headed for the dining room.

Hmmm, so she waited tables at one time, Coreen concluded when she observed the ease with which Star lifted and carried two plates in each hand. Must have worked her way through school. Not a bad recommendation.

When Coreen took her seat at the table, the conversation no longer centered on Frieda Davis's likeness to her, but on Star's choice of a venue for her wedding.

"I haven't been in a lot of churches," she said, "but I do know they are a great place to show off a fine wedding dress."

A frown crossed Bates's face. "They're also the place to ask the Lord to bless your relationship with your new husband, Star. You can get married according to your own custom, but you have to get the Lord on your side, too."

"Oh, I will," Star said. "We worship the Lord; we just call him the Great Spirit."

After dinner, Eric and Star went to see a movie, and Glen and Bates played Scrabble. Coreen folded herself in a living room chair and pretended to sleep, but in fact, she was ruminating about her resemblance to the woman in the photograph. Her mind told her that she had at last seen what her own child looked like, and that the woman sought out Glen in order to get more information about her. When she could barely hold back the sobs, she crept slowly up the stairs, brushed her teeth, and crawled into bed.

My goodness, she said to herself, *I made a real blunder when I didn't ask Glen any questions about that woman. Eric and Bates are probably already tossing that around in their heads, ready to blow it up into a cause célèbre.*

Suddenly, she sat up. If the woman was her child and if she had located her birth mother, wouldn't she have asked Glen whether he knew Coreen Treadwell? *I may be getting paranoid for no reason,* Coreen surmised. However, her mind told her the ax would fall, and soon.

The scheme in which Frieda had so prided herself had begun to lose its glitter, and along with that its usefulness. *I'll have to wean myself away from Glen,* she admitted as she worried increasingly about him and the way he treated her. *And I will, even if I have to go to prayer meeting and confess what I've been doing. I hate myself for the way I let him use me.*

Myriad thoughts rushed through her mind. If she broke up with Glen, she would lose the opportunity to greet Coreen Treadwell while holding the hand of her beloved son. But she would find other ways to make her pay. She had dreamed at night and daydreamed in the daytime about the treatment she would mete out to her birth mother. And the more she learned of Coreen's spiraling professional career, the more determined was she to inflict what she considered a fitting reprisal. Her resolve had never been stronger.

As she dressed before daybreak that October morning for the drive to Rocky Mount, North Carolina, to see her sisters, she switched off the telephone so that Glen couldn't call her. She didn't trust herself not to drop her plans and run to meet him or go to his apartment, whatever he asked.

She reached Portia's house shortly after ten, parked in front of the gray Cape Cod structure, and walked up the winding, gray stone walk that led to the front steps. The house sat well back from the street, and weeping willows adorned its sides. She liked it at once and quickened her steps, sniffing as she did so the scent of autumn leaves smoldering somewhere nearby.

The door opened, and Portia and Julie rushed out to greet her. "Good Lord," Portia exclaimed. "Girl, what have you done to yourself? You're a regular movie queen."

Julie stepped back and looked at her. "I always knew you'd be beautiful if you just paid a little bit of attention to yourself." Julie's arms went around her and tightened. "You look wonderful."

The three sisters walked arm in arm into the house. "Now

this is what I call a classy place," Frieda said in a voice tinged with admiration. "Portia, honey, you didn't get this with one of those nine hundred telephone numbers, did you?"

The three of them enjoyed hearty laughter, for it was a joke among them that Portia abstained with such assiduousness that the lock on her vaginal portal was second in security only to the gold in Fort Knox.

"You've found a man," Portia said.

Frieda sat down on the living room sofa and kicked off her shoes. "You could say that. But it's going nowhere. It didn't stand a chance from the start, and soon as I can get the guts, I'm gonna break it off." She crossed her left knee over her right one, leaned back, and smiled, as if savoring a notion she'd been nurturing for a long time. "You have to watch a sweet man; after he gets what he wants, he can turn on you like a pit bull. But you know and I know that if anybody does me wrong, they'll hear from me. The mailman may be slow, but he always gets there."

"Be careful," Julie said. "You know my views on vengeance. You must like him a lot if it's hard to break with him."

"I don't know if like's the word. Sometimes I dislike him, but I can't get him out of my system. He taught me what it means to be a female."

She saw Julie and Portia exchange glances and explained, "When a man does that for you, you'll be forever in his debt, no matter how you feel about him. What are you two doing these days?"

They talked well into the afternoon, bringing each other up to date on their lives. They ate hamburgers and apple pie for lunch and around four o'clock, Julie drove them to the cemetery to visit their mother's grave.

"Don't expect me to even glance at Papa's grave," Frieda told them.

"You needn't worry about that," Julie said.

They left the cemetery and drove through the city to Thelonious Monk Park on South Washington Street to watch a parade honoring the "going home" of an old man who, for the previous fifty years, had played a twelve-string blues guitar at the entrance of the old market place.

Frieda could barely control the churning inside of her, the

feeling—like a bulb bursting into bloom—that she had con-
quered herself, that she could shake Glen's hold on her. And she
would give him good reason to regret his maltreatment of her.
Plenty of it.

"You've definitely had a change of mood or something since
you got here yesterday," Portia said as they stood beside Frieda's
car, telling her good-bye.

"I made up my mind about something."

"You're going to break up with that guy?" Julie asked.

Frieda nodded. "Yessiree, and in a big way."

"If you do something you can't be proud of," Portia warned,
"you'll regret it."

To Frieda's way of thinking, that depended on how you
viewed the situation. She had been farther down than she would
ever allow herself to go again. As if she had swum from muddy
water into a clear blue sea, she felt cleansed. She had needed the
company of her sisters to remind her of what she had been
through and of her resolve never to let another man use her.
Heading for Baltimore, Frieda was happier than she had been in
weeks.

She took her time answering the telephone when it rang almost as soon as she got home. If Glen was calling. she would
plead exhaustion after the long drive and deal with him another
time. However, when she answered it was Thelma's voice she
heard.

"The pastor asked about you," Thelma said. "Twice recently,
you skipped service. You finished knitting those caps and mit-
tens?"

"Long ago. I'm working on some matching scarves. Of course,
if we don't have enough caps to go around, we can give the
scarves separately. I picked up some plays for young people—
Old Testament stories somebody dramatized. The teens will love
that."

"That's good, 'cause they get bored quicker than they can
count to a hundred. You coming to church next Sunday?"

"Sure. I was out of town today. Just got back."

"Well, you never mind about the pastor's griping; you're a
good person, and everybody knows it."

Once, she had thought of herself as a woman who always

tried to do what was right, but from the time she began to search for her birth mother, she hadn't been a good person. She vowed to herself that as soon as she confronted Coreen Treadwell and gave the woman a piece of her mind, she would seek forgiveness and be her old self once more.

Events the following day, Monday, bestowed upon Coreen the fulfillment of her dream, and by coincidence brought Frieda closer to her goal.

Coreen stood at the stove stirring chicken soup with her nose turned up at the smell of grease that had dripped from the muffin tin and was burning on the bottom of the hot oven. Exasperated at the odor and the fumes that escaped the oven, she left the stove and raised the kitchen window as high as it would go. They needed a brand-new, modern kitchen, but she didn't dare mention that, not with the slowdown at Bates's shop.

"That person who calls here, says nothing, and hangs up is at it again," Bates said. "He blocked his number again, so I'm going to ask the phone company to trace every call that comes in here."

The phone rang again, and he rushed back to answer it. She didn't doubt that he'd give the prankster an earful.

"It's for you," he said. "A woman with an accent. Said her name's Kuti."

Coreen dashed past him, nearly slipping on the highly polished parquet floor. "This is Coreen," she said. "How are you, Nana?"

"Great. We won, Coreen. Hands down. You received seventy-three percent of the vote. You're our president for the next four years."

Coreen stared at the receiver and at Bates, who stood nearby. "You mean I won?" she asked. "Well, I . . . I . . . that's really something."

"When can you meet with the board? All of our meetings are in Brussels, usually once a month, but we try to accommodate our presiding officer."

She tried to focus on the woman's words, but they seemed surreal, like a genie with three wishes to give in a fantasy movie, magically offering the impossible one minute, and in the next nowhere to be seen.

"It'll take me a little while to digest this, Nana. Is it all right if I call you tomorrow?"

"Of course. You're the boss now, and we take our cue from you."

Coreen didn't believe the board gave the president that much power. "Thanks for being so considerate," she said. "I'll phone you at about four o'clock your time." She hung up and stood catatonic-like, staring into space, unable to believe that she'd made it. Coreen Treadwell was the top of the heap.

"When are you leaving?"

She swung around, almost surprised to see Bates standing there. "In about two weeks, I guess. I . . . I can't believe it. Did you hear what she said? *I won.* I'm president of the International Society of Social and Welfare Agencies."

"Congratulations. You worked hard and you got what you wanted. Hats off to you."

He smiled when he said it, but everything else about him said he didn't rejoice with her. That he'd fallen another step behind.

Unable to concentrate on the meal she was preparing, Coreen over-seasoned the pork chops and burned them while she daydreamed.

"You'd better let me do this," Bates said, "otherwise we won't have anything fit to eat for dinner."

He cooked the food and put it on the table. "Are you aware," he asked her, "that you haven't said one word since we sat down to eat?"

She shook herself out of the trance, stopped eating, and looked at her husband. "I've been thinking that I finally have the recognition I worked so hard for, but it's going to cost me dearly, starting right here at home."

Bates didn't stop eating, nor did he take his gaze from his food. "You could've said no thanks. You still can. But I guess you're willing to pay the price."

He concentrated then on finishing his meal, in effect terminating the discussion. After dinner, he put the dishes in the dishwasher, washed the pots and pans, and cleaned the kitchen, whistling "Amazing Grace" as he did so.

He's too happy or he's pretending, she thought, and waited for the ax to fall, as it did when he put on a jacket and called to her, "I'm going out."

A gust of wind and the click of the front door lock were her confirmation that he had gone without telling her where he headed or when she could expect him home. Loneliness enveloped her, and for the first time in her life, she wished for a sister, a girlfriend, a buddy who knew everything about her and didn't judge her. Someone with whom she could share all of her fears and longings. Coreen knew that that role belonged to her husband, but he didn't and couldn't fulfill it, because she had never confided in him. He didn't know her, her roots, her life. If only she could expect from him understanding and compassion, but she didn't because he found imperfections in every person he judged. And he judged most of the people he met.

I'll just have to tough it out for now, she told herself. *He'll come around when his libido starts to throttle him. Then he'll be willing to take a good look at our future.*

Bates didn't have any place special to go when he left home. He'd gotten out of there so that he wouldn't grovel at Coreen's feet. He had wanted to beg her not to take on the responsibility of leading the world's most important social agency. She deserved the status and a chance to enjoy the returns from her hard work. But what about him? He hadn't sold a ticket in the last three days, and his telephone didn't ring a dozen times that day.

He was taught that a man should provide for his wife and children, should take care of them. He figured he did his best for his sons, and both of them made a living and didn't ask their parents for help.

He ambled along Queen Street, deep in thought. If he passed anyone, he didn't know it. The breeze picked up, blowing sticks around his feet and bringing the scent of salty ocean air to his nostrils. He focused on his shadow, long and slender, marching ahead of him, a phantom in the moonlit night.

He tried to remember when Coreen sped past him, leaving him to trail along in the wake of the windblown dust of her climb to fame. He went into Bakerville Drugs and Notions to use the pay phone. As a business man, he ought to have a cell phone, but he'd as soon spend the forty dollars a month on something else. When Jessie answered the phone, he relaxed against the wall beside it.

"Hi, Jessie. This is Bates. I'm out for a walk. Feel like coming along for a beer or something? I thought I'd stop at the Inn," a place where he thought a Christian man could go without indicting himself. "A cup of coffee is about all I want."

"Say, man." He knew from the tone of his friend's greeting that he didn't plan to leave home. Jessie confirmed that when he said, "I'd love to, but I'll have to make it another time. Lorna's got some plans, and you know how that is, man."

He did, indeed. He crossed Courthouse Square to the public library and didn't think he'd ever been so happy to see a lighted building. He went in, grateful that he didn't have to walk the streets in order to kill time. Inside, he got a book on the Galapagos Islands and pretended to read.

He had made Coreen unhappy, probably suspicious, as well, and he wasn't proud of himself. After frittering away twenty minutes of his life, he went home.

"I didn't expect you back so soon," Coreen said when he walked in. For some reason, it didn't surprise him that she remained as she was when he left home, for his behavior even troubled him.

"I just went to take in a little fresh air," he said, knowing that if he had found a pleasant way to while away some time, he would still be out. "Did you call that woman back yet?"

"I'll . . . uh . . . I'll call her Monday. It's well after midnight over there." She stood as if to move in his direction. "You . . . uh . . . turning in now?"

Intimacy was the last thing he wanted, and he couldn't think of a single pose she could strike—and she had many of them—that would induce him to have an erection.

"You go ahead," he said. "I think I'll sort through those travel catalogues I put downstairs. I'll be up later."

She nodded and spoke with halting speech and evident reluctance. "Well . . . all right. Good night."

Coreen awakened the next morning, Saturday, to hear the ringing of the telephone beside the bed. The only evidence that Bates had slept there was the crumpled pillow and sheets. He had managed to sleep without touching her.

"Good morning," she said, and cleared her throat. "Treadwell residence."

"Girl, did I wake you up?"

She recognized Lizette's voice. "Doesn't matter. Why?"

"Honey, I need to talk to somebody and I have to be at the shop."

Coreen swung her feet over the side of the bed and allowed herself an expansive yawn. "All right. I'll be over there in an hour. Make some coffee."

"Thanks. You will be blessed."

Funny how some people could become so righteous as soon as they had problems. She parked in her agency's parking lot and walked down Rust Street to Lizette's beauty shop.

"Got your coffee right here," Lizette said when Coreen walked in to a chorus of greetings from Lizette's customers.

"Hi, Miss Treadwell," they said in unison.

"Hi all," she answered, stopped, and looked around. She didn't know any of the women who greeted her.

"Come on back here," Lizette said, leading Coreen to her private sanctuary in the rear of the shop. "They're all under the dryer except Miss Horn, and she's waiting for her coloring to take."

"Did you get to the supermarket before Porgy left?" Coreen asked Lizette.

"I got there fast as I could, but I didn't see hide nor hair of him. I finally heard from him, though."

Coreen sat forward and gulped down the coffee she sipped, nearly burning her mouth. "He called you?"

"No. That would be too normal a thing to do. He wrote me a letter and mailed it or had it mailed in Elizabeth City."

"You don't seem happy. What did he say?"

"He wants me to drive over to Elizabeth City tonight after I get off from work and meet him at a hotel. Can you beat that?"

"So what's the problem? Don't tell me that after practically dying of grief over Porgy for the past six months, you're going to put your behind on your shoulders and act like you don't care."

"I didn't say anything like that. But why doesn't he come home?"

"Maybe he wants the two of you to meet on neutral ground. If you act nonchalant about this, Lizette, Porgy may give you the lesson of a lifetime."

"I don't feel nonchalant, it's just that—"

"You're hardheaded. The longer a man stays away from you, the easier it is for him to do it. It's like giving up smoking; each day you don't smoke, the less your craving for nicotine."

"I sure know what that means; it took me almost two years to get over the feeling that I just had to smoke. Porgy didn't say nothing in that letter about loving me; just said he wanted us to talk and see if we had anything going."

"You close the shop today at six. By nine-thirty, you should be in Elizabeth City, allowing for an hour and a half at home to get your negligeé and perfume."

"You'd go, no questions asked?"

Coreen thought of her problems with Bates, leaned back, and closed her eyes so that Lizette couldn't read her thoughts. "In your place, I would close this shop early, go home, soak in a bubble bath, doll up, pack my lures, and head for that hotel."

"Maybe I'll do that. Can you come back around five and give me a little moral support?"

The word "yes" lay on the tip of Coreen's tongue, but she remembered that when she walked into the shop, six strange women had greeted her as if they knew her personally. Her belly began to churn, and she swallowed several times. Fearing the onset of nausea, she asked Lizette for cold water.

"I'm fine, but work's been too exciting lately, so I'd better rest this afternoon. Be smart and tell Porgy you want him to come home, and if he asks you to marry him, say yes."

"I don't know what I'd do without you, Coreen. Thanks for being there for me."

"Don't thank me. Just act smart."

As she drove home, she couldn't stop thinking that, in her hometown, she had become a public person, one whom strangers easily recognized. Soon, she would have international status and the recognition that went with it. If anyone wanted to find her, she was about to simplify their task, for she couldn't refuse the chance to wear the crown.

How could life be so unfair? Accept the opportunity of a lifetime, and as a consequence probably lose her husband, her family and friends, and all she had worked for. If she were to turn it down—and she had no intention of doing that—Bates would torment her with his suspicions until she confessed everything. She parked at the corner of Queen Street and Rhimes Court and gave herself a good talking-to. The idea that somebody wanted to find her had no basis, and she was going to stop being paranoid about it.

After a few minutes, she put the car into gear and headed home. "If I fall," she said aloud with vehemence hardening her voice, "I'm going to fall from a great height." And as if the thought cheered her, she accelerated the vehicle and sped home in record time, arriving almost simultaneously with Bates.

"Hi. You're home early. It's only one o'clock."

He shrugged. "No point in using up heat and electricity for nothing. Nobody came in, so I closed."

She clamped her mouth shut or she would have gaped at him. He was telling her that on Saturday, his busiest day, he hadn't had a single customer from eight-thirty until one o'clock. "Thank goodness for answering machines," she said, hoping he had at least had callers that morning.

"All I did for four and a half hours was work the crossword puzzle and read travel magazines. I didn't even have to answer the telephone."

Coreen took his hand in her left one, and with her right one, used her key to unlock the front door. She didn't let him see her reaction to his permitting her to open the door and hold it for him, for she had thought him seriously ill before his demeanor told her that he was merely preoccupied.

"Maybe it's the changing seasons," she said, hoping to raise his spirits.

He shook his head. "No, it isn't. My shop is redundant. The people can get my services on the Internet with a discount. I can't match that."

As much as she sympathized with him, she couldn't let him fool himself. "Honey, most of your customers are retirees, and the older ones probably haven't even learned how to operate a computer. I think we need to mount a publicity campaign, do some real promotional work."

He released her hand, braced his waist with his knuckles, and stared at Coreen. "*We?* Do you mean you have found a way to help?"

She bit her tongue and squashed her annoyance. "Yes, we." She looked at her watch. "We've got plenty of time. Let's go to the office supply store and get some glossy photocopy paper and a couple of reams of paper for flyers."

To her amazement, he agreed, and they spent the remainder of the afternoon designing and printing a flyer that advertised vacation specials at good rates.

"If that doesn't help, I may have to close," he said when they finished.

"Never" was as much as she could manage, for she hadn't guessed his situation and wouldn't have imagined it if he hadn't worn the look of a defeated man. "Let's go for a drive," she said, hoping to enliven both their spirits.

"We could stop by the Octoberfest if you like."

She jumped at the chance to go someplace with him other than a restaurant. "Great. Let's wash up and go. It's been ages since I had hot dogs and beer." She ignored his raised eyebrow, for she knew he regarded beer drinking as low-class and de-grading. "Don't worry," she said, needling him, "I wouldn't dare drink it straight from the bottle."

They sat on a bench in the big tent, watching three men juggle with colorful bottles. "You know," she said as if amazed, "I'm enjoying these hot dogs and this pilsner beer as much as, if not more than, filet mignon and fine red wine. What are you looking at?"

"Do you know that man who's sitting on the edge of that wooden table over there?"

She followed his gaze. "Never saw him before. Why?"

"Let's go before I punch him out. No man's going to gaze at my wife like that when I'm two inches from her."

"But, Bates, we just got here, and I'm—"

"I don't care. We're leaving. This is why I don't go to these places—too many ill-bred people."

"As soon as I finish my beer," she said, defiant and not caring about his reaction to it. *If he's this insecure,* she thought, *how will he behave when he sees what I have to do as president of ISSWA. Or if you are exposed,* her niggling conscience prodded.

He grabbed her seconds after he locked the front door and pinned her to him. "I don't want any man looking at you that way, undressing you with his eyes."

"I didn't even see him," she said, her body warming to the sure signs of his rising passion.

"I wanted to smash him," he murmured, and brushed her lips with his own. When she opened her mouth for his entrance, he stepped back and looked at her, searching for evidence of desire. She knew he would find what he sought when her breathing shortened and she began to rub her hands up and down her sides. He released an expletive, rare for him, picked her up, and carried her to bed. When she awakened hours later, he sat on the edge of their bed with a tray of potato salad, smoked tongue with mustard sauce, and deviled eggs.

"We left before you had time to finish eating, so I cooked." He opened a bottle of beer, poured a glassful, and handed it to her, a concession, she knew, since he disapproved of beer drinking.

"Sometime I think we'll never make it," he said, "and then on days like today, I don't see how we can fail."

But she did, for like the ocean tide slashing its way to shore, she seemed headed for a day of reckoning.

Chapter Thirteen

Frieda left Wednesday night prayer meeting, the first she had attended in several months, and walked out into the crisp October night. She had just taken her first step toward ridding her body of its passion for Glen Treadwell. She hadn't confessed, because she considered most of her fellow parishioners petty gossipers and as much a sinner as she. Still, she had said her prayers and expected forgiveness. Mt. Zion AME Church was home to those who worshipped there, and Pastor Hall was the earthly man to whom they looked for guidance. He always said you were forgiven if you asked.

As she got into her car, Frieda couldn't help wondering how Pastor Hall could be so perfect, and especially with so many of the single sisters grinning at him all the time. She wished she could ask him how to wean herself from Glen, but she didn't dare, fearing that she might lower herself in Pastor Hall's esteem. She found a spot in front of her building, got out, and kicked aside the black plastic garbage bags blocking her way. As she parked, a new plan formed in her head: She didn't need Glen in order to humiliate Coreen Treadwell; in her mind's eye, she envisaged other equally effective, less costly ways.

Armed with her new resolve, she telephoned Glen as soon as she walked into her apartment. It was time to end it.

"Hi, babe," he said in a voice suggestive of one lying down and half asleep. "I called you three times. Where were you? Woman, I'm dying over here."

"I . . . uh, just got in from church."

"Church? Today's Wednesday. Grab your toothbrush and get over here before I burst. I'm hard as a rock."

She swallowed hard. "Uh . . . that's what I called you about. I'm not seeing you again. Okay?"

His voice lost its sexy come-on and reached her strong, even imperious. "Hell no, it's not okay. Forget that foolishness. I'm in your blood, and you may as well accept it. We'll break up *when I say so.*"

"I told you. That's over. I'm not going to your place again, and you're not coming here."

"The hell you say. Just wait till you start thinking about the way I make you howl. How good it is when I'm inside you, rocking you and driving you out of your senses. Remember how you clawed and—?"

"No, I don't. I wiped you out of my mind."

"I don't believe that and neither do you. Just listen to you. If I went over there right now, I'd be inside you in ten minutes, and you know it."

Unable to think of an alternative, she hung up and knew at once that she had done the wrong thing. That he would pursue her as he did when they first met, seduce her, and then drop her like a load of cement. She called him back.

"I apologize for hanging up on you, Glen, but you—"

"Yeah. It got too hot for you, didn't it? You coming over here or not?"

"I'm going to bed, and if anybody knocks on my door tonight, I'm calling the cops." Even as she said the words, liquid accumulated in her mouth, she crossed her knees, and the nerve endings in her vagina began to torture her for the friction that would bring relief.

She imagined that his eyes narrowed as they did when something displeased him. "When I see you next, and I will see you, I'm going to make you burn if it takes me all night. You write that down."

She barely recognized the uncertainty and lack of conviction in his voice and responded to the man she knew as being overbearing. "It's time you took a good look at yourself, Glen."

"What? So now you're into psychoanalysis."

Weary and caught in a libidinous snare of her own making, she stood up and spoke firmly. "Nice knowing you, Glen. 'Bye." She hung up and turned off her telephone. The following day, she went out on her lunch hour and took the first steps toward implementing Plan B.

That weekend, Coreen flew to Brussels for her inauguration as president of ISSWA and to receive her credentials from the board. "We've arranged for television interviews on BBC in London and the three major broadcast networks and CNN in the United States. We're also sending your photo and bio to international news services and major newspapers worldwide," the board chairman told her, obviously pleased with that accomplishment.

Coreen pressed her teeth together and spread her lips in what she hoped was a smile, or at the least a grin, and clasped her shaking hands behind her.

"I thank you for the effort you're making to ensure the success of my t-tenure," she said, stuttering for the first time since the afternoon on which Leon Farrell invaded her body against her will. "Th-this is overwhelming," she managed to say and sank into the nearest chair. "I'm humbled."

Although she feared the board members would discern her anxiety, she managed to smile and communicate a feeling of satisfaction with the board's plans. She was grateful that the nine trusted members of the ISSWA inner circle couldn't see the tears that drenched her insides or taste the brine they left on her nerve endings. She took a deep breath and stood, like Marie Antoinette, a queen awaiting the guillotine.

"Thank you for your confidence. I promise to do my best."

In the afternoon, instead of going to bed in order to avoid jet lag, she telephoned the psychoanalyst and went to see him.

"There's no point in another prolonged session in which you try to remember everything that ever happened to you," he said. "You're using me for a confessor, and I don't have the power to forgive you." He rang for his assistant. "Give my client a glass of water, please."

He then said what she most dreaded hearing. "Until you go back to Pick-Up, North Carolina, you're going to be half a person riddled with guilt and fear. And you can save yourself a lot of pain if you accept your husband for what he is, and if you tell him what you've told me. Those are my last words on the subject. Visit a hundred analysts and every competent one will tell you the same thing."

She left him, more disheartened that ever. Flying back to the States the next morning, she tried to imagine Bates's reaction if he knew she had borne a child and given it up for adoption. In her mind's eye, she could see him walking away from her. But when she got home, he greeted her at the front door and carried her bag and briefcase up to their bedroom. She told herself that she had worried for no reason, that whatever happened, he would stick with her. She wanted badly to believe that.

"Your mail's in there on the desk," Bates said. "I'll get some supper together."

She stared at the small box, not more than five inches square, and finally forced herself to look for the return address. Who would send her a package to her home? She couldn't read the name, and could barely make out the remainder of the address, though she had no trouble reading the Owings Mills, Maryland, postmark. She opened the box with a sense of dread, and her lower lip dropped when her gaze captured the contents, a small black edition of the New Testament. She picked it up, opened it to the page marked with a paper clip, and began to read the words underlined in green ink—Galatians 6:7, "Be not deceived; God is not mocked: for whatsoever a man soweth, that shall he also reap."

Stunned, Coreen threw the little book across the bed, sat down, and buried her face in her hands. She rocked in grief, but no tears dampened her eyes. The sound of Bates's footsteps on the stairs startled her, and she rushed to retrieve the little Bible, planning the explanation she would give him.

"Someone sent me this New Testament," she said with her face wreathed in smiles as he walked in. "I can't make out the name and address, can you?"

He shook his head. "Next thing you know, some of your fans will send you a cow. Well, as long as it isn't something you have to pay income tax on."

"Tell me about it." His jovial mood buoyed her spirits, and when he slung an arm around her waist and walked down the stairs to the kitchen with her, she thought her heart would burst with joy. He really cared for her, in spite of his sometimes difficult ways, and if she was lucky, maybe he would stand with her through whatever she had to face.

As they ate the supper of fried catfish, corn muffins, and string beans, he questioned her about her inauguration, how frequently she would fly to Brussels, and what her work would entail. She told him that her election to the presidency would receive international news coverage.

"Yeah? Your face will be as familiar to people as U.N. Secretary-General Kofi Annan's. I wouldn't be surprised if he invited you to dinner with him and that nice Swedish wife of his."

Coreen stopped eating, for her stomach had begun to churn and cramp. She sprang from the table and ran to the bathroom. Half an hour later, lying across the bed while Bates put cold, wet towels to her forehead and the back of her neck, she told herself that she couldn't continue as she was. She had to go back to Pick-Up. If that was her only chance of finding her way out of the inferno that threatened to engulf her, she had no choice. Maybe she would at least free herself of the guilt.

When she turned over on her back, she saw that Bates scrutinized her as if she were a stranger, and she wondered if he associated her stomach disorder with his remark about her celebrity. She didn't dare ask him, and when he saw the question mirrored in her eyes, he changed his facial expression as one draws a window shade, leaving her to pretend the moment hadn't occurred. But she knew that one day he wouldn't remain quiet, that he would pour out his beliefs and suspicions in bitter words.

He brought her gown and robe and dropped them on the foot of the bed. "Why don't you get some sleep. You've had a long day."

That was his way of telling her he didn't expect them to make love, and she had never been more grateful. "Thanks. It's two in the morning in Brussels. Are you . . . going out?"

He didn't look at her. "Hadn't planned to. Think I'll watch that tape of Halle Berry."

"What's the name of the movie?" she asked, attempting to show interest.

He lifted his right shoulder in a dismissive shrug. "Who cares?"

As the sound of his steps receded, she got the wrapping from the box that contained the New Testament and studied the return address. According to law, one's return address on a package had to match the ID of the person mailing the package. She couldn't decipher it, not even with the aid of a magnifying glass. She got the atlas and found Owings Mills in the vicinity of Baltimore, and surmised that not more than a twenty-minute train ride separated them.

Her mental wheels began turning and finally stopped when she connected Owings Mills, Baltimore, Glen, and the picture of the woman who looked so much like her. She knew when Bates got in bed and when he arose the next morning, for she hadn't slept. She wanted to go to church with him; she wanted to tell him everything; she did neither, but put on a face and moved about as if life were as it had been a year earlier.

At work the next day, Coreen received a letter from Becky Smith. She opened it with reluctance, for she had hoped that time would cut the girl's dependence on her. She read:

> Dear Miss Treadwell, I love my job, and I'm crazy about my little apartment. Just wanted you to know that I have enrolled for my GED, and my boss gives me plenty of time for my studies. Thanks for everything. Becky.

She reread the letter, closed it, and put it in her drawer. Life had set itself straight for at least one person. If she could, she would warn Becky not to live a lie, that before she married, she should tell the man about her past. She would tell the girl that secrets circumscribe a person, limit one's life as fetters hobble a horse. However, the opportunity for such counsel had passed, and she could only hope that Becky wouldn't win the game but in the process lose the prize.

She answered her phone, hearing, "Ms. Treadwell, Mr. Treadwell is on two." She could almost measure her husband's fumes at having to go through her secretary in order to reach her.

"I forgot to tell you," he said, "that while you were away this past weekend, I got four phone calls in which the person just listened to me say hello and then hung up. The phone company said the calls come from public telephones and nothing can be done about it. So I want us to change the phone number and not list it. We can give it to the people we want to have it. Problem is, you have to pay extra to have an unlisted number."

"Are the calls local or from out of town?"

"Local, of course," he said, in a tone suggesting the ludicrousness of the question.

She'd erred in asking that, but maybe he wouldn't catch the significance. "You want me to have the number changed or will you do it?"

"I'll do it right now. See you this evening."

"Right. See you then."

The words "I love you" seemed to have vanished from their vocabularies; they didn't even say them when they made love. "Is this all that there is?" she wondered aloud. It was far from ideal, but it was all she had.

She dialed Bates's number. "I didn't tell you that I have to go to Rocky Mount this weekend, and I'll probably leave Saturday morning and come back Sunday morning. I don't see how I can get back Saturday night."

She waited interminable minutes for his response before he asked, "Is this for work or for that outfit in Europe?" At last the hostility she had suspected toward her presidency of ISSWA colored his voice.

"I know it's tiresome my taking off unexpectedly this way, and I'll probably have to do it from time to time, but I hope you'll understand," she said, avoiding answering his question.

"At least leave me a number, so I'll know where you are."

She gave him her cellular phone number, because she had no idea where or if she would sleep. After he hung up, she made the flight reservation and ordered a rental car. She'd find a hotel in Rocky Mount.

* * *

The next Saturday morning, Coreen got up at around five o'clock, having slept fitfully and very little the previous night. After showering and dressing, she took her overnight bag and briefcase downstairs, went into the kitchen, and made a pot of coffee. She didn't bother with breakfast, because she knew she wouldn't eat any. As the hot liquid slid down her throat, she tried not to think, and to comfort herself, gazed eastward to see the sun rise from her kitchen window. The gray skies would soon be streaked with orange, purple, red, and yellow, but she turned away, unable to appreciate beauty or to find pleasure in anything. She didn't believe Bates was asleep at a quarter of six in the morning, and her sinking feeling that he had deserted her when she most needed him caused her almost to strangle herself with the hot coffee.

That assessment of her husband wasn't fair, and she didn't pretend to herself that it was. She equivocated as to whether she should go back upstairs and tell him good-bye or leave him a note and head for the airport. If she left without speaking with him, he would wash her face with it as often as it pleased him to do so. And he would have just cause. She walked back up the stairs.

"Bates, I'm leaving now. Are you awake?" When he turned over and opened his eyes, she knew he had been awake for a long time.

"Yeah."

She leaned forward and brushed his lips with her own, but without an invitation, she couldn't linger. "I'll see you tomorrow morning. My phone number is on the kitchen table." When he didn't respond, she could only say, "Gotta go. 'Bye."

She thought he said, " 'Bye," but she wasn't sure.

Although normally a fast driver, Coreen took her time on the drive to Elizabeth City to get her flight to Rocky Mount. *I must be trying to miss the plane* was her thought as she moved up Route 17 at a mere forty miles an hour. The closer she got to the airport, the more depressed she became, as a heaviness settled over her. When cramps knifed through her belly, she told herself to turn around and go home.

But if she did that, she would only have to begin the trip another day. Besides, what reason would she give Bates? By the time she drove into the airport parking lot, her sweat-soaked shirt and undergarments were sticking to her body, so much so that she removed her jacket and turned on the heater so as to dry herself before stepping out into the October air.

She had expected, even hoped for a long line at the ticket counter—anything that would prolong the time until she reached the point of no return—but only two people preceded her. Finally, with ticket in hand, she located the waiting section at the departure gate and sat down.

"Can I help you, ma'am?"

Coreen looked up into the face of a young woman whose age she guessed at about twenty-two. "Uh . . . I'm fine. Thanks." She wasn't fine, she was terrified, but she cloaked her feelings as best she could.

"You're sure? I noticed you shaking, and you didn't seem to be aware of the tears on your face. But if you're okay—"

"I'm all right. Thanks. Just a little tired, but I'm okay."

Disconcerted by the woman's penetrating look, Coreen forced a smile. "You're a kind person and I appreciate your concern, but I'm fine."

The woman went back to her seat, and Coreen took a copy of the *Journal of Social Work* from her briefcase and tried to read an article about the attraction of street gangs for young boys. Unable to concentrate, however, she put it away and closed her eyes.

"Flight 611 to Rocky Mount now boarding."

She couldn't force herself to move.

"Last call for Flight 611."

She gathered her overnight bag and briefcase and walked with feet of lead down the ramp to the MD-80. Later, as the big McDonald Douglas jet sped through the sky, she prayed that it would slow down. Foolish, she knew, but she couldn't shake the feeling that each minute took her closer to her doom.

A flight attendant asked if she needed help, and it occurred to Coreen that a fellow passenger must have noticed her demeanor and called the attendant. She removed her hands from their tight grip on her belly, sat up straight, and pressed her teeth together in what she hoped passed for a smile.

"I would like some water, please," Coreen said. "Otherwise, I'm fine. Thanks."

A change in the sound of the plane's engine further unnerved Coreen, for she knew it signaled an approach to landing. She fought the feeling of nausea and calmed herself by saying the Lord's Prayer. In spite of her dread and apprehension, Coreen walked through the half-empty terminal with head high and shoulders back.

"I'm not going to let it kill me," she said aloud, attempting to infuse herself with a strong dose of courage. "I'm here, and I intend to find out whether that analyst is worth what I paid him," she murmured to herself, adopting an attitude that she hoped would help her survive the weekend and possibly her greatest ordeal since she left Pick-Up.

"Pick-Up's about a forty-five minute drive out Route 91 heading south," the clerk at Budget Rent A Car told her. "It's not much of a place, though."

Coreen tried not to think during her drive to Pick-Up, but scenes from those days long past seeped into her head, crowding out every other image. She drove faster and faster, as if flying from demons until, needing directions, she stopped at a little café that joined a filling station.

"I'm looking for Pick-Up," she told the proprietor.

"A bit farther on, you'll see a little white church on the corner of Creek Road. Take the next exit and you'll be there in no time."

She thanked the man, then bought coffee and a hot dog, scraped the raw onions off it with the edge of a paper napkin, and walked out eating it. She ate as she drove, denying herself an excuse to linger in the café and further postpone returning to the place she had tried for thirty years to erase from her memory.

She turned off Route 91 and onto the dirt road leading to her destination, and stopped a woman who struggled with a loaded tow sack on her shoulder.

"Good afternoon, miss. I'm looking for the Agatha Monroe place in Pick-Up. Do you know it?"

"I sure do. Who is it around here that don't know it?. Agatha's been dead for months, but the place is just like she left it. She didn't have no kin, and she kept to herself like she didn't need nobody. Ain't nobody wants nothing she had. Place is sitting there just like it was when they took her out of there."

Nothing the woman said surprised Coreen, for not only had she been a victim of her aunt's cruelty and selfishness, but in the five and a half months that she lived with the woman, her aunt had no visitors. She didn't even have a telephone, because, as she said, "I don't know anybody who's got anything to say to me, and I don't have time to sit and talk to people. I greet people when I go to church, and that's plenty."

"If you're going to Pick-Up, I'll be glad to give you a lift," she said to the woman, opening the trunk of the car. "Put your bag back there."

As Coreen drove, the woman pointed out places that should have had meaning to a young girl living in a small town—the post office, bus station, one-room elementary school, beauty parlor, the *Sentinel* office, two churches, and the general store—but none registered with Coreen. She had never seen them. Her aunt had secluded her from the minute she got off the bus until she left Pick-Up to go to North Carolina Central University in Durham.

"Go about half a mile farther till you see a filling station, turn in there, and drive to the end of the road. It's the only house there."

Coreen thanked the woman, who continued down the road with the tow sack once more weighing her down. About a quarter of a mile before she reached the house, Coreen stopped the car and lectured to herself, pumping up her courage. Her fingers gripped the steering wheel so tightly that pain streaked to her wrists. Every atom of her being seemed to shout, *Don't go there.*

After a few minutes, she was able to loosen her grip on the wheel and drive on to Agatha Monroe's deserted house. Dying weeds choked the rosebushes and other perennials in the front yard. She looked up at the pecan tree, bare but for a brown leaf here and there, and then rested her gaze on the earth below it. More than a bushel of nuts lay scattered about. Unwanted. In that poor community, there had lived a woman of such selfishness and self-absorption that people in need refused to touch what she left behind.

Although certain that she wouldn't be able to enter the house, nevertheless she turned the knob on the front door, and to her astonishment the door opened. It occurred to her that she had never before walked through that door, but at her aunt's admonishment always used the back way.

The old treadle sewing machine hadn't been moved from its place in the hallway. Agatha's hand-crocheted doilies still covered the backs of her living room couch and chairs. She stared at the hooked rug she once scrubbed with a brush while crawling on her hands and knees with her belly dragging the floor. She walked through the house, tightening her nostrils against the stale, musty smell of a closed house that had known months of nonuse.

The room she had occupied had been converted to a storage room for her aunt's canned foods, but the cot—with its two-inch-thick mattress on which she had twisted and turned during the late months of her pregnancy and on which she gave birth without even an aspirin to relieve the pain—remained in the place where she last saw it. A house deserted, its front door unlocked for months, and not even thieves disturbed its contents.

Coreen leaned against the doorjamb and tried to deal with the numbness that seeped through her, giving her hands and feet the sensation of frostbite. As she gazed, catatonic-like, at that cot, that symbol of all her problems, pain shot from her back to her pelvis, simulating the onset of childbirth. She caught herself as she was about to scream.

"I've got to get out of here," she said, and rushed toward the back door. When she couldn't open it, her heartbeat accelerated and her breathing shortened. She scampered to the front door, which remained ajar, and ran outside.

Every unpleasantness that she experienced that long-ago summer came back to her, and she was once more seventeen, pregnant, and scared. She heard her aunt's voice, "Don't sit there. Get up and make yourself useful. Nobody told you to lie down and let that boy use you, pouring his junk into you."

"But Aunt Agatha, I begged him not to do it, to stop, and I fought him as best I could, but he was stronger and he wouldn't listen to me."

"That's what they all say. You're not going to eat me out of house and home without paying your way. Go pick those peas."

"Yes, ma'am."

A gust of wind brought Coreen back to the present. She closed the front door and walked around the side of the house to the gardens. *Justice can be furious*, she thought, and laughed for the first time since she awoke that morning in Bakerville. She laughed at the rotted heads of lettuce, the pea bushes heavy with an unpicked and dead crop, the rows of onions decaying in the ground, and the thicket of dried weeds where she had once been forced to clean away every blade of grass. She stood there laughing until tears cascaded down her cheeks.

She walked around to the front of the house with one thought: *Why should I feel guilt about giving up a child for which I suffered such anguish?*

As she stood in the front yard, she let her gaze roam, taking in everything about the place, hoping to put the past to rest. She gazed at the pecan tree and the nuts beneath it.

"Damned if I'm going to leave all of these here," she said aloud. "The locals may be too proud to take them, but I *earned* them."

She took a plastic shopping bag from her overnight bag, filled it with pecans, and put it in the trunk of the car. "I wish I could take every one of them."

On the way back, she stopped in Wilson for a tank of gas, then drove on to Rocky Mount. She hated driving strange roads at night, but darkness had set in before she arrived in Rocky Mount, forcing her to drive slowly. After getting a hotel room and registering, she found a novelty store, bought a newspaper, some snacks, and a copy of *Blues From Down Deep*, went back to the hotel, and ordered dinner in her room. While she waited for the food to arrive, she telephoned Bates.

Coreen listened to the rings and counted each one. After fifteen of them, she left a message, hung up, and looked at her watch. Maybe he went out to eat dinner with Jessie. After all, it was only nine o'clock. But wouldn't Jessie eat with Lorna? She didn't know what she would have said to him if he had answered, but at least she wouldn't feel so alone.

She began to dial Glen on her cellular phone, and hung up; Bates said she should loosen her ties with Glen, that he needed to mature, to stand on his own. She didn't agree with Bates, but she wanted the best for Glen, and if she was going to follow her analyst's advice, she had better start. Being at her aunt's place in Pick-Up had stretched her to her limits, but she survived it, and in reliving a part of her past torment gained strength for the next battle. She opened the bag of dried cranberries, and for diversion tuned the television to a pay station and watched *The Color Purple*. However, unable to concentrate on the movie, she flipped off the television and read until she became drowsy.

After a meal of club steak, French fries, sauteed spinach, and apple crumb cake, which she ate in her room, she showered, brushed her teeth, and got in bed. The twang of a country music singer over a local radio station served as company. She didn't like country music, but she didn't want to hear the sound of silence. An hour passed and Bates hadn't called, so she turned off the lights and the radio and tried to sleep.

Drip. Drip. Drip. She dashed into the bathroom, tightened the faucet in the sink, and went back to bed. *Drip. Drip. Drip.* On it went until she couldn't bear the eerie sound. A call to management assured Coreen that the plumber had gone for the night, and she could either change rooms or put a pillow over her head. She opted for the pillow.

Well after midnight, she finally dozed off, only to awaken around four o'clock, panting and out of breath. She switched on the light over the bed and sat up, shaking. For hours, it seemed, her aunt Agatha chased her down a long, endless row of lettuce, a row that stretched for as far as the eye could see. And although she stumbled and staggered from fatigue as she ran, Agatha was always two arm lengths behind her. When she thought she would fall into the woman's clutches, she could see the end of the road, but as she neared it, there stood Bates, his arms folded across his chest and a censorial expression on his face.

She got out of bed, unlocked the bar, got a three-jigger bottle of Hines cognac, and was about to drink it when she remembered that cognac always gave her a headache. She got back in bed but didn't attempt to sleep. Instead, she tried to figure out how she would tell Bates that she was the mother of a child, and what she would do if, upon learning of it, he disdained her. Worse still, what would she do if she lost her profession and her family all at once.

I can't think like this. I've given everything to my job, and I've been a loving and supportive wife and mother. Who is perfect? If the worse happens, I'm going to fight for my family and for my job.

She got up, dressed, put her briefcase in her overnight bag, and finished packing it. She could only have two items on the plane, and one of them would be the pecans in the trunk of the rented car. She wondered if her aunt had chased her in the dream because she disapproved of her taking the pecans.

"Tough," she said. "I earned them and much more."

At six o'clock, she telephoned Bates.

"Hello," he said in that deep masculine voice that once sent shivers along her spine, but which had long ago become more comfortable and assuring than exciting.

"Hi," she said. "I called last night, but you were out. I wanted to catch you before you went to church—"

"You're kidding. I don't leave for church for another four and a half hours."

If she told him she was confused, he would ask why. In truth, when she dialed, she was thinking the day was Saturday, but by the time he answered, she remembered that it was Sunday.

"I hardly slept," she said, and told him about the leaking faucet. "It was in a corner of the room beside the bathroom."

They made small talk, but he offered no explanation as to his whereabouts the evening before, and she didn't ask. "My plane gets into Elizabeth City at ten-thirty, so I'll be home before noon."

"Then you'll be there when I get home from church. By the way, Glen called. He said the station's audience increased by twenty-five percent since he's been manager and he got a raise."

"Wonderful," she said, tempering her response. "If he'll just continue this way."

"What did you say?" Bates asked her.

She repeated it. "Maybe he's found his life's work. I certainly hope so. See you when I get home."

"Looks like it, and seems he found it without any help from Mama. Drive carefully. 'Bye."

Nettled at his words, her next thought was to call Glen and congratulate him, extolling his achievements, but she restrained her enthusiasm, and when she remembered the time, was glad she hadn't awakened him.

"Have I been so far off track with my family?" she wondered as she checked the room for any belongings she might have overlooked and as her mind revisited times that she had made an unfair difference between Eric and Glen. She hadn't seen it as unfair, rationalizing that Glen was the baby and that he needed her more, but looking back, she wished she had been wiser. Only the Lord knew what she was going home to. In some days recently, Bates had been as cold as winter frost, and she knew the temperature would continue to fall unless she found a way to change the direction in which their relationship seemed headed.

If Coreen had taken the first step toward ridding herself of guilt, Frieda Davis embedded herself more deeply in it. She spent Veterans Day parked first across from the Treadwell home at 38 Queen Street North and then directly in front of Lizette's House of Style.

"I'm going to make her as miserable as she made me," she vowed as she drove back to Baltimore. When she turned into Franklin Street, the first thing she saw was Glen's red Mercury Cougar parked in front of 2900, the building in which she lived. She slowed down, and her first inclination was to turn around and spend the night at the hospital.

"I'm not afraid to confront him," she said to herself, stopped parallel to him, rolled down her window, and tapped her horn.

"Would you please get out of my parking spot before I call the police?"

"This spot belongs to the city of Baltimore. I'm staying here, baby, till you get out of that car."

She drove to the end of the block and parked. "Lord, I need you right now, so please don't let me down. Just please don't let him touch me." She started to get out, remembered that she wasn't on the best of terms with the Lord, turned the ignition key, and headed for the hospital.

"This is one hell of a mess," she said after she crawled onto her bunk. "I can't even stay in my own apartment."

The next morning, she called him at work, greeted him, and said, "Glen, I told you it was over and I mean it. So let's part on good terms. I wish you well."

His laughter shook her, its sound reverberating in the pit of her belly. If only she had never seen him, never fallen in love with him. If only she didn't want to be with him this minute so badly that she ground her teeth and crossed her knees as she pulsated with desire.

"You've got to be kidding. No woman has ever walked away from me, and you're the first to try it. *I say when it's over.* And this is *not* over." This time, she noticed his softer manner and less-ened resolve—speaking as if from habit rather than feeling—and she tried to put aside her distress.

"You'll see," she said in a voice that wouldn't have convinced a two-year-old, and hung up.

That afternoon, she made it a point to leave the building along with her supervisor, a middle-aged woman who loved young and handsome men. It didn't surprise her that Glen's Cougar blocked the walkway leading to the street so that one had to step off the concrete and walk on the grass in order to reach the street. As she neared the car, he got out and stood lean-ing against the front passenger door with his arms folded against his chest. Impressive by any measure.

When they reached him, Frieda smiled. "Hi, Glen. This is my supervisor, Miss Randolph. Vernice, this is *the* Glen Treadwell, the voice of WBCC."

By that time, Vernice Randolph stood as close to Glen as de-cency would permit. "You go 'way from here. You really are that fabulous voice that just kinda wraps around a girl and leaves her breathless?"

Frieda walked as fast as she could to her car farther down the street, as Glen's ego trapped him in a conversation with Vernice Randolph. However, Vernice's holding power was not as Frieda hoped, for Glen's car was parked in front of her house when she got there. She wondered if he'd gotten a speeding ticket. This time, it was not desire but anger that motivated her. She got out of her car before he could get out of the Cougar and rushed to meet him. When he reached out to her, she kicked his shin.

"Don't touch me. You used me; that's all you did. I had sworn never again to let a man use me the way my adoptive father did. But you did, and I let you."

When she saw that she shocked him, she pulled in a long deep breath and plowed on. "The worst was that night when you flipped me over on my stomach like my adoptive father did—exactly the same way—pulled my hips up and plowed into me as if I wasn't human with feelings. You didn't even ask me if you could do it. Then you let me walk out of there alone at midnight when you knew it was hot and men would be prowling the streets. I've never been so humiliated in my life. But it was all my fault. I had planned to use you, but you beat me to it. I fell in love with you, but that didn't stop me from hating you sometimes."

"How were you planning to use me?" He projected none of his usual masculine swagger, and his voice lacked the mellifluous quality that reeled in women the way a fisherman hooked fish.

"How?" she asked him. "You'll know soon enough. Just leave me alone."

She had confounded him, but she loved it. A small sense of triumph over herself and her need of him enabled her to hold up her head and walk back to her car. She got inside, drove to the far end of the block to park, and walked back to the building in which she lived, not fearing an encounter with him, for she had seen him abashed, lacking his powerful public persona. When she reached the house, he still sat in the red Cougar looking straight ahead, but she ignored him and went home.

For the next several hours, Frieda sat on the side of her bed reviewing her life. She relived the day she discovered that Claude and Beatrice Davis were not her birth parents; the night Claude Davis took her virginity, and the many nights thereafter that he used her to suit his pleasure; and the night she ran away from home wearing sneakers and her adoptive mother's robe for warmth, carrying one hundred and seventy-three dollars stolen from Claude Davis's pocket. And she recalled all the nights that Glen Treadwell used her. Several men had courted her, wanted her, and wanted to marry her, but she had fallen in love with the only louse among them.

Frieda got up, threaded her way to the kitchen, and began cooking her supper. It was time she settled the score and got on with her life.

Chapter Fourteen

Coreen returned home from Pick-Up around twelve o'clock that Sunday after one of the harshest ordeals of her life. As she unpacked, she knew she would either have to lie to Bates or tell him everything, and she had neither the strength to tell him the truth nor the will to lie. She sat on the side of her bed, exhausted from the ordeal and the restless night, and stretched out and fell asleep.

She awoke after four o'clock in an empty house, and was beset with a sense of dread. If nothing untoward had happened to Bates, he was showing her that he didn't care and wasn't anxious to see her. She forced down a peanut butter and jelly sandwich, dressed in a woolen suit and raincoat, and drove down to the beach. As she strolled, she gazed at the Albermarle, content to dance, slosh, and ripple as nature commanded. Tiredness set in, and she sat on the pier where she once encountered Porgy, alone and meditative, sat there until the water and the sky became almost indistinguishable.

As darkness encroached, she wished for a place to go other than home, a home that might be dark and empty and where a marriage seemed on the verge of splintering. And she wished, not for the first time in recent months, that she had a girlfriend and buddy to whom she could reach out in times like these. But when she might have developed close friends, she had been busy repairing her life; molding herself, Bates, and his sons into a family; and struggling to succeed in her profession. Lacking an acceptable alternative, she went home.

She walked into the kitchen where Bates stood akimbo, his gaze searching the room as if seeing it for the first time.

"Hi," she said. "Somehow I didn't expect to see you here. Where've you been?" she asked, departing from her longstanding practice of not asking him where he'd been.

"I could ask you the same."

"When you weren't home at four, I went down to the beach and sat on the pier. If I'd had someplace to go, I wouldn't be here right now."

He relaxed his stance and leaned against the kitchen counter. "Where'd you get all those pecans? They look as if you picked them up off the ground yourself. The hull is still on some of 'em."

She had just made a statement relative to the tenuous nature of their relationship, and he responded with a comment about pecans. "That's right. I gathered them from beneath somebody's pecan tree. You want to go out for supper, skip food, or have you already eaten somewhere?"

"Whose tree?"

"You never heard of her. What are we doing for supper?"

He stepped closer to her. "When you get mad, you don't usually make it so obvious. It's more important that you behave like a lady. Lose your temper? Not the president of ISSWA. Getting furious is beneath her."

She took several steps back and pointed her right index finger at him. "Keep it up. You'll get more than you asked for, and you will remember it for a long time."

His face relaxed into the kind of easy, self-assured grin that first attracted her to him, one that promised every pleasure a woman could tolerate.

"Go ahead. I'm waiting for you to get either scared enough, mad enough, or sensible enough to level with me. Until you do—for whatever reason—things are going to stay exactly like they are. I'll cook supper."

He cooked a meal of shrimp scampi, noodles tossed with butter and minced Italian parsley, steamed asparagus, and green salad. "There's ice cream for dessert," he said at the end of their mostly silent meal. "I get tired of soul food sometimes. How'd you like the scampi?"

She didn't feel like making small talk, but she didn't want the wedge between them to get larger. "Delicious. Where'd you learn to cook that?"

He raised an eyebrow. "In Italy. San Vincenzo near Pisa. A woman there taught me how to cook it because I liked it so much."

"Did you have an affair with her?" She didn't want to hear him say yes, and she definitely didn't want him to tell her what the woman was like, but she couldn't control the need to know.

"When you ask a question, be sure you want the answer. I'll get the ice cream."

After dinner, he settled in front of the television set, put his tape of Halle Berry in the VCR, and opened a bottle of ginger ale. She wanted to wreck the television set and force him to talk to her, to tell her why he hadn't come home after church, why he hadn't asked her whether her trip was successful.

"I'm going to work for about an hour and then turn in," she said as she started up the stairs. "Good night."

" 'Night," he replied without glancing in her direction.

It's all up to you, her conscience nagged. *Only you can change this situation.* She had to, and she knew it, but finding the courage to do it, to expose herself to the most critical person she ever knew . . . She climbed the stairs thinking how hopeless it was.

Bates sat before a blank television screen, angry at himself. He hadn't handled it right. Rather than being remorseful for having dashed off with short notice and being away most of the weekend, Coreen was mad and it was his fault. He'd chosen the wrong way of letting her know he was near the breaking point, that he'd reached the limit of his tolerance for the kind of relationship they had, and that he wasn't willing to pretend otherwise. Yet, if he went up those stairs, both of them would get angry and self-righteous. He wished to heaven he knew how to put an end to their misery and get them back to laughing, teasing, and making love, the way they were before the boys left home. And before Coreen embarked on her ascent to glory.

Abruptly, he sat forward, his ears cocked. That coughing, gagging sound! In his rush to the stairs, he nearly knocked over the coffee table.

"What's the matter with you?" he asked Coreen, who sat up in bed, shaking. "What's wrong?"

"I . . . d-don't know. I was asleep, and it was like I was choking. I woke up."

"Were you having a nightmare?"

"I don't know. I was choking until I woke up," she said, still trembling.

He sat down on the edge of the bed and pulled her into his arms. "You're all right now. What you need is a good rest. Can you . . . ?" He didn't finish it because he knew she wouldn't stay home from work to rest. She had trudged to that office when her car wouldn't move and icicles hung from its roof and wheels, and when she had a temperature of one hundred and two degrees.

"I'll go down and get you a glass of warm milk." But when he would have released her, she clung to him. Not from desire or in an attempt at seduction, he realized, but stark fear. *Fear of what?* He eased her away, stared into her face, and saw terror. Terror that he knew she wouldn't share with him. He hugged her to him, wishing he could do that with a full heart. When she appeared more calm, he went down to the kitchen, warmed a glassful of milk, and stirred a tablespoon of cognac in it.

When he handed her the milk, he told her that it contained the cognac. "Now you'll sleep peacefully."

"Thanks. I just pray I never have another experience like that one. I couldn't swallow. I couldn't breathe. It was awful."

"Don't think about it anymore. Try to think of something pleasant."

"Thanks for being there for me. I know you won't believe me, but I always need you."

What could he say to that? Maybe she did, but he wouldn't mind having more evidence of it than she'd given him during the last few months. He needed her, but she didn't seem to see that.

"Sleep well. I'll be downstairs if you want me for anything." Time was when he'd have held her in his arms all night. But that was then. Maybe they'd find their way out of this morass. Maybe not.

So much remained a mystery: Coreen's bouts of gloominess; her secretiveness; the way she would bounce from her normal self to depression in a second and often in the middle of a conversation; the sudden trip this weekend for which she'd given no satisfactory explanation; her blindness in respect to the poor state of his business. *I could pry it out of her, but something tells me I'd regret it as long as I live.*

He walked over to the living room window and looked out at the moonlit night. Crisp, cool, and barren. The phone rang and he looked at his watch. Nine-thirty. He answered on the third ring.

"Treadwell residence. Hello."

Only silence greeted him. "I've got the phone company on your trail, and when they catch you—" The caller hung up. He released some of his frustration with a kick at the carpet. Down in his gut, he knew that the anonymous calls were in some way related to Coreen. He looked around for anything that would take the brunt of his discomfiture, and finding nothing, knocked his left fist into his right palm and expelled a long breath. It would come to a head, and soon, for he sensed that she was nearing the point of capitulation.

Several days later, Coreen received a call from Lieutenant Mitchell requesting that she go to the police station at once. Coreen didn't mind going, even though Mitchell didn't give her an explanation. She thought of telephoning Bates, decided that there wasn't time, and left the office.

"Thank you for coming, Ms. Treadwell. I'd like you to identify this suspect. We're holding him for harassing you and your husband with anonymous calls."

She walked into the room where three men stood under

lights and scrutinized them. "I don't recognize any of them, Lieutenant. I don't deal with many cases; the caseworkers handle most face-to-face consultations."

"You're some hot stuff," one of them yelled out. "I'd recognize that twang of yours in my sleep. You told Becky to get rid of my kid. Yeah, I put it there, and you should have minded your own business."

Mitchell dismissed the other two men and handcuffed the one who had indicted himself. Coreen didn't recognize the offender, about twenty-two, tall, arrogant, and reeking of a sweet-smelling cologne, the kind she hated. The type of man who would violate a girl while eight other hoodlums watched.

Saddened, she shook her head. "If you don't need me for anything else, Lieutenant, I'll get back to work. You may want to speak with my husband about this, as well. He answered the phone more often than I did."

"Thanks. I'll call him when we get down to cases."

Back in her office, Coreen was glad for a reason to telephone Bates, for their conversation had become stilted and superficial.

"Hi," she said, when he answered. "The phone company caught our anonymous caller, and he's been locked up. I just left the police station."

"Do you know him?" His question set her aback.

"No. Never saw him before." She explained her involvement with the man. "Becky didn't get rid of the child; she gave it up for adoption, but I suppose she told him that to make certain she didn't hear from him again."

"How did he know where she was?"

Coreen thought for a minute. "You know, that question hadn't crossed my mind. Thanks. I know just where the leak is. I demoted her earlier, but this time she is out."

"If you mean Maddie Franks, I say it's past time you got rid of her. From the things you've told me about her, she was definitely not an asset."

"It wasn't obvious to me until recently," Coreen said in self-defense.

"Well, one less puzzle to deal with."

"What do you mean by that?"

"You ask? Our life together is one big puzzle, although something tells me it's starting to untangle."

Shaken by Bates's strange and, to her, almost mystic observations over the past several days—as if he had access to her unspoken thoughts—Coreen decided she needed respite from it, and a trip to Brussels was one certain way to get it. In fairness to her husband, she reflected, more than his tart and incisive observations contributed to her nervousness and almost constant agitation. She had a feeling that a bell tolled for her and that she could do nothing to stop it. Her relationship with Bates had deteriorated so badly that she doubted him capable of the love and understanding she would need when he learned all of her truths, and the African-American media were already celebrating her elevation to leadership of ISSWA. If only she had said no to Nana Kuti.

At the end of the week, Coreen left for Brussels, giving an unscheduled conference call as the reason. To her amazement, Bates displayed no reaction; from his behavior, she might as well have been going to her office eleven blocks away on Poplar Neck Road. And at the international office of ISSWA, she learned that her impulsive act was unwelcome.

"Madam President," the board chairman said, "we need ample time to prepare for the visits of our president. Three days' notice is not sufficient. And we also must have an agenda that warrants the cost and use of the president's time."

Shocked though she was, she presented a stern face and replied, "The president also needs to know what her duties are and how she is expected to perform them. If the president is merely a front who rubber-stamps the policies and actions of the board, I want out right now." She braced herself against the back of her chair and hid her hands so that her nervousness and fear wouldn't be apparent.

"Why, Mrs. Treadwell, I do apologize. I have no desire to be discourteous. Please forgive me."

She wondered if the man had meant to test her mettle, to find out how much jostling she'd take. She looked him in the eye."I suppose you know that we Americans smile a lot and African-Americans smile and laugh even more. But don't be misled. Half the time, those smiles and grins are merely a show of politeness."

"We have needed some direction for a long time," Nana Kuti said, associating herself with Coreen's comment. "We're in a rut, and I'm glad to see we have a president who wants to be a real president."

However, not even Kuti's support soothed Coreen; she had done a hasty and ill-advised thing, and the experience mortified her. Worse, she didn't expect warmth and understanding when she arrived home. However, it relieved her to find that Bates had cooked supper, and although he didn't meet her at the airport, he was at home when she got there.

"How'd it go?" he asked, surprising her again.

"Couldn't have been much worse. They have to get used to me and vice versa."

"I'm going out," he said. "I'll be back in time to serve supper."

She took her bag upstairs, showered, and stretched out on the bed. When she awoke, Bates was sitting on the side of the bed holding a plate of food. Politically correct, she thought, but not a kiss, a stroke of his hand, or a word of love.

One afternoon about two weeks later, Bates rested his elbows on his desk and gave thanks. His take in the previous two weeks doubled receipts for the previous two months, and his orders were continuing the trend. The buzzer sounded as it always did when the front door opened. He sat up straight, glanced toward the door, and nearly bounded out of his seat. He knew his lower jaw dropped, and he couldn't manage to close his mouth.

Finally, the woman standing before him arranged her face in a smile that was anything but sincere; indeed, it was both cocky and arrogant, so much so that he recovered his aplomb. "May I help you?" he asked her, already certain of what he faced.

"I'm looking for my birth mother."

The similarity struck him when he looked up and saw her

standing there, her face the picture of triumph. "Why are you telling me? I'm not a private investigator." He didn't imagine that her sails lost some wind, as it were, for she was immediately less cocky.

"This is a travel agency," he went on, biding his time while he studied her demeanor. "If you need a tour, a ticket, or a hotel, I can help you; if not, I'm busy."

"Coreen Treadwell is my birth mother," she replied, adding to his suspicion. With such a strong resemblance, he had practically reached that conclusion.

"Then why don't you contact *her?* What are you bothering *me* for?"

"Well, I . . . I didn't know how she would react to seeing me."

He didn't believe her. If she was after blackmail, she'd picked the wrong couple. He got up, went to the front door, and looked out; as he suspected, the blue Plymouth was parked in front of his shop.

"You know where she lives, because I've seen your car parked across the street from our house at least three times, and I'll bet you know where she works, so don't play innocent with me. If you want to see her, you know where to go. Otherwise, you can leave a message with me and I'll give it to her."

He gazed intently at her and at the change in her, so obviously flustered and, it seemed, disappointed, for he had deprived her of whatever she hoped to gain by approaching him rather than Coreen.

"I'll . . . Sorry I bothered you."

He watched as she walked to her car, the image of Coreen right down to her magnificent, long-lashed eyes, the curve of her bottom lip, and the stateliness of her carriage. Pandora's box was about to open, but he wouldn't be the one to pop the lid.

He didn't tell Coreen of his encounter with the woman who claimed to be her daughter, for he feared she would have disowned her. Instead, he watched his wife for clues.

"Supper's ready," Coreen called to him one afternoon the following week, early in November. When he reached the kitchen, he saw in her stance the demeanor of the woman who claimed to be her daughter, and it occurred to him that he might not have associated the two right then if he hadn't remembered that woman's voice. Tremors shot through him when he recalled that dark and melodious sexy voice, identical to Coreen's.

Bates scrutinized Coreen's hands and saw in them her daughter's fingers, identical in shape and size but more weathered. He wondered about the kind of work her daughter did. But the more convinced he became of the veracity of the woman's claim, the more certain he was that somewhere therein lay the root of their marital problems. *It's Coreen's duty to solve this. When she does, maybe we can have a marriage.*

On an impulse, he telephoned Eric one night after Coreen had gone to bed early, a habit she had developed, he suspected, to minimize the periods of awkwardness when they weren't eating or watching television.

"What did you do with that picture you had of Glen's girlfriend?"

"It's somewhere around here. You want it? I don't think she's his girlfriend, Dad."

"Drop it in the mail, would you? She reminds me of someone."

"Sure thing. You guys all right?"

"Thanks. How're the wedding plans coming along?"

"I'd like to chuck it all and go to a justice of the peace, but Star won't hear of that. She is one organized woman. I sure hope I survive this."

Bates laughed as the memory of his first marriage flashed through his mind. "You will. It's what's in the pocketbook that shrivels up and dies."

They enjoyed a laugh, and Bates hung up with the shaky feeling that when he got that picture, he would discover more than he wanted to.

Frieda drove back to Baltimore chastened, but none the less resolute, for she knew she would never rest until she confronted Coreen Treadwell. Bates Treadwell wasn't what she had expected, though she could see in him Glen's good looks and smooth tongue. Maybe he already knew about her, but from the surprise on his face when she walked into his place of business, she doubted it.

She recalled her last, painful tryst with Glen, which brought back to her with thundering force her trials with her adoptive father, the source of her animosity toward the woman who gave her life. She checked her answering machine when she returned home, and to her surprise Glen had called her. She prayed for the strength to put him out of her life and erased the message, but for the remainder of the day and on into the night, her nipples ached as desire shackled her, forcing her to acknowledge that she would be vulnerable to Glen Treadwell for a long time.

At midnight, half asleep, she answered the telephone. "Hello. Who's this?"

"Glen. Why didn't you return my call?"

"Glen, leave me alone, will you? I was asleep."

"Well, I can't sleep. You're on my mind day and night."

She awakened more fully. "Now, that's a twist. It used to be your penis I was bothering; now it's your mind. Well, do tell! Would you please hang up and let me get some sleep? I have to be at work at eight o'clock. Good-bye."

She hung up and unplugged the telephone. She couldn't guarantee that she wouldn't go to him or let him come to her if he called her again that night. When the alarm went off at six-thirty, she disentangled her body from the wrinkled, twisted sheets and rolled out of bed. As she dressed, it occurred to her that Glen hadn't been arrogant or strident, that he had been almost reticent.

"Too late for that," she said to herself, for she had already exposed herself to Glen's father. "Too much pain and dishonesty." She shook her head, remembering the seeds that she, too, had sowed. "Too many lies."

All day at work, she mulled over her encounter with Glen's father and his seeming lack of concern for her existence. *Glen's like that, too,* she recalled, *clever at hiding what he thinks and feels.* A man who could find physical release in lovemaking and not make a sound, an actor who believed in getting ahead of a person and staying there.

You're not fooling me, Bates Treadwell. If Coreen Treadwell had ever told her family about me, Glen would have asked some questions when he saw that photo and maybe even when he was looking down in my face riding me senseless. Oh, no, Mr. Bates. You may not have been surprised to see me, but I guarantee you, your wife will get the shock of her life.

It was Sunday evening, a week before Thanksgiving, and Bates sat across the table from his wife toying with his dessert. He liked pecan pie, but not after a meal that included both candied sweet potatoes and baked corn bread.

"You don't like it?" Coreen asked him, one of the few words she had said during the meal.

"Sure I like it, but I'm too—Wonder who that is?" He went to answer the front door bell.

"What the . . . ?" *So this is it,* he thought, regaining his composure. "I suppose you want to see your mother. Come on in, and have a seat in the living room."

Nothing could have given him more pleasure than the expression of defeat on her face, the realization that her plan to disrupt her birth mother's life and marriage hadn't worked. But he had a score to settle with the woman who bore his name and neglected to share with him her troubles and the experiences that shaped her life. He walked back into the kitchen where Coreen had finished the remainder of her pecan pie and faced her.

"Your daughter is here to see you. She's in the living room."

A loud gasp escaped Coreen seconds before she slumped in the chair. He checked her heartbeat and her pulse, got a wad of paper towel, and applied cold water to her forehead and the back of her neck. Passing by the living room on his way to the linen closet for a pillow and towel, he leaned in and said, "She'll be here a few minutes. You came in right at dinnertime."

When he returned to the kitchen, Coreen was struggling to get her bearings. Her glance darted from place to place as though she sought an avenue of escape, but as far as he was concerned, it was D-Day.

"She's waiting for you in the living room."

She got up slowly, and he took her arm and accompanied her to meet her daughter.

* * *

Coreen looked at the woman whose picture she saw weeks earlier and who looked as she had thirty years earlier. "I knew you would come one day," she said. "Why are you here now?" At Bates's urging, she took a seat in the big chair across from the sofa where Frieda sat.

Frieda stood up. "I've been looking for you for the better part of a year, and let me tell you I went to a whole lot of trouble to find you. Spent the money I've been saving to buy me a little house somewhere near the water, struck deals with unsavory characters to get your address, and demeaned myself with a man all in order to get to you. And when I found out who you were, what you did, and how you lived, I thought about the pigsty I lived in as a child while you lived in wealth and comfort, mothering and loving somebody else's children."

"What is your name?"

"When I was born, it was 'Baby Holmes' or maybe 'Baby Monroe,' whatever name you went by. Now it's Frieda Davis, a name given me by Beatrice and Claude Davis, the people who adopted me after you decided you didn't want me." She ignored Coreen's gasp.

"That's right, and I don't plan to forgive you for it. If you knew the hell I lived in while you were living and acting like royalty, you might even be ashamed. Imagine. You got a job helping other peoples' girls, and you didn't know whether yours was dead or alive."

"Watch your tongue, woman," Bates said. "This is my house, and while you're in it you will respect my wife."

"Your wife didn't go through what I went through." She walked to within inches of Coreen and looked down at her. "Thanks to you, the man I called Father raped me a couple of days after my twelfth birthday. And from then until I was seventeen, used me whenever he felt like it and any way he wanted to, hurting me and slamming into me, making me take him any way he wanted it. I used to run to the bathroom and vomit as soon as he left me. Five long years of that, until I stole away from home one night in the dead of winter wearing sneakers, a thin dress, my mother's robe for warmth, and carrying nothing but the little money I stole from his pocket."

Coreen covered her ears with her hands. "I don't want to hear any more. You've had your fun, now please go. Please."

"But I don't owe nobody a cent," Frieda went on. "I work eight hours a day and I've never stooped to prostituting myself for money. I hope you can say as much about yourself."

Furor rushed through Coreen as she stared at the child whose coming into the world had caused her such anguish. She got up and faced the woman. Head to head and toe to toe they stood. No longer fearing reprisals of any kind, not from Bates, the city of Bakerville, or the world of social work, she pointed her right index finger into the chest of Frieda Davis.

"Who are you to judge me? If you had walked in my shoes, would you have done differently? You are what I got when I was raped while I begged, screamed, kicked, and scratched for help, fighting to get away from him. You were violated. Well, so was I, and with my back crushed against the bark of a tree bleeding from his pushing and slamming into me. A virgin. I was an honor student. The whole town expected me to do big things. My father was so proud of me that he stopped roughing up my mother. And two months later, the doctor said I was pregnant. *With you.*" Frieda's eyes widened, and she took a step back.

"Oh, I haven't finished," Coreen said. "In fact, I just started, so you sit down over there and listen. You came here to disrupt my life, to destroy my marriage and my family, so I'm having my say. Do you think I could love the child of a man who did that to me, a man I loathed? No, hated. Do you? Every time I looked at you, I would remember him and what he did to me. To my life.

"My mother sent me off to my aunt in a little place called Pick-Up, North Carolina. Agatha Monroe must have been the meanest woman on earth. I slept on a cot with a two-inch mattress and gave birth to you on that same cot. All summer I slaved, crawling up and down her long rows of lettuce, string beans, and berries with my huge belly dragging the ground. I still remember the pain in my back that never went away. I peeled fruit, strung beans, dug potatoes, chopped corn, and she didn't even give me an aspirin for the pain in my back."

Coreen brushed away her tears with the back of her hand. "The only thing she did for me in those five and a half months was deliver you, and for that searing pain that went on for thirty-six hours, she didn't even give me an aspirin. And when I begged her to call a doctor, she said the doctor cost money. I never looked at you after she took you out of me, and all this time, I didn't know whether I'd had a boy or a girl."

She wiped her eyes with the tail of her shirt. "You came here for revenge, as if I had deliberately given you to a sadistic child abuser. I didn't know who adopted you, and I never tried to find out. I'm terribly sorry for what you suffered. If I could change it, I would, but I feel no guilt whatsoever. I, too, am a victim."

"What's my birth father's name, and where is he?"

"I have no idea where he is; as for his name, that secret will die with me. He was my high school classmate, and to this day I can hardly bear the thought of him. I'm tired." She turned her back, no longer able to control her tears. "I hope you're satisfied."

Bates stood. "I'll walk you to the door, Miss Davis. I hope you got what you came for and that you won't bother my wife again. If you harass her, I'll get a restraining order against you."

Frieda stopped walking toward the door and whirled around. "I'm a law-abiding citizen," she said, "and harassing people is against the law. 'Scuse me." She brushed past him and into the living room where Coreen had taken a seat on the sofa and buried her head in her arms.

"I may as well get it all out now," she said to Coreen. "I had planned to meet you holding hands with your stepson, but he got to be so obnoxious, I couldn't tolerate him long enough to get him going my way. A born user."

Coreen slapped her hand over her mouth and squeezed her eyes tight. "Please go."

She heard the door close, got up, and trudged up the stairs. She didn't think she could stand a confrontation with Bates or one of his prosecutorial grillings. He would either leave her or forgive her, and at the moment she didn't have the strength to make a case for herself.

"Are you coming back down?" he called up to her as she neared the top of the stairs.

"Not tonight, if you don't mind. I'm exhausted."

"Yeah. I guess you are."

* * *

Bates sat on the bottom stair step and rested his palms on his widespread knees. So this was it, the crux of the problem. But how did it figure in Coreen's changed behavior during the last half year or more? He didn't fault her for giving up the child. To his way of thinking, if a girl couldn't love a child, she should give it to someone she hoped would. And how had the woman found Glen? He was glad his son hadn't fallen for her, and that must have taken some doing, for she was every bit the looker Coreen was at that age.

He pulled air through his front teeth and pounded his right knee with his fist. Coreen would wonder why he didn't appear upset at the gut-wrenching revelations that she and Frieda Davis poured out in his presence. She didn't know that he had had over two weeks in which to digest the fact that, as a teenager, she had borne a child. The woman's crassness in coming to their home to vent her animosity shocked him, but he did his best to hide that.

He got up and flipped on the television. He didn't trust his mild attitude about Coreen's withholding such an important thing from him; by morning, he could be in a rage. He had a feeling that if Coreen had told him about that time in her life, the crisis they were experiencing would not have happened. He'd give her time and then he would talk to her, find out what, if anything, she still hadn't told him and clear the slate. He got ready for bed, and it shamed him that, between him and his wife there was a distance equal to one half of the bed.

Damn, he muttered to himself. *I'm tired of lying here night after night hard as a rock and not daring even to touch my wife. This is going to end, and soon.*

Chapter Fifteen

Frieda shook out her uniform, hung it in her locker, and put on her coat. Out of habit, she glanced at the mirror, but her gaze lingered only briefly upon the new and improved Frieda whose image she saw there, but which no longer interested her. To her mind, the good looks she had cultivated over the past half year had brought her only pain and self-disgust.

She slipped her shoulder bag over her right shoulder and slammed the locker shut. Another day of the same old thing.

"How ya'll doing, Mr. Jackson?" she asked the man who shuffled along with his IV and catheter bags attached to a pole, the strange odor of his deteriorating body enveloping him like a cloud.

"Pretty good, Miss Davis, pretty good."

She knew he would say that seconds before he took his last breath. She walked on down the long corridor toward the front door of the hospital on her way home. On her way to what? As she had done for the last twenty-four hours, she relived the confrontation with her birth mother, searching for the victory she had anticipated for years. Looking for the goal that had driven her since she was twelve years old. After all she'd done, she knew no triumph, not a modicum of satisfaction for having accomplished her aim.

Her steps slowed as she reached the front door, hoping to dissipate the emptiness inside of her.

"How y'all doing?" she asked the nurse who rushed into the

building reporting late for work, but she didn't listen for the woman's answer. Her attention was on the pain inside of her and on her prayer that the Lord would forgive her for the thing she'd done. And if only she could get rid of this awful hunger deep inside of her, this longing for peace and for . . . for Glen.

The deep breath she inhaled after stepping outside did nothing to relieve her sadness. She walked, unseeing, toward the steps and stopped short.

His fingers barely touched her elbow. "Wh-what are you doing here?" she asked Glen. "I thought I told you—"

"I had to come. I . . . I . . . Come with me. Will you?"

She faced him, but stepped away from his outstretched hand. "Glen, please leave me alone. You had your fun, and it's over."

"Frieda, you can't know what I'm going through. At least let me talk with you. Please."

She summoned what strength she could muster and stamped her foot. "I am not—we're speaking *not*—going home with you, and you are *not* going to my place. Is that clear? So get in your car and go on about your business."

"I didn't drive. My car is at the radio station. I knew if you saw it, you'd get the wrong idea. Mind if I walk along with you?"

"It's a free country," she said with a toss of her head, "but when I get to my car, I'm getting in it and driving home. Alone."

His fingers on her arm shocked her through the fabric of her coat, blouse, and suit. "Let's stop here in the Bread Basket. I need to talk with you."

She gazed at him, taking in his diffidence, and wondered at the change in him, whether he was sincere or acting.

"*Please*, Frieda."

She looked hard at him. All of him. Thoroughly. She couldn't associate his demeanor with the Glen she knew. Ignoring her feelings, she refused to waver, and without answering him, walked to the restaurant, opened the door, and allowed him to follow her. When he heard what *she* had to say, she didn't doubt that he would leave her alone. "I'm only having coffee," she said, "and I'm paying for that."

He chose a table in a far corner, waited until she sat down, and sat facing her. After ordering coffee for her and hot chocolate for himself, he spread his hands on the table, palms up.

"I can't stop thinking about you, Frieda. I know I behaved badly, and I know I hurt you, but it wasn't deliberate. I'm—"

She leaned forward. "No? Then you must have been a madman." She shook her head as if disbelieving what she knew to be the truth. "Glen. The things you did, Glen . . ."

"I know, and you'll never guess how sorry I am. It was pure meanness. I hated how I felt about you, how you were embedded in me like a hook. And how you strung me along for months—the only woman I ever wanted that I didn't get within a week. You made me beg."

"You could have walked away. There isn't a single thing special about *me*."

He went on as if he hadn't heard her. "I always got whatever I wanted. My dad was strict, but my older brother and my stepmother pampered me. My teachers let me get away with all kinds of things. People treated me as if I were special. All but you and maybe my dad. You made me suffer because I wanted you so badly. Not at first. At first, I was after a few rolls in the hay."

She could feel her bottom lip curl in anger. "You're a man who only wants what he can't have. As soon as I gave in, you started showing me your ugly behind, treating me like I was nothing because you knew how I felt about you."

He shook his head as if denying it, but he said, "I know. I didn't think you were good enough for me. I'm ashamed of that."

He grasped both of her hands and held them firmly. "I don't want to go on without you. I can't. That day in the park when you were telling our inquiring reporter about your life, and then when you compared me to your adoptive father, I realized what I'd done and what you mean to me."

She tried to free her hands, but he refused to release them. "Listen to me, Frieda. I love you. I love you. Do you hear me?"

Frieda stared at him, her mouth open, but he continued to talk. "You said you love me. Can't we start over? Please let me show you who I really am. Let me love you and cherish you. Frieda, for heaven's sake, say something."

When she thought the blood racing through her veins and arteries and the hot churning in her belly would overwhelm her and that his aura would finally engulf her, she jumped to her feet, braced her hips with her fists, and glared down at him.

"Say something? *You want me to say something?* Well, here it is. Nothing else is ever going to happen between you and me. It's over. You used me. Well, that makes two of us."

She brushed her damp cheeks with her coat sleeve and leaned over him. "I didn't meet you by accident. I looked you up and planned it." He seemed startled. "Oh, yes. I meant to walk into Coreen Treadwell's house holding your hand and wearing your ring but—"

Now he was standing and staring down into her face. "What the hell are you talking about?" he hissed barely above a whisper.

She didn't back away. He would hurt, but wasn't her own pain so acute that she felt she would suffocate? "I'm talking about your stepmother, the woman who gave me away to that pig who busted into me, a twelve-year-old virgin, and left me so I could hardly walk for a week. That's right," she said as horror shrouded his face.

"Your stepmother who pampers and coddles *you* gave away her own child." He sat down and lowered his head into his hands. "Yes. She's my birth mother."

"Don't lie to me, Frieda. This is too much of a coincidence. I don't believe you planned all this. Adoption records are sealed in North Carolina. Isn't that where you said you were born?"

"I went another route."

"Hey, wait a minute," he said, reached up, grasped her hand, and pulled her down into the seat facing him. "That photograph. My brother Eric showed it to her, and she pretended surprise."

"I guess she wasn't pretending. She hadn't seen me since I was born, if she saw me then. Didn't you ever notice how much I look like her? If I removed these contact lenses, you'd see eyes identical to hers. I got them in case I looked like her and you noticed the similarity.

"Funny thing," she went on, "I went to your father's travel agency first and told him who I was, but he didn't seem interested. You woulda thought I was giving him the weather fore-cast. He couldn't have cared less. He acted the same way when I went to his house and he opened the front door."

"You went to my parents' home to upset them? How could you do that?"

"How could you do what you did to me? If you walked in my shoes, you wouldn't ask that question. Let's go. There's nothing for you and me," she said, and hearing the words added to her pain.

"No," he said. "You don't mean that. I love you and you said you love me. You can't—"

She gripped her shoulder bag and looked into the distance. "This isn't easy, but I brought it all on myself. It's over, Glen, and I'm sorry, but Coreen Treadwell and I will never be able to toler-ate each other. I'd better be going."

Her lips quivered and her eyes blinked rapidly as she dropped two quarters on the table to pay for the coffee. "I wish you luck."

He didn't look at her. "Just tell me this. You've probably thrown a bomb into my parents' relationship. Are you also plan-ning to ruin my mother professionally?"

"It . . . wasn't what I always thought it would be. I've fin-ished with it. She can go her own way, and I'll go mine."

She left the restaurant with her shoulders back and head high, walked the three blocks to her car, opened it, sank into the driver's seat, and let the tears flow. The only man she ever loved, but thanks to her hatred and mistreatment of Coreen Treadwell, she could forget about him. For Glen, she would soon cease to exist, and as much as she had prayed to the Lord to forgive her for what she had planned to do, He hadn't heard her. Nobody had to tell her that her punishment had just begun. She turned the ignition key, put the car in drive, and headed for home. This time, the red Cougar would not be sitting in front of 2911 Franklin Street.

Frieda had faced the consequences of her folly, but Coreen had yet to deal with repercussions of choices she made, with questions she hadn't answered, and problems she hadn't solved. She couldn't understand why Bates hadn't grilled her about

Frieda Davis, why he tiptoed around her as if the least jarring would shatter her. She became more and more frustrated waiting for him to bring up the subject.

In two days, Glen, Eric, and Star would arrive for Thanksgiving and for Eric's marriage to Star, and they would sense the tension between Bates and her, as well as Bates's subtle hostility. The atmosphere of discontent wouldn't escape any adult. The more she fretted about it, the more frustrated and wound up she became. That Sunday night after supper, Bates cleared the table of dishes and cleaned the kitchen, all the time whistling as if he were a child on Christmas morning. She'd had a week of his feigned contentment and his pretense. That and the conflict within her, her uncertainty about what he would do, and her fear that Frieda Davis might carry her vengeful tale to the media, churned within her until she thought she would explode.

When Bates headed for the stairs, still whistling "Eleanor Rigby," Coreen raced after him and grabbed his arm.

He spun around. "Woman, what on earth is the matter with you?"

"With me? What about you? You can't continue walking around here, hardly saying a word, as if you're living alone. As though I'm not here. When are you going to ask me about Frieda Davis?"

Bates retraced his steps, took his time walking into the living room, and sat down. "When are *you* going to tell *me* what she left out or didn't know? I don't want to hear that old background stuff again. Start with the day you agreed to marry me, and tell me why you forgot to say you'd had a baby and given it up for adoption. Didn't you think I had a right to know?

"I don't fault you for doing that; you went through hell for something thrust upon you against your will. What I fault you for is not telling me. You didn't have a thing to be ashamed of."

"I know I should have told you, but I was afraid you wouldn't understand. And as time went on, it got harder and harder until I stopped trying to get up the courage to tell you and just started hoping and praying you'd never find out."

"Really?" His soft voice and subdued manner didn't fool her; he was biding his time. "I've got a lot of questions. For starters, why you were scared to appear before that Senate committee? You made all kinds of excuses, but I know when you're scared.

Why do you get so shook up about doing anything that might draw media attention? We can be having a pleasant conversation, I'll make a harmless statement, and immediately you fold up as if you've seen a ghost.

"And I'll tell you something. When you want to, you can be as phony as a four-dollar bill. I almost believed you saw no reason why the woman in that photo was the spitting image of you. That is, until she came to my shop—" At her gasp, he said, "That's right. I met her two weeks before you did."

"And you didn't . . ." Coreen had been leaning against the doorway. She moved away from it, walked into the living room, and sat down. "You can't imagine what it's like to live in fear. Morning, noon, and night. It's—"

He slapped his right thigh in a gesture of impatience. "And that was unnecessary. All you had to do was tell me, and your fear would have been over."

"I didn't know that, Bates. From the time I went before that committee, I've been afraid that if my son or daughter wanted to find me, that exposure would simplify the task.

"I didn't want to be found, didn't want to relive that period of horror in my life every time I looked at that child, and I was willing to go to great lengths to avoid being found.

"I didn't want to be exposed to my family and to lose their affection and respect. And the higher up I went professionally, the more vulnerable I became to censorship by my peers. My job is helping girls in trouble, and I didn't even know where my own child was. The media would enjoy that."

With his legs widespread and his hands resting on his thighs, he looked at her, saying nothing, for a long time. Then he said, "You let us flounder through some difficult times, quarrels, tension, hostility, and weeks without sex because you didn't have the guts to tell me what you should have told me twenty years ago. You risked a lot. If we're going to put this behind us, I'll need to know that you trust me, that we won't have any more secrets like that one."

"Bates, whenever I think of that time in my life, I feel demoralized. I've done the best I could."

"Let's start from here and get our lives back on track. I'm tired of—"

The phone rang. "Don't answer it," she said.

"It may be one of the boys," Bates said, and rushed to the phone.

"Hello." He listened for a minute. "Lizette, we're busy right now. Can't it wait?"

He turned to her. "Lizette wants to come over and bring Porgy. Why, I don't know."

"Tell her to come on."

"All right. In about forty-five minutes."

He hung up and walked over to Coreen. "If you're willing to work at getting back to where we were, the least I can do is try. Let's leave this for now. Lizette and her . . . uh . . . *whatever* will be here in a few minutes."

Coreen made coffee, got the Pillsbury cookie roll out of the freezer, cut the cookies, and put them in the oven. She knew Lizette would prefer beer and cheese sticks, but probably not with Porgy present. She chilled a bottle of chardonnay and looked around for something else to do.

Without warning, she had to grope for the edge of the kitchen counter, weakened as she was by the recollection of what had just passed between Bates and herself. He hadn't judged her harshly, and he was willing to help her strengthen their relationship. Frieda Davis had failed to destroy Coreen's marriage. But what about her career?

No matter what else happens, she told herself, *I will be thankful for this blessing. I still have my family.*

After the doorbell rang repeatedly, she heard Lizette say, "Hi, bro, I thought you weren't going to let us in. Where's Coreen?"

"In the kitchen. If you'd mend your ways, you wouldn't be so ready to think I'd mistreat you. Y'all come on in."

"What's wrong with her ways?" Porgy asked him, his voice bearing a hint of testiness.

"You don't want me to get on that subject," Bates said.

"Oh, but I do. I want to know where, in your opinion, Lizette comes up short?"

Sensing the approaching unpleasantness and aware that Bates never backed away from a set-to, Coreen rushed to the foyer to greet Lizette and Porgy.

"Hi, you two. Come on in. Porgy, this is the first time you've been here in ages. Sit down over here. I just finished making coffee. Or would you rather have some crisp cold, white wine?" She was overdoing it, but she had to defuse the situation.

Porgy spared her a slow grin. "Wine's good. Thanks. I imagine Lizette wants beer."

Coreen stopped in her tracks. Either Porgy had loosened up or he was being solicitous of Lizette.

"I'll take whatever's handy," Lizette said, "but first come in here. I have something to tell you."

"This I gotta hear," Coreen heard Bates say as she entered the living room.

Lizette leaned against the back of the sofa, crossed her knees, and assumed a superior air. "Just wanted y'all to know I swapped Treadwell for Jenkins."

Coreen rushed over to hug her sister-in-law, but Lizette held out her hand, palm forward to ward off the contact, when Bates said, "It's time he made a decent woman out of you. Responsible people make a commitment and get married."

Porgy stood. "It's time I did what?"

"Don't take him on, Porgy," Lizette said. "The trouble with my brother is that he doesn't remember where we came from. He went to Europe and came back thinking he was better than everybody else. Anybody born in a house that had never seen paint, didn't have window screens, central heating, or indoor plumbing ought to have compassion for the underprivileged. Shouldn't look down on other people, either. But not my brother."

Coreen stared at Lizette, not believing what she heard. "According to Bates," Lizette went on, "drinking beer means you're low-class, but I bet that was the first thing he ever smelled on Papa's breath."

Porgy sat down, shaking his head as if in disbelief. "Well, I'll be damned. Who would have thought it? That speaks well for you, honey. You've done more with what you had than many people born to the rich." He walked over and kissed her.

Dumbfounded, Coreen tried to think of something to say that would sweeten the atmosphere. "All the experiences—good and bad—that Bates had growing up made him a fine, upright, and honorable man." She went to the kitchen, steadied herself, and returned with a plate of cookies and a bottle of wine. Bates opened the wine, got four stem glasses, and poured a round.

"Congratulations," Bates said to Porgy, " I'm glad you finally did it."

"For twelve years, I asked Lizette to marry me at least once every day, and for twelve years, she said no at least once a day. When I got tired of it, I left her and stayed away till she agreed to get married." With a broad grin that spelled happiness, he looked at his wife. "Hasn't killed you, has it?" She shook her head, and he put the glass to his lips and let the wine ease down his throat.

"I was always ashamed of my father and all he stood for," Bates said later when he and Coreen were alone. "He worked hard sharecropping, but that only guaranteed him poverty. He didn't drink all the time, only beer mostly on Saturday nights, and he wasn't violent or abusive. Just poor and downtrodden." With his eyes, he beseeched her for understanding. "I promised myself I wouldn't live that way and, when I see people who had a more promising beginning than I had throwing away their lives, I just can't find compassion for them. I don't even try."

"Let's put this behind us, too," she said, but he held up his hand palm out. At last they had a basis for understanding each other, and he wanted the slate clean.

"I thought you were upper class, and I resented it. The way you set the table, the kind of linens you bought, your insistence on fresh flowers and your distaste for artificial ones—that and heaven knows how many other habits of yours had me believing you were born to wealth. And I thought that till Frieda Davis came here. While I'm forgiving you, you're going to have to absolve me."

She took his hand. "Let's go see a movie, eat dinner out, and come back home."

He thought she emphasized the word "home" and began to anticipate the minute when they would return and close the door behind them.

As they left the movie and walked to the car, he held her hand, squeezing her fingers and tugging her close to him. "Did I ever tell you I've had three straight weeks of great sales at the store? Those flyers we put out must have done it." He dropped her hand and put his right arm around her waist. "I'm sure that's what did the trick, and I have to thank you for that."

She felt like stretching out her arms and running with the wind at her back. She didn't know when she had felt so good. "Honey," she said, "I'm so happy."

They returned home anxious to be alone, but the light blazing in the foyer and living and dining rooms served as notice that they would have to postpone lovemaking for a time.

"Well, what do you know?" Bates said when Glen opened the door and, to his surprise, enveloped him in a hug, according him the affection normally reserved for Coreen. Glen hugged his stepmother and stepped away.

"Sorry I didn't cook dinner, but I can fix you something in a hurry," Coreen said to Glen. "We ate out."

Drawn and seemingly washed out, he said, "I already ate."

Bates scrutinized him, seeing in his younger son a different demeanor, one that he couldn't fathom. "What's up, Glen?" he asked.

"Nothing, Dad. Oh, heck. *Everything.*" He walked into the living room and flopped on the sofa as if knowing that, after his provocative reply, his parents would follow him.

Glen braced his elbows on his thighs and supported his head with both hands. "Has either of you met Frieda Davis?" At their gasps, he said. "I see." He repeated what she told him of her encounter with each of them and added, "I don't know why I didn't see the resemblance right away. She held me off till I nearly lost my mind over her, and all the time she was plotting revenge against Mom."

Coreen rested her hand on his left knee. "She said you were obnoxious. How was that possible if you nearly lost your mind over her?"

"She told the truth. I was getting even for the way she strung me along, dangled me as if I were a puppet. When I finally got her, I mistreated her."

"It's over, I hope," Bates said.

Glen looked at his father. "Yeah, it's over. The problem is, I fell in love with her."

"You what?" they said in unison.

"Right. And she's in love with me, but it's over and we both know it. Of all the women I've met, had fun with, and gotten close to, I finally fall in love with the one I can't have and no longer want to have. I thought I was using her, and she was using me. Both of us are paying for our sins." He spread his hands and looked at his palms. "I have a good career, I'm gaining some stature in the broadcast field, I'm taking courses to finish my college degree, but the rest of my life is shot."

"You didn't tell me this. I'm proud of you, son," Bates said. "Keep busy and pay attention to other girls, and your feelings for Frieda will fade. Not all at once, but they will fade away."

"I sure hope you're right." He looked at Coreen. "How do you feel about this, Mom? I mean this whole bizarre scene?"

She cleared her throat. "Your father and I have dealt with this, and it's a page we've turned. I pray that you can do the same."

Bates stood. "She had her revenge, and I hope that satisfies her."

"She told me it was an empty victory, and she's going to put her thirst for vengeance behind her."

Bates gave thanks for the relief mirrored in his wife's eyes. "I hope she was telling the truth."

"Oh, she meant it, all right," Glen assured him. "Frieda's as straight as the crow flies."

Coreen shifted in her seat, troubled that the child she bore brought such unhappiness to her beloved Glen. "Are we . . . I mean, does Eric know?'

Glen nodded. "He said that from the minute he saw that photo, he knew that unless you were sisters, you were mother and daughter. He didn't think she was your sister."

"How does he . . . I mean, what did he say?" Coreen probed.

"He said he sympathized with both of you, and that I should get here early, tell what I know and clear the air of it so he can enjoy his wedding. Star figured it out, too. She said she followed you into the kitchen to give you some support, but didn't have the nerve to let you know she understood that Frieda was your daughter."

*   *   *

Coreen donned a silver gray lace dinner dress and broad-brimmed silk hat of matching color. She hadn't seen Bates in a tuxedo since their marriage, and she took pride in walking beside him up the aisle of Mt. Airy church toward the alter. She had thought that Star might wear something traditionally native, but she stood adorned in traditional ivory silk, a white-beaded tiara, and a long white silk and lace train. Her maid of honor wore a white gown with tiny sculptured peach flowers on the bodice and sleeves and peach-colored silk hat with a white band.

After the half-hour service, they sipped wine and danced at the St. Marks hotel. Very soon, Coreen's gaze was fixed on Glen, and she knew from his attentiveness to the maid of honor that Frieda would one day be only a memory for him. She said as much to Bates as they prepared for bed that night.

"Yeah," he said, "I was thinking the same thing. And I got the impression that she flipped over him. Maybe this time . . ."

"I think he learned his lesson, and he's ready for a stable relationship with a woman who makes some constructive demands on him. At least, I hope so."

He kissed the side of her neck and slipped her gown to the floor. *How could I have been so foolish?* she thought later, as her blood pounded and her arteries throbbed when she burst open from the pleasure of his thrusting inside of her.

Later, contented in his arms, she promised herself that one day she would set things right with Frieda Davis.

Ever since she drove away from Bakerville, Frieda had felt the need to be with her sisters, to bond with them. It was a feeling she hadn't previously experienced. She knew that the encounter with her birth mother the previous Sunday left her in emotional disarray. Guilty and ashamed. Lacking purpose, without the bitterness she had nursed for more than half her life. She left Baltimore that Friday afternoon after work and headed for Charlotte, not bothering to tell her sisters to expect her.

"Frieda," Portia exclaimed. "What are you doing here? What's the matter? Julie," she called, "it's Frieda."

"Honey, what is it?" Julie asked after they found their way

into the living room and sat down. "You're so . . . so subdued. Oh, my goodness. *You met her.*"

Frieda nodded. "Yes, and I should have let it go, just like you said." She leaned back in her chair and took them through each page of her life from the time she learned that she could get her birth certificate until she walked away from Glen for the last time. She didn't spare herself.

"It was terrible," she said, emptying the words out of herself with great care, as if they might poison her. "Terrible for me and for her, too. And as badly as Glen hurt me, I still love him. The sad part is, he loves me, too." She took a deep breath as though renewing herself.

"It's over, though; it has to be, and I want it to be over." She closed her eyes and whispered, "Would you believe I'm the spitting image of her?"

"You must feel awful," Portia said, "and I hope you've finished with it. The whole thing was unhealthy. I almost said 'unsavory'."

"I know," Frieda said. "I'd give anything if I hadn't started it. The Lord is punishing me for it, too, because I miss Glen like . . ." She threw up her hands. "Don't worry about me; I'll get over him as soon as I find somebody else."

Portia and Julie exchanged knowing looks, and she knew they didn't believe her. "Of course you will," they said in unison.

She nodded. "Yeah. Sure."

That night after she got home, Frieda sat on her living room sofa and forced herself to open the letter she had carried in her handbag since Tuesday, fearing its contents. With a cup of coffee for fortification, she slit the envelope, said a word of prayer, and began to read.

Dear Frieda,

I had always feared that the child I bore would one day search for and find me, and I did not want to be found. But I had never imagined that, if we met, the encounter would be characterized by such anger and bitterness as you and I experienced. I am truly sorry that our meeting was so unpleasant, though I suppose, in our case, it was unavoidable.

My family and I are putting it all behind us now, and I hope you will be able to do the same and that you will be happy. I thank you for not pursuing this any further. We may not ever be good friends, but you know where I live, and if you ever really need me, you have only to let me know.

Warm regards,
Coreen Treadwell

Frieda hadn't expected such kindness and forgiveness from her birth mother, and she was overcome with gratitude. Her pastor had tongue-lashed her for knowingly sinning against her "neighbors," and she hadn't told him half of what she'd done. She and Coreen Treadwell wouldn't be close, but she cherished the offer of help if she ever needed it. She folded the letter and put it in the box where she stored receipts for her monthly payments on a plot of land close to the Chesapeake Bay.

"Maybe the Lord heard some of my prayers after all," she said to herself, got her stationery and a pen, and began to write.

Coreen found the letter in the mailbox when she got home the following Wednesday afternoon. One glance at the return address and she nearly lost her balance. Frieda Davis was capable of sending a hate letter. She put the missive on the table in the foyer. *I don't want to deal with it now, and I'm not sure I want a running correspondence with her, at least not if she retains the attitude she showed here.*

"Did you see this?" Bates asked her when he arrived home from work.

"Uh . . . yes, but—"

"Open it."

Reminding herself that she had promised to be open with him, to share the bad as well as the good, she sat down on the living room sofa and slit the envelope with her right middle finger.

"Tell me what it says," he urged, demanding that she be straightforward with him, that she share it no matter its content.

She opened the letter and read it aloud.

Dear Coreen,

I can't undo what I did, and I'm sorry. I learned an awful lesson and I'm paying for it. I'm glad things are fine with you and your family, and I hope Glen is getting on all right. Too bad things happened as they did.

Thank you for forgiving me. If you ever need me, just let me know. God bless both of us. Frieda.

With gratitude that she knew her eyes reflected, she looked up at her husband as his fingers entwined with hers.

"Maybe things had to happen they way they did," he said, "in order for all of us to have this . . . this renewal, this blessed catharsis. I wish her the best."

"I do, too. I haven't felt so free, so unfettered in thirty years." Feeling as if she could fly, she settled into the curve of his arms.

"The store's coming along nicely. How about a Caribbean cruise the first of the year?"

"I'd love it," she said, without thought as to time away from the agency or that someone in Brussels might need to speak with her. "You know, we never had a honeymoon."

"True, but we'll have one come January."

IF YOU WALKED IN MY SHOES

GWYNNE FORSTER

ABOUT THIS GUIDE

The suggested questions are intended to enhance
your group's reading of Gwynne Forster's
IF YOU WALKED IN MY SHOES.

You can contact the author at:

Gywnne Forster
P.O. Box 45
New York, NY 10044
e-mail: *GwynneF@aol.com*
website: *www.gwynneforster.com*

DISCUSSION QUESTIONS

1. When Coreen's child was born, how did she rationalize the decision she made?

2. Did she have other options and, if so, what were they?

3. What major error did she make that guaranteed her decision would haunt her?

4. Why do you think Coreen's aunt Agatha treated her as she did, and what effect did that time in Coreen's life have upon her work as head of a social agency?

5. Many young girls suffer abuse by a male family member. How would you describe a man who molests his own daughters? Emotionally ill? Inordinately possessive? Given to incontinence? Criminally immoral?

6. There have been many case studies of families in which mothers, fearing for their own safety, did not intervene when their husband molested their daughter; some case studies document that the mother knew her husband would go to their daughter when she rejected intimacy with him, yet, she did not intervene on her daughter's behalf. What is your estimation of these mothers, bearing in mind that their husbands were usually abusers and bullies?

7. Frieda Davis struck out on her own at night, stealing away from home at age seventeen to avoid further molestation. We meet her when she is twenty-nine, a hard worker in a job that requires training and skill, both of which she acquired on her own. Do you admire her for this?

8. Does her struggle justify her single-minded pursuit of her birth mother?

9. When individuals agree to marry, do you think they are obligated to reveal everything in their pasts that could become the subject of conflict or that could embarass their spouse?

10. Why is Coreen reluctant to appear before the Senate committee, and why does she finally decide to do that?

11. How does Coreen's driving ambition conflict with the prospect of fame?

12. Does Bates elicit sympathy? Why? What are his laudable traits as a husband and father? Where does he fall short?

13. Discuss the conflict that Frieda experiences within herself.

14. What conflicting goals of Frieda and Coreen drive the story and dominate their lives?

15. Has Coreen dealt fairly with her two stepsons, Eric and Glen? How does she rationalize her different treatment of them?

16. What does Star symbolize for Coreen?

17. How does Frieda find her birth mother?

18. How does Frieda learn about Glen, and how does she foist herself upon him?

19. Why and in what way is Glen susceptible to Frieda when he first meets her? How does this change? What explanation does Glen give Frieda and his parents for having mistreated Frieda?

20. What solution did the psychoanalyst give Coreen to the problem of her growing paranoia about being discovered and disgraced? How does she deal with it, and what is the outcome?

21. What are the effects of Coreen's professional achievements coupled with her fears that her past will be exposed upon Coreen's marriage? Give some examples of Coreen's and Bates's lack of knowledge of each other.

22. What price does Glen pay for his womanizing, and what price does Frieda pay for deceiving Glen?

23. As a result of the explosive encounter between Coreen and Frieda, their lives are forever changed. How?

24. In an exchange of letters, Coreen and Frieda effect a modest accommodation to each other. What, in light of this, do you envisage as the nature of their relationship in the future?